An Open Letter About
BLACK ORDER
by James Rollins

Writing my past seven no___ ___ ___ ___ ___ science with historical m___ ___ ___ ___ ___ in
religious texts and my ___ ___ ___ ___ e
blending science and r___ ___ ___ mystery
above all others: the co___ ___ intelligent Design
and Evolution. It was ba___ in our classrooms, in the halls
of State, in newspapers, on television. So perhaps it was
time for Sigma Force to delve into this controversy.

First, as to my own background, I have a doctorate in vet-
erinary medicine. And as a veterinarian, I was trained in the
anatomy, the physiology, and the medicine of a wide range
of animals. To me, evolution was as plain as the difference
between a Chihuahua and a Great Dane.

Still, I also knew there were some questions surrounding
evolutionary theory that remained unanswered. So I spent
six months immersing myself in the current debate. And
in the course of this study, I came across a revolutionary
approach to this controversy, one involving the very
latest scientific theory (which is explored in this novel).
But it was also during the course of writing this story that
I discovered something surprising: an answer to this
debate arose within the pages that startled even me.

So while at its heart, BLACK ORDER is a wild and
wooly adventure thriller spanning continents—from Copenhagen, to Nepal, to South Africa—it also offers some
thoughtful reflections on the potentiality of life and offers
a new theory that straddles the line between Intelligent
Design and Evolution, bringing a new understanding of life
and our place in the greater scheme of existence.

I hope you enjoy the journey!

By James Rollins

Coming Soon in Hardcover

THE DEVIL COLONY

JAMES ROLLINS

A Σ SIGMA FORCE THRILLER

BLACK ORDER

HARPER

An Imprint of HarperCollinsPublishers

HARPER

An Imprint of HarperCollins*Publishers*
10 East 53rd Street
New York, New York 10022-5299

Copyright © 2006 by Jim Czajkowski
Excerpt from *The Judas Strain* copyright © 2007 by Jim Czajkowski
ISBN 978-0-06-202235-6

First Harper paperback international printing: June 2010
First Harper paperback printing: June 2007
First William Morrow hardcover printing: July 2006

10 9 8 7 6 5 4 3 2 1

TO DAVID,
for all the adventures

ACKNOWLEDGMENTS

Novel writing, despite the time spent alone with the blank page, is a collaborative process. There are scores of people whose fingerprints are all over this book. First, let me especially acknowledge Penny Hill, for the long lunches, the thoughtful commentary, but mostly for her friendship. And the same goes for Carolyn McCray, who still kicks my butt to challenge me to stretch a little further. Then, of course, I'm honored to acknowledge my friends who meet every other week at Coco's Restaurant: Steve and Judy Prey, Chris Crowe, Lee Garrett, Michael Gallowglas, Dave Murray, Dennis Grayson, Dave Meek, Jane O'Riva, Dan Needles, Zach Watkins, and Caroline Williams. They are the cabal behind this writer. And a special shout out to author Joe Konrath for his energy, support, and thoughtful debate on some of the topics in this book, and to David Sylvian for lugging a camera everywhere, even atop the highest peak in the Sierras. As to the inspiration behind this story, I must credit the books by Nick Cook and the intriguing research of Johnjoe McFadden. Finally, the four people instrumental at all levels of production: my editor, Lyssa Keusch, her colleague May Chen, and my agents, Russ Galen and Danny Baror. And as always, I must stress any and all errors of fact or detail fall squarely on my own shoulders.

NOTE FROM THE
HISTORICAL RECORD

In the last months of World War II, as Germany fell, a new war began among the Allies: to plunder the technology of Nazi scientists. A race between the Brits, Americans, French, and Russians was every country for itself. Patents were stolen: for new vacuum tubes, for exotic chemicals and plastics, even for pasteurizing milk with UV light. But many of the most sensitive patents disappeared into the well of deep black projects, like *Operation Paper Clip*, where hundreds of Nazi V-2 rocket scientists were recruited in secret and brought into the United States.

But the Germans did not give up their technology easily. They also fought to secure their secrets in the hopes of a rebirth of the Reich. Scientists were murdered, research labs destroyed, and blueprints hidden in caves, sunk to the bottom of lakes, and buried in crypts. All to keep them from the Allies.

The search became daunting. Nazi research and weapons labs numbered in the hundreds, many underground, spread across Germany, Austria, Czechoslovakia, and Poland. One of the most mysterious was a converted mine outside the small mountain town of Breslau. The research at this facility was code-named *die Glocke* or "the Bell." People in the surrounding countryside reported strange lights and mysterious illnesses and deaths.

The Russian forces were the first to reach the mine. It was deserted. All sixty-two scientists involved in the project had been shot. As for the device itself . . . it had vanished to God knows where.

All that is known for sure: the Bell was real.

NOTE FROM THE
SCIENTIFIC RECORD

Life is stranger than any fiction. All the discussions raised in
this novel about quantum mechanics, intelligent design, and
evolution are based on facts.

The fact that evolution is the backbone of biology, and biology is thus in the peculiar position of being a science founded on an improved theory—is it then a science or faith?

— CHARLES DARWIN

Science without religion is lame, religion without science is blind.

—ALBERT EINSTEIN

Who says I am not under the special protection of God?

—ADOLF HITLER

BLACK
ORDER

1945

MAY 4
6:22 A.M.
FORTRESS CITY OF BRESLAU, POLAND

The body floated in the sludge that sluiced through the dank sewers. The corpse of a boy, bloated and rat gnawed, had been stripped of boots, pants, and shirt. Nothing went to waste in the besieged city.

SS *Obergruppenführer* Jakob Sporrenberg nudged past the corpse, stirring the filth. Offal and excrement. Blood and bile. The wet scarf tied around his nose and mouth did little to ward off the stench. This was what the great war had come to. The mighty reduced to crawling through sewers to escape. But he had his orders.

Overhead the double *crump-wump* of Russian artillery pummeled the city. Each explosion bruised his gut with its concussive shock. The Russians had broken down the gates, bombed the airport, and even now, tanks ground down the cobbled streets while transport carriers landed on Kaiserstrasse. The main thoroughfare had been converted into a landing strip by parallel rows of flaming oil barrels, adding their smoke to the already choked early morning skies, keeping dawn at bay. Fighting waged in every street, in every home, from attic to basement.

Every house a fortress.

That had been *Gauleiter* Hanke's final command to the populace. The city had to hold out as long as possible. The future of the Third Reich depended on it.

And on Jakob Sporrenberg.

"Mach schnell," he urged the others behind him.

His unit of the *Sicherheitsdienst*—designation Special Evacuation *Kommando*—trailed him, knee-deep in filthy water. Fourteen men. All armed. All dressed in black. All burdened with heavy packs. In the middle, four of the largest men, former *Nordsee* dockmen, bore poles on their shoulders, bearing aloft massive crates.

There was a reason the Russians were striking this lone city deep in the Sudeten Mountains between Germany and Poland. The fortifications of Breslau guarded the gateway to the highlands beyond. For the past two years, forced labor from the concentration camp of Gross-Rosen had hollowed out a neighboring mountain peak. A hundred kilometers of tunnels clawed and blasted, all to service one secret project, one kept buried away from prying Allied eyes.

Die Riese . . . the Giant.

But word had still spread. Perhaps one of the villagers outside the Wenceslas Mine had whispered of the illness, the sudden malaise that had afflicted even those well outside the complex.

If only they'd had more time to complete the research . . .

Still, a part of Jakob Sporrenberg balked. He didn't know all that was involved with the secret project, mostly just the code name: Chronos. Still, he knew enough. He had seen the bodies used in the experiments. He had heard the screams.

Abomination.

That was the one word that had come to mind and iced his blood.

He'd had no trouble executing the scientists. The sixty-two men and women had been taken outside and shot twice in the head. No one must know what had transpired in the depths of the Wenceslas Mine . . . or what was found. Only one researcher was allowed to live.

Doktor Tola Hirszfeld.

Jakob heard her sloshing behind him, half dragged by one of his men, wrists secured behind her back. She was tall for a woman, late twenties, small breasted but of ample waist and shapely legs. Her hair flowed smooth and black, her skin as pale as milk from the months spent underground. She was to have been killed with the others, but her father, *Oberarbeitsleiter* Hugo Hirszfeld, overseer of the project, had finally shown his corrupted blood, his half-Jewish heritage. He had attempted to destroy his research files, but he had been shot by one of the guards and killed before he could firebomb his subterranean office. Fortunately for his daughter, someone with full knowledge of *die Glocke* had to survive, to carry on the work. She, a genius like her father, knew his research better than any of the other scientists.

But she would need coaxing from here.

Fire burned in her eyes whenever Jakob glanced her way. He could feel her hatred like the heat of an open furnace. But she would cooperate . . . like her father had before her. Jakob knew how to deal with *Juden,* especially those of mixed blood. *Mischlinge.* They were the worst. Partial Jews. There were some hundred thousand *Mischlinge* in military service to the Reich. Jewish soldiers. Rare exemptions to Nazi law had allowed such mixed blood to still serve, sparing their lives. It required special dispensation. Such *Mischlinge* usually proved to be the fiercest soldiers, needing to show their loyalty to Reich over race.

Still, Jakob had never trusted them. Tola's father proved the validity of his suspicions. The doctor's attempted sabotage had not surprised Jakob. Juden were never to be trusted, only exterminated.

But Hugo Hirszfeld's exemption papers had been signed by the führer himself, sparing not only the father and daughter, but also a pair of elderly parents somewhere in the middle of Germany. So while Jakob had no trust of the *Mischlinge,* he placed his full faith in his führer. His orders had been letter specific: evacuate the mine of the necessary resources to continue the work and destroy the rest.

That meant sparing the daughter.

And the baby.

The newborn boy was swaddled and bundled into a pack, a Jewish infant, no more than a month old. The child had been given a light sedative to keep him silent as they made their escape.

Within the child burned the heart of the abomination, the true source of Jakob's revulsion. All of the hopes for the Third Reich lay in his tiny hands—the hands of a *Jewish* infant. Bile rose at such a thought. Better to impale the child on a bayonet. But he had his orders.

He also saw how Tola watched the boy. Her eyes glowed with a mix of fire and grief. Besides aiding in her father's research, Tola had served as the boy's foster mother, rocking him asleep, feeding him. The child was the only reason the woman was cooperating at all. It had been a threat on the boy's life that had finally made Tola acquiesce to Jakob's demands.

A mortar blast exploded overhead, dropping all to their knees and deafening the world to a sonorous ring. Cement cracked, and dust trickled into the foul water.

Jakob gained his feet, swearing under his breath.

His second in command, Oskar Henricks, drew abreast of him and pointed forward to a side branch of the sewer.

"We take that tunnel, *Obergruppenführer.* An old storm drain. According to the municipal map, the main trunk empties into the river, not far from Cathedral Island."

Jakob nodded. Hidden near the island, a pair of camouflaged gunboats should be waiting, manned by another *Kommando* unit. It was not much farther.

He led the way at a more hurried pace as the Russian bombardment intensified overhead. The renewed assault plainly heralded their final push into the city. The surrender of its citizenry was inevitable.

As Jakob reached the side tunnel, he climbed out of the sluicing filth and onto the cement apron of the branching passageway. His boots squelched with each step. The gangrenous reek of bowel and slime swelled momentarily worse, as if the sewer sought to chase him from its depths.

The rest of his unit followed.

Jakob shone his hand-torch down the cement drain. Did the air smell a touch fresher? He followed the beam with renewed vigor. With escape so near, the mission was almost over. His unit would be halfway across Silesia before the Russians ever reached the subterranean warren of rat runs that constituted Wenceslas Mine. As a warm welcome, Jakob had planted booby traps throughout the laboratory passages. The Russians and their allies would find nothing but death among the highlands.

With this satisfying thought, Jakob fled toward the promise of fresh air. The cement tunnel descended in a gradual slope. The team's pace increased, hastened by the sudden silence between artillery bursts. The Russians were coming in full force.

It would be close. The river would only remain open for so long.

As if sensing the urgency, the infant began a soft cry, a thready whine as the sedative wore off. Jakob had warned the team's medic to keep the drugs light. They dared not risk the child's life. Perhaps that had been a mistake . . .

The timbre of the cries grew more strident.

A single mortar shell blasted somewhere to the north.

Cries became wails. The noise echoed down the tunnel's stone throat.

"Quiet the child!" he ordered the soldier who bore the baby.

The man, reed thin and ashen, bobbled the pack from his shoulder, losing his black cap in the process. He struggled to free the boy but only earned more distressed screeches.

"L-let me," Tola pleaded. She fought the man holding her elbow. "He needs me."

The child bearer glanced to Jakob. Silence had fallen over the world above. The screaming continued below.

Grimacing, Jakob nodded his head.

Tola's bonds were cut from her wrists. Rubbing circulation into her fingers, she reached for the child. The soldier gladly relinquished his burden. She cradled the baby in the crook of her arm, supporting his head and rocking him gently. She leaned over him, drawing him close. Soothing sounds, wordless and full of comfort, whispered through his wails. Her whole being melted around the child.

Slowly the screeching ebbed to quieter cries.

Satisfied, Jakob nodded to her guard. The man raised his Luger and kept it pressed to Tola's back. In silence now, they continued their trek through the subterranean warren beneath Breslau.

In short order, the smell of smoke overtook the reek of the sewers. His hand-torch illuminated a smoky pall that marked the exit of the storm drain. The artillery guns remained quiet, but an almost continuous pop and rattle of gunfire continued—mostly to the east. Closer at hand, the distinct lap of water could be heard.

Jakob gestured to his men to hold their position back in the tunnel and waved his radioman to the exit. "Signal the boats."

The soldier nodded crisply and hurried forward, disappearing into the smoky gloom. In moments, a few flashes of light passed a coded message to the neighboring island. It would only take a minute for the boats to cross the channel to their location.

Jakob turned to Tola. She still carried the child. The boy had quieted again, his eyes closed.

Tola met Jakob's gaze, unflinching. "You know my father was right," she said with quiet certainty. Her gaze flicked to the sealed crates, then back to him. "I can see it in your face. What we did . . . we went too far."

"Such decisions are not for either of us to decide," Jakob answered.

"Then who?"

Jakob shook his head and began to turn away. Heinrich Himmler had personally given him his orders. It was not his place to question. Still, he felt the woman's attention on him.

"It defies God and nature," she whispered.

A call saved him from responding. "The boats come," the radioman announced, returning from the mouth of the storm drain.

Jakob barked final orders and got his men into position. He led them to the end of the tunnel, which opened onto the steep bank of the River Oder. They were losing the cover of darkness. Sunrise glowed to the east, but here a continuous cloud of black smoke hung low over the water, drawn thick by the river draft. The pall would help shelter them.

But for how long?

Gunfire continued its oddly merry chatter, firecrackers to celebrate the destruction of Breslau.

Free of the sewer's stink, Jakob pulled away his wet mask and took a deep clean breath. He searched the lead gray waters. A pair of twenty-foot low boats knifed across the river, engines burbling a steady drone. At each bow, barely concealed under green tarps, a pair of MG-42 machine guns had been mounted.

Beyond the boats, a dark mass of island was just visible. Cathedral Island was not truly an island, as it had accumulated enough silt back in the nineteenth century to fuse to the far bank. A cast-iron emerald green bridge dating back to the same century crossed to this side. Beneath the bridge, the two gunboats skirted its stone piers and approached.

Jakob's eyes were drawn upward as a piercing ray of sunlight struck the tips of the two towering spires of the cathedral that gave the former island its name. It was one of a half-dozen churches crowded on the island.

Jakob's ears still rang with Tola Hirszfeld's words.

It defies God and nature.

The morning chill penetrated his sodden clothes, leaving his skin prickling and cold. He would be glad when he was well away from here, able to shut out all memory of these past days.

The first of the boats reached the shoreline. Glad for the distraction, even happier to be moving, he hurried his men to load the two boats.

Tola stood off to the side, babe in her arms, flanked by the one guard. Her eyes had also discovered the glowing spires in the smoky skies. Gunfire continued, moving closer now. Tanks could be heard grinding in low gears. Cries and screams punctuated it all.

Where was this God she feared defying?

Certainly not here.

With the boats loaded, Jakob moved to Tola's side. "Get on the boat." He had meant to be stern, but something in her face softened his words.

She obeyed, her attention still on the cathedral, her thoughts even further skyward.

In that moment, Jakob saw the beauty she could be . . . even though she was a *Mischlinge*. But then the toe of her boot stubbed, she stumbled and caught herself, careful of the babe. Her eyes returned to the gray waters and smoky pall. Her face hardened again, gone stony. Even her eyes turned flinty as she cast about for a seat for her and the baby.

She settled on a starboard bench, her guard moving in step with her.

Jakob sat across from them and waved to the boat's pilot to set out. "We must not be late." He searched down the river. They were headed west, away from the eastern front, away from the rising sun.

He checked his watch. By now, a German Junker Ju 52 transport plane should be waiting for them in an abandoned airfield ten kilometers away. It had been painted with a German Red Cross, camouflaging it as a medical transport, an added bit of insurance against assault.

The boats circled out into the deeper channel, engines trebling up. The Russians could not stop them now. It was over.

Motion drew his attention back to the far side of the boat.

Tola leaned over the baby and delivered a soft kiss atop the boy's wispy-haired pate. She lifted her face, meeting Jakob's gaze. He saw no defiance or anger. Only determination.

Jakob knew what she was about to do. "Don't—"

Too late.

Shifting up, Tola leaned back over the low rail behind her and kicked off with her feet. With the baby clutched to her bosom, she flipped backward into the cold water.

Her guard, startled by the sudden action, twisted and fired blindly into the water.

Jakob lunged to his side and knocked his arm up. "You could hit the child."

Jakob leaned over the boat's edge and searched the waters. The other men were on their feet. The boat rocked. All Jakob saw in the leaden waters was his own reflection. He motioned for the pilot to circle.

Nothing.

He watched for any telltale bubbles, but the laden boat's

wake churned the waters to obscurity. He pounded a fist on the rail.

Like father . . . like daughter . . .

Only a *Mischlinge* would take such a drastic action. He had seen it before: *Jüdische* mothers smothering their own children to spare them greater suffering. He had thought Tola was stronger than that. But in the end, perhaps she had no choice.

He circled long enough to make sure. His men searched the banks on each side. She was gone. The whistling passage of a mortar overhead discouraged tarrying any longer.

Jakob waved his men back into their seats. He pointed west, toward the waiting plane. They still had the crates and all the files. It was a setback, but one that could be overcome. Where there was one child, there could be another.

"Go," he ordered.

The pair of boats set out again, engines winding up to a full throttle.

Within moments, they had vanished into the smoky pall as Breslau burned.

Tola heard the boats fade into the distance.

She treaded water behind one of the thick stone pylons that supported the ancient cast-iron Cathedral Bridge. She kept one hand clenched over the baby's mouth, suffocating him to silence, praying he gained enough air through his nose. But the child was weak.

As was she.

The bullet had pierced the side of her neck. Blood flowed thickly, staining the water crimson. Her vision narrowed. Still she fought to hold the baby above the water.

Moments before, as she tumbled into the river, she had intended to drown herself and the baby. But as the cold struck her and her neck burned with fire, something tore through her resolve. She remembered the light glowing on the steeples. It was not her religion, not her heritage. But it was a reminder that there was light beyond the current darkness. Somewhere men did not savage their brothers. Mothers did not drown their babies.

She had kicked deeper into the channel, allowing the current to push her toward the bridge. Underwater, she used her own air to keep the child alive, pinching his nose and exhaling her breath through his lips. Though she had planned for death, once the fight for life had ignited, it grew more fierce, a fire in her chest.

The boy never had a name.

No one should die without a name.

She breathed into the child, shallow breaths, in and out as she kicked with the current, blind in the water. Only dumb luck brought her up against one of the stone pilings and offered a place to shelter.

But now with the boats leaving, she could wait no longer.

Blood pumped from her. She sensed it was only the cold keeping her alive. But the same cold was chilling the life from the frail child.

She kicked for shore, a frantic thrashing, uncoordinated by weakness and numbness. She sank under the water, dragging the infant down with her.

No.

She struggled up, but the water was suddenly heavier, harder to fight.

She refused to succumb.

Then under her toes, slick rocks bumped against her boots. She cried out, forgetting she was still underwater, and gagged on the mouthful of river. She sank a bit more, then kicked one last time off the muddy rocks. Her head breeched, and her body flung itself toward shore.

The bank rose steeply underfoot.

On hand and knee, she scrabbled out of the water, clutching the baby to her throat. She reached the shoreline and fell facedown onto the rocky bank. She had no strength to move another limb. Her own blood bathed over the child. It took her last effort to focus on the baby.

He was not moving. Not breathing.

She closed her eyes and prayed as an eternal blackness swallowed her.

Cry, damn you, cry . . .

Father Varick was the first to hear the mewling.

He and his brothers were sheltered in the wine cellar beneath Saints Peter and Paul Church. They had fled when the bombing of Breslau began last night. On their knees, they had prayed for their island to be spared. The church, built in the fifteenth century, had survived the ever-changing masters of the border city. They sought heavenly protection to survive once more.

It was in such silent piety that the plaintive cries echoed to the monks.

Father Varick stood, which took much effort for his old legs.

"Where are you going?" Franz asked.

"I hear my flock calling for me," the father said. For the past two decades, he had fed scraps to the river cats and the occasional cur that frequented the riverside church.

"Now is not the time," another brother warned, fear ripe in his voice.

Father Varick had lived too long to fear death with such youthful fervor. He crossed the cellar and bent to enter the short passage that ended at the river door. Coal used to be carted up the same passage and stored where now fine green bottles nestled in dust and oak.

He reached the old coal door, lifted the bar, and undid the latch.

Using a shoulder, he creaked it open.

The sting of smoke struck him first—then the mewling drew his eyes down. *"Mein Gott im Himmel . . ."*

A woman had collapsed steps from the door in the buttress wall that supported the channel church. She was not moving. He hurried to her side, dropping again to his knees, a new prayer on his lips.

He reached to her neck and checked for a sign of life, but found only blood and ruin. She was soaked head to foot and as cold as the stones.

Dead.

Then the cry again . . . coming from her far side.

He shifted to find a babe, half-buried under the woman, also bloody.

Though blue from the cold and just as wet, the child still lived. He freed the infant from the body. His wet swaddling shed from him with their waterlogged weight.

A boy.

He quickly ran his hands over the tiny body and saw the blood was not the child's.

Only his mother's.

He glanced sadly down at the woman. So much death. He searched the far side of the river. The city burned, roiling smoke into the dawning sky. Gunfire continued. Had she swum across the channel? All to save her child?

"Rest," he whispered to the woman. "You have earned it."

Father Varick retreated to the coal door. He wiped the blood and water from the baby. The child's hair was soft and thin, but plainly snowy white. He could be no more than a month old.

With Varick's ministrations, the boy's cries grew stronger, his face pinched with the effort, but he remained weak, limp limbed, and cold.

"You cry, little one."

Responding to his voice, the boy opened his swollen eyes.

Blue eyes greeted Varick. Brilliant and pure. Then again, most newborns had blue eyes. Still, Varick sensed that these eyes would keep their sky blue richness.

He drew the boy closer for warmth. A bit of color caught his eye. *Was ist das?* He turned the boy's foot. Upon the heel, someone had drawn a symbol.

No, not drawn. He rubbed to be sure.

Tattooed in crimson ink.

He studied it. It looked like a crow's foot.

But Father Varick had spent a good portion of his youth in Finland. He recognized the symbol for what it truly was: one of the Norse runes. He had no idea which rune or what it meant. He shook his head. Who had done such foolishness?

He glanced at the mother with a frown.

No matter. The sins of the father were not the son's to bear.

He wiped away the last of the blood from the crown of the boy's head and snugged the boy into his warm robe.

"Poor *Junge* . . . such a hard welcome to this world."

FIRST

FIRST

I

ROOF OF THE WORLD

PRESENT DAY
MAY 16, 6:34 A.M.
HIMALAYAS
EVEREST BASE CAMP, 17,600 FEET

Death rode the winds.

Taski, the lead Sherpa, pronounced this verdict with all the solemnity and certainty of his profession. The squat man barely reached five feet, even with his battered cowboy hat. But he carried himself as if he were taller than anyone on the mountain. His eyes, buried within squinted lids, studied the flapping line of prayer flags.

Dr. Lisa Cummings centered the man in the frame of her Nikon D-100 and snapped a picture. While Taski served as the group's guide, he was also Lisa's psychometric test subject. A perfect candidate for her research.

She had come to Nepal under a grant to study the physiologic effects of an oxygen-free ascent of Everest. Until 1978, no one had summited Everest without the aid of supplemental oxygen. The air was too thin. Even veteran mountaineers, aided by bottled oxygen, experienced extreme fatigue, impaired coordination, double vision, hallucinations. It was considered impossible to reach the

summit of an eight-thousand-meter peak without a source
of canned air.

Then in 1978, two Tyrolean mountaineers achieved the
impossible and reached the summit, relying solely on their
own gasping lungs. In subsequent years, some sixty men and
women followed in their footsteps, heralding a new goal of
the climbing elite.

She couldn't ask for a better stress test for low-pressure
atmospheres.

Prior to coming here, Dr. Lisa Cummings had just
completed a five-year grant on the effect of *high*-pressure
systems on human physiological processes. To accomplish this, she had studied deep-sea divers while aboard a
research ship, the *Deep Fathom*. Afterward, circumstances
required her to move on . . . both with her professional life
and personal. So she had accepted an NSF grant to perform
antithetical research: to study the physiologic effects of *low*-
pressure systems.

Hence, this trip to the Roof of the World.

Lisa repositioned for another shot of Taski Sherpa. Like
many of his people, Taski had taken his ethnic group as his
surname.

The man stepped away from the flapping line of prayer
flags, firmly nodded his head, and pointed a cigarette
pinched between two fingers at the towering peak. "Bad
day. Death ride deese winds," he repeated, then replaced his
cigarette and turned away. The matter settled.

But not for the others in their group.

Sounds of disappointment flowed through the climbing
party. Faces stared at the cloudless blue skies overhead.
The ten-man climbing team had been waiting nine days for
a weather window to open. Before now, no one had argued
against the good sense of not climbing during the past
week's storm. The weather had been stirred up by a cyclone
spinning off the Bay of Bengal. Savage winds had pum-

meled the camp, reaching over a hundred miles per hour, kiting away one of the cook tents, knocking people over bodily, and been followed by spats of snowfall that abraded any exposed skin like coarse sandpaper.

Then the morning had dawned as bright as their hopes. Sunlight glinted off the Khumbu glacier and icefall. Snow-capped Everest floated above them, surrounded by its serene sister peaks, a wedding party in white.

Lisa had snapped a hundred shots, catching the changing light in all its shifting beauty. She now understood the local names for Everest: Chomo-lungma, or Goddess Mother of the World, in Chinese, and Sagarmatha, the Goddess of the Sky, in Nepalese.

Floating among the clouds, the mountain was indeed a goddess of ice and cliff. And they had all come to worship her, to prove themselves worthy to kiss the sky. And it hadn't come cheap. Sixty-five thousand dollars a head. At least that included camping equipment, porters, Sherpas, and of course all the yaks you could want. The lowing of a female yak echoed over the valley, one of the two dozen servicing their climbing team. The blisters of their red and yellow tents decorated the camp. Five other camps shared this rocky escarpment, all waiting for the storm gods to turn their back.

But according to their lead Sherpa, that would not be today.

"This is so much bull," declared the manager of a Boston sporting goods company. Dressed in the latest down-duvet one-piece, he stood with his arms crossed beside his loaded pack. "Over six hundred dollars a day to sit on our asses. They're bilking us. There's not a cloud in the damn sky!"

He spoke under his breath, as though trying to incite an uprising that he had no intention of leading himself.

Lisa had seen the type before. Type A personality . . . *A* as in asshole. Upon hindsight, perhaps she shouldn't have slept with him. She cringed at the memory. The rendezvous had been back in the States, after an organizational meeting at the Hyatt in Seattle, after one too many whiskey sours. Boston Bob had been just another port in a storm . . . not the first, probably not the last. But one thing was certain: this was one port she would not be dropping anchor in again.

She suspected this reason more than any other for his continued belligerence.

She turned away, willing her younger brother the strength to quell the unrest. Josh was a mountaineer with a decade of experience and had coordinated her inclusion in one of his escorted Everest ascents. He led mountaineering trips around the world at least twice a year.

Josh Cummings held up a hand. Blond and lean like herself, he wore black jeans, tucked into the gaiters of his Millet One Sport boots, and a gray expedition-weight thermal shirt.

He cleared his throat. "Taski has scaled Everest twelve times. He knows the mountain and its moods. If he says the weather is too unpredictable to move forward, then we spend another day acclimating and practicing skills. If anyone would like, I can also have a pair of guides lead a day trip to the rhododendron forest in the lower Khumbu valley."

A hand rose from the group. "What about a day trip to the Everest View Hotel? We've been camping in these damn tents for the past six days. I wouldn't mind a hot bath."

Murmurs of agreement met this request.

"I don't know if that's such a good idea," Josh warned. "The hotel is a full day's trek away, and the rooms at the hotel have oxygen pumped into them, to stave off altitude sickness. It could weaken your current acclimation and delay any ascent."

"Like we're not delayed enough already!" Boston Bob pressed.

Josh ignored him. Lisa knew her younger brother would not be pressured to do something as stupid as risk an ascent against inclement weather. Though the skies were blue, she knew that could change in a matter of minutes. She had grown up on the sea, off the Catalina coast. As had Josh. One learned to read signs beyond the lack of clouds. Josh might not have developed a Sherpa's eye to read the weather up at these heights, but he certainly knew to respect those who did.

Lisa stared up at the plume of snow blowing off the tip of Everest's peak. It marked the jet stream, known to gust over two hundred miles an hour across the summit. The plume stretched impossibly long. Though the storm had blown itself out, the pressure pattern still wreaked havoc above eight thousand meters. The jet stream could blow a storm back over them at any moment.

"We could at least make for Camp One," Boston Bob persisted. "Bivouac there and see what the weather brings."

An irritating whine had entered the sports-store manager's voice, trying to wheedle some concession. His face had reddened with frustration.

Lisa could not fathom her prior attraction to the man.

Before her brother could respond to the lout, a new noise intruded. A *thump-thump* like drums. All eyes swung to the east. Out of the glare of the rising sun, a black helicopter appeared. A hornet-shaped B-2 Squirrel A-Star Ecuriel. The rescue chopper had been designed to climb to these heights.

A silence settled over the group.

A week ago, just before the recent storm broke, an expedition had gone up on the Nepal side. Radio communication had put them up at Camp Two. Over twenty-one thousand feet in elevation.

Lisa shaded her eyes. Had something gone wrong?

She had visited the Himalayan Rescue Association's health clinic down in Pheriche. It was the point of triage for all manner of illnesses that rolled down the mountainside to their doorstep: broken bones, pulmonary and cerebral edema, frostbite, heart conditions, dysentery, snow blindness, and all sorts of infections, including STDs. It seemed even chlamydia and gonorrhea were determined to summit Everest.

But what had gone wrong now? There had been no Mayday on the radio's emergency band. A helicopter could only reach a little above Base Camp due to the thin air up here. That meant rescues from air often required trekking down from the most severe heights. Above twenty-five thousand feet, the dead were simply left where they fell, turning the upper slopes of Everest into an icy graveyard of abandoned gear, empty oxygen containers, and frost-mummified corpses.

The beat of the rotors changed pitch.

"They're coming this way," Josh said and waved everyone back to the nests of four-season storm tents, clearing the flat expanse that served as the camp's helipad.

The black helicopter dropped over them. Rotor wash swirled sand and bits of rock. A Snickers wrapper blew past Lisa's nose. Prayer flags danced and twisted, and yaks scattered. After so many days of quiet in the mountains, the noise was deafening.

The B-2 settled to its skids with a grace that belied its size. Doors swung open. Two men stepped out. One wore a green camouflage uniform and shouldered an automatic weapon, a soldier of the Royal Nepalese Army. The other stood taller, in a red robe and cloak sashed at the waist, head shaved bald. A Buddhist monk.

The pair approached and spoke rapidly in a Nepalese dialect to a pair of Sherpas. There was a short bout of gesturing, then an arm pointed.

At Lisa.

The monk led the way to her, flanked by the soldier.

From the sun-crinkles at the corners of his eyes, the monk appeared to be in his midforties, skin the color of latte, eyes caramel brown.

The soldier's skin was darker, his eyes pinched closer together. His gaze was fixed below her neckline. She had left her jacket unzipped, and the sports bra she was wearing beneath her fleece vest seemed to have captured his attention.

The Buddhist monk, on the other hand, kept his eyes respectful, even bowing his head slightly. He spoke precise English touched by a British accent. "Dr. Cummings, I apologize for the intrusion, but there has been an emergency. I was informed by the HRA clinic that you are a medical doctor."

Lisa frowned, her brow furrowing. "Yes."

"A nearby monastery has been struck by a mysterious ailment, affecting almost all the inhabitants. A sole messenger, a man from a neighboring village, had been dispatched on foot, traveling three days to reach the hospital in Khunde. Once alerted, we'd hoped to ferry one of the HRA doctors up to the monastery, but an avalanche has the clinic already shorthanded. Dr. Sorenson told us of your presence here at Base Camp."

Lisa pictured the short Canadian doctor, another woman. They had shared a six-pack of Carlsberg lager along with sweet milk tea one evening. "How can I be of service?" she asked.

"Would you be willing to accompany us up there? Though isolated, the monastery is serviceable by helicopter."

"How long . . . ?" she asked and glanced in Josh's direction. He had moved over to join them.

The monk shook his head, his eyes concerned and slightly abashed at imposing upon her. "It is about a three-hour ride. I don't know what we'll find." Another worried shake of his head.

Josh spoke up. "We're held up here for the day anyway."

He touched her elbow and leaned closer. "But I should go with you."

Lisa balked at this suggestion. She knew how to take care of herself. But she had also been instructed on the tense political climate in Nepal since 1996. Maoist rebels had been waging a guerrilla war in the highlands, seeking to overthrow the constitutional monarchy and replace it with a socialist republic. They were known to hack off victims' limbs—one by one—with farm sickles. Though there was currently a cease-fire, occasional atrocities were still committed.

She eyed the well-oiled automatic rifle in the soldier's hands. When even a holy man needed an armed escort, perhaps she had better reconsider her brother's offer.

"I . . . I have little more than a first aid kit and some monitoring equipment," she said haltingly to the monk. "I'm hardly suited for a major medical situation involving multiple patients."

The monk nodded and waved to the idling helicopter. Its rotors still spun. "Dr. Sorenson has stocked us with everything we should need for the short term. We don't expect to impose upon your services for more than a day. The pilot has a satellite phone to relay your findings. Perhaps the matter has already been resolved, and we could return here as soon as midday."

A shadow passed over his features with this last statement. He didn't believe it. Worry threaded his words . . . that and perhaps a trace of fear.

She took a deep breath of the thin air. It barely filled her lungs. She had taken an oath. Besides, she had snapped enough photographs. She wanted to get back to real work.

The monk must have noted something in her face. "So you'll come."

"Yes."

"Lisa . . . ," Josh warned.

"I'll be fine." She squeezed his arm. "You have a team to keep from mutinying on you."

Josh glanced back to Boston Bob and sighed.

"So hold the fort here until I get back."

He faced her again, not swayed, but he did not argue. His face remained tight. "Be careful out there."

"I have the very best of the Royal Nepalese Army to watch my back."

Josh stared at the lone soldier's oiled weapon. "That's what I'm worried about." He tried to lighten it with a snort, but it came out more bitter.

Lisa knew that was the best she'd manage out of him. She quickly gave him a hug, gathered her medical backpack from her tent, and in moments, she was ducking under the razored threat of the spinning rotors and climbing into the backseat of the rescue helicopter.

The pilot did not even acknowledge her. The soldier took the copilot seat. The monk, who introduced himself as Ang Gelu, joined her in the backseat.

She donned a set of sound-dampening headphones. Still, the engines roared as the blades spun faster. The craft bobbled on its treads as the rotors tried to grip the thin air. A whine ratcheted up into subsonic ranges. The craft finally lifted free of the rocky helipad and rose rapidly.

Lisa felt her stomach sink below her navel as the craft circled out over a neighboring gorge. She stared through the side window and down to the clutter of tents and yaks below. She spotted her brother. He had an arm lifted in farewell, or was it just raised against the sun's glare? Next to him stood Taski Sherpa, easily identifiable by his cowboy hat.

The Sherpa's earlier assessment followed her into the sky, icing through her thoughts and worries.

Death rides these winds.

Not a pleasant thought at the moment.

Beside her, the monk's lips moved in silent prayer. He

remained tense . . . whether from their mode of transport or in fear of what they might discover at the monastery.

Lisa leaned back, the Sherpa's words still echoing in her head.

A bad day indeed.

9:13 A.M.
ELEVATION: 22,230 FEET

He moved along the chasm floor with easy strides, steel crampons gouging deep into snow and ice. To either side rose cliffs of bare stone, pictographed in brown lichen. The gorge angled upward.

Toward his goal.

He wore a one-piece goose-down suit, camouflaged in shades of white and black. His head was covered by a polar-fleece balaclava, his face hidden behind snow goggles. His climbing pack weighed twenty-one kilos, including the ice ax strapped to one side and a coil of poly rope on the other.

He also carried a Heckler & Koch assault rifle, an extra twenty-round magazine, and a satchel holding nine incendiary grenades.

He had no need for additional oxygen, not even at this elevation. The mountains had been his home for the past forty-four years. He was as well habituated to these highlands as any Sherpa, but he didn't speak their language and a different heritage shone from his eyes: one eye a glacial blue, the other a pure white. The disparity marked him as surely as the tattoo on his shoulder. Even among the *Sonnekönige,* the Knights of the Sun.

The radio in his ear buzzed.

"Have you reached the monastery?"

He touched his throat. "Fourteen minutes."

"No word must escape of the accident."

"It will be handled." He kept his tone even, breathing through his nose. He heard as much fear as command in the other's voice. Such weakness. It was one of the reasons he seldom visited the *Granitschloß,* the Granite Castle, preferring to live on the fringes, as was his right.

No one asked him to move any closer.

They only asked for his expertise when it was most needed.

His earpiece crackled. "They will reach the monastery soon."

He didn't bother to answer. He heard a distant *thump* of rotors. He calculated in his head. No need to hurry. The mountains taught patience.

He steadied his breathing and continued down toward the cluster of stone buildings with red-tile roofs. Temp Och Monastery sat perched at the edge of a cliff, approachable only by a single path from below. The monks and students seldom had to worry about the rest of the world.

Until three days ago.

The accident.

It was his job to clean it up.

The bell-beat of the approaching helicopter grew louder, rising from below. He kept his pace steady. Plenty of time. It was important that those who approached enter the monastery.

It would be much easier to kill them all.

9:35 A.M.

From the helicopter, the world below had frozen into a stark photographic negative. A study in contrasts. Blacks and whites. Snow and rock. Mist-shrouded peaks and shadowed gorges. The morning light reflected achingly off ice ridges and glacial cliffs, threatening snow blindness from the aerial glare.

Lisa blinked away the brightness. Who would live so far from everything? In such an unforgiving environment? Why did mankind always find such inhospitable places to claim when much easier lives were available to them?

Then again, her mother often posed the same riddle to Lisa. Why such extremes? Five years at sea on a research vessel, then another year training and conditioning for the rigors of mountain climbing, and now here in Nepal, preparing to assault Everest. Why such risks when an easier life was readily available?

Lisa's answer had always been a simple one: *for the challenge of it.* Hadn't George Mallory, mountaineering legend, answered similarly when asked why he climbed Everest? *Because it was there.* Of course, the true story behind that famous line was that Mallory had issued it in exasperation to a badgering journalist. Had Lisa's response to her mother's inquiries been any less a knee-jerk reaction? What *was* she doing up here? Everyday life offered enough challenges: making a living, saving for retirement, finding someone to love, surviving loss, raising children.

Lisa balked at these thoughts, recognizing a twinge of anxiety and realizing what it might imply. *Could I be living a life on the edge to avoid living a real one? Is that perhaps why so many men have passed through my life without stopping?*

And here she was. Thirty-three, alone, no prospects, only her research for company, and a one-person sleeping bag for a bed. Maybe she should just shave her head and move into one of these mountaintop monasteries.

The helicopter jittered, angling up.

Her attention focused back to the moment.

Oh, crap . . .

Lisa held her breath as the helicopter skimmed a sharp ridge. Its skids barely cleared the windswept lip of ice and dove into the neighboring gorge.

She forced her fingers to unlock from the seat's armrest. Suddenly a three-bedroom cottage with two-point-five kids didn't sound so bad.

Beside her, Ang Gelu leaned forward and pointed between pilot and soldier, motioning below. The roar of the rotors swallowed his words.

Lisa leaned her cheek against the door's window to peer outside. The curve of cold Plexiglas kissed her cheek. Below, she spotted the first bit of color. A tumble of red-tile roofs. A small collection of eight stone lodges perched on a plateau, framed by twenty-thousand-foot peaks on three sides and a vertical cliff on the fourth.

Temp Och Monastery.

The helicopter dropped precipitously toward the buildings. Lisa noted a terraced potato field to one side. Some corrals and barns sprawled on the other. No movement. No one came out to greet the noisy newcomers.

More ominously, Lisa noted a collection of goats and blue bharal sheep gathered in the penned corrals. They weren't moving either. Rather than driven into a panic by the descending helicopter, they were all sprawled on the ground, legs twisted, necks bent, unnatural.

Ang Gelu noted the same and sank into the seat. His eyes found hers. What had happened? Some argument was under way between pilot and soldier in the front seat. Plainly the pilot didn't want to land. The soldier won the argument by placing a palm on the butt of his rifle. The pilot scowled and snugged his oxygen mask tighter over his nose and mouth. Not because he needed the additional air, but in fear of contagion.

Still, the pilot obeyed the soldier's orders. He strangled the controls and lowered the craft earthward. He aimed as far from the corrals as possible, dropping toward the edge of the monastery's potato fields.

The fields rose in an amphitheater of tiers, lined by rows

of tiny green sprouts. High-altitude potato farming had been introduced by the British in the early nineteenth century and potatoes had become one of the subsistence crops of the area. With a jarring bump, the helicopter's skids struck the rocky soil, crushing a row of plants. Neighboring sprouts whipped and waved in the rotor wash.

Still no one acknowledged their arrival. She pictured the dead livestock. Was there even anyone to rescue? What had happened here? Various etiologies ran through her head, along with routes of exposure: ingestion, inhalation, contact. Or was it contagious? She needed more information.

"Perhaps you should stay here," Ang Gelu said to Lisa while unbuckling his seat straps. "Let us check out the monastery."

Lisa grabbed her medical pack from the floor. She shook her head. "I have no fear of the sick. And there may be questions only I can answer."

Ang Gelu nodded, spoke hurriedly to the soldier, and cracked open the rear hatch. He climbed out, turning to offer a hand to Lisa.

Cold winds swept into the heated interior, aided by the rush of the rotors. Pulling up her parka's hood, Lisa found the frigid draft drained whatever oxygen was still in the air at this altitude. Or maybe it was her fear. Her earlier words were braver than she felt.

She took the monk's hand. Even through her woolen mittens, she felt his strength and warmth. He did not bother covering his shaved head, seemingly oblivious to the icy cold.

She clambered out but stayed ducked under the sweep of the helicopter blades. The soldier left last. The pilot remained inside the cabin. Though he might land the helicopter as ordered, he was taking no chances in leaving its canopy.

Ang Gelu slammed the hatch closed and the trio hurried across the potato field toward the jumble of stone buildings.

From the ground, the red-shingled lodges were taller than they seemed from the air. The centermost structure looked to be three stories tall, topped with a pagoda-style roof. All the buildings were elaborately decorated. Rainbow-hued murals framed doors and windows. Gold leaf brightened lintels, while carved stone dragons and mythic birds sneered and leered from roof corners. Covered porticos linked the various buildings, creating little courtyards and private spaces. Wooden prayer wheels, carved with ancient lettering, were mounted on poles throughout the structures. Multicolored prayer flags draped from rooflines, snapping in the intermittent gusts.

While it had a fairy-tale appearance to it, a mountaintop Shangri-La, Lisa still found her steps slowing. Nothing moved. Most of the windows were shuttered. Silence weighed heavily.

Then there was the distinct taint to the air. Though mostly a researcher, Lisa had experienced her share of death while a medical resident. The fetid miasma of rot could not be so easily blown away. She prayed it was coming only from the livestock on the far side of the pavilion. But from the lack of response to their presence, she didn't hold out much hope.

Ang Gelu led the way, flanked by the soldier. Lisa was forced to hurry to keep up with them. They passed between two buildings and headed toward the central towering structure.

In the main courtyard, farm implements lay strewn haphazardly, as if abandoned in a hurry. A cart tethered to a yak stood overturned on its side. The animal was dead, too, sprawled on its flank, belly distended with bloat. Milky eyes stared at them. A distended tongue protruded from black swollen lips.

Lisa noted the lack of flies or other tiny opportunists. Were there flies at this altitude? She wasn't sure. She searched the skies. No birds. No noise except the hushed wind.

"This way," Ang Gelu said.

The monk headed for a set of tall doors that led into the central dwelling, clearly the main temple. He tested the latch, found it unlocked, and pulled it open with a moan of hinges.

Beyond the threshold, the first sign of life flickered. To either side of the doorway, barrel-size lamps glowed with a dozen flaming wicks. Butter lamps, fueled by yak butter. The fetid odor was worse inside. It did not bode well.

Even the soldier now held back from crossing the threshold, shifting the automatic weapon from one shoulder to the other, as if to reassure himself. The monk simply strode inside. He called out a greeting. It echoed.

Lisa entered behind Ang Gelu. The soldier kept a station at the doorstep.

A few more barrel lamps illuminated the temple's interior. To either side, towering prayer wheels lined the walls, while juniper-scented candles and incense sticks burned near an eight-foot-tall teak statue of Buddha. Other gods of the pantheon were lined behind his shoulders.

As Lisa's eyes adjusted to the gloomy interior, she noted the numerous wall paintings and intricately carved wooden mandalas, depicting scenes that in the flickering light seemed demonic. She glanced upward. Raftered tiers climbed two stories, supporting a nest of hanging lamps, all dark and cold.

Ang Gelu called again.

Somewhere above their heads, something creaked.

The sudden noise froze them all. The soldier flicked on a flashlight and waved it above. Shadows jittered and jumped, but nothing was there.

Again the creak of planks sounded. Someone was moving on the top floor. Despite the positive sign of life, Lisa's skin pebbled with goose bumps.

Ang Gelu spoke. "A private meditation room overlooks the temple. There are stairs in back. I will check. You stay here."

Lisa wanted to obey, but she felt the weight of both her medical backpack and her responsibility. It wasn't the hand of man that had slain the livestock. That she was certain. If there was a survivor, anyone to tell what happened here, she was best suited for this task.

She hefted her pack higher on the shoulder. "I'm coming."

Despite her steady voice, she let Ang Gelu go first.

He crossed around behind the Buddha statue to an arched doorway near the back. He pushed through a drape of gold-embroidered brocade. A small hallway led deeper into the structure. Shuttered windows allowed a few slivers of light into the dusty gloom. They illuminated a whitewashed wall. The splash of crimson and smear along one wall did not require closer inspection.

Blood.

A pair of slack naked legs stuck out of a doorway half-way down the hall . . . resting in a black pool. Ang Gelu motioned her back into the temple. She shook her head and moved past him. She didn't expect to save whoever lay there. It was plain he must already be dead. But instinct drew her forward. In five strides, she was at the body.

In a heartbeat, she took in the scene and fell back.

Legs. That's all there was left of the man. Only a pair of chopped limbs, cleaved midthigh. She stared deeper into the room—into the slaughterhouse. Arms and legs lay stacked like cords of firewood in the center of the room.

And then there were the severed heads, neatly aligned along one wall, staring inward, eyes wide with the horror of it all.

Ang Gelu was at her side. He stiffened at the sight and mumbled something that sounded like half prayer, half curse.

As if hearing him, something stirred in the room. It

rose from the far side of the pile of limbs. A naked figure, shaven-headed, drenched in blood like a newborn. It was one of the temple's monks.

A guttural hiss rose from the figure. Madness shone damply. Eyes caught the meager light and reflected back, like a wolf at night.

It lumbered toward them, dragging a three-foot-long sickle across the planks. Lisa fled several steps down the hall. Ang Gelu spoke softly, palms raised in supplication, plainly trying to placate the ravening creature.

"Relu Na," he said. "Relu Na."

Lisa realized Ang Gelu recognized the madman, someone he knew from an earlier visit to the monastery. The simple act of giving the man a name both humanized him and made the awfulness all that more horrific.

With a grating cry, the monk leaped at his fellow brother. Ang Gelu easily ducked the sickle. The figure's coordination had deteriorated along with his mind. Ang Gelu bearhugged the other, grappling him, pinning him to one side of the doorframe.

Lisa acted quickly. She dropped her pack, tugged down a zipper, and removed a metal case. She popped it open with her thumb.

Inside lay a row of plastic syringes, secured and preloaded with various emergency drugs: morphine for pain, epinephrine for anaphylaxis, Lasix for pulmonary edema. Though each syringe was labeled, she had their positions memorized. In an emergency, every second counted. She plucked out the last syringe.

Midazolam. Injectable sedative. Mania and hallucinations were not uncommon at severe altitudes, requiring chemical restraint at times.

Using her teeth, she uncapped the needle and hurried forward.

Ang Gelu had the man still trapped, but the monk thrashed

and bucked in his grip. Ang Gelu's lip was split. He had gouges along one side of his neck.

"Hold him still!" Lisa yelled.

Ang Gelu tried his best—but at that moment, perhaps sensing the doctor's intent, the madman lashed forward and bit deep into Ang Gelu's cheek.

The monk screamed as his flesh was torn to bone.

But he still held tight.

Lisa rushed to his aid and jammed the needle into the madman's neck. She slammed the plunger home. "Let him go!"

Ang Gelu shoved the man hard against the frame, cracking the monk's skull against the wood. They backed away.

"The sedative will hit him in less than a minute." She would have preferred an intravenous stick, but there was no way to manage that with the man's wild thrashings. The deep intramuscular injection would have to suffice. Once quieted, she would be able to finesse her care, perhaps glean some answers.

The naked monk groaned, pawing at his neck. The sedative stung. He lurched again in their direction, reaching down again for his abandoned sickle. He straightened.

Lisa tugged Ang Gelu back. "Just wait—"

—*crack*—

The rifle blast deafened in the narrow hall. The monk's head exploded in a shower of blood and bone. His body fell back with the impact, crumpling under him.

Lisa and Ang Gelu stared aghast at the shooter.

The Nepalese soldier held his weapon on his shoulder. He slowly lowered it. Ang Gelu began berating him in his native tongue, all but taking the weapon from the soldier.

Lisa crossed to the body and checked for a pulse. None. She stared at his body, trying to determine some answer. It would take a morgue with modern forensic facilities to ascertain the cause for the madness. From the messenger's story, whatever had occurred here hadn't affected just the one man. Others must have been afflicted to varying degrees.

But by what? Had they been exposed to some heavy metal in the water, a subterranean leak of poisonous gas, or some toxic mold in old grain? Could it be something viral, like Ebola? Or even a new form of mad cow disease? She tried to remember if yaks were susceptible. She pictured the bloated carcass in the courtyard. She didn't know.

Ang Gelu returned to her side. His cheek was a bloody ruin, but he seemed oblivious to his injury. All his pain was focused on the body beside her.

"His name was Relu Na Havarshi."

"You knew him."

A nod. "He was my sister's husband's cousin. From a small rural village in Raise. He had fallen under the sway of the Maoist rebels, but their escalating savagery was not in his nature. He fled. For the rebels, it was a death sentence to do so. To hide him, I secured him a position at the monastery . . . where his former comrades would never find him. Here, he found a serene place to heal . . . or so I had prayed. Now he will have to find his own path to that peace."

"I'm sorry."

Lisa stood. She pictured the pile of limbs in the neighboring room. Had the madness triggered some post-traumatic shock, causing him to act out what horrified him the most?

Overhead another popping creak sounded.

All eyes turned upward.

She had forgotten what had drawn them all back here. Ang Gelu pointed to a steep narrow stair beside the draped doorway to the temple. She had missed it. It was more a ladder than a stair.

"I will go," he said.

"We all stick together," she argued. She crossed to her bag and preloaded another syringe of sedative. She kept it in her hand. "Just make sure Quick Draw McGraw over there keeps his finger off the trigger."

The soldier went up the ladder first. He scouted the immediate vicinity and waved them up. Lisa climbed and discovered an empty room. Stacks of thin pillows were piled in one corner. The room smelled of resin and the waft of incense from the temple room below.

The soldier had his weapon trained on a wooden door on the far side. Flickering light leaked under the jam. Before anyone could move closer, a shadow passed across the bar of light.

Someone was in there.

Ang Gelu stepped forward and knocked.

The creaking halted.

He called through the door. Lisa didn't understand his words, but someone else did. A scrape of wood sounded. A latch was lifted. The door teetered slightly open—but no farther.

Ang Gelu put his palm on the door.

"Be careful," Lisa whispered, tightening her grip on her syringe, her only weapon.

Beside her, the soldier did the same with his rifle.

Ang Gelu pushed the door the rest of the way open. The room beyond was no larger than a walk-in closet. A soiled bed stood in the corner. A small side table supported an oil lamp. The air was ripe with the fetid tang of urine and feces from an open chamber pot at the foot of the bed. Whoever had holed up here had not ventured out in days.

In a corner, an old man stood with his back to them. He wore the same red robe as Ang Gelu, but his clothes were ragged and stained. The owner had tied the lower folds around his upper thighs, exposing his bare legs. He worked on a project, writing on the wall. Fingerpainting, in fact.

With his own blood.

More madness.

He carried a short dagger in his other hand. His bared legs were striped with deep cuts, the source of his ink. He continued to work, even as Ang Gelu entered.

"Lama Khemsar," Ang Gelu said, concern and wariness in his voice.

Lisa entered behind him, syringe ready in her fingers. She nodded to Ang Gelu when he looked back at her. She also waved the soldier back. She didn't want a repeat of what had happened below.

Lama Khemsar turned. His face was slack, and his eyes appeared glassy and slightly milky, but the candlelight reflected brightly, too brightly, fever-bright.

"Ang Gelu," the old monk muttered, staring in a daze at the hundreds of lines of script painted across all four walls. A bloody finger raised, ready to continue the work.

Ang Gelu stepped toward him, plainly relieved. The man, master of the monastery, was not too far gone yet. Perhaps answers could be obtained. Ang Gelu spoke in their native tongue.

Lama Khemsar nodded, though he refused to be drawn from his opus in blood. Lisa studied the wall as Ang Gelu coaxed the old monk. Though she was not familiar with the script, she saw the work was merely the same grouping of symbols repeated over and over again.

Sensing there must be some meaning here, Lisa reached to her bag and freed her camera with one hand. She aimed it at the wall from her hip and snapped a picture. She forgot about the flash.

The room burst with brilliance.

The old man cried out. He swung around, dagger in hand. He swiped through the air. Ang Gelu, startled, fell back. But Ang Gelu had not been the target. Lama Khemsar cried out a smattering of words in abject fear and drew the blade's edge across his own throat. A line of crimson became a pulsing downpour. The cut sliced deep into the trachea. Blood bubbled with the old monk's last breaths.

Ang Gelu lunged and knocked aside the blade. He caught Lama Khemsar and lowered him to the floor, cradling him. Blood soaked the robe and across Ang Gelu's arms and lap.

Lisa dropped her camera and bag and hurried forward. Ang Gelu tried to put pressure on the wound, but it was futile.

"Help me get him to the floor," Lisa said. "I have to secure an airway . . ."

Ang Gelu shook his head. He knew it was hopeless. He simply rocked the old lama. The man's breathing, marked by the bubbling from the slash, had already stopped. Age, blood loss, and dehydration had already debilitated Lama Khemsar.

"I'm sorry," Lisa said. "I thought . . ." She waved an arm at the walls. "I thought it might be important."

Ang Gelu shook his head. "It's gibberish. A madman's scribblings."

Not knowing what else to do, Lisa freed her stethoscope and slipped it under the edge of the man's robe. She sought to mask her guilt with busywork. She listened in vain. No heartbeat. But she discovered odd scabbing across the man's ribs. Gently she peeled back the soaked front of his robe and bared the monk's chest.

Ang Gelu stared down and exhaled sharply.

It seemed the walls were not the only medium upon which Lama Khemsar chose to work. A final symbol had been carved into the monk's chest, sliced by the same dagger, by the same hand most likely. Unlike the strange symbols on the walls, the twisted cross could not be mistaken.

A swastika.

Before they could react, the first explosion rocked the building.

9:55 A.M.

He woke in a panic.

The rumble of thunder shook him out of a feverish darkness. Not thunder. An explosion. Plaster dusted down from the low ceiling. He sat up, disoriented, struggling to fix himself in time and place. The room spun a bit around him. He searched down, throwing back a soiled woolen blanket. He lay in a strange cot, wearing nothing but a linen breechclout. He lifted an arm. It trembled. His mouth tasted of warm paste, and though the room was shuttered against the light, his eyes ached. A paroxysmal bout of shivering shook through him.

He had no idea where or even *when* he was.

Shifting his legs off the cot, he attempted to stand. Bad idea. The world went black again. He slumped and would have slipped into oblivion, but a spat of gunfire centered him. Automatic fire. Close. The short burst died away.

He tried again, more determined. Memory returned as he lurched toward the only door, struck it, held himself up by his arms, and tried the knob.

Locked.

9:57 A.M.

"It was the helicopter," Ang Gelu said. "It's been destroyed."

Lisa stood to one side of the high window. Moments before, as the explosive blast echoed away, they had freed the window latches and shoved the shutters wide. The soldier had thought he'd seen movement in the courtyard below and strafed wildly.

There was no return fire.

"Could it have been the pilot?" Lisa asked. "Maybe there was a problem with the engine and he evacuated in a panic."

The soldier kept his post by the window, resting his stock on the sill, one eye to the scope, scanning and sweeping.

Ang Gelu pointed to the roil of oily smoke rising from the potato fields. Exactly where the helicopter had been parked. "I don't believe that was a mechanical accident."

"What do we do now?" Lisa asked. Had another of the crazed monks blown up the chopper? If so, how many other maniacs were loose in the monastery? She pictured the sickle-wielding wild man, the self-mutilation of the monk . . . what the hell was happening here?

"We must leave," Ang Gelu said.

"And go where?"

"There are tiny villages and occasional homesteads within a day's walk. Whatever has transpired here will require more than three people to discern."

"What of the others here? Some may not be as far gone as your brother-in-law's cousin. Should we not try to help them?"

"My first concern must be for your safety, Dr. Cummings. Additionally word must reach someone in authority."

"But what if whatever agent struck here is contagious? We could spread it by traveling."

The monk fingered his wounded cheek. "With the helicopter destroyed, we have no means of communication. If we stay here, we die, too . . . and no word reaches the outside world."

He made a good point.

"We can minimize our exposure to others until we know

more," he continued. "Call out for help, but maintain a safe distance."

"No physical contact," she mumbled.

He nodded. "The information we bear is worth the risk."

Lisa slowly nodded. She stared at the column of black smoke against the blue sky. Possibly one of their party was already dead. There was no telling the true number of afflicted here. The explosion would surely have roused others. If they were to make their escape, it would have to be quickly.

"Let's go," she said.

Ang Gelu spoke sharply to the soldier. He straightened with a nod and retreated from his post at the window, his gun at the ready.

Lisa gave the room and the monk one last worried glance, considering the possibility of contagion. Were they already infected? She found herself internally judging her status as she followed the others out of the room and down the ladder. Her mouth was dry, her jaw muscles ached, and her pulse beat heavily in her throat. But that was just the fear, wasn't it? A typical flight-or-fight response to the situation, normal autonomic responses. She touched her forehead. Damp, but not feverish. She took a deep breath to steady herself, to recognize the foolishness. Even if the agent was infectious, the incubation period would be longer than an hour.

They crossed through the main temple with its teak Buddha and attendant gods. Daylight glared exceptionally bright through the doorway.

Their armed escort checked the courtyard for a full minute, then waved an all clear. Lisa and Ang Gelu followed.

As Lisa stepped into the courtyard, she searched the dark corners for sudden movement. All seemed quiet again.

But not for long . . .

With her back turned, a second detonation tore through the building across the courtyard. The force blew her to her hands and knees. She ducked, rolling on one shoulder to stare behind her.

Roof tiles sailed skyward amid flames. A pair of fireballs blasted out of shattered windows, while the door to the lodge exploded into a splintery ruin, belching out more smoke and fire. Heat washed over her like the exhalation from a blast furnace.

The soldier, a few steps ahead, had been knocked onto his backside by the blast. He'd kept his gun only by locking his fingers on its leather strap. He scrambled up as a rain of broken tiles fell from the sky.

Ang Gelu gained his own feet and offered a hand to Lisa.

It was his undoing.

A sharper blast punctuated the clatter of tiles and roar of flames. A gunshot. The upper half of the monk's face blew away in a mist of blood.

But this time it was not the handiwork of her armed escort.

The soldier's rifle still hung from its strap as the man fled the rain of stone tiles. He seemed deaf to the shot, but his eyes widened as Ang Gelu toppled over. Reacting on pure reflex, he dodged to the right, throwing himself into the shadow of the neighboring lodge. He yelled at Lisa, unintelligible in his panic.

Lisa crab-crawled back toward the temple doorway. Another shot sparked off the rocky courtyard. At her toes. She flung herself across the threshold and into the dark interior.

Ducking around a corner, she watched the soldier sidle along the wall, careful to keep clear of where he estimated the sniper might be perched.

Lisa forgot how to breathe, eyes fixed wide. She searched the rooflines, the windows. Who had shot Ang Gelu?

Then she saw him.

A shadow sprinted through the smoke billowing out of the far building. She caught a reflection of flames off gun-metal as the man ran. A weapon. The sniper had fled his original position and was tacking for a new vantage.

Lisa moved back into the open, praying the shadows hid her well. She called and waved to the soldier. He had his back to the wall, sliding toward her location, toward the main temple. His gaze and weapon focused on the roofline overhead. He had not seen the flight of the sniper.

She yelled again. "Get out!" She didn't speak the language, but her panic must've been plain. His eyes met hers. She urged him over to her hiding place. She pointed, trying to illustrate the path the sniper had fled. But where had he gone? Was he already in position?

"Run!" she screamed.

The soldier took a step toward her. A flash over the man's shoulder revealed Lisa's mistaken assumption. The sniper hadn't been sprinting to gain a new vantage. Flames danced behind a window in the neighboring building. Another bomb.

Oh, God . . .

The detonation caught the soldier in midstep. The doorway behind him exploded outward with a thousand fiery shards, piercing through the soldier at the same time the blast lifted him off his feet and tossed him across the yard. He landed hard on his face and slid.

Once stopped, he did not move, even as flames ignited his clothing.

Lisa dodged into the depths of the main temple, eyes searching the doorway. She retreated toward the rear exit, back toward the narrow hall. She didn't have a plan. In fact, she barely had control of her own thoughts.

She was certain of only one thing. Whoever had murdered Ang Gelu and their escort had been no maddened monk. The actions had been too calculated, the execution too planned.

And now she was alone.

She checked the narrow hallway, spotted the bloody body

of Relu Na. The rest of the hallway appeared clear. If she could get the dead man's abandoned sickle . . . at least have some weapon in hand . . .

She stepped into the hall.

Before she could take a second step, a form materialized behind her. A bare arm clamped tight around her neck. Hoarse words barked at her ear. "Don't move."

Never one to obey, Lisa drove her elbow into the gut of her attacker.

A satisfying *oof* and the arm fell away. The attacker fell back through the embroidered brocade drapery across the doorway, tearing it down with his weight. He landed on his backside.

Lisa spun, crouched and ready to run.

The man wore only a loincloth. His skin was deeply tanned but roped here and there with old scars. Lank black hair, disheveled, half-obscured his face. From his size, musculature, and broad shoulders, he appeared more Native American than Tibetan monk.

Then again, it could just be the loincloth.

With a groan, he looked up at her. Ice blue eyes reflected the lamplight.

"Who are you?" she asked.

"Painter," he said with a groan. "Painter Crowe."

2

DARWIN'S BIBLE

MAY 16
6:05 A.M.
COPENHAGEN, DENMARK

What was it with bookstores and cats?

Commander Grayson Pierce crunched another chewable Claritin tablet as he left Hotel Nyhavn. Yesterday's research among Copenhagen's bibliophile community had led him through a half dozen of the city's literary establishments. In every bookstore, colonies of dander-rich felines seemed to have taken up residence, lounging on counters, prowling the top of teetering bookshelves filled with dust and moldering leather.

He suffered for it now, stifling a sneeze. Or maybe it was simply the beginning of a cold. Spring in Copenhagen was as damp and cold as any New England winter. He had not packed warmly enough.

He wore a sweater he had purchased from an overpriced boutique neighboring his hotel. The turtleneck was corded merino wool, undyed and plain. And it itched. Still, it warded off the early morning chill. Though dawn was an hour past, the cold sun in a slate-gray sky offered no hope of a warmer day. Scratching at his collar, he headed toward the central train station.

His hotel was located beside one of the city's canals. Gaily painted row houses—a mix of shops, hostelries, and private homes—lined both sides of the waterway, reminding Gray of Amsterdam. Along the banks, a motley assortment of watercraft were moored tightly together: faded low-slung sloops, bright excursion boats, stately wooden schooners, gleaming white yachts. Gray passed one with a shake of his head. It looked like a floating wedding cake. Already at this early hour, a few camera-laden visitors wandered about or took up posts along the bridge rails, snapping away.

Gray crossed the stone span and followed the canal's bank for a half block, then stopped and leaned against the brick parapet that overlooked the waterway. His reflection in the still water appeared below, startling him a moment. Half-shadowed, his father's face stared back up at him; coal black hair hung lankily over blue eyes, a crooked cleft divided the chin, the planes of his face were all sharp angles defining a stony Welsh heritage. He was definitely his father's son. A fact Gray had been dwelling on a bit too much lately, and it was keeping him up at night.

What else had he inherited from his father?

A pair of black swans glided past his position, disturbing the waters, trembling apart the reflection. The swans headed for the bridge, their long necks sashaying, eyes searching with a nonchalant air.

Gray followed their example. Straightening, he feigned interest in taking a photo of the line of boats while actually studying the bridge he had just crossed. He watched for any stragglers, any familiar faces, anyone suspicious. It was one advantage of residing near the canal. The bridges were perfect squeeze points to observe anyone trailing him. By crisscrossing the stone spans, he would force any tail into the open. He watched for a full minute until satisfied, memorizing faces and gaits, then continued on.

On such a minor assignment as this one, the habit was more paranoid than necessary, but he carried a reminder around his neck of the importance of diligence: a chain from which hung a small silver dragon charm. It had been a gift from an operative playing on the other side of the fence. He carried it as a reminder. To be wary.

As he set off again, a familiar vibration stirred in his pocket. He retrieved his cell phone and flipped it open. Who was calling him at this early hour?

"Pierce here," he answered.

"Gray. Good, I reached you."

The familiar silkiness of the voice warmed through his morning chill. A smile softened his hard features. "Rachel . . . ?" His steps faltered with concern. "Is something wrong?"

Rachel Verona was the primary reason Gray had asked for this assignment, winging across the Atlantic to Denmark. While the current investigation could have been handled by any low-level research assistant at Sigma, the mission offered a perfect opportunity to reconnect with the beautiful dark-haired lieutenant of the Italian carabinieri. The two had met while working a case last year in Rome. Since then they had fabricated whatever excuse to meet. Still, it had proven difficult. Her position kept her landlocked in Europe, while his position with Sigma Force limited his time away from Washington. It had been almost eight weeks since they'd last been together.

Much too long.

Gray pictured their last rendezvous, at a villa in Venice, Rachel's form silhouetted against the open balcony door, her skin aglow in the light of the setting sun. They'd spent that entire evening in bed. Memories washed through him: the cinnamon-and-chocolate taste of her lips, the rich perfume of her damp hair, the heat of her breath on his neck, the soft moans, the rhythm of their entwined bodies, the caress of silk . . .

He prayed she remembered to pack that black teddy.

"My flight's been delayed," Rachel said, interrupting his reverie with reality.

"What?" He straightened beside the canal, unable to keep the disappointment from his voice.

"I've been rerouted on a KLM flight. I now land at twenty-two hundred."

Ten o'clock. He frowned. That meant canceling their sunset dinner reservations at St. Gertruds Kloster, a candlelit restaurant nestled inside the medieval monastery vault. He'd had to book it a full week in advance.

"I'm sorry," Rachel said, filling his silence.

"No . . . no worries. As long as you get here. That's all that matters."

"I know. I miss you so much."

"Me, too."

Gray shook his head at his lame response. He had so much more in his heart, but the words refused to come. Why was it always like this? The first day of every rendezvous required overcoming a certain formality between them, an awkward shyness. While it was easy to romanticize that they would simply fall easily and immediately into each other's arms, the reality was different. For the first hours, they were merely strangers with a shared past. They would certainly hug, kiss, say the right things, but the deeper intimacy required a span of time, hours necessary to catch up on each other's lives on either side of the Atlantic. But more importantly, they sought to find their rhythm again, that warm cadence that would smolder into the more passionate.

And each time Gray feared they would not find it.

"How is your father doing?" Rachel asked, beginning the first steps of the dance.

He welcomed the diversion, while not necessarily the

subject matter. But at least he had good news. "He's actually doing very well. His symptoms have pretty much stabilized as of late. Only a few bouts of confusion. My mother is convinced the improvement is due to curry."

"Curry? As in the spice?"

"Exactly. She read an article that curcumin, the yellow pigment in curry, acts as an antioxidant and anti-inflammatory. Possibly it even helps break down the amyloid plaques attributable to Alzheimer's."

"That does sound promising."

"So now my mother puts curry into everything. Even my father's scrambled eggs in the morning. The whole house smells like an Indian restaurant."

Rachel's soft laughter brightened the dreary morning. "At least she's cooking."

Gray's smile broadened on its own. His mother, a tenured biology professor at George Washington University, had never been known for her homemaking skills. She'd been too busy building her career, a necessity after an industrial accident had disabled Gray's father almost two decades ago. Now the family was struggling with a new issue: the early stages of his father's Alzheimer's. Recently, Gray's mother had taken a short leave of absence from the university to help care for her husband, but now there was talk of her returning to the classroom. With everything going so well, it had proven a good time for Gray to escape D.C. for this short trip.

Before he could respond, his phone chimed with another call. He checked the caller ID. *Damn . . .*

"Rachel, I've got a call coming in from central command. I'll need to take this. I'm sorry."

"Oh, then I'll let you go."

"Wait, Rachel. Your new flight number."

"It's KLM flight four zero three."

"Got it. I'll see you tonight."

"Tonight," she echoed back and clicked off.

Gray pressed his flash button to activate the other call. "Pierce here."

"Commander Pierce." The speaker's clipped New England accent identified the man immediately as Logan Gregory, second in command of Sigma Force, serving directly under Director Painter Crowe. In his usual perfunctory manner, Logan did not waste words.

"We've new chatter to report that may relate to your search in Copenhagen. Interpol reports a sudden increase in interest in today's auction."

Gray had crossed another bridge. He stopped again. Ten days ago, a database at the National Security Agency had flagged a series of black market trades, all pertaining to historical documents that once belonged to Victorian-era scientists. Someone was collecting manuscripts, transcripts, legal documents, letters, and diaries from that era, many with shady trails of ownership. And while normally this would be of little interest to Sigma Force, which concentrated on global security issues, the NSA database tied several of the sales to factions within terrorist organizations. And such organizations' money trails were always scrutinized.

Still it made no sense. While certainly such historical documents had proven to be a growing market for speculative investment, it was not the bailiwick of most terrorist organizations. Then again, times were changing.

Either way, Sigma Force had been tapped to investigate the principals involved. Gray's assignment was to get as much background on the by-invitation-only sale that was to occur later this afternoon, which included researching items of particular interest, several being put up by local collectors and shops in the area. Hence he had spent the past two days visiting the dusty bookstores and antiquary establishments in the narrow backstreets of Copenhagen. He discovered the most help at a shop on Højbro Plads, owned by an ex-lawyer from Georgia. With the ex-pat's help, Gray felt prepared. His plan this morning had been to canvass the auction site and secure a few buttonhole cameras near all entrances and exits. At the auction, Gray was merely to observe the principals and get head shots when possible. A minor assignment, but if it extended the database of peripheral players in the war on terror, all the better.

"What's stirred up the pot?" Gray asked.

"A new line item. It's attracted the attention of several of the principals we're investigating. An old Bible. Just put up by a private party."

"And what's so exciting about that?"

"According to the line item description, the Bible originally belonged to Darwin."

"As in *Charles* Darwin, the father of evolution?"

"Exactly."

Gray tapped a knuckle on the brick parapet. Another Victorian-era scientist. As he contemplated this, he studied the neighboring bridge.

He found himself fixated on a teenage girl in a dark blue zippered sweater-jacket with the hood pulled up. Seventeen . . . eighteen. Smooth-faced, her skin was the color of burnt caramel. Indian? Pakistani? What he could see of her black hair was long, spilling out one side of the hood in a single thick braid. She carried a green, battered pack over her left shoulder, like many of the backpacking college students.

Except Gray had seen the young woman before . . . crossing the first bridge. Her eyes met his for a moment across the fifty yards. She turned away too quickly. Sloppy.

She was following him.

Logan continued, "I've uploaded the seller's address into your phone's database. You should have enough time to interview the owner before the auction."

Gray glanced to the address that appeared on the screen, pinpointed on a city map. Eight blocks away, just off the

Strøget, the main pedestrian plaza that ran through the heart of Copenhagen. Not far.

But first . . .

From the corner of his eye, Gray continued to monitor the reflection of the bridge in the canal's still waters below. In the wavering mirror, he watched the girl hunch her shoulders, pulling her backpack higher in a weak attempt to hide her features.

Did she know her cover had been blown?

"Commander Pierce?" Logan said.

The girl reached the end of the bridge, strode away, and vanished down a side street. He waited to see if she doubled back.

"Commander Pierce, did you get that address?"

"Yes. I'll check into it."

"Very good." Logan signed off.

From the canal railing, Gray canvassed his surroundings, watching for the girl's return or the appearance of any accomplices. He regretted leaving his 9mm Glock in the hotel safe. But the instructions from the auction house warned that all invited participants would be searched upon entering, including passing through a metal detector. Gray's only weapon was a carbonized plastic knife in a boot sheath. That was it.

Gray waited.

Foot traffic flowed around him as the city woke. Behind him, a cadaverous shop owner was icing down a stack of street-side crates and slapping out a selection of fresh fish: Dover sole, cod, sand eel, and the ubiquitous herring.

The smell finally drove him from his post by the canal. He headed out, extra attentive to his back trail.

Perhaps he was being too paranoid, but in his profession, such a neurosis was healthy. He fingered the dragon pendant around his neck and continued into the city.

After several blocks, he felt secure enough to pull out a notepad. Written on the first page were items of particular interest, set for auction that afternoon.

1. A copy of Gregor Mendel's 1865 paper on genetics.

2. Max Planck's books on physics: *Thermodynamik* from 1897 and *Theorie der Wärmestrahlung* from 1906, both signed by the author.

3. Botanist Hugo de Vries's 1901 diary on plant mutations.

Gray had annotated as much information as he could about these items, from his research yesterday. He jotted down the latest item of interest.

4. Charles Darwin's family Bible.

Flipping the notebook closed, he wondered for the hundredth time since flying here: *What was the connection?*

Perhaps it was a puzzle best left to someone else at Sigma. He thought about having Logan run some of the details past his colleagues Monk Kokkalis and Kathryn Bryant. The pair had proven to be experts at piecing together details and constructing patterns where none existed. Then again, maybe there really was *no* pattern here. It was still too early to tell. Gray needed to gather a bit more intelligence, a few more facts, especially about this last item.

Until then, he'd leave the two lovebirds alone.

9:32 P.M. EST
WASHINGTON, D.C.

"It is true?"

Monk rested his palm on the bare belly of the woman he loved. He knelt beside the bed in orange-and-black Nike sweatpants. His shirt, wet after his evening jog, lay on the hardwood floor, where he had dropped it. His eyebrows, the only hair on his shaved head, were raised in hopeful expectation.

"Yes," Kat confirmed. She gently removed his hand and rolled out the other side of the bed.

Monk's grin grew broader. He could not help it. "Are you sure?"

Kat strode toward the bathroom, wearing only a pair of white panties and an oversize Georgia Tech T-shirt. Her straight auburn hair draped loose to her shoulders. "I was five days late," she answered sullenly. "I took an EPT test yesterday."

Monk stood up. "Yesterday? Why didn't you tell me?"

Kat disappeared into the bathroom, half closing the door.

"Kat?"

He heard the water turn on in the shower. He circled the bed and crossed to the bathroom doorway. He wanted to know more. She had dropped the bombshell when he returned from his jog to find her curled in bed. Her eyes had been swollen, her face puffy. She had been crying. It had taken some coaxing to discover what had been troubling her all day.

He rapped on the door. The noise was louder and more demanding than he intended. He scowled at the offending hand. The five-fingered prosthesis was state-of-the-art, chock full of the latest in DARPA gadgetry. He had received the hand after losing his own on a mission. But plastic and metal were not flesh. Rapping on the wood door had sounded like he was trying to batter it down.

"Kat, talk to me," he said gently.

"I'm just going to take a quick shower."

Despite her sighed words, Monk heard the strain. He peeked into the bathroom. Though they had been seeing each other for almost a year now and he had his own drawer in her apartment here, there were limits of propriety.

Kat sat atop the closed toilet, her head resting in her hands.

"Kathryn . . ."

She glanced up, plainly startled at the intrusion. "Monk!" She leaned to the door to push it the rest of the way closed.

He blocked it with his foot. "It wasn't like you were *using* the bathroom."

"I was waiting for the shower to warm up."

Monk noted the steam-fogged mirror as he entered. The chamber smelled of jasmine. A scent that evoked all manner of stirrings inside him. He stepped and knelt again before her.

She leaned back.

He placed his hands, one flesh, one synthetic, atop her knees.

She would not meet his eyes, head still hanging.

He pushed apart her knees, leaned between them, and slid his hands up along her outer thighs and cupped her buttocks. He pulled her to him.

"I have to—" she started.

"You have to come here." He lifted her and lowered her to his lap, straddling him now. His face was a breath from hers.

She finally met his eyes. "I . . . I'm sorry."

He leaned closer. "For what?" Their lips brushed each other's.

"I should've been more careful."

"I don't remember complaining."

"But this sort of mistake—"

"Never." He kissed her hard, not in anger but in firm assurance. He whispered between their lips. "Never call it that."

She melted into him, her arms entwining behind his neck. Her hair smelled of jasmine. "What are we going to do?"

"I may not know everything, but I *do* know that answer."

He rolled to the side and lowered her down to the bathroom rug beneath him.

"Oh," she said.

7:55 A.M.
COPENHAGEN, DENMARK

Gray sat in the café opposite the small antiquarian shop. He studied the building across the street.

SJÆLDEN BØGER was stenciled on the window. RARE BOOKS. The bookstore occupied the first floor of a two-story row house topped by a red-tile roof. It appeared identical to its neighbors, lined one after the other down the street. And like the others in this less affluent section of town, it had fallen into disrepair. The upper windows were boarded up. Even the first-floor shop was secured behind a steel drop-gate.

Closed for now.

As Gray waited for the shop to open, he eyed the building more clinically, sipping what passed for hot chocolate here in Denmark, so thick it tasted like a melted Hershey's bar. He searched beyond the boarded windows. Though the building had faded, its Old World charm persisted: owl-eyed dormers peered out from the attic, heavy exposed beams crisscrossed the upper story, and a steep pitch of the roofline stood forever ready to shrug off a long winter's snowfall. Gray even spotted old scars below the windows where flower boxes had once been bolted.

Gray contemplated ways of renovating the house back to its original glory, rebuilding it in his head, a mental exercise balancing engineering with aesthetics.

He could almost smell the sawdust.

This last thought suddenly soured the daydream. Other memories intruded, unbidden and unwanted: his father's woodshop in the garage, working alongside him after school. What usually started out as a simple renovation project often ended up in shouting matches and words too hard to take back. The warring had eventually driven Gray out of high school and into the military. Only lately had son and father found new ways to communicate, finding common ground, accepting differences.

Still, Gray was haunted by an offhand remark of his mother's. How father and son were more alike than they were different. Why had that been bothering him so much lately? Gray pushed the thoughts away and shook his head.

With his concentration broken, he checked his watch, anxious to get on with the day. He had already canvassed the auction site and secured two cameras at the front and rear access points. All he had to do was interview the shop owner here about the Bible and take some snapshots of the principals involved—then he was finished, opening up a long weekend to spend with Rachel.

The thought of her smile eased the knot that had developed between his shoulder blades.

Finally, across the street, a bell chimed. The door to the shop opened and the security gate began to roll up.

Gray sat straighter, surprised by who opened the shop. Black braided hair, mocha complexion, wide almond-shaped eyes. She was the one who had followed him earlier this morning. She even wore the same zippered sweater-jacket and green, battered pack.

Gray scooped out a bundle of bills and left it on the café table, glad to get out of his head and back to the business at hand.

He strode across the narrow street as the girl finished securing the gate. She glanced over at him, unsurprised.

"Let me guess, mate," she said in crisp English, flavored with a British accent, eyeing him up and down. "American."

He frowned at her abrupt manner. He hadn't said a word yet. But he kept his face mildly curious, offering no clue that he knew she had been following him earlier. "How did you know?"

"The way you walk. Stick up your bum. Gives all you away."

"Is that so?"

She locked the gate. He noted she wore several pins on her jacket: a rainbow Greenpeace flag, a silver Celtic symbol, a gold Egyptian ankh, and a colorful assortment of buttons with slogans in Danish and one in English that read GO LEMMINGS GO. She also wore a white rubber bracelet with the word HOPE stamped into it.

She waved him out of her way but bumped past him when he didn't move quick enough. She walked backward across the street. "Shop don't open for another hour. Sorry, mate."

Gray stood on the stoop, glancing between the shop door and the girl. She crossed the street and headed to the café. Passing the table he'd just vacated, she picked up one of the bills Gray had left and went inside. Gray waited. Through the window, he watched her order two large coffees and pay with the pilfered bill.

She returned, a tall Styrofoam cup in each hand.

"Still here?" she asked.

"Don't have anywhere else to be at the moment."

"Shame." The girl nodded to the closed door and lifted both hands. "Well?"

"Oh." Gray turned and opened the door for her.

She brushed inside. "Bertal!" she boomed—then glanced back at him. "Are you coming inside or not?"

"I thought you said—"

"Bollocks." She rolled her eyes. "Enough with the act. Like you didn't see me earlier."

Gray tensed. So it wasn't just coincidence. The girl *had* been following him.

She called into the shop. "Bertal! Get your tail over here!"

Confused and wary, Gray followed her into the shop. He stayed by the door, ready to move if necessary.

The shop was as narrow as an alley. To either side, rows of bookshelves rose from floor to ceiling, crammed with all manner of book, volume, text, and pamphlet. A few steps inside, two glass cabinets flanked the center aisle, plainly locked. Inside were crumbling leather-bound books and what looked like scrolls bound in acid-free white tubes.

Gray searched deeper.

Dust motes floated through the space in the slanting morning sunlight. The air tasted old, moldering as much as the shop's paper stock. It was like much of Europe. Age and ancientness were a part of everyday life here.

Still, despite the decrepitude of the building, the shop shone with a welcoming grace, from the stained-glass wall sconces to the handful of ladders that leaned against bookshelves. There was even an inviting pair of overstuffed chairs near the front window.

And best of all . . .

Gray took a deep breath.

No cats.

And the reason why became apparent.

Around one of the shelves, a large shaggy shape lumbered into view. It looked like a Saint Bernard cross, an elderly fellow with baggy brown eyes. The dog sullenly shambled toward them, hobbling on its left front limb. The paw on that side was a gnarled lump.

"There you are, Bertal." The girl bent down and poured the contents of one of her Styrofoam cups into a ceramic bowl on the floor. "The mangy sot's useless before his first morning latte." This last was said with obvious affection.

The Saint Bernard reached their side and began lapping the bowl eagerly.

"I don't think coffee's good for a dog," Gray warned.

The girl straightened, tossing her braid over her shoulder.

"No worries. It's decaffeinated." She continued into the shop.

"What happened to his paw?" Gray asked, making small talk while he adjusted to the situation. He patted the dog on the side as he passed, earning a thump of a tail.

"Frostbite. Mutti took him in a long time ago."

"Mutti?"

"My grandmother. She's been waiting for you."

A voice called from the rear of the shop. *"Er det ham der vil købe bøgerne, Fiona?"*

"Ja, Mutti! The American buyer. In English please."

"Send ham ind paa mit kontor."

"Mutti will see you in her office." The girl, Fiona, led him toward the rear. The dog, finished with his morning coffee, followed at Gray's heels.

In the middle of the shop, they passed a small cash-register desk set up with a Sony computer and printer. It seemed the modern age had found its foothold here.

"We have our own website," Fiona said, noting his attention.

They passed the register and entered a back room through an open door. The space here was more parlor than office. There was a sofa, a low table, and two chairs. Even the desk in the corner seemed more in place to support the hot plate and teakettle than for any clerical function. One wall, though, was lined by a row of black filing cabinets. Above them, a barred window let in cheery morning light, illuminating the office's sole occupant.

She stood and offered her hand. "Dr. Sawyer," she said, using his assumed name for this mission. She had clearly reviewed some background on him. "I am Grette Neal."

The woman's grip was firm. She was rail thin, and though her skin was pale, the indomitable health of her countrymen shone from her pores. She waved Gray to one of the chairs. Her whole manner was casual, even her clothes: navy jeans, a turquoise blouse, and modest black pumps. Her long silver hair was combed straight, accentuating a serious demeanor, but her eyes sparkled with wry amusement.

"You have met my granddaughter." Grette Neal's fluency in English was smooth, but the Danish accent was evident. Unlike her granddaughter.

Gray glanced between the pale elderly woman and the dark girl. There was no family resemblance, but Gray kept silent on this matter. He had more important matters to clarify.

"Yes, we've met," Gray said. "In fact, it seems I've met your granddaughter *twice* today."

"Ah, Fiona's curiosity will get her in real trouble one of these days." Grette's chastisement was softened by a smile. "Has she returned your wallet?"

Gray's brow wrinkled. He patted his back pocket. Empty.

Fiona reached into a side pouch of her pack and held out his brown leather wallet.

Gray snatched it back. He remembered her bumping into him as she left to get the coffee. It had been more than impatient rudeness.

"Please don't take offense," Grette assured him. "It's her way of saying hello."

"All his ID checked out," Fiona said with a shrug.

"Then please return the young man's passport, Fiona."

Gray checked his other pocket. Gone. For the love of God!

Fiona tossed the small blue chapbook with the U.S. eagle on the cover.

"Is that everything?" Gray asked, patting himself down.

Fiona shrugged.

"Again, please excuse my granddaughter's exuberance. She gets overly protective sometimes."

Gray stared at the two of them. "Would either of you care to explain what's going on?"

"You've come to inquire about the Darwin *Bibel,*" Grette said.

"The Bible," Fiona translated.

Grette nodded at her granddaughter. The slip of tongue plainly revealed some anxiety about the object.

"I represent a buyer who might be interested," Gray said.

"Yes. We know. And you spent all day yesterday questioning others about additional items for bid at the Ergenschein Auction?"

Gray's brows rose in surprise.

"We are a small community of bibliophiles here in Copenhagen. Word travels quickly among us."

Gray frowned. He had thought he'd been more discreet.

"It was your very inquiry that helped me decide to submit my Darwin Bible to the auction. The entire community is stirred up by the growing interest in Victorian-era scientific treatises."

"Making it a good time to sell," Fiona said a bit too firmly, as if this were the tail end of a recent argument. "The flat lease is a month past—"

Her words were waved away. "It was a difficult decision. The Bible was purchased by my father in 1949. He treasured the volume. There are handwritten names of the Darwin family, going back ten generations before the illustrious Charles. But the Bible is also of historic interest. It journeyed with the man on his around-the-world trip aboard the HMS *Beagle*. And I don't know if you knew this or not, but Charles Darwin once considered entering the seminary. In this one Bible, you find the juxtaposition of the religious man and the scientist."

Gray nodded. Plainly the woman was attempting to intrigue him. Was all this a ploy to get him to pitch into the auction? To get the best price? Either way, Gray could use that to his advantage.

"And the reason Fiona followed me?" he asked.

Grette's demeanor grew tired. "My apologies again for the intrusion. Like I mentioned before, there has been much interest of late in Victorian-era memorabilia, and it is a small community. We all know some of the transactions have been . . . shall we say . . . if not across the *black* market, then definitely the gray."

"So I've heard rumors," he said coyly, hoping to tease out more information.

"There have been some buyers who have reneged on bid prices or paid with illicit proceeds, bounced checks, et cetera. Fiona was only trying to protect my best interest. And sometimes she goes too far, falling back on talents best left behind." The woman raised a single scolding eyebrow at her granddaughter.

Fiona suddenly found the floorboards of particular interest.

"There was one gentleman a year ago who spent an entire month searching through my files of provenance, the historical records of ownership." She nodded to the wall of file cabinets. "Only to pay for the privilege with a stolen credit card. He showed particular interest in the Darwin Bible."

"So we can't be too careful," Fiona said, emphasizing again.

"Do you know who this gentleman was?" Gray asked.

"No, but I'd remember him if I saw him again. A strange, pale fellow."

Fiona stirred. "But a fraud investigation administered by the bank traced his trail through Nigeria to South Africa. That's as far as it could be followed. Bloody bastard covered his tracks."

Grette frowned. "Language, young lady."

"Why such diligent investigation for a bad debt?" he asked.

Fiona again found the floorboards fascinating.

Grette stared hard at her granddaughter. "He has the right to know."

"Mutti . . ." Fiona shook her head.

"Know what?"

Fiona glared at him, then away. "He'll tell others, and we'll get half the price for it."

Gray held up a hand. "I can be discreet."

Grette studied him, one eye narrowing. "But can you be truthful . . . that I wonder, Dr. Sawyer."

Gray felt himself scrutinized by both females. Was his cover as secure as he hoped? The weight of their combined gazes made his back stiffen.

Grette finally spoke. "You should know. Shortly after the pale gentleman absconded with the knowledge here, there was a break-in at the shop. Nothing was stolen, but the display where we normally showcased the Darwin Bible was picked and opened. Fortunately for us, the Bible and our most valuable items are kept hidden in a floor vault at night. Also, the police responded promptly to the alarm, chasing them off. The burglary remained unsolved, but we knew who came after it."

"The sniveling prat . . . ," Fiona mumbled.

"Since that night, we've kept the Bible in a safe-deposit box in a bank around the corner. Still, we've been vandalized twice this past year. The culprit bypassed the alarm, and the place was ransacked each time."

"Someone was searching for the Bible," Gray said.

"So we supposed."

Gray began to understand. It wasn't just monetary gain that was the deciding factor in unloading the Bible, but also to relieve themselves of the burden. Someone wanted the Bible, and eventually the pursuit might escalate into more violent means to gain possession of it. And that threat might pass on to the new buyer.

From the corner of his eye, Gray studied Fiona. All her

actions were done to protect her grandmother, to protect their financial security. He noted the fire in her eyes even now. The girl plainly wished her grandmother had remained more reticent.

"The Bible might be safer in a private collection in America," Grette said. "Such troubles might not pass over the proverbial Pond."

Gray nodded, reading the sales pitch behind the words.

"Did you ever find out what so possessed the stranger to pursue the Bible?" he asked.

Now it was Grette's turn to search off into the distance.

"Such information can only make the Bible more valuable to my client," Gray pressed.

Grette's eyes flicked to him. Somehow she knew the lie behind his words. She studied him again, weighing something more than just the truth of his words, looking deeper.

At that moment, Bertal shambled into the office, nosed longingly at a set of tea cakes beside the kettle on the desk, then crossed to Gray's side and slumped to the floorboards with a sigh. His muzzle came to rest atop Gray's boot, plainly comfortable with this stranger to their shop.

As if this were enough, Grette sighed and closed her eyes, and whatever hard edge softened. "I don't know for sure. I only have some suppositions."

"I'll take what you can give."

"The stranger came here looking for information regarding a library that was sold piecemeal after the war. In fact, four such items are up for auction this afternoon. The de Vries diary, a copy of Mendel's papers, and two texts by the physicist Max Planck."

Gray was well aware of the same list on his notepad. They were the very items that had sparked special attention among the questionable entities. Who was buying them up and why?

"Can you tell me anything else about this old library collection? Is there any provenance of significance?"

Grette stood and stepped toward her files. "I have the original receipt from my father's purchase back in 1949. It names a village and a small estate. Let me see if I can find it."

She moved into a shaft of sunlight below the back window and pulled open a middle drawer. "I can't give you the original, but I'd be happy to have Fiona photocopy it for you."

As the old woman rustled through her files, Bertal raised his nose from Gray's right shoe, trailing a rope of drool. A low growl burbled from the dog.

But it was not directed at Gray.

"Here it is." Grette turned and held out a sheet of yellowed paper in a plastic protective sleeve.

Gray ignored her extended arm and concentrated on her toes. A thin shadow shifted across the patch of sunlight where Grette stood.

"Get down!"

Gray leaped toward the sofa, reaching for the old woman.

Behind him, Bertal barked sharply, almost masking the *crack* of glass.

Gray, still reaching, was too late. All he could do was catch Grette Neal's body as the front of her face dissolved in a shower of blood and bone, shot from behind by a sniper outside the window.

Gray caught her body and pitched down to the sofa.

Fiona screamed.

Through the shattered rear window, two distinct *pop*s sounded along with the shatter of glass. Two black canisters jetted into the office, struck the far wall, and clattered down, bouncing.

Gray leaped off the sofa, shouldering into Fiona. He shoved her bodily out of the office and around the corner.

The dog scrambled after them.

Gray half carried Fiona behind a sheltering bookcase as

twin detonations ripped through the office, blasting apart the wall in a fiery explosion of plaster and splintered wood.

The bookcase toppled over, crashing into its neighbor and leaning precariously. Gray sheltered Fiona under him.

Overhead, texts burst into flame and fiery ash rained down.

Gray spotted the old dog. He had moved too slowly, hobbled by the bad paw. The concussion had slammed the poor dog into the far wall. He did not move. His fur smoldered.

Gray shielded Fiona from the sight. "We have to get clear."

He pulled her shocked form from under the leaning bookcase. Flames and smoke already filled the back half of the shop. Overhead sprinklers burst with tepid sprays. Too little, too late. Not with this much tinder on hand.

"Out the front!" he urged.

He stumbled forward with her.

Too slowly.

Before them, the outer security gate crashed down, sealing the front door and window. Gray noted shadows fading to either side of the barred gate. More gunmen.

Gray glanced behind him. A churning wall of flame and smoke filled the back of the shop.

They were trapped.

11:57 P.M.
WASHINGTON, D.C.

Monk drowsed in that happy place between bliss and sleep. He and Kat had moved from the bathroom floor to the bed as passion dissolved to soft whispers and even softer touches. The sheets and comforters were still knotted around their naked forms; neither was ready to untie themselves, not physically, not in any way.

Monk's finger traced the curve of Kat's breast, lazily, more in reassurance than arousal. The smooth arch of her foot gently caressed his calf.

Perfection.

Nothing could ruin this—

A piercing warble erupted in the room, tensing them both.

It rose from the side of the bed, where Monk had dropped his sweatpants . . . or rather had them yanked off him. The pager was still clipped to the elastic waist. He knew he had switched the device to vibration when he returned from his evening jog. Only one manner of call broke through that mode.

Emergency.

On the other side of the bed, from the nightstand, a second pager burst with a matching clarion call.

Kat's.

They both pushed up, eyes meeting with worry.

"Central command," Kat said.

Monk reached down and grabbed his pager, dragging his sweatpants up with it. He confirmed her assessment.

He rolled his feet to the floor and reached for the phone. Kat sat up next to him, pulling the sheets to cover her bare breasts, as if some manner of decency was necessary to call into central command. He dialed the number for Sigma Force's direct line. It was picked up immediately.

"Captain Bryant?" Logan Gregory answered.

"No, sir. It's Monk Kokkalis. But Kat . . . Captain Bryant is here with me."

"I need you both back at command immediately."

Logan filled him in tersely.

Monk listened, nodding. "We're leaving now," he finished and hung up.

Kat met his gaze, brows pinched together. "What's wrong?"

"Trouble."

"With Gray?"

"No. I'm sure he's fine." Monk climbed into his sweats. "Probably having a great time with Rachel."

"Then—?"

"It's Director Crowe. Something's happened in Nepal. Details are sketchy. Something about a plague."

"Has Director Crowe reported in?"

"That's just it. His last report was three days ago, but a storm had closed off communication. So there was not too much concern. Then the storm broke today, and still no communication. And now there're rumors of plague, death, and some uprising out there. Possibly a rebel attack."

Kat's eyes widened.

"Logan is calling everyone into command."

Kat slid out of bed and reached for her own clothes. "What could be going on out there?"

"Nothing good, that's for damn sure."

9:22 A.M.
COPENHAGEN, DENMARK

"Is there a way upstairs?" Gray asked.

Fiona stared at the closed gate, rooted in place, eyes wide and unblinking. Gray read the signs of shock in the girl.

"Fiona . . ." Gray stepped around and leaned close, nose to nose, filling her vision. "Fiona, we must get away from the fire."

Behind her, the firestorm spread rapidly, fueled by the stacks of dry books and broken pine shelving. Flames had climbed and lapped to the ceiling. Smoke churned and rolled along the roof. Sprinklers continued to leak tepidly into the conflagration, adding steam to the toxic pall.

The heat intensified with each breath. Still, as Gray took

Fiona's hands in his, she shivered, her whole body trembling. But at least his touch finally focused her eyes on him.

"Is there a way upstairs? To another level?"

Fiona glanced up. A pall of smoke obscured the tin ceiling tiles. "Some old rooms. An attic . . ."

"Yes. Perfect. Can we get up there?"

She shook her head at first slowly, then more firmly, reviving to the danger. "No. The only stairs are . . ." She waved feebly toward the fire. "At the back of the building."

"On the outside."

She nodded. Ash swirled in fiery eddies around them as the wall of fire advanced.

Gray cursed silently. There must've once been an interior staircase, before the building was split into a shop and upper rooms. But no longer. He'd have to improvise.

"Do you have an ax?" he asked.

Fiona shook her head.

"How about a crowbar? Something to open crates or boxes?"

Fiona stiffened and nodded. "By the cash register."

"Stay here." Gray edged along the left-hand wall. It offered the clearest path back toward the central desk. The fire had not quite reached it.

Fiona followed.

"I told you to stay back."

"I know where the soddin' crowbar is," she snapped at him.

Gray recognized the terror behind her anger, but it was an improvement over the limp-limbed shock from a moment ago. Plus it matched his own fury. At himself. It was bad enough the girl had tailed him earlier, but now he'd allowed himself to be trapped by unknown assassins. He'd been too distracted by thoughts of Rachel, too dismissive of this mission and its parameters, and now it wasn't only his life in jeopardy.

Fiona pushed ahead of him, red-eyed and coughing from

the smoke. "It's over here." She leaned across the desk, reached behind it, and tugged free a long green steel bar.

"Let's go." He led the way back toward the advancing flames. He pulled out of his wool sweater and traded it for the crowbar.

"Wet the sweater down. Soak it good in that sprinkler." He pointed with the crowbar. "And yourself, for that matter."

"What are you going to—?"

"Try to make our own staircase."

Gray mounted one of the bookshelf ladders and scrambled up. The smoke churned above his upraised face. The very air burned. Gray poked the crowbar at one of the tin ceiling tiles. It was easily dislodged and nudged aside. As he had hoped, the shop roof was a cantilevered drop ceiling. It hid the rafter-and-plank floor of the story above.

Gray climbed to the top of the ladder and scaled the last few shelves of the bookcase. He perched atop it. Using this vantage, he jammed his crowbar between two of the planks. It sank deep. He shouldered and levered the crowbar. The steel bar ripped through the old wood. Still, he barely managed to gouge out a mouse hole.

Eyes watering and burning, Gray leaned down. A racking cough shook through him. Not good. It would be a race between his crowbar and the smoke. Gray glanced back to the fire. It grew fiercer. The smoke belched thicker.

He'd never make it at this rate.

Movement drew his gaze back down. Fiona had scrambled up the ladder. She had found a kerchief, soaked it, and had it wrapped around the lower half of her face like a bandit, a fitting disguise in her case.

She held up his soggy wool sweater. She had soaked herself, too, seeming to shrink in size like a wet puppy. Gray realized she was younger than the seventeen he had guessed earlier. She could be no more than fifteen. Her eyes were red-rimmed with panic—but also shone with hope, placing some blind faith in him.

Gray hated when people did that . . . because it always worked.

Gray tied the arms of his sweater around his neck and let the rest drape over his back. He tugged up a flap of sodden wool to cover his mouth and nose, offering some insulation from the ash-thickened air.

With water soaking through the back of his shirt, Gray knelt up again, ready to attack the stubborn planks. He sensed the presence of Fiona below. And the responsibility.

Gray searched the space between the drop ceiling and the rafters for any other means of escape. All around, piping and wiring crisscrossed in a haphazard pattern, plainly added piecemeal after the two-story home had been sectioned into a lower shop and upper apartment. The newer renovations appeared shoddy, the difference between Old World crafts-manship and modern slipshod construction.

As he searched, Gray spotted a break in the uniform run of planks and rafters. A boxed-off section, three feet square, framed by thicker bracing. Gray recognized it immediately. He'd been right earlier. The bracing marked the opening where a long-demolished interior staircase had once passed through to the floor above.

But how securely had it been sealed up?

Only one way to find out.

Gray rose up on his heels, stood atop the bookcase, and followed it like a balance beam in the direction of the framed opening. It was only a few yards—but it led deeper into the shop, toward the fire.

"Where are you going?" Fiona demanded from atop the ladder.

Gray didn't have the breath to explain. The smoke choked thicker with every step. The heat grew to an open-furnace intensity. He finally reached the section of bookshelf below the sealed stairwell.

Glancing down, Gray saw that the bookcase's lower shelves already smoldered. He'd reached the firestorm's leading edge.

No time to waste.

Bracing himself, he slammed his crowbar up.

The tip plunged easily through the thinner wood planking. It was no more than pressed fiberboard and vinyl tiles. Shoddy, as he'd hoped. Thank God for the lack of modern work ethic.

Gray hauled on his crowbar, cranking like a machine as the air burned and the heat blistered. Soon he had created an opening wide enough to climb through.

Gray tossed the crowbar through the opening. It clattered above.

He turned to Fiona and waved her to him.

"Can you get on top of the bookshelves and—?"

"I saw how you got over there." She scrambled up onto the bookcase.

A *pop* drew Gray's attention below. The bookcase shuddered under him.

Uh-oh . . .

His weight and the burning lower tiers were rapidly weakening his perch. He reached to the hole and half pulled himself up, shifting his weight off the shelf.

"Hurry," he urged the girl.

With her arms held out for balance, Fiona edged along the top of the bookcase. About a yard away.

"Hurry," he repeated.

"I heard you the first—"

With a resounding *crack,* the section of bookcase under Gray collapsed. He gripped the edges of the hole tighter as the case toppled away, crashing into the fire. A fresh wash of heat, ash, and flames swept high.

Fiona screamed as her section shook, but held.

Hanging by his arms, Gray called to her. "Leap over to me. Grab around my shoulders."

Fiona needed no further encouragement as her case wobbled. She jumped and struck him hard, arms latching around his neck, legs clinging around his waist. He was almost knocked from his perch. He swung in place.

"Can you use my body to climb up through the hole?" he asked with a strain.

"I . . . I think so."

She hung a moment longer, not moving.

The rough edges of the hole tore at his fingers. "Fiona . . ."

She trembled against him, then worked her way around to his back. Once moving, she climbed quickly, planting a toe into his belt, then pushing off his shoulder. She was through the hole with all the agility of a spider monkey.

Below, a bonfire of books and shelving raged.

Gray gladly hauled himself up after her, worming through the hole and beaching himself on the floor. He was in the center of a hallway. Rooms spread out in either direction.

"Fire's up here, too," Fiona whispered, as if afraid to attract the flames' attention.

Rolling to his feet, Gray saw the flickering glow from the back half of the apartment. Smoke choked these halls, even thicker than below.

"C'mon," he said. It was still a race.

Gray hurried down the hall away from the fire. He ended at one of the boarded upper windows. He peeked between two slats. Sirens could be heard in the distance. People gathered in the street below: onlookers and gawkers. And surely hidden among them was a gunman or two.

Gray and the girl would be exposed if they tried climbing out the window.

Fiona studied the crowd, too. "They won't let us leave, will they?"

"Then we'll get out on our own."

Gray backed away and searched up. He pictured the attic dormer window he'd spotted earlier from the street. They needed to reach the roof.

Fiona understood his intention. "There's a pull-down ladder in the next room." She led the way. "I would come up here to read sometimes when Mutti . . ." Fiona's voice cracked, and her words died.

Gray knew the girl would be haunted by the death of her grandmother for a long time. He put his arm around her shoulder, but she shrugged out of it angrily and stepped away.

"Over here," she said and entered what once must have been a sitting room. Now it held only a few crates and a faded, ripped sofa.

Fiona pointed to a frayed rope hanging from the ceiling, attached to a trapdoor in the roof.

Gray tugged it down, and a collapsible wooden ladder slid to the floor. He climbed first, followed by Fiona.

The attic was unfinished: just insulation, rafters, and rat droppings. The only light came from a pair of dormer windows. One faced the front street, the other toward the back. Thin smoke filled the space, but so far no flames.

Gray decided to try the rear window. It faced west, leaving the roof in shadow this time of day. Also, that side of the row house was on fire. Their attackers might be less attentive to it.

Gray hopped from rafter to rafter. He could feel the heat from below. One section of insulation was already smoldering, the fiberglass melting.

Reaching the window, Gray checked below. The roof pitch was such that he could not see into the courtyard behind the shop. And if he couldn't see them, they couldn't see him. Additionally, smoke roiled up from the broken windows below, offering additional cover.

For once, the fire was to their advantage.

Still, Gray stood well to the side as he unhooked the window latch and pushed it open. He waited. No gunshots. Sirens could now be heard converging on the street outside.

"Let me go first," Gray whispered in Fiona's ear. "If all's clear—"

A low roar erupted behind them.

They both turned. A tongue of flame shot out of the heart of the burning insulation, licking high, cracking and smoking. They were out of time.

"Follow me," Gray said.

He edged out the window, staying low. It was wonderfully cool out on the roof, the air crisp after the perpetual stifle.

Buoyed by the escape, Gray tested the roof tiles. The pitch was steep, but he had good grip with his boots. With care, walking was manageable. He stepped away from the shelter of the window and aimed for the roofline to the north. Ahead, the gap between the row houses was less than three feet. They should be able to leap the distance.

Satisfied, he turned back to the window. "Okay, Fiona . . . be careful."

The girl popped her head out, searched around, then crept onto the roof. She stayed crouched, almost on all fours.

Gray waited for her. "You're doing fine."

She glanced over to him. Distracted, she failed to spot a cracked tile. Her toe shattered through it. It broke away, causing her to lose her balance. She landed hard on her belly—and began to slide.

Her fingers and toes fought for purchase, but to no avail.

Gray lunged for her. His fingers found only empty air.

Her speed increased as she skated over the tiles. More tiles broke away in her frantic attempt to halt her plummet. Shards of pottery chattered and bounced ahead of her, becoming an avalanche of roof tiles.

Gray lay splayed on his belly. There was nothing he could do to help.

"The gutter!" he called after her, forgoing caution. "Grab the gutter!"

She seemed deaf to his words, fingers scrabbling, toes gouging out more tiles. She bumped over on her side and began to roll. A fluttering scream escaped her.

The first few broken tiles rained over the edge. Gray heard them shatter to the stone courtyard below with firecracker pops.

Then Fiona followed, tumbling over the roof edge, arms flailing.

And she was gone.

3

UKUFA

Six thousand miles and a world away from Copenhagen, an open-air Jeep trundled across the trackless wilderness of South Africa.

The heat already sweltered, searing the savanna and casting up shimmering mirages. In the rearview mirror, the plains baked brilliantly under the sun, interrupted by thorny thickets and solitary stands of red bush willow. Immediately ahead rose a low knoll, studded thickly with knobby acacia and skeletal leadwood trees.

"Is that the place, Doctor?" Khamisi Taylor asked, twisting the wheel to bounce his Jeep across a dry creekbed, the dust rising in a rooster tail. He glanced at the woman beside him.

Dr. Marcia Fairfield half stood in the passenger seat, her hand clamped on the windshield's edge for balance. She pointed an arm. "Around to the west side. There's a deep hollow."

Khamisi downshifted and skirted to the right. As the current game warden on duty for the Hluhluwe-Umfolozi Game Preserve, he had to follow protocol. Poaching was a serious offense—but also a reality. Especially in the lonelier sections of the park.

Even his own people, his fellow Zulu tribesmen, sometimes followed the traditional way and practices. It required even fining some of his grandfather's old friends. The elders had given him a nickname, a word in Zulu that translated as "Fat Boy." It was said with little outward derision, but Khamisi knew there was still an undercurrent of distaste. They considered him less a man for taking a white man's job, living *fat* off of others. He was still a bit of a stranger around here. His father had taken him to Australia when he was twelve, after his mother died. He had spent a good portion of his life outside the city of Darwin on Australia's north coast, even spent two years at university in Queensland. Now at twenty-eight, he was back, having secured a job as a game warden—partly from his education, partly from his ties to the tribes here.

Living fat off of others.

"Can't you go any faster?" his passenger urged.

Dr. Marcia Fairfield was a graying biologist out of Cambridge, well respected, a part of the original Operation Rhino project, often called the Jane Goodall of rhinos. Khamisi enjoyed working with her. Maybe it was just her lack of pretense, from her faded khaki safari jacket to her silver-gray hair tied back in a simple ponytail.

Or maybe it was her passion. Like now.

"If the cow died birthing, her calf might still be alive. But for how long?" She pounded a fist against the edge of the windshield. "We can't lose both."

As game warden, Khamisi understood. Since 1970, the population of black rhinos had decreased ninety-six percent in Africa. The Hluhluwe-Umfolozi reserve sought to remedy that, as it had the white rhino population. It was the chief conservation effort of the park.

Every black rhino was important.

"The only reason we found her was the tracking implant," Dr. Fairfield continued. "Spotted her by helicopter. But if she gave birth, there'll be no way to track her calf."

"Won't the baby stay close to its mother?" Khamisi asked. He had witnessed the same himself. Two years ago, a pair of lion cubs had been found huddling against the cold belly of their dam, shot by a sport poacher.

"You know the fate of orphans. Predators will be drawn by the carcass. If the calf is still around, bloody from birth . . ."

Khamisi nodded. He punched the gas and bounced the Jeep up the rocky slope. The rear end fishtailed in some loose scree—but he kept going.

As they cleared the hill, the terrain ahead broke apart into deep ravines, cut by trickling streams. Here the vegetation thickened: sycamore figs, Natal mahogany, and nyala trees. It was one of the few "wet" areas of the park, also one of the most remote, well away from the usual game trails and tourist roads. Only those with permits were allowed to traverse this section under strict limitations: daylight hours only, no overnight stays. The territory ran all the way to the park's western border.

Khamisi scanned the horizon as he inched the Jeep down the far slope. A mile away, a stretch of game fencing broke across the terrain. The ten-foot-high black fence divided the park from a neighboring private preserve. Such reserves often shared a park's borders, offering the more affluent traveler a more intimate experience.

But this was no ordinary private preserve.

The Hluhluwe-Umfolozi Park had been founded in 1895, the oldest sanctuary in all of Africa. As such, the neighboring private reserve was also the oldest. The chunk of family-owned land predated even the park, owned by a living dynasty of South Africa, the Waalenberg clan, one of the original Boer families, whose generations stretched back to the seventeenth century. This particular reserve was a quarter the size of the park itself. Its grounds were said to be teeming with wildlife. And not just the big five—the elephant, rhinoceros, leopard, lion, and cape buffalo—but also predators and prey of every ilk: the Nile crocodile, hippo, cheetah, hyena, wildebeest, jackal, giraffe, zebra, waterbuck, kudu, impala, reedbuck, warthog, baboons. It was said that the Waalenberg preserve had unknowingly sheltered a pack of rare okapi, well before this relative of the giraffe had even been discovered back in 1901.

But there were always rumors and stories associated with the Waalenberg preserve. The park was only accessible by helicopter or small plane. The roads that once led to it had long since returned to the wild. The only visitors, occasional as they were, were major dignitaries from around the world. It was said Teddy Roosevelt once hunted on the reserve and even fashioned the United States national park system after the Waalenberg preserve.

Khamisi would give his eyeteeth to spend a day in there.

But that honor was limited only to the head warden of Hluhluwe. A tour of the Waalenberg estate was one of the perks upon acquiring that mantle, and even then it took a signed affidavit of secrecy. Khamisi hoped one day to achieve that lofty goal.

But he held out little hope.

Not with his black skin.

His Zulu heritage and education might have helped him get this job, but even after apartheid, there remained limits. Traditional ways die hard—for both black and white men. Still, his position was an inroad. One of the sad legacies of apartheid was that an entire generation of tribal children had been raised with little or no education, suffering under the years of sanctions, segregation, and unrest. A lost generation. So he did all he could do: opened what doors he could and held them for those who would come after.

He would play the Fat Boy, if that's what it took.

In the meantime . . .

"There!" Dr. Fairfield shouted, startling Khamisi back to the tortuous unmarked track. "Make a left at that baobab at the bottom of the hill."

Khamisi spotted the prehistoric giant tree. Large white flowers drooped mournfully from the ends of its branches. To its left, the land dropped away, descending into a bowl-shaped depression. Khamisi caught a sparkle of a tiny pool near the bottom.

Water hole.

Such springs dotted the park, some natural, some man-made. They were the best places for a glimpse of wildlife—and also the most dangerous to traverse on foot.

Khamisi braked to a halt by the tree. "We'll have to walk in from here."

Dr. Fairfield nodded. They both reached for rifles. Though both were conservationists, they were also familiar with the ever-present danger of the veldt.

As he climbed out, Khamisi shouldered his large-bore double rifle, a .465 Nitro Holland & Holland Royal. It could stop a charging elephant. In dense brush, he preferred it to any bolt-action rifle.

They headed down the slope, prickling with basket grass and shrubby sicklebush. Overhead, the higher canopy shielded them from the sun but created deep shadows below. As he marched, Khamisi noted the heavy silence. No bird-song. No chatter of monkeys. Only the buzz and whirring of insects. The quiet set his teeth on edge.

Beside him, Dr. Fairfield checked a handheld GPS tracker.

She pointed an arm.

Khamisi followed her direction, skirting the muddy pool. As he stalked through some reeds, he was rewarded by a growing stench of rotting meat. It didn't take much longer to push into a deep-shadowed copse and discover its source.

The black rhino cow must have weighed three thousand pounds, give or take a stone. A monster-size specimen.

"Dear God," Dr. Fairfield exclaimed through a handkerchief clutched over her mouth and nose. "When Roberto pinpointed the remains by helicopter . . ."

"It's always worse on the ground," Khamisi said.

He marched to the bloated carcass. It lay on its left side. Flies rose in a black cloud at their approach. The belly had been ripped open. Intestines bulged out, ballooned with gas. It seemed impossible that all this had once fit inside the abdomen. Other organs were draped across the dirt. A bloody smudge indicated where some choice tidbit had been dragged into the surrounding dense foliage.

Flies settled again.

Khamisi stepped over a section of gnawed red liver. The rear hind limb appeared to have been almost torn off at the hip. The strength of the jaws to do that . . .

Even a mature lion would've had a hard time.

Khamisi circled until he reached the head.

One of the rhino's stubby ears had been bitten off, its throat savagely ripped open. Lifeless black eyes stared back at Khamisi, too wide, appearing frozen in fright. Lips were also rippled back as if in terror or agony. A wide tongue protruded, and blood pooled below. But none of this was important.

He knew what he had to check.

Above the scum-flecked nostrils curved a long horn, prominent and perfect.

"Definitely not a poacher," Khamisi said.

The horn would've been taken. It was the main reason rhino populations were still in rapid decline. Powdered horn sold in Asian markets as a so-called cure for erectile dysfunction, a homeopathic Viagra. A single horn fetched a princely sum.

Khamisi straightened.

Dr. Fairfield crouched near the other end of the body. She had donned plastic gloves, leaning her rifle against the body. "It doesn't appear she's given birth."

"So no orphaned calf."

The biologist stepped around the carcass to the belly again. She bent down and, without even a wince of squeamishness, tugged a flap of torn belly up, and reached inside.

He turned away.

"Why hasn't the carcass been picked clean by carrion feeders?" Dr. Fairfield asked as she worked.

"It's a lot of meat," he mumbled. Khamisi circled back around. The quiet continued to press around him, squeezing the heat atop them.

The woman continued her examination. "I don't think that's it. The body's been here since last night, near a watering hole. If nothing else, the abdomen would have been cleaned out by jackals."

Khamisi surveyed the body again. He stared at the ripped rear leg, the torn throat. Something large had brought the rhino down. And fast.

A prickling rose along the back of his neck.

Where *were* the carrion feeders?

Before he could contemplate the mystery, Dr. Fairfield spoke. "The calf's gone."

"What?" He turned back around. "I thought you said she hadn't given birth."

Dr. Fairfield stood up, stripping off her gloves and retrieving her gun. Rifle in hand, the biologist stalked away from the carcass, gaze fixed to the ground. Khamisi noted she was following the bloody path, where something was dragged away from the belly, to be eaten in private.

Oh, God . . .

He followed after her.

At the edge of the copse, Dr. Fairfield used the tip of her rifle to part some low-hanging branches, which revealed what had been dragged from the belly.

The rhino calf.

The scrawny body had been shredded into sections, as if fought over.

"I think the calf was still alive when it was torn out," Dr. Fairfield said, pointing to a spray of blood. "Poor thing . . ."

Khamisi stepped back, remembering the biologist's earlier question. Why hadn't any other carrion feeders eviscerated the remains? Vultures, jackals, hyenas, even lions. Dr. Fairfield was right. This much meat would not have been left to flies and maggots.

It made no sense.

Not unless . . .

Khamisi's heart thudded heavily.

Not unless the predator was *still* here.

Khamisi lifted his rifle. Deep in the shadowed copse, he again noted the heavy silence. It was as if the very forest were intimidated by whatever had killed the rhino.

He found himself testing the air, listening, eyes straining, standing dead still. The shadows seemed to deepen all around him.

Having spent his childhood in South Africa, Khamisi was well familiar with the superstitions, whispers of monsters that haunted and hunted the jungles: the *ndalawo,* a howling man-eater of the Uganda forest; the *mbilinto,* an elephant-size hippo of the Congo wetlands; the *mngwa,* a furry lurker of coastal coconut groves.

But sometimes even myths came to life in Africa. Like the *nsui-fisi.* It was a striped man-eating monster of Rhodesia, long considered a folktale by white settlers . . . that is, until decades later it was discovered to be a new form of cheetah, taxonomically classified as *Acinonyx rex.*

As Khamisi searched the jungle, he recalled another monster of legend, one that was known across the breadth of Africa. It went by many names: the *dubu,* the *lumbwa,* the *kerit,* the *getet.* Mere mention of the name evoked cries of fear from natives. As large as a gorilla, it was a veritable devil for its swiftness, cunning, and ferocity. Over the centuries, hunters—black and white—claimed to have caught glimpses of it. All children learned to recognize its characteristic howl. This region of Zululand was no exception.

"*Ukufa . . . ,*" Khamisi mumbled.

"Did you say something?" Dr. Fairfield asked. She was still bent down by the dead calf.

It was the Zulu name for the monster, one that was whispered around campfires and kraal huts.

Ukufa.

Death.

He knew why such a beast came to mind now. Five months ago, an old tribesman claimed to have seen an *ukufa* near here. *Half beast, half ghost, with eyes of fire,* the old man had railed with dead certainty. Only those as old as the leathery elder took heed. The others, like Khamisi, pretended to humor the tribesman.

But here in the dark shadows . . .

"We should go," Khamisi said.

"But we don't know what killed her."

"Not poachers." That's all Khamisi needed or wanted to know. He waved his rifle toward the Jeep. He would radio the head warden, get the matter signed off and settled. Predator kill. No poaching. They'd leave the carcass to the carrion. The cycle of life.

Dr. Fairfield reluctantly rose.

Off to the right, a drawn-out call split through the shadowy jungle—*hoo eeee OOOO*—punctuated by a high-pitched feral scream.

Khamisi trembled where he stood. He recognized the cry, not so much with his head as with his bone marrow. It echoed back to midnight campfires, to stories of terror and bloodshed, and even further back, to something primeval, to a time before speech, where life was instinct.

Ukufa.

Death.

As the scream faded away, silence again fell heavily over them.

Khamisi mentally measured the distance between them and the Jeep. They needed to retreat, but not in a panic. A fearful flight would only whet a predator's bloodlust.

Out in the jungle, another scream growled.

Then another.

And another.

All from different directions.

In the sudden quiet afterward, Khamisi knew they had only one chance.

"Run."

9:31 A.M.
COPENHAGEN, DENMARK

Gray lay on his belly across the roof tiles, head down, sprawled where he'd missed grabbing Fiona. The image of her tumbling over the smoky edge of the roof seared into his mind's eye. His heart thudded in his chest.

Oh, God . . . what've I done . . . ?

Over his shoulder, a fresh spat of flames burst out the attic dormer, accompanied by a growled rush of heat and smoke. Despite his distress, he had to move.

Gray willed himself up onto his elbows, then hands, pushing up.

To the side, the fire took a momentary breath, falling back. In the lull, he heard voices below, urgent, furtive. Also closer to him . . . . a low moan. Just beyond the roofline.

Fiona . . . ?

Gray dropped back to his belly and scooted in a controlled slide to the roof's edge. Smoke choked up from the shattered windows directly below. He used the pall to cloak his approach.

Reaching the guttered edge, he glanced down.

Directly under him stretched a wrought-iron balcony . . . no, *not* a balcony. It was a landing to a staircase. The exterior stairs that Fiona had mentioned.

Sprawled across the landing was the girl.

With a second groggy groan, Fiona rolled over and began to haul herself up, using the railing posts.

Others noted her movement.

Out in the courtyard below, Gray spotted two figures. One stood in the middle of the flagstones, a rifle raised to his shoulder, searching for a clear shot. Black smoke belched out the broken apartment door window, obscuring Fiona from view. The sniper waited for the girl to get her head above the landing's railing.

"Stay down," he hissed at Fiona.

She glanced up. Bright blood dribbled across her brow.

The second gunman circled, a black pistol clutched double-fisted. He aimed for the stairs, intent to block any escape.

Gray motioned Fiona to remain crouched, then rolled along the roofline until he was above the second gunman. The churning smoke continued to keep him hidden. Most of the assassins' attention remained focused on the stairs. Once in position, Gray waited. He clutched a heavy roof tile in his right hand, one of the stone tiles Fiona had loosened during her tumble.

He would have only one shot.

Below, the man held his pistol at the ready and placed one foot on the lowermost stair.

Gray leaned over the edge, arm raised.

He whistled sharply.

The gunman glanced up, swiveling his weapon and dropping to a knee. Damned fast . . .

But gravity was faster.

Gray chucked the tile. It spun through the air like an ax and struck the gunman in his upraised face. Blood spurted from the man's nose. He fell back hard. His head hit the flagstones, bounced, then didn't move.

Gray rolled again—back toward Fiona.

A shout rose from the rifleman.

Gray kept his gaze fixed on him. He had hoped downing the man's partner would chase the other off. No such luck. The rifleman fled to the opposite side, finding shelter near a trash bin but leaving him a clear shot still. His sniping position was close to the burning rear of the shop, taking advantage of the smoke billowing out a neighboring window.

Gray reached Fiona again. He waved her to stay low. It would be their deaths to attempt to haul Fiona up. Both would be exposed too long.

That left only one choice.

Gripping the gutter with one hand, Gray lunged and swung down. He dropped to the landing with a ring of steel, then ducked low.

A brick above his head shattered.

Rifle shot.

Gray reached to his ankle sheath and pulled his dagger free.

Fiona eyed it. "What are we—?"

"*You* are going to stay here," he ordered.

Gray reached a hand to the railing above. All he had was the element of surprise. No body armor, no weapon except his dagger.

"Run when I tell you," he said. "Straight down the stairs and over your neighbor's fence. Find the first policeman or firefighter. Can you do that?"

Fiona met his eyes. It looked as if she were about to argue, but her lips tightened and she nodded.

Good girl.

Gray balanced the dagger in his hand. One chance again. Taking a deep breath, Gray leaped up, pinioned off the railing, and vaulted over it. As he fell toward the flagstones, he did two things at the same time.

"Run!" he hollered and tossed the dagger toward the sniper's hiding place. He didn't hope for a kill, just a distraction long enough to close quarters with the man. A rifle was ungainly in tight situations.

As he landed, he noted two things.

One good, one bad.

He heard Fiona's ringing footsteps down the metal staircase.

She was fleeing.

Good.

At the same time, Gray watched his dagger wing through the smoky air, bang the trash bin, and bounce off. His toss hadn't even been close.

That was bad.

The sniper rose from his spot unfazed, rifle ready, aimed straight at Gray's chest.

"No!" Fiona screamed as she reached the bottom of the stairs.

The rifleman didn't even smile as he pulled the trigger.

11:05 A.M.
HLUHLUWE-UMFOLOZI GAME PRESERVE
ZULULAND, SOUTH AFRICA

"Run!" Khamisi repeated.

Dr. Fairfield needed no further prodding. They fled in the direction of their waiting Jeep. Reaching the watering hole, Khamisi waved Dr. Fairfield ahead of him. She shouldered through the tall reeds—but not before silently meeting his gaze. Horror shone in her eyes, mirroring his own.

Whatever creatures had screamed in the forest had sounded large, massive, and whetted from the recent kill. Khamisi glanced back at the rhino's macerated carcass. Monsters or not, he needed no other information about what might be hidden in the maze of heavy forest, trickling streams, and shadowed gullies.

Twisting back around, Khamisi followed the biologist. He checked over his shoulder frequently, ears straining for any sound of pursuit. Something splashed into the neighboring pond. Khamisi ignored it. It was a small splash. Too small. His brain teased out extraneous details, sifting through the buzz of insects and crunch of reeds. He concentrated upon real danger signals. Khamisi's father had taught him how to hunt when he was only six years old, drilling into him the signs to watch when stalking prey.

Only now, he was the hunted.

The panicked whir of wings drew his ear and eye.

A flick of movement.

Off to the left.

In the sky.

A single shrike took wing.

Something had frightened it.

Something on the move.

Khamisi closed the distance with Dr. Fairfield as they cleared the reeds. "Hurry," he whispered, senses straining.

Dr. Fairfield craned her neck, her rifle swiveling. She was breathing hard, face ashen. Khamisi followed her gaze. Their Jeep stood at the ridgeline above, parked in the shade of the baobab tree at the edge of the deep hollow. The slope seemed steeper and longer than it had coming down.

"Keep moving," he urged.

Glancing back, Khamisi spotted a tawny klipspringer doe leap from the forest edge and skip-hop its way up the far slope, kicking up dirt.

Then it was gone.

They needed to heed its example.

Dr. Fairfield headed up the slope. Khamisi followed, side-stepping, fixing his double-barreled rifle toward the forest behind them.

"They didn't kill to eat," Dr. Fairfield gasped ahead of him.

Khamisi studied the dark tangle of forest. Why did he know she was right?

"Hunger hadn't goaded them," the biologist continued, as if struggling to qualm her panic with deliberation. "Hardly anything was eaten. It was as if they had killed for pleasure. Like a house cat hunting a mouse."

Khamisi had worked alongside many predators. It wasn't the way of the natural world. Lions, after a meal, seldom proved a threat, usually lounging about, even approachable, up to a distance. A sated predator would not tear apart a rhino, rip its calf from its belly, just for the sport of it.

Dr. Fairfield continued her litany, as if the present danger were a puzzle to solve. "In the domesticated world, it is the well-fed house cat that hunts *more* often. It has the energy and the time for such play."

Play?

Khamisi shuddered.

"Just keep moving," he said, not wanting to hear more.

Dr. Fairfield nodded, but the biologist's words stayed with

Khamisi. What sort of predator kills just for the sport of it? Of course, there was one obvious answer.

Man.

But this was not the work of any human hand.

Movement again captured Khamisi's gaze. For just a moment, a pale shape shifted behind the fringe of dark forest, caught out of the corner of the eye. It vanished like white smoke as he focused on the spot.

He remembered the words of the wizened Zulu tribesman.

Half beast, half ghost . . .

Despite the heat, his skin went cold. He increased his pace, almost shouldering the older biologist up the slope. Loose shale and sandy dirt shifted treacherously underfoot. But they were almost at the top. The Jeep was only thirty meters away.

Then Dr. Fairfield slipped.

She went down on a knee and fell backward, knocking into Khamisi.

He took a stumbled step back, missed his footing, and went down hard on his rear. The angle of the slope and momentum tumbled him ass over end. He rolled halfway down the hill before he finally braked his fall using his heels and the butt of his rifle.

Dr. Fairfield still sat where she had fallen, eyes wide with fear, staring back down.

Not at him.

At the forest.

Khamisi twisted around, gaining his knees; his ankle screamed, sprained, maybe broken. He searched and saw nothing, but he raised his rifle.

"Go!" he screamed. He had left the keys in the ignition. "Go!"

He heard Dr. Fairfield scramble to her feet with a crunch of shale.

From the forest edge, another ululating cry arose, cackling and inhuman.

Khamisi aimed blindly and pulled the trigger. The *boom* of his rifle shattered through the hollow. Dr. Fairfield cried out behind him, startled. Khamisi hoped the noise also startled off whatever lurked out there.

"Get to the Jeep!" he bellowed. "Just go! Don't wait!"

He stood, leaning his weight off his bad ankle. He kept his rifle poised. The forest had gone quiet again.

He heard Dr. Fairfield reach the top of the slope. "Khamisi . . . ," she called back.

"Take the Jeep!"

He risked a glance behind him, over his shoulder.

Dr. Fairfield turned from the ridgeline and stepped toward the Jeep. Above her, movement in the branches of the baobab drew his eye. A few of the tree's droopy white flowers swayed gently.

There was no wind.

"Marcia!" he yelled. "Don't—!"

A savage cry erupted behind him, drowning out the rest of his warning. Dr. Fairfield turned half a step in his direction.

No . . .

It leaped down from the deep shadows of the giant tree, a pale blur. It struck the biologist and knocked them both out of sight. Khamisi heard a curdling scream from the woman, but it was ripped away in half a breath.

Silence again settled.

Khamisi faced the forest edge again.

Death above and below.

He had only one chance.

Ignoring the pain in his ankle, Khamisi ran.

Down the slope.

He simply let gravity take hold of him. It wasn't so much a sprint as a freefall. He raced back to the bottom of the hill, legs struggling to keep him upright. Reaching the bottom, he pointed his gun toward the forest and squeezed out a second shot from his double barrel.

Boom.

He had no hope of scaring off the hunters. He sought only to buy himself an extra fraction of life. The rebound of the rifle also helped him keep his feet as the slope leveled out. He kept running, ankle on fire, heart thundering.

He spotted or maybe merely sensed the movement of something large just at the forest edge. A slightly paler shade of shadow.

Half beast, half ghost . . .

Though unseen, he knew the truth.

Ukufa.

Death.

Not today . . . he prayed not today.

Khamisi crashed through the reeds—

—and dove headlong into the water hole.

9:32 A.M.
COPENHAGEN, DENMARK

Fiona's scream punctuated the sniper's rifle blast.

Gray twisted, hoping to escape mortal injury. As he turned, a blur of something large crashed out through the remains of the smoky shop window.

The gunman must have caught the same movement a fraction before Gray, enough to throw his aim off by a hair-breadth.

Gray felt the sear of the bullet's passage under his left arm.

He continued to spin farther out of point-blank range.

From the window, the large shape bounded atop the trash bin and bowled into the rifleman.

"Bertal!" Fiona yelled.

The shaggy Saint Bernard, soaked to the skin, clamped

his jaws onto the rifleman's forearm. The sudden and unexpected attack caught the man off guard. He fell back into the shadows behind the trash bin. His rifle clattered to the flagstones.

Gray lunged for it.

A canine yelp sounded near at hand. Before Gray could react, the assassin leaped out, high. He planted a boot heel into Gray's shoulder, smashed him into the stones, and bolted over him.

Gray flipped to his side, aiming the captured rifle. But the man moved like a gazelle. Flagging a black trench coat, he vaulted over a garden stone fence and ducked away. Gray heard his footfalls retreating down the alley.

"Bastard . . ."

Fiona ran up to Gray. She had a pistol in hand. "The other man . . ." She pointed behind her. "I think he's dead."

Gray shouldered the rifle and took the pistol from her hand. She didn't argue, too intent on another concern.

"Bertal . . ."

The dog came out, tottering, weak, one side was severely scorched.

Gray glanced back to the burning shop. How had the poor guy survived? Gray pictured where he had last seen the dog: blasted by the initial firebombs into the back wall, knocked unconscious.

Fiona hugged the soaked brute.

The dog must have landed under a sprinkler.

She lifted the Saint Bernard's face, staring nose to muzzle. "Good dog."

Gray agreed. He owed Bertal. "All the Starbucks you want, buddy," he promised under his breath.

Bertal's limbs trembled. He sank to his haunches, then to the stones. Whatever adrenaline had sustained the poor brute was giving out.

Off to the left, raised voices reached them, calling out in

Danish. A spray of jetted water sailed high. Firefighters were headed around the far side of the shop.

Gray could stay no longer.

"I have to go."

Fiona stood up. She glanced between Gray and the dog.

"Stay with Bertal," he said, backing a step. "Get him to a doctor."

Fiona's gaze hardened. "And you're just going to leave . . ."

"I'm sorry." It was a lame response to encompass the horrors: the murder of her grandmother, the burning down of their shop, the hairbreadth escape. But he didn't know what else to say, and he had no time to explain more.

He turned and headed toward the rear garden wall.

"Yeah, go ahead, sod off!" Fiona yelled after him.

Gray hopped the fence, face burning.

"Wait!"

He hurried down the alley. He hated abandoning her—but there was no choice. She was better off. Within the circle of emergency personnel, she would be sheltered, protected. Where Gray had to go next was no place for a fifteen-year-old. Still, his face continued to burn. Deeper down, he could not deny a more selfish motivation: he was simply glad to be rid of her, of the responsibility.

No matter . . . it was done.

He stalked quickly down the alley. He tucked the pistol into the waistband of his pants and ejected all the shells from the rifle. Once finished, he shoved the rifle behind a stack of lumber. Carrying it would be too conspicuous. As he continued, he pulled his sweater back on. He needed to abandon his hotel and change identities. The deaths here would be investigated. It was time to let the persona of Dr. Sawyer die.

But before that, he had one more task to complete.

He freed his cell phone from a back pocket and hit speed

dial for central command. After a few moments, he was connected with Logan Gregory, his op mission leader.

"We have a problem out here," Gray said.

"What's wrong?"

"Whatever is going on is bigger than we initially thought. Big enough to kill over." Gray debriefed his morning. A long stretch of silence followed.

Logan finally spoke, a strain of tension in his voice. "Then it's best if we scrub this mission until you have more resources on the ground."

"If I wait for backup, it'll be too late. The auction is in a few more hours."

"Your cover's blown, Commander Pierce."

"I'm not sure it is. As far as the principals know, I'm an American buyer who asks too many questions. They won't try anything in the open. There'll be plenty of people in attendance at the auction, and the house has tight security. I can still canvass the site and perhaps ascertain some clues about who or what's really behind all this. Afterward, I'll disappear, go low until I have more help."

Gray also wanted to get his hands on that Bible, if only to inspect it.

Logan spoke. "I don't think that's wise. The potential risk outweighs the potential gain. Especially as a solo op."

Gray's response grew heated. "So the bastards try to fry my ass . . . and now you want me to sit on it?"

"Commander."

Gray's fingers tightened on the phone. Logan had plainly spent too much time as a paper pusher at Sigma. For a research mission, Logan was adequate as an ops leader—but this was no longer a fact-gathering assignment. It was turning into a full-blown Sigma Force op. And if that was the case, Gray wanted someone with real leadership backing him up.

"Maybe we should get Director Crowe involved," Gray said.

Another long pause followed. Perhaps he had said the wrong thing. He didn't mean to insult Logan, to go over his head, but sometimes you simply had to know when to step aside.

"I'm afraid that would be impossible at the moment, Commander Pierce."

"Why?"

"Director Crowe is currently incommunicado in Nepal."

Gray frowned. "In Nepal? What's he doing in Nepal?"

"Commander, *you* sent him."

"What?"

Then it dawned on Gray.

The call had come in a week ago.

From an old friend.

Gray's mind slipped into the past, back to his first days with Sigma Force. Like all other Sigma agents, Gray had a background with Special Forces: joining the army at eighteen, the Rangers at twenty-one. But after being court-martialed for striking a superior officer, Gray had been recruited by Sigma Force, straight out of Leavenworth. Still, he had been leery. There had been a good reason he'd struck that officer. The man's incompetence had resulted in needless deaths in Bosnia—deaths of children—but Gray's anger had deeper roots. Tangled issues with authority, going back to his father. And while those hadn't been completely resolved, it had taken a wise man to show Gray the path.

That man had been Ang Gelu.

"Are you saying Director Crowe is out in Nepal because of my friend the Buddhist monk?"

"Painter knew how important the man was to you."

Gray stopped walking and stepped into the shadows.

He had spent four months studying with the monk in Nepal, alongside his training for Sigma. In fact, it was through Ang Gelu that Gray had developed his own unique curriculum at Sigma. Gray had been fast-tracked to study biology and physics, a dual degree, but Ang Gelu elevated Gray's studies, instructing him how to search for the balance between all things. The harmony of opposites. The Taoist yin and yang. The one and the zero.

Such insight eventually helped Gray confront demons of his past.

Growing up, he had always found himself stuck between opposites. Though his mother had taught at a Catholic high school, instilling a deep spirituality in Gray's life, she was also an accomplished biologist, a devout disciple of evolution and reason. She placed as much faith and trust in the scientific method as in her own religion.

And then there was his father: a Welshman living in Texas, a roughneck oilman disabled in midlife and having to assume the role of a housewife. As a result, his life became ruled by overcompensation and anger.

Like father, like son.

Until Ang Gelu had shown Gray another way.

A path between opposites. It was not a short path. It extended as much into the past as the future. Gray was still struggling with it.

But Ang Gelu had helped Gray take his first steps. He owed the monk for that. So when the call for help reached Gray a week ago, he had not wanted to ignore it. Ang Gelu reported strange disappearances, odd maladies, all in a certain region near the Chinese border.

The monk had not known to whom to turn. His own government in Nepal was too focused on the Maoist rebels. And Ang Gelu knew Gray was involved in a nebulous chain of command in covert ops. So he had appealed to Gray for help. But already assigned to this current mission, Gray had turned the matter over to Painter Crowe.

Passing the buck . . .

"I had only meant for Painter to send a junior operative,"

Gray stumbled out, incredulous. "To check it out. Certainly there were others who—"

Logan cut him off. "It was slow here."

Gray bit back a groan. He knew what Logan meant. The same lull in global threats had brought Gray to Denmark.

"So he went?"

"You know the director. Always wants to get his hands dirty." Logan sighed in exasperation. "And now there's a problem. A storm blanketed communication for a few days, but now that it's cleared, we've still not heard an update from the director. Instead we're hearing rumors through various channels. The same stories as reported by your friend. Sickness, plague, deaths, even possible rebel attacks in the region. Only it's escalating."

Gray now understood the strain he'd been hearing in Logan's voice.

It seemed it was not only Gray's mission that was going tits up.

When it rains, it pours.

"I can send you Monk," Logan said. "He and Captain Bryant are on their way here. Monk can be on the ground there in ten hours. Stand down until then."

"But the auction will be over—"

"Commander Pierce, you have your orders."

Gray spoke rapidly, his voice tightening again. "Sir, I've already set up buttonhole cameras at entry and egress points around the auction house. It would be a waste to ignore them."

"All right. Monitor the cameras from a secure location. Record everything. But no more. Is that understood, Commander?"

Gray bristled, but Logan had his hands full. All because of a favor to Gray. So he had little reason to object. "Very good, sir."

"Report in after the auction," Logan said.

"Yes, sir."

The line clicked off.

Gray continued through the backstreets of Copenhagen, alert to all around him. But worry nagged him.

For Painter, for Ang Gelu . . .

What the hell was happening in Nepal?

4

GHOST LIGHTS

11:18 A.M.
HIMALAYAS

"And you're sure Ang Gelu was killed?" Painter asked, glancing back.

A nod answered him.

Lisa Cummings had finished her story, having told how she'd been enlisted from an Everest climbing team to investigate an illness at the monastery. She had quickly related the horrors that followed: the madness, the explosions, the sniper.

Painter reviewed her story in his head as the pair wound deeper into the monastery's subterranean root cellar. The narrow stone maze was not meant for one his size. He had to keep tucked low. Still, the top of his head brushed across some hanging bundles of drying juniper branches. The aromatic sprays were used to make ceremonial smudge sticks for the temple overhead, a temple that was now just one large smudge stick, burning and smoking into the midday sky.

Weaponless, they had fled into the cellars to escape the flames. Painter had stopped only long enough to grab a heavy poncho and a pair of fur-lined boots from a cloakroom. In the current getup, he almost looked the part of a

Pequot Indian, even if he was only half-blooded. He had no recollection of where his own clothes or packs had been taken.

Three days had vanished from his life.

Along with ten pounds.

While donning the robe earlier, he noted the prominence of his ribs. Even his shoulders seemed bonier. He had not fully escaped the illness here. Still, at least his strength continued to improve.

It needed to.

Especially with an assassin still on the loose.

Painter had heard the occasional spats of gunfire as they fled below. A sniper was killing anyone who fled the burning monastery. Dr. Cummings had described the attacker. Only one man. Surely there were others. Were they Maoist rebels? It made no sense. What end did their slaughter serve?

Bearing a penlight in hand, Painter led the way.

Dr. Cummings followed closely.

Painter had learned she was an American medical doctor and a member of an Everest climbing party. He studied her glancingly, evaluating her. She was long-legged with an athletic physique, blond and ponytailed, her cheeks rosy from windburn. She was also terrified. She kept close to him, jumping at the occasional muffled pop of the firestorm overhead. Still, she didn't stop, no tears, no complaints. It seemed she staved off any shock by sheer will.

But for how long?

Her fingers trembled as she moved aside a drying bouquet of lemongrass from her face. They continued onward. As they moved deeper into the root cellar, the air grew redolent from all the sprigs: rosemary, artemisia, mountain rhododendron, khenpa. All ready to be prepared into various incense sticks.

Lama Khemsar, the head of the monastery, had taught Painter the purposes of the hundreds of herbs: for purification, to foster divine energies, to dispel disruptive thoughts, even to treat asthma and the common cold. But right now, all Painter wanted to remember was how to reach the cellar's back door. The root cellar connected all the monastery's buildings. Monks used the cellars during the winter's heavy snowfall to pass underground from structure to structure.

Including reaching the barn at the outskirts of the grounds. It stood well away from the flames and out of direct sight.

If they could reach it . . . then escape to the lower village . . .

He needed to contact Sigma Command.

As his mind spun with possibilities, so did the passageway.

Painter leaned a hand on the cellar wall, steadying himself.

Dizzy.

"Are you all right?" the doctor asked, stepping to his shoulder.

He took a few breaths before nodding. Since he had awakened, bouts of disorientation continued to plague him. But they were occurring less frequently—or was that wishful thinking?

"What really happened up there?" the doctor asked. She relieved him of his penlight—it was actually hers, from her medical kit—and pointed it into his eyes.

"I don't . . . I'm not sure . . . But we should keep moving."

Painter tried to push off the wall, but she pressed a palm against his chest, still examining his eyes. "You're showing a prominent nystagmus," she whispered and lowered the penlight, brow crinkled.

"What?"

She passed him a canteen of cold water and motioned for him to sit on a wrapped bale of hay. He didn't argue. The bale was as hard as cement.

"Your eyes show signs of horizontal nystagmus, a twitch of the pupils. Did you take a blow to the head?"

"I don't think so. Is it serious?"

"Hard to say. It can be the result of damage to the eye or brain. A stroke, multiple sclerosis, a blow to the head. With the dizziness, I'd say you've had some insult to your vestibular apparatus. Maybe in the inner ear. Maybe central nervous system. Most likely it's not permanent." This last was mumbled in a most disconcerting voice.

"What do you mean by *most likely*, Dr. Cummings?"

"Call me Lisa," she said, as if attempting to divert attention.

"Fine. Lisa. So this could be permanent?"

She glanced away. "I'd need more tests. More background," she said. "Maybe you could start by telling me how all this happened."

He took a swig. He wished he could. An ache settled behind his eyes as he tried to remember. The last days were a blur.

"I was staying at one of the outlying villages. In the middle of the night, strange lights appeared up in the mountains. I didn't see the fireworks. By the time I'd woken, they'd subsided. But by the morning, everyone in the village complained of headaches, nausea. Including me. I asked one of the elders about the lights. He said they would appear every now and then, going back generations. Ghost lights. Attributed it to evil spirits of the deep mountains."

"Evil spirits?"

"He pointed to where the lights were seen. Up in a remote region of the mountains, an area of deep gorges, ice water-falls, stretching all the way to the Chinese border. Difficult to traverse. The monastery sits on a shoulder of mountain overlooking this no-man's-land."

"So the monastery was closer to the lights?"

Painter nodded. "All the sheep died within twenty-four

hours. Some dropped where they stood. Others bashed their heads against boulders, over and over again. I arrived back the next day, aching and vomiting. Lama Khemsar gave me some tea. That's the last thing I remember." He took another sip from the canteen and sighed. "That was three days ago. I woke up. Locked in a room. I had to smash my way out."

"You were lucky," the woman said, collecting back her canteen.

"How's that?"

She crossed her arms, tight, protective. "Lucky to be away from the monastery. Proximity to the lights appears to correlate to the severity of symptoms." She glanced up and away, as if trying to see through the walls down here. "Maybe it was some form of radiation. Didn't you say the Chinese border was not far? Maybe it was a nuclear test of some sort."

Painter had wondered the exact same thing days earlier.

"Why are you shaking your head?" Lisa asked.

Painter hadn't realized he was. He raised a palm to his forehead.

Lisa frowned. "You never did say what *you* are doing way out here, Mr. Crowe."

"Call me Painter." He offered her a crooked smile.

She wasn't impressed.

He debated how much more to say. Under the circumstances, honesty seemed the most prudent. Or at least as honest as he could be.

"I work for the government, a division called DARPA. We—"

She cut him off with a flip of her fingers, arms still crossed. "I'm familiar with DARPA. The U.S. military's research and development division. I had a research grant with them once. What's their interest out here?"

"Well, it seems you were not the only one Ang Gelu recruited. He contacted our organization a week ago. To investigate rumors of strange illnesses up here. I was just getting the lay of the land, determining what experts to bring into the area—doctors, geologists, military—when the storms blew in. I hadn't planned on being cut off for so long."

"Were you able to rule anything out?"

"From initial interviews, I was concerned that perhaps the Maoist rebels in the area had come into possession of some nuclear waste, preparing a dirty bomb of some sort. Along the lines of what you were conjecturing with the Chinese. So I tested for various forms of radiation as I waited out the storms. Nothing unusual registered."

Lisa stared at him, as if studying a strange beetle.

"If we could get you to a lab," she said clinically, "we might come up with some answers."

So she didn't consider him so much a beetle as a *guinea pig*.

At least he was moving up the evolutionary scale.

"First we have to survive," Painter said, recalling her to the reality here.

She glanced at the cellar's ceiling. It had been a while since they heard any gunfire. "Maybe they'll think everyone's dead. If we just stay down here—"

Painter pushed off the bale and stood. "From your description, the attack here was methodical. Planned in advance. They'll know about these tunnels. They'll eventually search here. We can only hope they'll wait for the fires to cool down."

Lisa nodded. "Then we keep going."

"And get clear. We can do this," he assured her. He placed a hand against the wall to steady himself. "We can do this," he repeated, more to himself this time than to her.

They set off.

After a few steps, Painter felt steadier.

Good.

The exit could not be much farther.

As if confirming this, a breeze whispered down the corridor, stirring the hanging bundles of herbs with a dry clacking. Painter felt the cold on his face. It froze him in place. A hunter's instinct took hold—half special ops training, half blood heritage. He reached behind him and took hold of Lisa's elbow, silencing her.

He flicked off the penlight.

Ahead, something heavy struck the floor, the sound echoing down the passage. Boots. A door slammed closed. The breeze died.

They were no longer alone.

The assassin crouched in the root cellar. He knew others were down here. How many? He shouldered his rifle and pulled out a Heckler & Koch MK23 pistol. He had already stripped his hands to fingerless wool undergloves. He stood his post, listening.

The faintest scuffle and scrape.

Retreating.

At least two . . . maybe three.

Reaching up, he pulled shut the trapdoor that led to the barn above. The cold breeze died with one last whispered rush as darkness clamped over him. He pulled down a pair of night-vision goggles and clicked on an ultraviolet lamp affixed to his shoulder. The passage ahead glowed in shades of a silvery green.

Near at hand, a wall of shelves was stacked with canned goods and rows of wax-sealed jars of amber honey. He slipped past, moving slowly, silently. There was no need to hurry. The only other exits led to fiery ruin. He had shot those monks with sense enough still in their addled heads to flee the flames.

Mercy killings, all of them.

As he knew too well.

The Bell had been rung too loudly.

It had been an accident. One of many lately.

For the past month, he had sensed the agitation among the others at the *Granitschloß*. Even before the accident. Something had stirred up the castle, felt as far as the hinterlands where he made his solitary home. He had ignored it. Why should it be his concern?

Then the accident . . . and it had become his problem.

To clean up their mistake.

It was his duty as one of the last surviving *Sonnekönige*. Such was the decline of the Knights of the Sun—both in numbers and in status, debilitated and shunned, anachronistic and an embarrassment. Before long, the last of them would be gone.

And just as well.

But at least this duty today was almost finished. He could return to his hovel after he cleared out this root cellar. The tragedy at the monastery would be blamed on Maoist rebels. Who else but the godless Maoists would attack a strategically unimportant monastery?

To ensure this deception, even his ammunition matched the rebels'.

Including his pistol.

With weapon ready, he edged by a row of open oak barrels. Grain, rye, flour, even dried apples. He stepped carefully, wary of any ambush. The monks might be damaged of mind, but even the mad could display cunning when cornered.

Ahead, the passageway jagged to the left. He hugged the right wall. He stopped to listen, ears pricked for any scuffle of heel. He flipped up his night-vision goggles.

Pitch dark.

He lowered the scopes over his eyes, and the passageway stretched ahead, limned in green. He would see any lurkers well before they saw him. There was no escape. They would have to get past him to reach the only safe way out.

He slid around the corner.

A low bale of hay sat crooked across the passage, as if knocked aside in a hurry. He searched the stretch of cellar ahead. More barrels. The roof was raftered with hanging bunches of drying branches.

No movement. No sound.

He reached a leg over the blocking bale and stepped to the far side.

Under his boot heel, a brittle juniper branch cracked.

His eyes flicked down. The entire floor was covered with a spread of branches.

Trap.

"Now!"

He glanced up as the world ahead burst into a strobing brilliance. Amplified by the goggles' sensitivity, the exploding supernovas seared the back of his skull, blinding him.

Camera flashes.

He fired instinctively.

The explosions were deafening in the tight cellar.

They must have lain in wait in the dark, listening until he stepped on the crackling branch, giving away his proximity, then ambushed him. He backed a step, half tripping on the bale of hay.

Falling back, his next shot fired high.

A mistake.

Taking advantage, someone barreled into him. Low. Hitting him in the legs and knocking him over the bale. His back slammed into the stone floor. Something stabbed into the meat of his thigh. He kneed up, earning a grunt from the attacker atop him.

"Go!" the attacker yelled, pinning down his pistol arm. "Get clear!"

His attacker spoke English. Not a monk.

A second figure leaped past their bodies, appearing shadowy as his vision began to return. He heard the steps retreating toward the barn trapdoor.

"*Scheiße,*" he swore.

He heaved his body around, flinging the man from him like a ragdoll. The *Sonnekönige* were not like other men. His attacker struck the wall, rebounded, and tried to leap after the other escapee. But vision returned rapidly, illuminated by the retreating light. Furious, he grabbed his attacker's ankle and dragged him back.

The man kicked with his other foot, catching him in the elbow.

Growling, he dug his thumb into a tender nerve behind the Achilles tendon. The man cried out. He knew how painful that pinch could be. Like having your ankle broken. He drew the man up by his leg.

As he straightened, the world turned in a heady spin. All the strength suddenly sputtered out of him as if he were a popped balloon. His upper thigh burned. Where he'd been stabbed. He stared down. Not stabbed. A syringe still protruded from his thigh, jammed to the hilt.

Drugged.

His attacker twisted and broke his weakening grip, rolling and scrambling away.

He could not let the man escape.

He lifted his pistol—as heavy as an anvil now—and fired after him. The shot ricocheted off the floor. Weakening rapidly, he fired a second shot—but the man was already out of sight.

He heard his attacker fleeing.

Limbs heavy, he sank to his knees. His heart pounded in his chest. A heart twice the average size. But normal for a *Sonnekönig*.

He took several deep breaths as his metabolism adjusted.

The *Sonnekönige* were not like other men.

He slowly pushed to his feet.

He had a duty to finish.

It was why he had been born.

To serve.

Painter slammed the trapdoor closed.

"Help me with this," he said, limping to the side. Pain prickled up his leg. He pointed to a stack of crates. "Stack them on the trapdoor."

He dragged off the topmost crate. Too heavy to carry, it crashed to the floor with a clang of rattling metal. He dragged it toward the door. He didn't know what was inside the crates, only that they were heavy, damn heavy.

He manhandled the box atop the trapdoor.

Lisa struggled with a second. He joined her, grabbing a third.

Together they hauled the load to the door.

"One more," Painter said.

Lisa stared at the pile of crates on the door. "No one's getting through that."

"One more," Painter insisted, panting and grimacing. "Trust me."

They dragged the last one together. It took both of them to lift it atop the others already piled on the trapdoor.

"The drugs will keep him out cold for hours," Lisa said.

A single gunshot answered her. A rifle round pierced through the loaded trapdoor and drilled into one of the barn rafters.

"I think I'm going to want a second opinion," Painter said, pulling her away.

"Did you get all of the midazolam . . . the sedative into him?"

"Oh yeah."

"Then how—?"

"I don't know. And right now, don't care."

Painter led her toward the open barn door. After searching for any other gunmen, they fled outside. To the left, the world was a fiery, smoky ruin. Flaming embers swirled into a lowering sky.

Clouds the color of granite obscured the summit overhead.

"Taski was right," Lisa mumbled, pulling up the hood of her parka.

"Who?"

"A Sherpa guide. He warned that another storm front would strike today."

Painter followed the flames twisting toward the clouds. Heavy white snowflakes began to sift downward, mixing with a black rain of glowing ash. Fire and ice. It was a fitting memorial to the dozen monks who had shared this monastery.

As Painter remembered the gentle men who made their home here, a dark anger stoked inside him. Who would slaughter the monks with such mercilessness?

He had no answer to the *who,* but he did know the *why.*

The illness here.

Something had gone wrong—and now someone sought to cover it up.

An explosion cut off any further contemplation. Flame and smoke belched out the barn door. One of the crate lids sailed out into the yard.

Painter grabbed Lisa's arm.

"Did he just blow himself up?" Lisa asked, staring aghast toward the barn.

"No. Just the trapdoor. C'mon. The fires will only hold him off so long."

Painter led the way across the ice-crusted ground, avoiding the frozen carcasses of the goats and sheep. They picked their way out the pen gate.

Snow grew heavier. A mixed blessing. Painter wore only a thick woolen robe and fur-lined boots. Not much insulation against a blizzard. But the fresh snowfall would help hide their path and shave visibility.

He led the way toward a path that ran along a sheer cliff face and trailed down to the lower village, the village he had visited a few days ago.

"Look!" Lisa said.

Below, a column of smoke churned into the sky, a smaller version of the one at their back.

"The village . . ." Painter tightened a fist.

So it wasn't just the monastery that was being eradicated. The scatter of huts below had been firebombed, too. The attackers were leaving no witnesses.

Painter pulled back from the cliff-side trail. It was too exposed.

The path would surely be watched, and others might still be below.

He retreated back toward the fiery ruins of the monastery.

"Where are we going to go?" Lisa asked.

Painter pointed beyond the flames. "No-man's-land."

"But isn't that where—?"

"Where the lights were last seen," he confirmed. "But the broken land is also a place to lose ourselves. To find shelter. To hole up and weather out the storm. We'll wait for others to come investigate the fire and smoke."

Painter stared at the thick black column. It should be visible for miles. A smoke signal, like his Native American ancestors once used. But was there anyone to see it? His gaze shifted higher, to the clouds. He tried to pierce the cover to the open skies beyond. He prayed someone recognized the danger.

Until then . . .

He had only one choice.

"Let's go."

1:25 A.M.
WASHINGTON, D.C.

Monk crossed the dark Capitol Plaza with Kat at his side. They marched in brisk stride together, not so much in simpatico as irritation.

"I'd prefer we wait," Kat said. "It's too early. Anything might happen."

Monk could smell the hint of jasmine from her. They had showered hurriedly together after the call from Logan Gregory, caressing each other in the steam, entwined as they rinsed, a final intimacy. But afterward, as they separately toweled and dressed, practicality began to intrude with every tug of a zipper and securing of a button. Reality set in, cooling their passion as much as the night's chill.

Monk glanced at her now.

Kat wore navy blue slacks, a white blouse, and a windbreaker emblazoned with the U.S. Navy symbol. Professional as always, as spit-and-polished as her black leather pumps. While Monk, in turn, wore black Reeboks, dark jeans, and an oatmeal-colored turtleneck sweater, topped by a Chicago Cubs baseball cap.

"Until I know for sure," Kat continued, "I'd prefer we keep silent about the pregnancy."

"What do you mean by *until I know for sure*? Until you know for sure you *want* the baby? Until you're sure about *us*?"

They had argued all the way from Kat's apartment at the edge of Logan Circle, a former Victorian bed-and-breakfast that had been converted into condos, within walking distance of the Capitol. This night, the short walk seemed interminable.

"Monk . . ."

He stopped. He reached a hand out to her, then lowered it. Still, she stopped, too.

He stared her square in the eye. "Tell me, Kat."

"I want to make sure the pregnancy . . . I don't know . . . *sticks*. Until I'm further along before telling anyone." Her eyes glistened in the moonlight, near tears.

"Baby, that's why we should let everyone know." He stepped closer. He placed a hand on her belly. "To protect what's growing here."

She turned away, his hand now resting on the small of her back. "And then maybe you were right. My career . . . maybe this isn't the right time."

Monk sighed. "If all kids were born only at the right time, the world would be a much emptier place."

"Monk, you're not being fair. It's not your career."

"Like hell it's not. You don't think a kid isn't going to alter my life, my choices from here? It changes everything."

"Exactly. That's what scares me the most." She leaned into his palm. He wrapped her in his arms.

"We'll get through this together," he whispered. "I promise."

"I'd still rather keep quiet . . . at least for a few more days. I haven't even been to a doctor yet. Maybe the pregnancy test is wrong."

"How many tests did you take?"

She leaned against him.

"Well?"

"Five," she whispered.

"Five?" He failed to keep the amusement from his voice.

She half punched him in the ribs. It hurt. "Don't make fun of me." He heard the smile in her voice.

He wrapped his arms tighter around her. "Fine. It'll be our secret for now."

She turned in his arms and kissed him, not deeply, not passionately, just in thanks. They separated, but their fingers remained entwined as they continued across the mall.

Ahead, brightly lit, was their destination: the Smithsonian Castle. Its red sandstone battlements, towers, and spires shone in the dark, an anachronistic landmark to the orderly city surrounding it. While the main building housed the Smithsonian Institution's information center, the old abandoned bomb shelter below had been converted into Sigma's central command, burying DARPA's covert force of military scientists in the heart of the Smithsonian's score of museums and research sites.

Kat's fingers slipped from his as they neared the castle grounds.

Monk studied her, a worry nagging him still.

Despite their agreement, he sensed the core of insecurity persisted behind her manner. Was it more than just the baby?

Until I know for sure.

Sure of what?

The worry nagged Monk all the way down to the subterranean offices of Sigma command. But once below, the debriefing with Logan Gregory, Sigma's interim director, added a whole new batch of worries.

"Storm cover is still blanketing the region, with electrical storms surging across the entire Bay of Bengal," Logan explained, seated behind an orderly desk. A bank of LCD computer screens lined one wall. Data scrolled across two of them. One showed a live feed from a weather satellite over Asia.

Monk passed Kat a photo of one of the satellite passes.

"Hopefully we'll hear some further word before sunrise," Logan continued. "Ang Gelu left at dawn in Nepal to helicopter some medical staff up to the monastery. They were attempting the flight during the break between storms. It's still early. Only noon there now. So hopefully we'll have some further intel soon."

Monk shared a glance with Kat. They had been briefed on the director's investigation. Painter Crowe had been out of communication for three days. From the haggard look of Logan Gregory, the man had been awake the entire time. He wore his usual blue suit, but it was slightly rumpled at elbow and knee, practically disheveled for the second in command of Sigma. His straw blond hair and tanned physique always gave him a youthful air, but this night, signs of his forty-plus years wore through: puffy eyes, a wan pallor, and a pair of wrinkles between his eyes as deep as the Grand Canyon.

"What about Gray?" Kat asked.

Logan straightened a file with a firm tap on the desk, as if this settled the prior matter. Ever efficient, he shifted a second folder to the forefront and opened it. "There was an attempt on Commander Pierce's life an hour ago."

"What?" Monk leaned forward, a bit suddenly. "Then what's with all the weather reports?"

"Calm down. He's secure and awaiting backup." Logan gave the bullet points of events in Copenhagen, including Gray's survival. "Monk, I've arranged for you to join Commander Pierce. There's a jet waiting in Dulles, scheduled for wheels up in ninety-two minutes."

Monk had to give the man credit. He didn't even check his watch.

"Captain Bryant," Logan continued, turning to Kat. "In the interim, I'd like to keep you here while we monitor situations in Nepal. I have calls into our embassy in Kathmandu. I can use your experience with intelligences, domestic and foreign."

"Certainly, sir."

Monk was suddenly glad Kat had risen through the ranks in the intelligence branch. She would be Logan's right-hand man during this crisis. He'd rather have her here, bunkered safely below the Smithsonian Castle, than out in the field. It would be one less thing to worry about.

He found Kat staring at him. There was an angry set to her eyes, as if she could read his mind. He kept his face fixed and immobile.

Logan stood up. "Then I'll let you both get situated." He held open the door to his office, effectively dismissing them.

No sooner had the door closed behind them than Kat grabbed his arm, above the elbow, hard. "You're heading over to Denmark?"

"Yeah, so?"

"What about . . . ?" She tugged him into the women's lavatory. It was empty at this late hour. "What about the baby?"

"I don't understand. What does—?"

"What if something happens to you?"

He blinked at her. "Nothing will happen."

She lifted his other arm, exposing his prosthetic hand. "You're not indestructible."

He lowered his arm, half hiding his hand behind him. His face heated up. "It's a babysitting operation. I'll support Gray as he finishes his work there. I mean, even Rachel's coming to town. Most likely I'll be their bloody chaperone. Then we'll be on the first flight back here."

"If it's so damn unimportant, let someone else go. I can tell Logan that I need your help here."

"Like he'll believe that."

"Monk . . ."

"I'm going, Kat. You're the one who wants to keep quiet about the pregnancy. I want to shout it out to the world. Either way, we have our duties. You have yours. I have mine. And trust me, I won't be reckless." He placed a hand on her belly. "I'll be protecting my ass for all three of us."

She covered his hand with her own and sighed. "Well, it is a pretty nice ass."

He smiled at her. She grinned back, but he also saw the exhaustion and worry in her eyes. He only had one answer for that.

He leaned in, lips touching, and whispered between them. "I promise."

"Promise what?" she asked, pulling back slightly.

"Everything," he answered and kissed her deeply.

He meant it.

"You can tell Gray," she said when they finally broke their embrace. "As long as you swear him to secrecy."

"Really?" His eyes brightened, then narrowed in suspicion. "Why?"

She stepped around him toward the mirror, but not before swatting his backside. "I want him watching your ass, too."

"All right. But I don't think he swings that way."

She shook her head and checked her face in the mirror. "What am I going to do with you?"

He stepped behind her and encircled her waist. "Well, according to Mr. Gregory, I do have ninety-two minutes."

12:15 P.M.
HIMALAYAS

Lisa scrambled after Painter.

With the skill of a mountain goat, he led the way down a steep pitch, boulder-strewn and treacherous with frozen shale. Snow fell thickly over them, a shifting, billowing cloud that lowered visibility to a few feet, creating a strange, gray twilight. But at least they were out of the worst of the icy gusts. The deep notch they had worked down ran counter to the wind's direction.

Still, there was no escaping the frigid cold as the temperature plummeted. Even in her storm parka and gloves, she shivered. Though they had traveled less than a full hour, the heat of the burning monastery was a distant memory. The inches of exposed skin on her face felt windburned and abraded.

Painter had to be faring worse. He had donned a pair of thick pants and woolen mittens, stripped off one of the dead monks. But he had no insulating hood, only a scarf tied over the lower half of his face. His breath puffed white into the frigid air.

They had to find shelter.

And soon.

Painter offered her a hand as she slid on her butt down a particularly steep patch and gained his side. They had reached the bottom of the notch. It angled away, framed by steep walls.

The fresh snow had already accumulated to a foot's depth down here.

It would be hard trekking without snowshoes.

As if reading her worry, Painter pointed off to one side of the narrow cut. An overhang lipped out, offering protection from the weather. They set out for it, trudging through the drifts.

Once they reached the overhang, it became easier.

She glanced behind her. Already their steps were filling up with new snow. In minutes, they would be gone. While this certainly helped hide their path from any trackers, it still unnerved her. It was as if their very existence were being erased.

She turned around. "Do you have any idea where we're going?" she asked. She found herself whispering—not so much in fear of giving away their position but as the blanketing hush of the storm intimidated.

"Barely," Painter said. "These borderlands are uncharted territory. Much of it never trod by man." He waved an arm.

"When I first arrived here, I did study some satellite survey shots. But they're not much practical use. The land's too broken. Makes surveys difficult."

They continued in silence for a few more steps.

Then Painter glanced back to her. "Did you know that back in 1999 they discovered Shangri-La up here?"

Lisa studied him. She couldn't tell if he was smiling behind his scarf, trying to ease her fear. "Shangri-La . . . as in *Lost Horizon*?" She remembered the movie and the book. A lost utopian paradise frozen in time in the Himalayas.

Turning back around, he trudged on and explained. "Two *National Geographic* explorers discovered a monstrously deep gorge in the Himalayas a few hundred miles south of here, tucked under a mountain spur, a place that failed to show up on satellite maps. At the bottom lay a subtropical paradise. Waterfalls, fir and pine trees, meadows full of rhododendrons, streams lined by hemlock and spruce trees. A wild garden landscape, teeming with life, surrounded on all sides by ice and snow."

"Shangri-La?"

He shrugged. "Just shows you that science and satellites don't always reveal what the world wants to hide."

By now his teeth were chattering. Even the act of talking wasted breath and heat. They needed to find their own Shangri-La.

They continued in silence. The snow fell thicker.

After another ten minutes, the notch cut to one side in a tight switchback. Reaching the corner, the protective overhang disappeared.

They stopped and stared, despairing.

The notch cut steeply down from here, widening and opening. A veil of snow fell ahead of them, filling the world. Through occasional gusts, fluttering glimpses of a deep valley appeared.

It was no Shangri-La.

Ahead stretched an icy, snow-swept series of jagged cliffs, too steep to traverse without ropes. A stream tumbled down through the precipitous landscape in a series of towering waterfalls—the course frozen to pure ice, locked in time.

Beyond, misted by snow and ice fog, lay a deep gorge, appearing bottomless from here. The end of the world.

"We'll find a way down," Painter chattered.

He headed into the teeth of the storm again. The snow quickly climbed above their ankles, then midcalf. Painter plowed a path for her.

"Wait," she said. She knew he couldn't last much longer. He had gotten her this far, but they were not equipped to go any farther. "Over here."

She led him toward the cliff wall. The leeward side was somewhat sheltered.

"Where—?" he tried to ask, but his teeth rattled away his words.

She just pointed to where the frozen stream tumbled past the cliff overhead. Taski Sherpa had taught them survival skills up here. One of his strictest lessons. Finding shelter.

She knew by heart the five best places to look.

Lisa crossed to where the waterfall of ice reached their level. As instructed, she searched where the black rock met the blue-white ice. According to their guide, summer snow-melt turned the Himalayan waterfalls into churning torrents, capable of carving a deep pocket out of the rock. And by summer's end, the water flow receded and froze, often leaving an empty space behind it.

With relief, she saw this waterfall was no exception.

She sent a prayer of thanks to Taski and all his ancestors.

Using her elbow, she shattered a crust of rime and widened a black gap between ice and wall. A small cave opened beyond.

Painter joined her. "Let me make sure it's safe."

Turning on his side, he squeezed through—and disappeared. A moment later, a small light bloomed, illuminating the waterfall.

Lisa peered through the crack.

Painter stood a couple of steps away, penlight in hand. He swept his beam around the small niche. "Looks safe. We should be able to weather out the storm in here for some time."

Lisa pushed through to join him. Out of the wind and snow, it already felt warmer.

Painter flicked off his penlight. A light source wasn't really necessary. The ice wall seemed to collect whatever daylight the storm let through and amplified it. The frozen waterfall scintillated and glowed.

Painter turned to her, his eyes exceptionally blue, a match to the glowing ice. She searched his face for signs of frostbite. The wind's abrasion had turned his skin a deep ruddy hue. She recognized his Native American heritage in the planes of his face. Striking with his blue eyes.

"Thanks," Painter said. "You may have just saved our lives."

She shrugged, glancing away. "I owed you the favor."

Still, despite her dismissive words, a part of her warmed at his appreciation—more than she would have expected.

"How did you know how to find—?" Painter's last words were lost to a hard sneeze. "Ow."

Lisa shrugged out of her pack. "Enough questions. We both need to warm up."

She opened her medical pack and tugged out an MPI insulating blanket. Despite its deceptive thinness, the Astrolar fabric would retain ninety percent of radiated body heat. And she wasn't counting on just body heat.

She pulled out a compact catalytic heater, vital gear in mountaineering.

"Sit," she ordered Painter, spreading the blanket over the cold rock.

Exhausted, he didn't offer any argument.

She joined him and swept it over them both, forming a cocoon. Nestling inside, she pressed the electronic ignition for her Coleman SportCat heater. The flameless device operated on a small butane cylinder that lasted fourteen hours. Using it sparingly and intermittently, along with the space blanket, they should be able to last two or three days.

Painter shivered next to her as the heater warmed.

"Take off your gloves and boots," she said, doing the same. "Warm your hands over the heater and massage fingers, toes, nose, ears."

"Against f . . . frostbite . . ."

She nodded. "Pile as much clothing between you and the rock to limit heat loss from conduction."

They stripped and feathered their nest with goose down and wool.

Soon the space felt almost balmy.

"I have a few PowerBars," she said. "We can melt snow for water."

"A regular backwoods survivalist," Painter said a bit more steadily, optimism returning as they warmed.

"But none of this will stop a bullet," she said. She stared over at him, almost nose to nose under the blanket.

Painter sighed and nodded. They were out of the cold, but not out of danger. The storm, a threat before, offered some protection. But what then? They had no means of communication. No weapons.

"We'll stay hidden," Painter said. "Whoever firebombed the monastery won't be able to track us. Searchers will come looking when the storm clears. Hopefully with rescue helicopters. We can signal them with that road flare I saw in your emergency pack."

"And just hope the rescuers reach us before the others."

He reached and squeezed her knee. She appreciated the fact that he didn't offer any false words of encouragement. No candy-coating their situation. Her hand found his and held tight. It was encouragement enough.

They remained silent, lost in their own thoughts.

"Who do you think they are?" she finally asked softly.

"Don't know. But I heard the man swear when I knocked into him. In German. Felt like hitting a tank."

"German? Are you sure?"

"I'm not sure of anything. Probably a hired mercenary. He obviously had some military training."

"Wait," Lisa said. She wiggled around to her pack. "My camera."

Painter sat straighter, shaking loose a corner of the blanket. He tucked it under to close the gap. "You think you might have a picture of him?"

"To operate the strobe flash, I set the camera to continuous shooting. In that mode, the digital SLR takes five frames per second. I have no idea what got captured." She twisted around, thumbing on the camera.

Shoulder to shoulder, they stared at the tiny LCD screen on the back of the camera body. She brought up the last shots. Most were blurry, but as she flipped through the series, it was like watching a slow-motion replay of their escape: the startled response of the assassin, his raised arm as he instinctively tried to shield his eyes, his gunfire as she ducked behind her barrel, Painter's crash into him.

A few shots had captured slices of the man's face. Piecing the jigsaw together, they had a rough composite: blond-white hair, brutish brow, prominent jaw. The last shot in the series must have been taken as she leaped over Painter and the assassin. She captured a great close-up of his eyes, his night-vision scopes knocked over one ear. Anger blazed, a wildness accentuated by the red-eyed pupils in the camera flash.

Lisa flashed back to Relu Na, the distant relation of Ang Gelu who had attacked them with a sickle. The maddened monk's eyes had glowed similarly. A chill that had nothing to do with the weather washed over her bare skin.

She also noted one other thing about the eyes.

They were mismatched.

One eye shone a brilliant Arctic blue.

The other was a dead white.

Maybe it was just flash washout . . .

Lisa hit the back arrow and recycled through the photos to the beginning. She overshot and brought up the last picture stored in the camera before the series in the root cellar. It was a picture of a wall, scrawled and scratched in blood. She had forgotten she had taken it.

"What's that?" Painter asked.

She had already related the sad story of the head of the monastery, Lama Khemsar. "That's what the old monk had been writing on the wall. It looks like the same series of marks. Over and over again."

Painter leaned closer. "Can you zoom in?"

She did, though some crispness and clarity pixilated away.

Painter's brow knit together. "It's not Tibetan or Nepalese. Look at how angular the script is. Looks more like Nordic runes or something."

"Do you think so?"

"Maybe." Painter leaned back with a tired groan. "Either way, it makes you wonder if Lama Khemsar knew more than he let on."

Lisa remembered something she had failed to tell Painter. "After the old monk cut his throat, we found a symbol carved into his chest. I dismissed it as just raving and coincidence. But now I'm not so sure."

"What did it look like? Can you draw it?"

"No need to. It was a swastika."

Painter's brows rose. "A swastika?"

"I think so. Could he have been flashing back to the past, acting out something that frightened him?"

Lisa related the story of Ang Gelu's relative. How Relu Na had fled the Maoist rebels, traumatized by their growing brutality as they took sickles to the limbs of innocent farmers. Then Relu Na did the same when the illness sapped the man's sanity, acting out some deep-seated trauma.

Painter frowned as she finished. "Lama Khemsar was somewhere in his midseventies. That would place him in his early to midteens during World War II. So it's possible. The Nazis had sent research expeditions into the Himalayas."

"Here? Why?"

Painter shrugged. "The story goes that Heinrich Himmler, the head of the SS, was fixated on the occult. He studied ancient Vedic texts of India, dating back thousands of years. The bastard came to believe that these mountains were once the birthplace of the original Aryan race. He sent expeditions looking for proof. Of course, the man was a few fries short of a Happy Meal."

Lisa smiled at him. "Still, maybe the old lama had some run-in with one of those early expeditions. Hired as a guide or something."

"Maybe. But we'll never know. Whatever secrets there were died with him."

"Maybe not. Maybe that was what he was trying to do up in his room. Letting go of something horrible. His subconscious trying to absolve itself by revealing what he knew."

"That's a lot of maybes." Painter rubbed his forehead, wincing. "And I have one more. *Maybe* it was just gibberish."

Lisa had no argument against that. She sighed, tiring rapidly as the adrenaline of their flight wore off. "Are you warm enough?"

"Yeah, thanks."

She switched off the heater. "Need to conserve the butane."

He nodded, then failed to stop a jaw-popping yawn.

"We should try to get some sleep," she said. "Take shifts."

Hours later, Painter woke, startled awake by someone shaking his shoulder. He sat up from where he had been leaning against the wall. It was dark out. The wall of ice before him was as pitch-black as the rock.

At least the storm seemed to have died down.

"What's wrong?" he asked.

Lisa had dropped a section of their blanket.

She pointed an arm and whispered, "Wait."

He shifted closer, shedding any sleepiness. He waited half a minute. Still nothing. The storm definitely seemed to have subsided. The wind's howl was gone. Beyond their cave, a winter's crystalline quiet had settled over the valley and cliffs. He strained to hear anything suspicious.

Something had definitely spooked Lisa.

He sensed her raw fear. It practically vibrated out of her tense body.

"Lisa, what's—?"

Suddenly the wall of ice flickered brilliantly, as if fireworks had ignited in the sky outside. There was no noise. The scintillating radiance cascaded up along the falls and away. Then the ice went dark again.

"The ghost lights . . . ," Lisa whispered and turned to him.

Painter flashed to three nights ago. When this had all started. *The illness in the village, the madness in the monastery.* He remembered Lisa's earlier assessment. Proximity to the strange lights was directly related to the severity of the symptoms.

And now they were in the heart of the badlands.

Closer than ever.

As Painter watched, the frozen waterfall flared again with a shining and deadly brilliance. The ghost lights had returned.

5

SOMETHING ROTTEN

Does nothing ever start on time in Europe?

Gray checked his wristwatch.

The auction had been slated to start at five o'clock.

Trains and buses might be efficient enough to set your clock by here, but when it came to scheduled events, it was anyone's guess. It was already after six. The latest consensus was that the auction's start would be closer to six-thirty, due to some late arrivals, as a storm off the North Sea was delaying air traffic into Copenhagen.

Bidders were still arriving below.

As the sun sank away, Gray had positioned himself on a second-story balcony of the Scandic Hotel Webers. It sat across the street from the home of Ergenschein Auction House, a modern four-story building that seemed more art gallery than auction establishment, with its modern Danish minimalist style, all glass and bleached woods. The auction was to take place in the house's basement.

And hopefully soon.

Gray yawned and stretched.

Earlier, he had stopped at his original hotel near Nyhavn, quickly collected his surveillance gear, and checked out. Under a new name with a new MasterCard, he had booked into this hotel. It offered a panoramic view of Copenhagen's City Square, and from the private balcony, he could hear the distant titter and music of one of the world's oldest amusement parks, Tivoli Gardens.

He had a laptop open with a half-eaten hot dog from a street vendor resting beside it. His only meal of the day. Despite rumors, the life of an operative was not all Monte Carlo casinos and gourmet restaurants. Still, it was a great hot dog, even if it cost almost five dollars American.

The image on the laptop screen shivered as the motion-sensitive camera snapped a rapid series of pictures. He had already captured two dozen participants: stiff bankers, dismissive Eurotrash, a trio of bull-necked gentlemen in shiny suits with mafioso stamped on their foreheads, a pudgy woman in professorial attire, and a foursome of white-suited nouveau riche wearing identical matching sailor caps. Of course, these last spoke American. Loudly.

He shook his head.

There couldn't possibly be too many more arrivals.

A long black limousine pulled up to the auction house. Two figures stepped out. They were tall and lean, dressed in matching black Armani suits. His and hers. He wore a robin's egg blue tie. She wore a silk blouse of a matching hue. Both were young, midtwenties at best. But they carried themselves as if much older. Maybe it was the bleached white hair, coiffed almost identically, short, pasted to the scalp, looking like a pair of silent-movie stars from the Roaring Twenties. Their manner gave them an ageless grace. No smiles, but not cold. Even in the snapshots, there was a friendly amusement in their eyes.

The doorman held the door open for them.

They each nodded their thanks—again not overly warm, but acknowledging the man's gesture. They vanished inside. The doorman stepped after them, turning a sign. Plainly this couple was the last, and perhaps in fact the very reason the auction had been delayed until now.

Who were they?

He stowed his curiosity. He had his orders from Logan Gregory.

He reviewed his pictures to ensure he had clean images of each participant. Satisfied, he backed the file onto a flash-disk and pocketed it. Now all he had to do was wait for the auction to end. Logan had arranged to obtain a list of sale items and names of successful bidders. Surely a few would be aliases, but the information would be shared with the U.S. task force on terrorism and eventually Europol and Interpol. Whatever was really afoot here might never be known to Gray.

Like why was he attacked? Why had Grette Neal been killed?

Gray forced his fist to relax. It had taken all afternoon, but in a calmer frame of mind, Gray had learned to accept the restraints Logan had placed on him. He had no idea what was really going on here, and to operate blindly, rashly, might only get more people killed.

Still, a large measure of guilt ached at the base of his spine, making it difficult to sit still. He had spent most of the afternoon pacing his hotel room. The past days had replayed in his mind over and over again.

If he had been more careful to start . . . taken more precautions . . .

Gray's cell phone vibrated in his pocket. Taking it out, he checked the incoming number. *Thank God.* He snapped open the phone, stood, and stepped to the balcony railing.

"Rachel . . . I'm glad you called back."

"I got your message. Are you all right?"

He heard both the personal concern and the professional interest in a more thorough debriefing. He had left her only a short note on her cell phone, warning that their rendezvous would have to be cut short. He hadn't gone into the details. Despite their relationship, there were security clearances involved.

"I'm fine. But Monk is flying in. He'll be here a little after midnight."

"I've just arrived in Frankfurt myself," Rachel said. "Laying over for my last leg to Copenhagen. I checked my messages after we landed here."

"Again. I'm sorry . . ."

"So I should head back?"

He feared involving her in any way. "It would be best. We'll have to reschedule. Perhaps if things calm down here, I can make a short side trip to Rome and visit you there before returning to the States."

"I would like that."

He heard the disappointment in her voice.

"I'll make it up to you," he said, hoping it was a promise he could keep.

She sighed—not in irritation, but in understanding. They were not naïve about their long-distance relationship. Two continents, two careers. But they were willing to work on it . . . to see where it would lead.

"I'd hoped we would have a chance to talk," Rachel said.

He knew what she meant, reading the deeper meaning behind her words. They had been through much together, witnessed both the good and the bad in each other, and still, despite the difficulty in a long-distance romance, neither had been willing to throw in the towel. In fact, both of them knew that it was time to discuss the next step.

Shortening that distance.

It was probably one of the reasons that they'd been so long apart since the last rendezvous. Some unspoken acknowledgment that they both needed time to think. Now it was time to lay the cards on the table.

Move forward or not.

But did he even have an answer? He loved Rachel. He was ready to make a life with her. They had even talked about kids. Still . . . something unsettled him. Made him almost relieved their tryst here had been delayed. It wasn't something as mundane as cold feet. So then what was it?

Maybe they *had* better talk.

"I'll get to Rome," he said. "I promise."

"I'm going to hold you to that. I'll even keep some of Uncle Vigor's *vermicelli alla panna* warming on the stove." He heard the tension easing from her voice. "I miss you, Gray. We—"

Her next words were cut off by the strident beep of a car horn.

Gray glanced down to the street. Below, a figure ran across two lanes, heedless of traffic. A woman in a cashmere jacket and ankle-length dress, hair bundled up in a bun. Gray almost didn't recognize her. Not until she flipped off the driver who had honked.

Fiona.

What the hell was the girl doing here?

"Gray—?" Rachel said in his ear.

He spoke in a rush. "I'm sorry, Rachel . . . I have to run."

He hung up, pocketing his cell phone.

Below, Fiona rushed to the auction house door and pushed inside. Gray darted back to his laptop. His camera captured the girl's image through the glass entrance. She was arguing with the doorman. Finally, the uniformed man checked a paper she shoved into his hands, scowled, and waved her farther inside.

Fiona bulled past him and disappeared. The camera went dark.

Gray glanced between laptop and street.

Damn it . . .

Logan would not be happy. No rash actions.

Still, what would Painter Crowe do?

Gray swung back inside and stripped out of his street clothes. His suit jacket lay on the bed. Ready in case of emergency.

Painter certainly would not sit calmly and do nothing.

10:22 P.M.
HIMALAYAS

"We have to remain calm," Painter said. "Sit tight."

Before them, the ghost lights continued to flare and subside, wintry and silent, igniting the icy waterfall into a shattering brilliance, then dying away. In the resulting darkness, the cave seemed colder and blacker.

Lisa shifted closer to him. Her hand found his, squeezing all the blood from his palm.

"No wonder they hadn't bothered tracking us," she whispered, breathless with fear. "Why hunt through this storm, when all they have to do is turn those damn lights back on and irradiate us? We can't hide from that."

Painter realized she was right. Maddened, they would be without defenses. In such a senseless state, the treacherous landscape and frigid cold would kill them as surely as any sniper's bullet.

But he refused to give up hope.

The madness took hours to take hold. He would not waste those hours. If they could reach help in time, perhaps there was a way to reverse the effect.

"We'll get through this," he said lamely.

This only irritated her.

"How?"

She turned to him as the lights flared again, sparkling the cavern with a diamondlike sheen. Lisa's eyes shone with less terror than he had imagined. She was fearful—and rightfully so—but there remained a hard glint, also diamondlike.

"Don't talk down to me," Lisa said, slipping her hand from his. "That's all I ask."

Painter nodded. "If they're trusting the radiation or whatever to kill us, they may not be watching the mountains that well. With the storm over, we can—"

A spatter of gunfire erupted, splintering the winter's quiet.

Painter met Lisa's gaze.

It sounded close.

Proving that, a spate of bullets cracked into the wall of ice. Painter and Lisa scrambled back, shedding their space blanket. They retreated to the rear of the small cave. There was no escape.

By now, Painter noted something else.

The ghost light had not faded as it had before. The frozen waterfall remained aglow with its deadly brilliance. The light held steady, pinning them down.

A bullhorn boomed. "Painter Crowe! We know you and the woman are hiding there!"

The commanding voice had a feminine lilt. Also accented.

"Come out! Hands high!"

Painter gripped Lisa's shoulder, squeezing as much reassurance into her as he could. "Stay here."

He pointed to their discarded outerwear, motioning Lisa to suit up. He shoved into his own boots, then edged to the break in the ice. He poked his head out.

As was common in the highlands, the storm had broken apart as quickly as it had struck. Stars shone across the black sky. The Milky Way arched over the wintry valley, etched in snow and ice, patched with mists of ice fog.

Closer at hand, a spotlight pierced the night, its beam centered on the frozen waterfall. Fifty yards away on a lower cliff, a shadowy figure straddled a snowmobile, operating the searchlight. It was only an ordinary lamp, possibly xenon from its intensity and bluish tint.

It was no mysterious ghost light.

Painter felt a surge of relief. Had that been the light all the time, marking the approach of the vehicles? Painter counted five of them. He also counted the score of figures in white parkas, spread across the lower tier and to either side. They all bore rifles.

With no other choice—and damn curious to boot—Painter held up his arms and stepped free of the cave. The nearest gunman, a hulk of a man, sidled closer, rifle leveled. A tiny beam of light traced Painter's chest. A laser sight.

Weaponless, Painter could only stand his ground. He weighed the odds of manhandling the rifle from the gunman.

Not good.

Painter met the eyes of the gunman.

One an icy blue, the other a frosted white.

The assassin from the monastery.

He remembered the man's ungodly strength. No, the odds were not good. And besides, with the number of men here, what would he do if he succeeded?

From behind the man's shoulder, a figure stepped into view. A woman. Perhaps the same who had used the bullhorn a moment ago. She reached and used a single finger to push the assassin's rifle down. Painter doubted any man would have the strength to do that.

As she stepped forward, Painter studied her in the spotlight's glare. She had to be in her late thirties. Bobbed black hair, green eyes. She wore a heavy white parka with a fur-lined hood. Her form was shapeless beneath her outerwear, but she appeared svelte and moved with a toned grace.

"Dr. Anna Sporrenberg," she said and held out a hand.

Painter stared at her glove. If he pulled her to him, got an arm around her throat, tried to use her as a hostage . . .

Meeting the assassin's eyes over her shoulder, Painter thought better. He reached out and shook the woman's hand. Since they hadn't shot him yet, he could at least be polite. He would play this game as long as it kept him alive. He had Lisa to consider, too.

"Director Crowe," she said. "It seems there has been much chatter over the past few hours across the international intelligence channels regarding your whereabouts."

Painter kept his face fixed. He saw no reason to deny his identity. Perhaps he could even use it to his advantage. "Then you know the extent to which those same resources will go to find me."

"Natürlich," she nodded, slipping into German. "But I would not count on their success. In the meantime, I must ask you and the young woman to accompany me."

Painter took a warding step back. "Dr. Cummings has nothing to do with any of this. She was only a health care worker coming to the aid of the sick. She knows nothing."

"We'll know the truth of that soon enough."

So there it was, plainly stated. They were alive for the moment only because of their suspected knowledge. And that knowledge would be extracted through blood and pain. Painter considered making a move now. Getting it over with. A fast death over a slow agonizing one. He had too much sensitive intel in his head to risk torture.

But he was not alone out here. He pictured Lisa, warming her hands with his. As long as they lived, there was hope.

Other guards joined them. Lisa was forced out of the cave at gunpoint. They were led to the snowmobiles.

Lisa met his eyes, fear shining bright.

He was determined to protect her to the best of his ability.

Anna Sporrenberg joined them as they were being bound. "Before we head out, let me speak plainly. We can't let you go. I think you understand that. I won't give you that false hope. But I can promise you a painless and peaceful end."

"Like with the monks," Lisa said harshly. "We witnessed your mercy there."

Painter tried to catch Lisa's eye. Now was not the time to antagonize their captors. The bastards obviously had no compunction against killing out of hand. They both needed to play the cooperative prisoner.

Too late.

Anna seemed to truly see Lisa for the first time, turning to her. A bit of heat entered the woman's voice. "It *was* mercy, Dr. Cummings." Her eyes flicked to the assassin who still kept guard. "You know nothing of the illness that struck the monastery. Of what horrors awaited the monks. We do. Their deaths were not murder, but *euthanasia*."

"And who gave you that right?" Lisa asked.

Painter shifted closer. "Lisa, maybe—"

"No, Mr. Crowe." Anna stepped closer to Lisa. "What right, you ask? Experience, Dr. Cummings. Experience. Trust me when I tell you . . . the deaths up there were a kindness, not a cruelty."

"And what about the men I came up here with in the helicopter? Was that a kindness, too?"

Anna sighed, tiring of their words. "Hard choices had to be made. Our work here is too important."

"And what about us?" Lisa called as the woman turned away. "It's a painless needle if we cooperate. But what if we don't feel like cooperating?"

Anna headed toward the lead snowmobile. "There will be no thumbscrews, if that's what you mean. Drugs only. We are not barbarians, Dr. Cummings."

"No, you're only Nazis!" Lisa spat at her. "We saw the swastika!"

"Don't be foolish. We're not Nazis." Anna glanced calmly back to them as she hiked her leg over the seat to the snow-mobile. "Not anymore."

6:38 P.M.
COPENHAGEN, DENMARK

Gray hurried across the street toward the auction house.

What was Fiona thinking, barging in here after what happened?

Concern for her safety weighed heavily. But Gray also had to admit that her intrusion offered him the excuse he needed. To attend the auction in person. Whoever had fire-bombed the shop, murdered Grette Neal, and tried to kill him . . . their trail led here.

Gray reached the sidewalk and slowed. The slanting rays of the setting sun turned the door to the auction house into a silvery mirror. He checked his clothes, having dressed in a frenzy of fine tailoring. The suit, a navy Armani pinstripe, fit well, but the starched white shirt was tight at the collar. He straightened the pale yellow tie.

Not exactly inconspicuous. But he had to play the role of the buyer for an affluent American financier.

He pushed through the door to the auction house. The lobby was pure Scandinavian design, meaning a total lack thereof: bleached wood, glass partitions, and little else. The only furniture was a bony sculptural chair positioned next to a side table the size of a postage stamp. It held up a single potted orchid. Its reedlike stem supported an anemic brown and pink blossom.

The doorman tapped his cigarette into the plant's pot and stepped toward Gray with a sour expression.

Gray reached to a pocket and pulled out his invitation. It had required wiring a quarter-million-dollar deposit into the house's fund, a guarantee that the buyer had the wherewithal to attend such an exclusive event.

The doorman checked his invitation, nodded, and strode over to a velvet rope that closed off a wide set of stairs that led to the lower level. He unhitched the rope and waved Gray through.

At the bottom of the stairs, a set of swinging doors opened into the main bidding floor. A pair of guards flanked the entrance. One held a metal-detecting wand. Gray allowed himself to be searched, arms out. He noted the video cameras posted to either side of the threshold. Security was snug. Once he was cleared, the other guard buzzed a button and pulled open the door.

The murmur of voices flowed out to him. He recognized Italian, Dutch, French, Arabic, and English. It seemed all the world had shown up for the auction.

Gray entered. A few glances were made in his direction, but most attention remained focused on the glass cases that lined the walls. Employees of the auction house, dressed in identical black attire, stood behind the counter, like at a jewelry store. They wore white gloves and helped patrons view the objects up for bid.

A string quartet played softly in one corner. A few servers circulated, offering tall glasses of champagne to the guests.

Gray checked in at a neighboring desk and was given a numbered paddle. He moved farther inside. A handful of patrons had already taken their seats. Gray spotted the pair of latecomers who had held up the auction, the pale young man and woman, the silent-movie stars. They sat in the front row. A paddle rested on the woman's lap. The man leaned over and whispered in his partner's ear. It was a strangely intimate gesture, perhaps enhanced by the woman's arched neck, long and lithe, tilted as if awaiting a kiss.

Her eyes flicked to Gray as he moved down the center aisle. Her gaze flowed over him and away.

No recognition.

Gray continued his own search, reaching the front of the room with its raised stage and podium. He turned in a slow circle. He saw no outward threat to his presence.

He also saw no sign of Fiona.

Where was she?

He edged to one of the glass cases and wandered down the far side. His ears were half tuned to the conversations around him. He walked past an attendant lifting and gently resting a bulky leather-bound book atop the display case for a portly gentleman. The interested party leaned close, a pair of spectacles resting at the tip of his nose.

Gray noted the particular book.

A treatise on butterflies with hand-drawn plates, circa 1884.

He continued down the aisle. Once near the door again, he found himself confronted by the dowdy woman he had filmed earlier. She was holding out a small white envelope. Gray accepted it, even before he wondered what it could be. The woman seemed disinterested in anything further and wandered away.

Gray smelled a hint of perfume on the envelope.

Strange.

He used a thumbnail to break the seal and pulled out a folded piece of stationery, expensive from its watermark. A short note was neatly written.

EVEN THE GUILD KNOWS BETTER THAN TO STRAY
TOO NEAR THIS FLAME. WATCH YOUR BACK.
KISSES.

The note was unsigned. But at the bottom, inked in crimson, was the symbol of a small curled dragon. Gray's other hand wandered to his neck, where a matching dragon hung in silver, a gift from a competitor.

Seichan.

She was an operative for the Guild, a shady cartel of terrorist cells that had crossed paths with Sigma Force in the past. Gray felt the hairs on his neck stand on end. He turned and searched the room. The dowdy woman who had handed him the note had vanished.

He glanced again at the note.

A warning.

Better late than never . . .

But at least the Guild was taking a pass here. That is, if Seichan could be believed . . .

Actually Gray was willing to take her at her word.

Honor among thieves and all that.

A commotion drew his attention toward the rear of the room.

A tall gentleman swept onto the bidding floor through a back door. Resplendent in a tuxedo, he was the esteemed Mr. Ergenschein himself, acting as auctioneer. He palmed his oiled black hair into place—clearly a dye job. Across his cadaverous features, a smile was fixed on his face, as if pasted from a book.

The reason for his clear discomfort followed behind. Or rather was being led by a guard who had a hand clamped on her upper arm.

Fiona.

Her face was flushed. Her lips set in a line of dread, bled of color.

Furious.

Gray headed toward them.

Ergenschein strode off to the side. He carried an object wrapped in a soft unbleached chamois. He stepped over to the main display case near the front. It had been empty before. One of the staff unlocked the cabinet. Ergenschein gently unwrapped the object and settled it into the case.

Noting Gray's approach, the auctioneer brushed his hands together and stepped over to meet him, allowing his palms to come to rest as if in prayer. Behind him, the cabinet was locked by an attendant.

Gray noted the addition to the case.

The Darwin Bible.

Fiona's eyes widened when she spotted Gray.

He ignored her and confronted Ergenschein. "Is there a problem here?"

"Of course not, sir. The young lady's being escorted out. She has no invitation to this auction."

Gray took out his own card. "I believe I'm allowed a guest in attendance." He held out his other hand for Fiona. "I'm glad to see she's already here. I was held up on a conference call with my buyer. I approached the young Ms. Neal earlier today to inquire about a private sale. One item in particular."

Gray nodded to the Darwin Bible.

Ergenschein's entire body sighed with feigned sadness. "A tragedy. About the fire. But I'm afraid that Grette Neal signed her lot to the auction house. Without a countermand from her estate's barrister, I'm afraid the lot must be put up for auction. That is the law."

Fiona tugged on the guard's arm, murder in her eyes.

Ergenschein seemed oblivious of her. "I'm afraid you'll have to bid yourself, sir. My apologies, but my hands are tied."

"Then in that case, you certainly wouldn't mind that Ms. Neal remains at my side. To aid me if I wish to inspect the lot?"

"As you wish." Ergenschein's smile wore into a brief frown. He made a vague dismissive wave to the guard. "But she must stay with you at all times. And as your guest, she is your responsibility."

Fiona was released. As Gray led her toward the back, he noted the guard flanked them along the edge of the room. It seemed they had gained their own personal bodyguard.

Gray herded Fiona into the last row. A chime sounded, announcing that the auction would commence in another minute. Seats began to fill, mostly near the front. Gray and Fiona had the back row to themselves.

"What are you doing here?" he whispered.

"Getting back my Bible," she said with thick disdain. "Or at least *trying* to."

She slumped back in her seat, arms crossed over her leather purse.

Off to the front, Ergenschein took the podium and made some formal introductions. The proceedings would be in English. It was the most common language among the auction's international clientele. Ergenschein elaborated on the rules of bidding, the house's premium and fees, even proper etiquette. The most important rule was that you were only allowed to bid up to ten times the amount placed and secured on deposit.

Gray ignored most of it, continuing with Fiona, earning a few disgruntled glances from those in the row ahead.

"You came back for the Bible? Why?"

The girl only tightened her arms.

"Fiona . . ."

She turned to him, hard and angry. "Because it was Mutti's!" Tears glistened. "They killed her over it. I won't let them have it."

"Who?"

She waved an arm. "Whoever sodding murdered her. I'm going to get it and burn it."

Gray sighed and leaned back. Fiona wanted whatever revenge she could get. She wanted to hurt them. Gray didn't blame her . . . but her reckless actions were only likely to get her killed, too.

"The Bible's ours. I should be able to take it back." Her voice cracked. She shook her head and swiped at her nose.

Gray put an arm around her.

She winced but didn't pull away.

In front, the auction began. Paddles rose and fell. Items came and went. The best would be held until last. Gray noted who bought what. He especially noted who were the final bidders for the items logged into his notebook, the three items of special interest: Mendel's genetics papers, Planck's physics, and de Vries's diary on mutations.

They all went to the pair of silent-movie stars.

Their identities remained unknown. Gray heard whispers among his fellow participants. No one knew who they were. Only their ever-rising paddle number.

Number 002.

Gray leaned to Fiona. "Do you recognize those buyers? Have you ever seen them before in your shop?"

Fiona straightened in her seat, stared for a full minute, then slunk down. "No."

"How about anyone else?"

She shrugged.

"Fiona, are you sure?"

"Yes," she snapped. "I'm bloody goddamn sure!"

This earned more exasperated glances in their direction.

At last the auction wound down to the final item. The Darwin Bible was unlocked from its case and carried like a religious relic to an easel that stood under a special halogen spot. It was an unimpressive tome: flaking black leather, tattered and stained, not even any lettering. It could be any old journal.

Fiona sat straighter. Plainly this was what had kept her in her seat this entire time. She grabbed Gray's wrist. "Are you really going to bid on it?" she asked, hope dawning in her bright eyes.

Gray frowned at her—then realized it wasn't a half-bad idea. If the others were willing to kill over it, maybe some clue to the entire house of cards could be discerned from it. Besides, he was aching to get a peek at it. And Sigma Force had poured 250,000 euros into the account here at the auction house. That meant he could bid up to 2.5 million. That was twice the maximum estimate for the Bible. If he won, he'd be able to inspect his purchase.

Still, he remembered Logan Gregory's admonishment. He had already disobeyed orders to follow Fiona here. He dared not involve himself even more intimately.

He felt Fiona's eyes on him.

If he started bidding, it would put their lives in danger, painting a bull's-eye on both of them. And what if he lost the bid? The risk would be for nothing. Hadn't he been foolhardy enough today?

"Ladies and gentlemen, how much to start the bidding on today's last lot?" Ergenschein said grandly. "Shall we open with one hundred thousand? Ah, yes, we have one hundred thousand . . . and from a *new* bidder. How wonderful. Number 144."

Gray lowered his paddle, all eyes on him, committed now.

Beside him, Fiona smiled widely.

"And we double the bid," Ergenschein said. "Two hundred thousand from number 002!"

The silent-movie stars.

Gray felt the room's focus shift back to him, including the pair in front. Too late to back down. He raised his paddle again.

The bidding continued for another ten tense minutes. The auction room remained full. Everyone was staying behind to see what the Darwin Bible would fetch. There was an undercurrent of support for Gray. Too many others had been outpaddled by number 002. And as the figure crossed the two million mark, well above the maximum estimate, murmurs of hushed excitement burbled around the room.

There was another flash of excitement when a phone bidder jumped into the fray, but number 002 outbid him, and he didn't counter.

Gray did. *Two mill three*. Gray's palms began to sweat.

"Two million four from number 002! Gentlemen and ladies, please keep your seats."

Gray raised his paddle one more time.

"Two million five."

Gray knew he was sunk. He could do nothing but watch as 002 rose again, unstoppable, relentless, merciless.

"Three million," the pale young gentleman said, tiring of the game. He stood and glanced back at Gray, as if daring him to challenge that.

Gray had reached his limit. Even if he wanted, he couldn't bet more. His hand ground on his paddle. Gray shook his head, admitting defeat.

The other bowed toward him, one adversary to another. The man tipped an imaginary hat. Gray noted a blue blemish on the fellow's right hand, at the webbing between thumb and forefinger. A tattoo. His companion, who by now Gray realized must be the young man's sister, perhaps even twin, bore the same mark on her left.

Gray fixed the tattoo in his mind's eye, perhaps a clue to their identity.

His attention was interrupted by the auctioneer.

"And it appears number 144 is finished!" Ergenschein said. "Any more bids. Once, twice, thrice." He raised the gavel, held it for a breathless moment, then tapped it on the edge of the podium. "Done!"

Polite applause met the concluding bid.

Gray knew it would have been more boisterous if he had won. Still, he was surprised to see who was clapping beside him.

Fiona.

She grinned at him. "Let's get out of here."

They joined the flow of people filing out the door. Gray was offered sympathy and condolences from a few of the other participants as he departed. Soon they reached the streets. They all went their separate ways.

Fiona tugged him a few shops down and directed him into a nearby patisserie, a French affair of chintz drapery and wrought-iron café tables. The girl picked a spot near a display filled with cream puffs, petits fours, chocolate éclairs, and *smørrebrød,* the ubiquitous Danish open-face sandwich.

She ignored the treats, beaming with a strange glee.

"Why are you so happy?" Gray finally asked. "We lost the bid."

Gray sat facing the window. They would have to watch their backs. Still, he hoped now, with the Bible sold, that perhaps the danger would subside.

"We stuck it to them!" Fiona said. "Drove it to three mill. Brilliant!"

"I don't think money means that much to them."

Fiona pulled the pin on her bun and shook her hair loose. She lost a decade of age in appearance. Amusement continued to shine in her eyes, with an edge of malicious delight.

Gray suddenly felt a sick twist of his stomach.

"Fiona, what have you done?"

She lifted her purse to the table, tilted it toward Gray, and held it open. He leaned forward.

"Oh, God . . . Fiona . . ."

A battered leather-bound tome rested in her purse.

A match to the Darwin Bible that had just been sold.

"Is that the *real* one?" he asked.

"I nicked it right from under that blind wanker in the back room."

"How—?"

"A bit of the old bait and switch. Took me all day to find a Bible the right size and shape. Course I had to tinker with it a bit afterward. But then all it took was lots of tears and shouting, a bit of fumbling . . ." She shrugged. "And Bob's your uncle, it was done."

"If you already had the Bible, why did you have me bid—?" Realization struck Gray. "You played me."

"To make those bastards shell out three mill for a two-pence fake!"

"They'll discover soon enough that it's not the real book," Gray said, horror rising.

"Yeah, but I plan to be long gone by then."

"Where?"

"Going with you." Fiona snapped the bag closed.

"I don't think so."

"You remember when Mutti told you about the disbanded library? Where the Darwin Bible came from?"

Gray knew what she was talking about. Grette Neal had hinted that someone was reconstructing some old scientist's library. She had been going to let him copy the original bill of sale, but then they'd been attacked, and it was lost to the flames.

Fiona tapped her forehead. "I have the address stored right here." She then held out a hand. "So?"

Frowning, he went to shake it.

She pulled her hand back in distaste. "As if." Extending her arm again, she turned her palm up. "I want to see your real passport, you wanker. You think I can't scope out a fake one when I see it."

He met her gaze. She had stolen his passport earlier. Her look now was uncompromising. Frowning, he finally reached to a concealed pocket of his suit and took out his real passport.

Fiona read it. "Grayson Pierce." She tossed it back on the table. "Nice to meet you . . . *finally*."

He retrieved his passport. "So the Bible. Where did it come from?"

"I'll only tell if you take me with you."

"Don't be ridiculous. You can't come with me. You're only a child."

"A child with the Darwin Bible."

Gray tired of her blackmail. He could snatch the Bible whenever he wanted to, but the same couldn't be said for her information. "Fiona, this isn't some goddamn game."

Her eyes hardened on him, aging before him. "And you don't think I know that." Her words were deadly cold. "Where were you when they took my Mutti out in bags? Bloody goddamn *bags*!"

Gray closed his eyes. She had struck a nerve, but he refused to relent. "Fiona, I'm sorry," he said with a strained voice. "But what you're asking is impossible. I can't take—"

The explosion shook the patisserie like an earthquake. The front glass rattled, dishes crashed. Fiona and Gray stood and went to the window. Smoke billowed across the street, fuming and roiling into the dusky sky. Flames danced and licked upward from the shattered side of a building across the street.

Fiona glanced to Gray. "Let me guess," she said.

"My hotel room," he admitted.

"So much for the head start."

11:47 P.M.
HIMALAYAS

Captured by the Germans, Painter rode behind Lisa on a sled pulled by one of the snowmobiles. They had been traveling for almost an hour, cinched in place with plastic straps and bound together. At least their sled was heated.

Still he kept hunched over Lisa, sheltering her as best he could with his body. She leaned back into him. It was all they could manage. Their wrists were bound to stanchions on either side.

Ahead, the assassin rode on the backseat of the towing snowmobile. He faced to the rear, rifle pointing at them, mismatched eyes never wavering. Anna Sporrenberg piloted the vehicle, the leader of this group.

A group of former Nazis.

Or *reformed* Nazis.

Or whoever the hell they were.

Painter shoved the question aside. He had a more important puzzle to solve at the moment.

Staying alive.

En route, Painter had learned how easily he and Lisa had been discovered hiding in their cave. Through infrared. Against the frigid landscape, their heat signature had been easy to pick up, revealing their hiding place.

The same would make flight across this terrain almost impossible.

He continued his deliberation, mind focused on one goal.

Escape.

For the past hour, the caravan of snowmobiles had trundled through the wintry night. The vehicles were equipped with electric motors, gliding with almost no noise. In silence, the five snowmobiles traversed the maze with practiced ease, gliding along cliff edges, diving down steep valleys, sweeping over bridges of ice.

He did his best to memorize their route. But exhaustion and the complexity of their path confounded him. It didn't help that his skull had begun to pound again. The headaches had returned—as had the disorientation and vertigo. He had to admit that his symptoms were *not* subsiding. He also had to admit that he was thoroughly lost.

Craning, he stared at the night sky.

Overhead, stars shone coldly.

Perhaps he could fix his position.

As he stared, the pinpoints of light spun in the sky. He tore his gaze away, a stabbing ache behind his eyes.

"Are you all right?" Lisa whispered back at him.

Painter grumbled under his breath, too nauseated to trust speaking.

"The nystagmus again?" she surmised on her own.

A harsh grunt from the assassin silenced any further communication. Painter was grateful. He closed his eyes and took deep breaths, waiting for the moment to pass.

Eventually it did.

He opened his eyes as the caravan edged up to a crest of rock and slowed to a stop. Painter searched around. Nothing was here. An icy cliff cracked the crest on the right. Snow began to fall again.

Why had they stopped?

Ahead, the assassin climbed from his seat.

Anna joined him. Turning a shoulder, the hulking man spoke to the woman in German.

Painter strained to hear and caught the assassin's last words.

"—should just kill them."

It was not said with any vehemence, only dread practicality.

Anna frowned. "We need to find out more, Gunther." The woman glanced in Painter's direction. "You know the problems we've been having lately. If he was sent here . . . if he knows something that can stop it."

Painter was clueless as to what they were talking about, but he allowed them this misconception. Especially if it kept him alive.

The assassin just shook his head. "He's trouble. I can smell it on him." He began to turn away, dismissive, done with the matter.

Anna stopped him with a touch to the man's cheek, tender, grateful . . . and maybe something more. "*Danke*, Gunther."

He turned away, but not before Painter noted the flash of pain in the man's eyes. The assassin trudged to the broken cliff face and disappeared through a crack in the wall. A moment later, a cloud of steam puffed out along with a bit of fiery light—then cut off.

A door opening and closing.

Behind him, one of the guards made a derisive noise, grumbling one word under his breath, an insult, heard by only those closest to him.

Leprakönig.

Leper King.

Painter noted the guard had waited until the hulking man named Gunther was out of earshot. He had not dared say it to the man's face. But from the hunch of the assassin's shoulders and gruff manner, Painter suspected he'd heard it before.

Anna mounted the snowmobile. A new armed guard took the assassin's seat, weapon pointing. They headed out again.

The path switchbacked around a spur of rock and down into an even steeper notch in the mountain. The way ahead was a sea of ice fog, obscuring what lay below. A heavy crest of the mountain overhung the misty sea, cupped low like a pair of warming hands.

They descended into the vast fog bank, lights spearing ahead.

In moments, visibility lowered to feet. Stars vanished.

Then suddenly the darkness deepened as they trundled under the shadow of the overhang. But rather than growing colder, the air grew notably warmer. As they descended farther, rocky outcroppings appeared out of the snow. Meltwater trickled around the boulders.

Painter realized there must be a localized pocket of geothermal activity here. Hot springs, while rare and known mostly to the indigenous people, dotted the Himalayas. Created by the intense pressures of the Indian continental plate grinding into Asia, such geothermal hot spots were believed to be the source of the Shangri-La mythology.

As the snow thinned, the caravan was forced to abandon the snowmobiles. Once parked, Painter and Lisa were cut free from their sled, hauled to their feet, and bound at the wrists. He kept close to Lisa. She met his eyes, mirroring his worry.

Where the hell were they?

Encircled by white parkas and rifles, they were led down the rest of the way. Snow turned to wet rock under their boots. Stairs appeared underfoot, cut into the rock, trickling with snowmelt. Ahead, the perpetual fog thinned and shredded.

Within a few steps, a cliff face appeared out of the gloom, sheltered by the shoulder of the mountain. A natural deep grotto. But it was no paradise—only craggy black granite, dripping and sweating.

More hell than Shangri-La.

Lisa stumbled beside him. Painter caught her as best he could with his wrists bound. But he understood her faltering step.

Ahead, out of the mists, appeared a castle.

Or rather *half* a castle.

As they neared, Painter recognized the shape as a façade, cut crudely into the back of the grotto. Two giant crenellated towers flanked a massive central keep. Lights burned behind thick, glazed windows.

"Granitschloß," Anna announced and led them toward an arched entrance, twice his height, flanked by giant granite knights.

A heavy oak door, studded and strapped in black iron, sealed the entryway. But as the group approached, the door winched up, rising like a portcullis.

Anna strode forward. "Come. It has been a long night, *ja*?"

Painter and Lisa were led at gunpoint toward the entrance. He studied the façade of battlements, parapets, and arched windows. Across the entire surface, the black granite sweated and trickled, wept and dripped. The water appeared like a run of black oil, as if the castle were dissolving before their eyes, melting back into the rock face.

The fiery illumination from a few of the windows made the castle's surface shine with a hellish glow, reminding him of a Hieronymus Bosch painting. The fifteenth-century artist had specialized in twisted depictions of hell. If ever Bosch had sculpted the gates to the Underworld, this castle would be it.

With no choice, Painter followed Anna and passed under the arched entrance of the castle. He looked up, searching for the words Dante had said were supposedly carved upon the gates to the Underworld.

All hope abandon, ye who enter here.

The words weren't here—but they might as well have been.

All hope abandon . . .

That about summed it up.

8:15 P.M.
COPENHAGEN, DENMARK

As the hotel explosion echoed away, Gray grabbed Fiona by the arm and rushed her out a side door of the French bakery. He aimed for a neighboring alley, pushing through the patrons gathered on the sidewalk patio.

Sirens erupted in the distance.

It seemed Copenhagen's firefighters were putting in a long day today.

Gray reached the corner of the alley, away from the smoke and chaos, Fiona in tow. A brick cracked near his ear, followed by a ricocheted *ping*. A gunshot. Spinning, he whipped Fiona into the alleyway and ducked low. He searched the street for the shooter.

And found her.

Close.

A half block back, across the street.

It was the white-blond woman from the auction. Only now she wore a black, tight-fitting running suit. She had also gained a new fashion accessory. A pistol with a silencer. She held it low by her knee, striding quickly toward his location. She touched her ear, lips moving.

Radio.

As the woman stepped under a streetlamp, Gray realized his mistake. It wasn't the same woman from the auction. Her hair was longer. Her face more gaunt.

An older sibling to the pair.

Gray swung away.

He expected Fiona to be halfway down the alley. She was only five yards back, straddling a rust-scarred lime green Vespa scooter.

"What are you—?"

"Getting us a ride." She had her purse open and dropped a screwdriver back into it.

Gray hurried to her side. "There's no time to hot-wire it."

Fiona glanced over a shoulder at him, while her fingers blindly fiddled with a nest of ignition wires. She twisted two, and the engine coughed, whined, and caught.

Damn . . .

She was good—but there were limits to trust.

Gray waved her back. "I'll drive."

Fiona shrugged and slid onto the backseat. Gray mounted

the bike, rolled it off its kickstand, and gunned the engine. Keeping the headlamp off, he took off down the dark alley. Or rather puttered.

"C'mon," he urged.

"Pop it into second," Fiona said. "Skip past third. You have to goose the crap out of these old ones."

"I don't need a backseat driver."

Still, Gray obeyed, popping the clutch and shifting. The scooter jumped like a startled filly. They sped faster down the alley, zigzagging around stacks of trashcans.

Sirens screamed behind them. Gray glanced back. A fire engine roared past the entrance to the alley, lights blazing, responding to the explosion. Before Gray turned back around, a dark figure strode into view, limned against the brighter streetlights.

The shooter.

He eked out a bit more power, swerving around a tall construction bin, putting it between him and the woman. If he stuck to the wall, he had a straight shot out of the alley from here.

At the other end, the far street glowed like a beacon.

It was their only chance.

Focused forward, he watched a second dark figure step into view and stop. A passing car's headlights turned his blond hair silver. Yet another sibling. The man wore a long black duster. He parted the trench coat and raised a shotgun.

The woman must have radioed him, setting up this ambush.

"Hold tight!" Gray called.

As the man lifted the gun one-armed, Gray noted the sling around his other arm, bandaged from wrist to elbow. Though his face was in shadows, Gray knew who blocked their escape.

It was the man who had murdered Grette Neal.

He still bore Bertal's bite wounds, bandaged now.

The shotgun pointed at Gray.

No time.

Gray twisted the scooter's handles and sent the bike into a smoking skid, tilted sideways, aiming for the man.

The shotgun exploded with a muffled blast, accompanied by a splintering crash as a fist of pellets struck a neighboring doorway.

Fiona yelped in fright.

But that was the man's only shot. He dove out of the way of the sliding bike. Once clear of the dark alley, Gray swung the bike out of its skid with a kick of the throttle and a scream of rubber on cement. He manhandled the scooter up and into traffic, earning a savage blast of a horn from a disgruntled Audi driver.

Gray headed away.

Fiona loosened her grip.

Gray maneuvered around the slower cars, gaining speed as the road sloped steeply downward. At the bottom, the avenue dead-ended into a tree-lined cross street. Gray braked for the sharp turn. The bike refused to obey. He glanced down. A cable bounced alongside the scooter's back tire.

The brake cable.

His skid-out must have dislodged it.

"Slow down!" Fiona yelled in his ear.

"Brake's out!" he called back. "Hang on!"

Gray choked out the engine, then fought to lose the bike's momentum by swerving and skidding, like a downhill skier. He dragged the rear tire alongside one curb, rubber smoking.

They reached the corner, going too fast.

Gray slewed the scooter on its side, metal scraping up fiery sparks. The bike slid across the intersection, passing in front of a flat-paneled truck. Horns blared. Brakes squealed.

Then they hit the far curb.

The bike flipped. Gray and Fiona flew.

A hedgerow broke the worst of their collision, but they still ended up rolling across the sidewalk and landing at the foot of a brick wall. Gaining his feet, Gray moved to Fiona's side.

"Are you all right?"

She stood up, more angry than hurt. "I paid two hundred kroner for this skirt." Her dress had a long rip up one side. She clutched it closed with one hand and bent down to retrieve her purse.

Gray's Armani suit fared even worse. One knee was ripped out, and the right side of his jacket looked like it had been scoured with a wire brush. But besides a few scrapes and abrasions, they were unharmed.

Traffic flowed past the site of their accident.

Fiona headed away. "Vespas crash around here all the time. And they're stolen just as often. Ownership of a scooter in Copenhagen is a general term. Need one? Grab one. Leave it behind for the next guy. No one really cares."

But somebody did.

A fresh squeal of tires drew their attention. A black sedan swung into the street two blocks back. It sped in their direction. It was too dark to identify the driver or passengers. Headlights speared toward them.

Gray hurried Fiona along the tree-lined sidewalk, seeking the deeper shadows. A tall brick wall framed this side of the street. No buildings, no alleys. Just a stretch of high wall. From beyond rose a merry twinkle of flutes and strings.

Behind them, the sedan slowed beside the crashed Vespa, searching.

No question their escape by scooter had been reported.

"Over here," Fiona said.

Hooking her purse over a shoulder, she led him to a

shadowy park bench and climbed on it—then using the seat back as a boost, she leaped up and grabbed one of the tree limbs overhead. She kicked up, hooking her legs over the branch.

"What are you doing?"

"Street kids do this all the time. Free admission."

"What?"

"C'mon."

Hand over hand, she followed the thick branch as it angled over the brick wall. She dropped on the far side and vanished.

Damn it.

The sedan began to drift up the street again.

With no choice, Gray followed Fiona's example. He mounted the bench and jumped up. Music wafted over the wall, scintillating and magical in the dark night. Once hanging upside down, he craned over the wall.

Beyond lay a wonderland of glowing lanterns, miniature palaces, and twirling amusements.

Tivoli Gardens.

The turn-of-the-century amusement park lay nestled in the heart of Copenhagen. From this height, Gray spotted the park's central lake. Its mirrored surface reflected thousands of lanterns and lights. Spreading outward, flower-lined paths led to lamplit pavilions, wooden roller coasters, carousels, and Ferris wheels. The old park was less a technocratic Disney and more an intimate neighborhood park.

Gray scuttled along the limb toward the park, passing over the wall.

On the far side, Fiona waited below and waved to him. She stood at the back of a utility or gardening shed.

Gray dropped his legs and dangled by his arms.

A chunk of bark exploded by his right hand. Shocked, he let go and fell, his arms cartwheeling for balance. He landed hard in a flower bed, jamming a knee, but the soft loam cushioned his fall. Beyond the wall, an engine growled, and a door slammed.

They'd been spotted.

Grimacing, Gray joined Fiona. Her eyes were wide. She had heard the shot. Without a word, they fled together toward the heart of Tivoli Gardens.

6

UGLY DUCKLING

1:22 A.M.
HIMALAYAS

Well past midnight, Lisa soaked in a steaming bath of naturally heated mineral waters. She could close her eyes and imagine herself in some expensive European spa. The room's accoutrements were certainly plush enough: thick Egyptian cotton towels and robes, a massive four-poster bed piled high with a nest of blankets on a foot-thick goose-down featherbed. Medieval tapestries hung on the walls, and underfoot, Turkish rugs covered the stone floors.

Painter was in the outer room, stoking their tiny fireplace.

They shared this pleasant little prison cell.

Painter had told Anna Sporrenberg that they were companions back in the States. A ruse intended to keep them from being separated.

Lisa hadn't argued against it.

She had not wanted to be alone here.

Though the water's temperature was only a few degrees lower than parboil, Lisa shivered. As a doctor, she recognized her own signs of shock as the adrenaline that had been sustaining her up to this point wore off. She remembered how earlier she had lashed out against the German woman, almost attacked her. What had she been thinking? She could've gotten them both shot.

And all that time, Painter had been so calm. Even now, she drew strength hearing Painter roll another log onto the fire, simple bits of caretaking and comfort. He must be exhausted. The man had already soaked in the massive tub, not so much for hygiene as a prescription against frostbite. Lisa had noted the white patches on the tips of his ears and insisted he go first.

More warmly dressed, she had fared better.

Still, she immersed herself fully into the tub, dunking her head under, her hair willowing out. The heat suffused through her, warming all her tissues. Her senses stretched. All she had to do was inhale, allow herself to drown. A moment of panic, and it would be over. All the fear, all the tension. She would be in control of her own fate—taking back what her captors held hostage.

Just a breath . . .

"Are you almost finished with your bath?" The muffled words reached her through the water, sounding far away. "They've brought us a late-night snack."

Lisa shifted, surfacing out of the steam, water sluicing from her hair and face. "I . . . I'll be out in another minute."

"Take your time," Painter called from the main room.

She heard him roll another log onto the fire.

How could he still be moving? Bedridden for three days, the fight in the root cellar, the frozen trek here . . . yet he still kept forging on. It gave her hope. Maybe it was just desperation, but she sensed a well of strength in him that went beyond the physical.

As she thought about him, her trembling finally slowed.

She climbed out of the bath, skin steaming, and toweled off. A thick robe hung from a hook. She left it hanging for a moment more. A floor-length mirror stood beside an antique washbasin. Its surface was misty, but her naked form was visible. She turned her leg, not in some narcissistic admiration, but to study the map of bruises down her limb. The deep ache in her calves reminded her of something essential.

She was still alive.

She glanced to the tub.

She would not give them the satisfaction. She would see it through.

She climbed into her robe. After snugging it tight around her waist, she lifted the heavy iron latch to the bathroom and opened the door. It was warmer in the next room. A steam register had kept the chamber livable, but the new fire in the hearth had stoked the room to a welcoming warmth. The tiny blaze snapped and crackled merrily, casting the room in a rich, flickering glow. A grouping of candles beside the bed added to the homey ambience, the only other illumination.

There was no electricity in the room.

While imprisoning them here, Anna Sporrenberg had explained proudly how most of their power was geothermally generated, based on a hundred-year-old design of Rudolf Diesel, the French-born German engineer who would go on to invent the diesel engine. Even still, electricity was not to be wasted and had been limited to select areas of the castle.

Not here.

Painter turned to her as she entered. She noted how disheveled his hair had dried, giving him a rakish, boyish appearance. Barefooted and in a matching robe, he filled a pair of stone mugs with a steaming brew.

"Jasmine tea," he said and waved her to a small sofa in front of the fire.

A platter rested on a low table: hard cheeses, a loaf of

dark bread, piled slices of roast beef, mustard, and a bowl of blackberries with a tiny decanter of cream.

"Our last meal?" Lisa asked, trying to sound flippant, but she couldn't carry it off. They were to be interrogated first thing in the morning.

Painter patted the seat next to him as he sat down.

She joined him.

As he sliced the bread, she picked up a sliver of sharp cheddar. She sniffed and set it down. No appetite.

"You should eat," Painter said.

"Why? So I'll be stronger when they drug us?"

Painter rolled a piece of beef and popped it into his mouth. He chewed as he spoke. "Nothing's certain. If I've learned nothing in life, I've at least learned that."

Unconvinced, she shook her head. "So what are you saying? Just hope for the best?"

"I personally prefer a plan."

She eyed him. "And you have one?"

"A simple one. Not exactly guns-blazing, grenades-exploding."

"Then what?"

He swallowed his roast beef and turned to her. "Something that I find works a surprising amount of the time."

She waited for an answer. "Well?"

"Honesty."

She slunk back, shoulders slumping. "Great."

Painter picked up a slice of bread, slathered it with some coarse mustard, added a slice of beef, and topped it with a piece of cheddar. He held it out toward her. "Eat."

Sighing, she took his creation in hand, only to appease him.

Painter made a second one for himself. "For instance, I'm the director for a division of DARPA named Sigma. We specialize in investigating threats to the U.S., employing a team of ex–Special Forces soldiers. The strong arm for DARPA out in the field."

Lisa nibbled at the edge of the sandwich's crust, catching a tangy bit of fresh mustard. "Can we expect some rescue by these soldiers?"

"Doubtful. Not in the time frame we have. It will take them days to discover that my body's not among the ruins of the monastery."

"Then I don't see—"

Painter held up a hand, munched a mouthful of sandwich, and mumbled around it. "It's about honesty. Putting it out there, plainly and openly. Seeing what happens. Something drew Sigma's attention out here. Reports of strange illnesses. After operating so covertly for so many years, why all these slips in the past months? I'm not one to place much stock in coincidence. I overheard Anna speaking to the soldier-assassin. She hinted at some problem here. Something that has them baffled. I think our two goals might not be at such cross-purposes. There may be room for cooperation."

"And they'd let us live?" she asked, half scoffing, but a part of her hoped. She bit into the sandwich to hide her foolishness.

"I don't know," he said, staying honest. "As long as we prove useful. But if we can gain a few days . . . it widens our chances for a rescue or maybe a change of circumstance."

Lisa chewed her food, contemplating. Before she knew it, her fingers were empty. And she was still hungry. They shared the bowl of blackberries, pouring cream over them.

She eyed Painter with a fresh perspective. He was more than stubborn strength. There was a brilliance behind those blue eyes and a wealth of common sense. As if sensing her scrutiny, he glanced at her. She quickly returned to studying the platter of food.

In silence, they finished their meal, sipping the tea. With

food in their bellies, exhaustion weighed on them both, making even talk a burden. Also she enjoyed the quiet, sitting next to him. She heard him breathing. She could smell his freshly scrubbed skin.

As she finished the last of her honeyed tea, she noted Painter rubbing at his right temple, one eye squinted. His headache was flaring up. She didn't want to play doctor, go clinical and worry him, but she studied him askance. The fingers of his other hand trembled. She noted the slight vibration in his pupils as he stared at the dying fire.

Painter had mentioned honesty, but did he want the truth about his condition? The attacks seemed to be coming on more frequently. And a part of her was selfish enough to fear—not for his health, but for the thin hope of survival he had instilled in her. She needed him.

Lisa stood. "We should get some sleep. Dawn cannot be far off."

Painter groaned but nodded. He stood. She had to grab his elbow as he teetered a bit.

"I'm fine," he said.

So much for honesty.

She guided him toward the bed and pulled back the blankets.

"I can sleep on the sofa," he said, resisting.

"Don't be ridiculous. Get in. Now's not the time to be concerned with any impropriety. We're in a Nazi stronghold."

"*Former* Nazi."

"Yeah, big comfort there."

Still, he climbed into the bed with a sigh, robe and all. Walking around the bed, she did the same, blowing out the bedside candles. The shadows thickened, but the dying firelight kept the room pleasantly aglow. Lisa didn't know if she could handle the total darkness.

She settled under the blankets, pulling them up to her chin.

She kept a space between the two of them, back to Painter. He must have sensed her fear and rolled to face her.

"If we die," Painter mumbled, "we'll die together."

She swallowed. Those were *not* the reassuring words she had expected to hear, but at the same time she was oddly comforted. Something in his tone, the honesty, the promise behind the words, succeeded where weak assertions of their safety would have failed.

She believed him.

Snuggling closer, her hand found his, fingers entwined, nothing sexual, just two people needing to touch. She pulled his arm around her.

He squeezed her hand, reassuring and strong.

She pulled deeper against him, and he rolled to hold her more snugly.

Lisa closed her eyes, not expecting to sleep.

But in his arms, she eventually did.

10:39 P.M.
COPENHAGEN, DENMARK

Gray checked his watch.

They'd been hiding for over two hours. He and Fiona had holed themselves up inside a service shaft for a ride called the *Minen*, or Mine. It was an old-fashioned animatronic amusement where cars rolled past cartoonish molelike animals in mining gear, working some whimsical subterranean quarry. The same musical refrain kept playing over and over again, an aural form of the Chinese water torture.

Shortly after disappearing into the crowds of Tivoli Gardens, Gray and Fiona had hopped on the old ride, playing father and daughter. But at the first unsupervised turn, they rolled out of their car and into a service cubby behind a swinging door with an electrical hazard sign on it. Never finishing the ride, Gray

could only imagine the end: the molelike creatures merrily ensconced in hospital beds, suffering from black-lung disease.

Or so he hoped.

The jaunty refrain in Danish continued for the thousandth
time. Maybe it wasn't as bad as the It's-a-Small-World ride
at Disneyland, but it was a close second.

In the cramped quarters, Gray had the Darwin Bible open
in his lap. He had been perusing the pages with a penlight,
searching for any clue to its importance, page by page. His
head throbbed in tune to the music.

"Do you have a gun?" Fiona asked, crunched in a corner,
arms crossed. "If you do, shoot me now."

Gray sighed. "We only have another hour."

"I'll never make it."

The plan was to wait for the park to close. The park only
had one official exit, but Gray was sure all exits were under
surveillance by now. Their only chance was to try to escape
during the park's mass exodus at midnight. He had tried to
confirm Monk's arrival at the Copenhagen airport, but the
iron and copper in the old building were playing havoc with
his cell phone reception. They needed to reach the airport.

"Have you learned anything from the Bible?" she asked.

Gray shook his head. It was fascinating to see the house
lineage graphed inside the front cover, the Darwin family's
personal evolutionary tree. But otherwise, of the remaining
pages he'd perused so far, the brittle and fragile sheets offered no clues. All he discovered were a few scribblings.
The same mark over and over, in many different positions
and incarnations.

Gray glanced at his notebook. He had jotted down the
symbols as they appeared, written in the margins of the
Bible—whether by the hand of Charles Darwin or a later
owner, he didn't know.

He nudged his notebook toward Fiona.

"Anything look familiar?"

Fiona sighed and leaned forward, uncrossing her arms. She squinted at the symbols.

"Bird scratches," she said. "Nothing worth murdering over."

Gray rolled his eyes, but he held his tongue. Fiona's mood had darkened. He preferred her vengeful amusement and manic anger. With their incarceration here, she seemed to have drawn inward. Gray suspected she had driven all her grief and energy into the ruse to obtain the Bible, her small act of revenge against her grandmother's murder. And now, in the dark, the reality was setting in.

What could he do?

Picking up pen and paper, he sought some means to keep her focused on the present. He drew another symbol, the small tattoo on the back of the male bidder's hand.

He slid it over. "How about this one?"

With an even louder, more dramatic sigh, she again leaned forward to stare. She shook her head. "A four-leaf clover. I don't know. What's that supposed to . . . wait . . ." She took the notebook and looked closer. Her eyes widened. "I've seen this before!"

"Where?"

"On a business card," Fiona said. "Only it wasn't like

this, more of an outline." She took up his pen and began to work.

"Whose business card?"

"The prat who came months ago and searched through our records. The guy who stiffed us with the fake credit card." Fiona continued to work. "Where did you see it?"

"It was drawn on the back of the man's hand, the one who bought the Bible."

Fiona practically growled. "I knew it! So it's been the same bastard behind this all along. First he tries to steal it. Then he tries to cover his tracks by killing Mutti and burning down the shop."

"Do you remember the name on the business card?" Gray asked.

She shook her head. "Only the symbol. Because I recognized it."

She slid her drawing over to him. It was a more detailed line-drawing of the solid tattoo, revealing more of a tangled nature to the symbol.

Gray tapped the page. "You recognized this?"

Fiona nodded. "I collect pins. Course I couldn't wear them with these naff clothes."

Gray remembered her hooded jacket, the one he had first spotted her wearing, festooned with buttons of every shape and size.

"I went through a Celtic phase," Fiona said. "It was the only music I'd listen to, and most of my pins had Celtic designs."

"And the symbol here?"

"Called an Earth Square or Saint Hans Cross. It's supposed to be protective, calling on the four corners of the earth for power." She tapped the cloverleaf circles. "That's why it's sometimes called a shield knot. Meant to protect you."

Gray concentrated but found no significance to the clue.

"It's why I told Mutti to trust him," Fiona said. She had sunk back. Her voice lowered to a whisper, as if afraid to talk. "She didn't like the man. On first sight. But when I saw that on his card, I thought he must be an okay bloke."

"You couldn't have known."

"Mutti did," she said sharply. "And now she's dead. Because of me." Guilt and anguish rang through her words.

"Nonsense." Gray moved closer and put his arm around her. "Whoever these people are, they were damned determined from the start. You know that. They would have found a way to get that information from your shop. They wouldn't have taken no for an answer. If you hadn't convinced your grandmother to let them look through the records, they might have killed you both on the spot."

Fiona leaned against him.

"Your grandmother—"

"She wasn't my grandmother," she interrupted hollowly.

Gray had figured as much, but he stayed silent, letting Fiona speak.

"She caught me when I tried to nick some stuff from her store. Two years ago. But she didn't call the police. Instead she made me soup. Chicken barley."

Gray didn't need to see in the dark to know Fiona had smiled slightly.

"That was the way she was. Always helping street kids. Always taking in strays."

"Like Bertal."

"And me." She stayed silent for a long moment. "My parents died in a car accident. They were Pakistani immigrants.

Punjabis. We had a small house in Waltham Forest in London, even a garden. We talked about getting a dog. Then . . . then they died."

"I'm sorry, Fiona."

"My aunt and uncle took me in . . . they had just arrived from the Punjab." Another long pause. "After a month, he started coming into my room at night."

Gray closed his eyes. Dear God . . .

"So I ran . . . I lived on the streets of London for a couple years, but I got in trouble with the wrong people. Had to run. So I left England and backpacked across Europe. Getting by. I ended up here."

"And Grette took you in."

"And now she's dead, too." Again that ring of guilt. "Maybe I'm just bad luck."

Gray pulled Fiona tighter. "I saw the way she looked at you. You coming into her life was *not* bad luck. She loved you."

"I . . . I know." Fiona turned her face away. Her shoulders shook as she quietly sobbed.

Gray just held her. She eventually turned and buried her face in his shoulder. Now it was Gray's turn to fight twinges of guilt. Grette had been such a generous woman, nurturing and instinctive, kind and empathetic. Now she was dead. He had his own culpability to balance here. If he had proceeded with more caution . . . been less reckless with this investigation . . .

And the cost for his neglect.

Fiona's sobbing continued.

Even if the murder and arson had been planned regardless of his own blundering inquiries, Gray judged his actions afterward. He had fled, abandoning Fiona to the chaos, leaving her to her grief. He remembered her calling out to him—at first angered, then pleading.

He hadn't stopped.

"I have no one now," Fiona cried softly into his suit.

"You have me."

She pulled back, teary-eyed. "But you're leaving, too."

"And you're coming with me."

"But you said—"

"Never mind what I said." Gray knew the girl was no longer safe here. She would be eliminated, if not to gain the Bible, then to shut her up. She knew too much. Like . . . "You mentioned you knew the address from the Bible's bill of sale."

Fiona stared at him with open suspicion. Her sobbing had stopped. She pulled back and eyed him, judging if his sympathy was a ruse to get her to cough up what she knew. He understood her wariness now, born of the streets.

Gray knew better than to push it. "I have a friend flying in on a private jet. He should be touching down at midnight. We can connect with him and fly anywhere. You can tell me where we have to go once we're on board." Gray held out a hand, prepared to seal the deal.

With one eye squinted in suspicion, Fiona took his hand. "Deal," she said.

It was a small patch on Gray's mistakes of the past day, but it was a start. She had to be removed from harm's way, and she should be safe once on board the plane. She could stay aboard, under guard, while he and Monk investigated further.

Fiona pushed his notebook back toward him with all the doodled symbols. "Just so you know . . . we need to go to Paderborn in Central Germany. I'll give you the specific address once we're there."

Gray took her concession as a tiny measure of trust. "Good enough."

She nodded.

The deal clinched.

"Now if only you could get this gormless music to stop," she added with a tired moan.

As if on cue, the incessant chant died. The constant low machinery hum and clacking of the cars over tracks also ceased. In the sudden quiet, footsteps sounded outside the narrow door.

Gray gained his feet. "Stay behind me," he hissed.

Fiona gathered up the Bible and tucked it into her purse. Gray grabbed a length of rebar he had found earlier.

The door opened and a bright light shone in their eyes.

The man barked sharply, startled. He spoke in Danish. "What are you two doing in here?"

Gray straightened and lowered the bar. He had almost speared the man in the maintenance uniform.

"Ride is closed," the man said, stepping aside. "Get out of here before I call security."

Gray obeyed. The man scowled at him as he passed. He knew how it must look. An older man with a teenaged girl holed up in a cubby of an amusement park.

"You all right, miss?" the worker asked. He must have noticed her puffy eyes, ripped clothes.

"We're fine." She hooked her arm into Gray's and sashayed her hips a bit. "He paid extra for *this* ride."

The man frowned in distaste. "Back door is over there." He pointed to a neon exit sign. "Don't let me catch you in here again. It's dangerous to be traipsing around back here."

Not as dangerous as outside. Gray led them to the door and pushed through. He checked his watch. It was only a bit after eleven. The park wouldn't close for another hour. Maybe they needed to try for an exit now.

As they cleared the corner of the ride's building, it looked like this section of the park was deserted. No wonder the ride had closed up early.

Gray heard music and merriment coming from the direction of the park's lake.

"Everyone's gathering for the electrical parade," Fiona said. "It closes up the park, along with fireworks."

Gray prayed tonight's fireworks didn't end up with people bleeding and screaming. He searched the immediate park grounds. Lanterns lit up the night. Tulips filled beds to overflowing. The concrete paths and aprons here were sparsely populated. They were too exposed.

Gray spotted a pair of park security guards, a man and a woman, striding a bit too purposefully in their direction. Had the maintenance worker gone ahead and alerted security after all?

"Time to get lost again," Gray said and tugged Fiona in the opposite direction of the approaching guards. He headed toward where the crowds gathered. They walked quickly, staying in shadows under trees. Just two visitors anxious to watch the parade.

They cleared the garden paths and entered the central plaza with its wide lake, aglow from all the lights and lanterns of the encircling pavilions and palaces. Across the way, a cheer arose as the first of the parade floats drifted into the plaza. It stood three stories, depicting a mermaid on a rock, emblazoned with emerald and azure blue lights. An arm waved in welcome. Other floats swept behind it, aglow with animated puppets, five meters tall. Flutes piped merrily, drums sounded.

"The Hans Christian Andersen parade," Fiona said. "Celebrating the writer's two hundredth anniversary. He's the patron saint of the city."

Gray marched with her toward the crowd lining the parade route around the center lake. Reflected in the still waters, a giant fiery bloom burst in the sky, accompanied by a sonorous *whump*. Fanciful cascades of sparkling streamers whistled and spiraled out across the night sky.

Nearing the edge of the surging parade crowd, Gray kept a constant vigil around him. He searched for any pale figure in black. But this was Copenhagen. Every fifth person was blond. And black, it seemed, was the new black this season in Denmark.

Gray's heart thumped in beat to the drums. A short volley of fireworks pummeled his chest and eardrums with their concussions. But they finally reached the crowds.

Directly overhead, another flaming flower, drizzling with fire, crackled and burst.

Fiona stumbled.

Gray caught her, his ears ringing.

As the explosion echoed away, Fiona stared up at him, shocked. She lifted a hand from her side. She held it out toward him as he pulled her into the crowd.

Her palm was covered in blood.

4:02 A.M.
HIMALAYAS

Painter woke into darkness, the fire cold. How long had he been asleep? Without windows, it was timeless. But he sensed not much time had passed.

Something had roused him.

He pushed up on an elbow.

On the other side of the bed, Lisa was also awake, glancing toward the door. "Did you feel—?"

The room shuddered with a violent shake. A distant *boom* reached them, felt in the gut.

Painter threw back the blankets. "Trouble."

He pointed to the pile of fresh clothes supplied by their hosts. They quickly dressed: long underwear, heavy worn jeans, and bulky sweaters.

Across the room, Lisa lit the bedside candles. She shoved

her feet into a pair of sturdy leather boots meant more for men. They waited in silence for a span of time . . . maybe twenty minutes, listening to the commotion slowly die down.

Both sank back to the bed.

"What do you think happened?" Lisa whispered.

Barked shouts echoed.

"Don't know . . . but I think we're about to find out."

Boots pounded down the stone passage beyond the thick oak door. Painter stood, craning an ear.

"Coming this way," he said.

Confirming this, a hard knock rattled the door. Holding up an arm, Painter held Lisa back, but he also took a step back himself. A heavy scrape sounded next, releasing the iron bar that sealed them inside.

The door was tugged open. Four men streamed into the room, rifles pointing at them. A fifth entered. He looked a lot like the assassin named Gunther. A giant bull of a man, thick necked, a stubble field for hair, silver or light gray. He wore baggy brown pants tucked into midthigh black boots and a matching brown shirt.

Except for the missing black armband and swastika, he looked the part of a Nazi storm trooper.

Or rather *former* Nazi storm trooper.

He also had the same pale face as Gunther, only something seemed wrong. The left side of his face drooped like a stroke victim. His left arm trembled with a palsy as he pointed toward the door.

"Kommen Sie mit mir!" he snapped.

They were being ordered out. The massive leader turned and strode away, as if any thought of disobeying was simply unfathomable. Then again, the rifles at their back certainly reinforced that assumption.

Painter nodded to Lisa. She joined him as they exited, trailed by the cadre of guards. The hallway was narrow, hewn from the rock, barely wide enough for two people. The only illumination came from flashlights secured to the guards' rifles, jittering shadows ahead of them. It was distinctly colder in the hallway than their room, but far from frigid.

They were not led far. Painter estimated that they were headed toward the front façade of the castle. He was right. He even heard a distant whistle of wind. The storm must have kicked up again outside.

Ahead, the massive guardsman knocked on a carved wooden door. A muffled response encouraged him to open the door. Warm light flowed out into the hall, along with a breath of heat.

The guard stepped through and held the door.

Painter led Lisa into the room and searched around him. It appeared to be a rustic study and library. It climbed two stories, all four walls covered in open bookshelves. The upper level was circled by an iron balcony, heavy and undecorated. The only way up was via a steep ladder.

The source of the room's heat was a large stone hearth, aglow with a small bonfire. An oil painting of a man in a German uniform glared down at them.

"My grandfather," Anna Sporrenberg said, noting Painter's attention. She rose from behind a carved monstrosity of a desk. She wore dark jeans and a sweater, too. Apparently it was the dress code for the castle. "He took over the castle after the war."

She motioned them to a circle of wingback chairs that fronted the fireplace. Painter noted the circles under her eyes. It looked like she hadn't slept at all. He also smelled smoke on her, an odor not unlike cordite.

Interesting.

Painter met her eyes as she approached the heavy chairs. The small hairs on the back of his neck prickled. Despite her exhaustion, her eyes were bright and sharp. Painter recognized a cunning, predatory, and calculating gleam. Here was someone to watch closely. She seemed to be appraising him just as intently, sizing him up.

What was going on?

"Setzen Sie sich, bitte," she said, nodding to the chairs.

Painter and Lisa took neighboring chairs. Anna chose one opposite them. The guard kept a post by the closed door, arms crossed. Painter knew the cadre of other guards still waited outside. He surveyed the room for escape routes. The only other exit was a deep-set glazed window, frosted to obscurity, crisscrossed with iron bars.

No escape that way.

Painter returned his attention to Anna. Maybe there was another way out. Anna's manner was cautious, but they had been called here for a reason. He needed as much information as possible, but he would have to handle this deftly. He noted Anna's family resemblance to the man in the oil painting. A place to start.

"You said your grandfather *took over* the castle," Painter said, prying for answers, sticking to safe ground. "Who held it before him?"

Anna leaned back into the seat, obviously relieved to sit in front of the fire for a quiet moment. Still, her manner was focused, hands folded on her lap, eyes passing over Lisa, then back to him. *"Granitschloß* has a long and dark history, Mr. Crowe. Are you familiar with Heinrich Himmler?"

"Hitler's second in command?"

"Ja. The head of the SS. Also a butcher and madman."

Painter was surprised to hear this characterization. Was this a trick? He sensed a game afoot. Only he didn't know the steps . . . at least not yet.

Anna continued, "Himmler believed himself to be the reincarnation of King Heinrich, a tenth-century German king of the Saxons. Even thought he received psychic messages from him."

Painter nodded. "I've heard he was interested in the occult."

"Obsessed actually." Anna shrugged. "It was a passion of many in Germany. Going back to Madame Blavatsky, who coined the term Aryan. She claimed to have gained secret knowledge while studying at a Buddhist monastery. Secret masters supposedly taught her how mankind had devolved from a superior race and would one day evolve back."

"The proverbial master race," Painter said.

"Precisely. A century later, Guido von List mixed her beliefs with German mythology, refining a Nordic origin to this mythic Aryan race."

"And the German people bought the story hook, line, and sinker," Painter said, baiting her a bit.

"And why not? After our defeat in World War I, such an idea was a flattering conceit. It was taken up in a flourish of occult lodges in Germany. The Thule Society, the Vril Society, the Order of the New Templars."

"And as I recall, Himmler himself belonged to the Thule Society."

"Yes, the *Reichsführer* believed fully in this mythology. Even in the magic of the Nordic runes. It was why he chose the double *sig* runes, twin lightning bolts, to represent his own order of warrior-priests, the *Schutzstaffel,* the SS. He became convinced, from studying Madame Blavatsky's work, that it was in the Himalayas that the Aryan race first arose, and that it was here that it would rise again."

Lisa spoke for the first time. "So Himmler did send expeditions out into the Himalayas." She shared a glance with Painter. They had talked about this earlier. So they weren't so far off base. But Painter still wondered about Anna's cryptic statement.

We're not Nazis. Not anymore.

He encouraged the woman to talk while she remained gregarious. He sensed a setup, but he had no idea where it was leading. He hated being in the dark, but he refused to show it.

"So what was Himmler searching for out here?" he asked. "Some lost tribe of Aryans? A white-supremacist's Shangri-La?"

"Not exactly. Under the guise of anthropological and zoological research, Himmler sent members of his SS to search for *evidence* of a long-lost master race. He became convinced that he would find traces of the old race here. And though he found nothing, he grew more determined, driven further into madness. When he started constructing an SS stronghold in Germany, a personal castle named Wewelsburg, he built a mirror image of the same here, airlifting a thousand slave laborers from German concentration camps. He also shipped a metric ton of gold bullion. To make us self-sufficient. Which it has, with careful investments."

"But why build here?" Lisa asked.

Painter could guess. "He believed that the Aryan race would again rise from these mountains. He was building their first citadel."

Anna nodded, as if conceding a point in a match. "He also believed the hidden masters who once taught Madame Blavatsky were still alive. He was building them a stronghold, a central place to bring all such knowledge and experience together."

"Did these hidden masters ever show up?" Painter asked mockingly.

"No. But my grandfather did at the end of the war. And he brought with him something miraculous, something that could make Himmler's dream a reality."

"And what was that?" Painter asked.

Anna shook her head. "Before we talk further, I must ask you a question. And I would appreciate a truthful answer."

Painter frowned at the sudden change of tack. "You know I can't promise that."

Anna smiled for the first time. "I appreciate even that much honesty, Mr. Crowe."

"So what's your question?" he asked, curious. Here must be the heart of the matter.

Anna stared at him. "Are you ill? I'm having a hard time telling. You seem very clear-headed."

Painter's eyes widened. He had not expected that question.

Before he could respond, Lisa answered, "Yes."

"Lisa . . . ," Painter warned.

"She'll know anyway. It doesn't take a medical degree to tell." Lisa turned to Anna. "He's showing vestibular signs, nystagmus, and disorientation."

"How about migraines with visual flashes?"

Lisa nodded.

"I thought as much." She leaned back. The information seemed to reassure the woman.

Painter frowned. Why?

Lisa pressed. "What is affecting him? I think we . . . he has a right to know."

"That will take some further discussion, but I can give you his prognosis."

"And that is?"

"He will die in another three days. Most horribly."

Painter forced himself not to react.

Lisa remained equally unfazed, her tone clinical. "Is there a cure?"

Anna glanced to Painter, then back to Lisa.

"No."

11:18 P.M.
COPENHAGEN, DENMARK

He had to get the girl to safety, to a doctor. Gray felt the blood seeping from Fiona's gunshot wound, soaking through her shirt as he supported her, an arm under her.

Around them, the crowds pressed. Cameras flashed, keeping Gray edgy. Music and song echoed off the lake as the electrical parade floated past. Giant animated puppets loomed high, nodding and lolling over the heads of the crowd.

Fireworks continued to boom and burst over the lake.

Gray ignored it all. He kept low, still searching for the sniper who shot Fiona. He had glanced briefly at her wound. Only a graze, skin burned, weeping blood, but she needed medical care. Pain blanched her face.

The shot had come from behind. That meant that the sniper had to be positioned among the trees and bushes. They had been lucky to reach the crowds. Still, with them spotted, the hunters were probably already converging. Surely there were some among the crowd already.

He checked his watch. Forty-five minutes until the park closed.

Gray needed a plan . . . a new plan. They could no longer wait until midnight to make their escape with the exiting crowd. They would be discovered before then. They needed to leave now.

But the stretch of park between the parade grounds and the exit was nearly deserted as all the visitors gathered around the lake. If they attempted a mad dash for the exit, they would be exposed again, caught out in the open. And surely the park gate was under watch, too.

Next to him, Fiona kept a hand clutched to her wounded side. Blood oozed between her fingers. Her eyes met his, panicked.

She whispered to him, "What are we going to do?"

Gray kept them moving through the crowd. He only had one idea. It was dangerous, but caution was not going to get them out of the park. He turned Fiona toward him.

"I need to bloody my hands."

"What?"

He motioned to her shirt.

Frowning, she lifted the edge of her blouse. "Be careful . . ."

He gently wiped the blood dribbling from the raw wound. She winced and let out a small gasp.

"Sorry," he said.

"Your fingers are freezing," she mumbled.

"Are you okay?"

"I'll live."

That was the goal.

"I'm going to have to carry you in a second," Gray said, standing up.

"What are you—?"

"Just be ready to scream when I tell you."

She wrinkled her nose in confusion, but nodded.

He waited for the right moment. Flutes and drums started in the distance. Gray edged Fiona in the direction of the main gates. Past the heads of a group of schoolchildren, Gray spotted a familiar figure in a trench coat, arm in a sling, Grette's murderer. He waded through the pocket of youngsters, eyes searching.

Gray retreated into a mob of Germans singing a ballad in tune with the flutes and drums. As the song ended, a burst of fireworks concluded in a tympani of crackling explosions.

"Here we go," Gray said, leaning down. He smeared his face with blood and picked Fiona up in his arms. Lifting her, he raised his voice and yelled in Danish. "Bomb!"

Crackling explosions punctuated his booming bellow.

"Scream," he whispered in Fiona's ear.

He lifted his face again, smeared in blood. On cue, Fiona wailed and shrieked in agony in his arms.

"Bomb!" Gray yelled again.

Faces turned in his direction. Fireworks boomed. The fresh blood glistened on his cheeks. At first no one moved. Then like a turning tide, one person backed away, bumping against another. Confused cries and calls rose. More people began to retreat.

Gray kept after those retreating, staying among the most panicked.

Fiona cried and thrashed. She waved an arm, fingers dripping with blood.

Confusion spread like wildfire. Gray's bellow caught on the dry tinder, whetted by attacks in London and Spain. More cries of *Bomb!* echoed through the crowd, carried from one breath to another.

Like a spooked herd of cattle, the crowd bristled and bumped against one another. Claustrophobia accentuated the anxiety. Fireworks died overhead, but by now, frightened cries erupted across the parade route. As one person fled, two more took flight, reflexive, growing exponentially. Feet pounded on pavement, retreating, aiming for the exit.

A trickle became a surge.

The stampede toward the exit began.

Gray allowed himself to be carried with it, Fiona in his arms. He prayed no one was trampled. But so far the retreat was not in full panic. With the boom of the fireworks ended, confusion reigned more than horror. Still, the flow of the crowd hastened toward the main gate.

Gray set Fiona down, freeing his arms. He wiped his face clean with the sleeve of his Armani jacket. Fiona stayed at his side, one hand clutching his belt to keep anchored to him amid the throng.

The gate appeared ahead.

Gray nodded toward it. "If anything happens . . . *run*. Keep going."

"I don't know if I can make it. Side hurts like a bitch."

Gray saw that she was limping now, scrunched over slightly.

Up ahead, Gray saw security guards trying to control the crowd through the gates, keeping the press of bodies from crushing anyone. As he watched, Gray spotted a pair of guards standing off to the side, conspicuously not helping with crowd control. A young man and woman. Both snowy blond. The bidders from the auction house. In disguise, they guarded the gates. Both had holstered pistols, palms resting on them.

For just a moment, the woman's eyes met his in the crowd.

But they shifted away.

Then snapped back again.

Recognition.

Gray backpedaled through the crowd, fighting the current.

"What?" Fiona asked, pushed behind him.

"Go back. We need to find another way."

"How?"

Gray edged off to the side, swimming against the riptide. It was too hard to retreat straight back. A moment later, he broke free. Only a handful of people still bustled around him, a small eddy in the greater current.

They needed better coverage.

Gray saw that they had reached the edge of the deserted parade route. The floats had ground to a stop, lights still blinking, but no music. It seemed the panic had spread to the float operators. They had abandoned their chariots and fled. Even the security guards had moved to the gates.

Gray spotted the open door to a cab of one of the floats.

"This way," he said.

He half carried Fiona away from the crowd and ran for the float. Over the cab towered a giant illuminated puppet of a gangly duck with an oversize head. Gray recognized the figure. From the Hans Christian Andersen fairy tale "The Ugly Duckling."

They dashed under one of its upraised wings aglow with twinkling yellow lights, plainly meant to flap. Gray helped Fiona into the cab, expecting to be shot in the back at any moment. He climbed in after her and closed the door, snapping it shut as quietly as he could.

As he glanced out the windshield, he appreciated his caution.

A figure appeared ahead, stepping out of the crowd, dressed in black. Grette's killer. He did not bother hiding his shotgun. All attention had diverted to the front of the park. He circled the edge of the retreating crowd, staring out toward the lake and parade circuit.

Gray ducked with Fiona.

The man passed within yards and continued down the line of abandoned floats.

"That was close," Fiona whispered. "We should—"

"Shh." Gray pressed a finger to her lips. His elbow nudged a lever. Something clicked in the dashboard.

Oh crap . . .

Speakers buried in the puppet overhead erupted.

—QUACK, QUACK, QUACK . . . QUACK, QUACK, QUACK—

The Ugly Duckling had awakened.

And everyone knew it.

Gray straightened. Thirty yards away, the gunman swung around.

There was no hiding now.

Suddenly the cab's engine growled. Glancing over, he saw Fiona sitting up, popping the clutch.

"Found the key in the ignition," she said and shifted into gear. The float lurched forward, swinging out of line.

"Fiona, let me—"

"You drove last time. And look where that got us." She aimed straight for the gunman with the shotgun. "Besides, I owe this bastard."

So she had recognized him, too. The man who murdered her grandmother. She had shifted into second by the time he raised his shotgun. She barreled toward him, careless of the threat.

Gray sought some way to help, searching the cab.

So many levers—

The assassin fired.

Gray winced, but Fiona had already twisted the wheel, anticipating. A corner of the windshield spiderwebbed, the shot wide. Fiona yanked the wheel back around, trying to run the man over.

With the sudden turn, the float, top-heavy, tipped over on two wheels.

"Hold on!" Fiona yelled.

The float crashed back down on four tires, but it bought the man an extra moment to sprint to the left. He was damn fast, already readying his shotgun, planning to shoot point-blank through the side window as the float passed.

They had no time to maneuver out of the way.

Returning his attention to the row of levers, Gray grabbed the left-most one. It only made sense. He yanked it down. Gears ground. The Duckling's left wing, raised a moment ago, flapped low. It struck the gunman in the neck, clothes-lining him from the side, shattering vertebrae. The man was lifted off his feet and tossed aside.

"Go for the gates!" Gray urged.

The Ugly Duckling had its first taste of blood.

—QUACK, QUACK, QUACK . . . QUACK, QUACK, QUACK—

The siren call of the float cleared a path. People scattered to the sides. The security guards were crushed back by the crowd. Even those in disguise. The service gate next to the main entrance, thrown wide earlier to ease the crush of flee-ing people, stood open.

Fiona aimed for it.

The duck shattered through it, tearing off its deadly left wing. The cab shuddered, and they were on the streets. Fiona headed away.

"Take the first corner," Gray said, pointing.

She obeyed, downshifting into the turn like a pro. The Duckling flew around the corner. After two more turns, Gray urged her to slow down.

"We can't keep driving this thing," he said. "It's too con-spicuous."

"You think?" Fiona glanced to him and shook her head in exasperation.

Gray found a long wrench in a tool kit. He had them stop at the top of a hill and waved Fiona out. Shifting over, Gray popped the clutch, jammed the wrench on the accelerator, and jumped to the curb.

The Ugly Duckling took off, lights blazing, clipping parked cars as it fled downhill. Wherever it finally came to roost, the crash site would divert the attention of any trackers.

Gray headed in the opposite direction. They should be safe for a few hours. He checked his watch. Plenty of time to reach the airport. And Monk. He would be touching down shortly.

Fiona limped beside him, eyes glancing back.

Behind them, the Duckling trumpeted into the night.

—QUACK, QUACK, QUACK . . . QUACK, QUACK, QUACK—

"I'm going to miss him," Fiona said.

"Me, too."

4:35 A.M.
HIMALAYAS

Painter stood by the hearth. He had risen from his chair upon the pronouncement of his death sentence.

The massive guard had come forward three steps when Painter rose to his feet, but Anna had held the man back with a raised hand. *"Nein, Klaus. Alles ist in Ordnung."*

Painter waited for the guard, Klaus, to return to his post by the door. "There's no cure?"

Anna nodded. "I spoke truly."

"Then why isn't Painter showing the same madness as the monks?" Lisa asked.

Anna glanced to Painter. "You were away from the monastery, *ja*? At the outlying village. Your exposure was less. Rather than the rapid neurological degeneration, you're experiencing a slower, more generalized *bodily* deterioration. Still, it is a death sentence."

Anna must have read something in his face.

"While there is no cure, there is a hope of slowing the deterioration. Over the years, experimenting with animals, we have devised some models that show promise. We can prolong your life. Or at least we could have."

"What do you mean?" Lisa asked.

Anna stood. "It is why I called you down here. To show you." She nodded to the guard, Klaus, who opened the door. "Follow me. And perhaps we'll find a way to help each other."

Painter offered Lisa a hand as Anna stepped away. He burned with curiosity. He sensed both a trap and a measure of hope.

What better bait?

Lisa leaned toward him as she stood. "What is going on?" she whispered in his ear.

"I'm not sure." He glanced to Anna as she spoke with Klaus.

Perhaps we'll find a way to help each other.

Painter had planned to propose the same to Anna, even discussed it with Lisa earlier, to bargain for their lives, to buy time. Had they been eavesdropped upon? Bugged? Or had matters simply grown so much worse here that their cooperation was truly needed?

Now he was worried.

"It must have something to do with that explosion we heard," Lisa said.

Painter nodded. He definitely needed more information. For now, he tabled any concern about his own health . . . though it was difficult, as another migraine built behind his eyes, aching in his back molars, reminding him of his illness with every throb.

Anna motioned them over. Klaus stepped back. He did not look happy. Then again, Painter had yet to see the man happy. And for some reason, he hoped never to. What made this man happy had to involve screaming and bloodshed.

"If you'll come with me," Anna said with cold politeness.

She headed out the door, flanked by two of the outer guardsmen. Klaus followed Lisa and Painter, trailed by another two armed men.

They headed in a direction different from their plush prison cell. After a few turns a straight tunnel, wider than any of the others, stretched into the heart of the mountain. It was also lit by a row of electric bulbs, lined up in wire cages along one wall. It was the first sign of any modern amenities.

They walked along the corridor.

Painter noted the smoky reek to the air. It grew stronger as they progressed. He returned his attention to Anna.

"So you know what made me sick," he said.

"It was the accident, as I said before."

"An accident involving *what*?" he pressed.

"The answer is not easy. It stretches far back into history."

"Back to when you were Nazis?"

Anna glanced to him. "Back to the origin of life on this planet."

"Really?" Painter said. "So how long is this story? Remember, I only have three days left."

She smiled at him again and shook her head. "In that case, I'll jump forward to when my grandfather first came to the *Granitschloß*. At the end of the war. Are you familiar with the turmoil at that time? The chaos in Europe as Germany crumbled."

"Everything up for grabs."

"And not just German land and resources, but also our research. Allied forces sent competing parties, scientists and soldiers, scouring the German countryside, pillaging for secret technology. It was a free-for-all." Anna frowned at them. "Is that the right word?"

Painter and Lisa both nodded.

"Britain alone sent in five thousand soldiers and civilians, under the code name T-Force. Technology Force. Their stated goal was to locate and preserve German technology from looting and robbery, when in fact *looting and robbery* was their true goal, competing against American, French, and Russian counterparts. Do you know who was the founder of the British T-Force?"

Painter shook his head. He could not help comparing his own Sigma Force to the earlier British World War II teams. Tech-plunderers. He would love to discuss the same with Sigma's founder, Sean McKnight. If he lived that long.

"Who was their leader?" Lisa asked.

"A gentleman named Commander Ian Fleming."

Lisa made a dismissive snort. "The writer who created James Bond?"

"The same. It was said he patterned his character on some

of the men on his team. That gives you some idea of the roughshod and cavalier exuberance of these plunderers."

"To the victor go the spoils of war," Painter quoted with a shrug.

"Perhaps. But it was my grandfather's duty to protect as much of that technology as possible. He was an officer in the *Sicherheitsdienst*." She glanced at Painter, testing him.

So the game was not over. He was up for the challenge. "The *Sicherheitsdienst* was the group of SS commandos involved in evacuation of German treasures: art, gold, antiquities, and technology."

She nodded at him. "In the final days of the war, as Russia pushed across the eastern lines, my grandfather was given what you Americans call a *deep black* mission. He received his orders from Heinrich Himmler himself, before the *Reichsführer* was captured and committed suicide."

"And his orders?" Painter asked.

"To remove, safeguard, and destroy all evidence of a project code-named Chronos. At the heart of the project was a device simply called *die Glocke*. Or the Bell. The research lab was buried deep underground, in an abandoned mine in the Sudeten Mountains. He had no idea what was the purpose of the project, but he would eventually. He almost destroyed it then, but he had his orders."

"So he escaped with the Bell. How?"

"Two plans were laid in place. One flight to the north through Norway, another to the south through the Adriatic. There were agents waiting to assist him on both routes. My grandfather opted to go north. Himmler had told him about *Granitschloß*. He fled here with a group of Nazi scientists, some with histories in the camps. All needed a place to hide. Plus my grandfather dangled a project that few scientists could resist."

"The Bell," Painter concluded.

"Exactly. It offered something many scientists at the time had been seeking through other means."

"And what was that?"

Anna sighed and glanced back to Klaus. "Perfection." She remained silent for a few moments, lost in some private sadness.

Ahead the passage finally ended. A pair of giant ironwood doors stood open at the end. Beyond the threshold, a crude staircase spiraled down into the mountain. It was cut from the rock, but the staircase circled around a center pillar of steel as thick as a tree's trunk. They wound down around it.

Painter stared up. The pillar pierced the top of the roof and continued higher . . . possibly all the way out the shoulder of the mountain. Lightning rod, he thought. He also smelled a hint of ozone in the air, stronger now than the smoke.

Anna noted his attention. "We use the shaft to vent excess energies out of the mountain." She pointed up.

Painter craned. He pictured the ghost lights reported in the area. Was this their source? Both of the lights and perhaps the illness?

Biting back his anger, Painter concentrated on the stairs. As his head pounded, the winding aggravated a growing vertigo. Seeking distraction, he continued their dialogue. "Back to the story of the Bell. What did it do?"

Anna broke out of her reverie. "At first no one knew. It came out of research into a new energy source. Some thought it might even be a crude time machine. That was why it was code-named Chronos."

"Time travel?" Painter said.

"You have to remember," Anna said, "the Nazis were light-years ahead of other nations in certain technologies. That was why there was such fervent scientific piracy after the war. But let me backtrack. During the early part of the century, two theoretical systems were in competition: the theory of relativity and quantum theory. And while they didn't necessarily contradict each other, even Einstein, the father of relativity, spoke of the two theories as incompatible. The theories split the scientific community into two camps. And we know very well on which side most of the Western world concentrated."

"Einstein's relativity."

Anna nodded. "Which led to splitting the atom, bombs, and nuclear energy. The entire world became the Manhattan Project. All based on Einstein's work. The Nazis went a different route, but with no less fervor. They had their own equivalent of the Manhattan Project, but one based on the *other* theoretical camp. Quantum theory."

"Why go that route?" Lisa asked.

"For a simple reason." Anna turned to her. "Because Einstein was a Jew."

"What?"

"Remember the context of the time. Einstein was a Jew. In the Nazis' eyes, that assigned lesser value to his discoveries. Instead, the Nazis took to heart the physical discoveries of pure German scientists, considering their works more valid and important. The Nazis based their Manhattan Project on the work of scientists like Werner Heisenberg and Erwin Schrödinger, and most importantly Max Planck, the father of quantum theory. All had solid roots in the Fatherland. So the Nazis proceeded on a course of practical applications based on quantum mechanics, work that even today is considered groundbreaking. The Nazi scientists believed a power source could be tapped based on experiments with quantum models. Something that is only being realized today. Modern science calls this power zero point energy."

"Zero point?" Lisa glanced to Painter.

He nodded, well familiar with the scientific concept. "When something is chilled to absolute zero—almost three hundred degrees below zero Centigrade—all atomic motion stops. A complete standstill. The zero point of nature. Yet even then, energy persists. A background radiation that shouldn't be there. The energy's presence could not be adequately explained by traditional theories."

"But quantum theory does," Anna said firmly. "It allows for movement even when matter is frozen to an absolute standstill."

"How is that possible?" Lisa asked.

"At absolute zero, particles might not move up, down, right, or left, but according to quantum mechanics, they could flash into and out of *existence,* producing energy. What is called zero point energy."

"Into and out of existence?" Lisa seemed little convinced.

Painter took the reins. "Quantum physics gets a bit weird. But while the concept seems crazy, the energy is real. Recorded in labs. Around the world, scientists are seeking ways to tap into this energy at the core of all existence. It offers a source of infinite, limitless power."

Anna nodded. "And the Nazis were experimenting with this energy with all the fervor of your Manhattan Project."

Lisa's eyes grew wide. "An unlimited source of power. If they had discovered it, it would have changed the course of the war."

Anna lifted one hand, correcting her. "Who is to say they *didn't* discover it? It is documented that in the last months of the war, the Nazis had achieved remarkable breakthroughs. Projects with the name *Feuerball* and *Kugelblitz*. Details of which can be found among the unclassified records of the British T-Force. But the discoveries came too late. Facilities were bombed, scientists killed, research stolen. Whatever was left disappeared into the deep black projects of various nations."

"But not the Bell," Painter said, drawing the discussion back to its original point. His nausea would not let the conversation stray too far afield.

"Not the Bell," Anna agreed. "My grandfather managed to escape with the heart of the Chronos Project, born of research into zero point energy. The project was given a new name by my grandfather. *Schwarze Sonne.*"

"Black Sun," Painter translated.

"Sehr gut."

"But what about this Bell?" Painter said. "What did it do?"

"It was what made you sick," Anna said. "Damaged you at the quantum level, where no pill or remedy can reach."

Painter almost tripped a step. He needed a moment to digest the information. *Damaged at the quantum level.* What did that mean?

The last stairs appeared ahead, blocked by a cordon of crossed wood beams, guarded by another pair of men with rifles. Though stunned, Painter noted the scorched rock along the roof of the last turn of the spiral.

Beyond opened a cavernous vault. Painter could not see far into it, but he could still feel the heat. Every surface was blackened. A row of humped shapes lay under tarps. Dead bodies.

Here was the blast zone from the explosions they had heard earlier.

Out of the ruin, a figure appeared, blackened with ash, but his features were still recognizable. It was Gunther, the massive guardsman who had burned down the monastery. It seemed those here had reaped what they had sown.

Fire for fire.

Gunther crossed to the cordon. Anna and Klaus joined him. With Klaus and Gunther side by side, Painter recognized a similarity between the two giants—not physical features, but in some hardness and foreignness that was hard to pin down.

Gunther nodded to Klaus.

The other barely noted his presence.

Anna bowed her head with Gunther, speaking rapidly in German. All Painter could make out was a single word. It was the same in German and English.

Sabotage.

So all was not right in the Granite Castle. Was there a traitor here? If so, who? And what was their purpose? Were they friend or another foe?

Gunther's eyes fell upon Painter. His lips moved, but Painter could not discern what he said. Anna shook her head, disagreeing. Gunther's eyes narrowed, but he nodded.

Painter knew he should be relieved.

With a final pinched stare, Gunther turned and strode back into the blackened ruins.

Anna returned. "This is what I wanted to show you." She waved an arm at the destruction.

"The Bell," Painter said.

"It was destroyed. An act of sabotage."

Lisa stared at the ruin. "And it was this Bell that made Painter sick."

"And held the only chance for a cure."

Painter studied the devastation.

"Do you have a duplicate Bell?" Lisa asked. "Or can you fabricate another?"

Anna slowly shook her head. "One of the key components can't be duplicated. Xerum 525. Even after sixty years, we've not been able to reformulate it."

"So no Bell, no cure," Painter said.

"But there might be a chance . . . if we help each other." Anna held out her hand. "If we cooperate . . . I give you my word."

Painter reached woodenly over and grasped her hand. Still, he hesitated. He sensed a level of subterfuge here. Something Anna had left unspoken. All her talk . . . all the explanations. They were all meant to misdirect. Why were they even offering him this deal?

Then it dawned on him.

He knew.

"The accident . . . ," he said.

He felt Anna's fingers twitch in his.

"It wasn't an *accident*, was it?" He remembered the word he had overheard. "It was *sabotage*, too."

Anna nodded. "At first, we thought it was an accident. We've had occasional problems with surges. Triggering spikes in the Bell's output. Nothing major. Venting the energies triggered a few illnesses locally. The occasional death."

Painter had to restrain himself from shaking his head. *Nothing major,* Anna had said. The illnesses and deaths were *major* enough to warrant Ang Gelu sending out an international call for help, drawing Painter here.

Anna continued, "But a few nights back, someone jinked with the settings during a routine test of the Bell. Exponentially increasing the output."

"And zapping the monastery and the village."

"That's right."

Painter tightened his grip on Anna's hand. It looked like she wanted to pull away. He wasn't about to let her. She was still hedging from full disclosure. But Painter knew the truth as surely as the headache that pressed now. It explained the offer of cooperation.

"But it wasn't just the monks and the village that were affected," Painter said. "Everyone *here* was, too. You're *all* sick like me. Not the rapid neurological degeneration seen at the monastery, but the slower bodily deterioration I'm experiencing."

Anna's eyes narrowed, studying him, weighing how much to tell—then she finally nodded. "We were partially shielded here, somewhat protected. We vented the worst of the Bell's radiation upward and out."

Painter remembered the ghost lights seen dancing in

the mountaintops. To spare themselves, the Germans had blasted the immediate area with radiation, including the neighboring monastery. But the scientists here had failed to escape totally unscathed.

Anna met his gaze, unflinching, unapologetic. "We're now all under the same death sentence."

Painter considered his options. He had none. Though neither side trusted the other, they were all in the same boat, so they might as well get closer. Gripping her hand, he shook it, sealing the pact.

Sigma and the Nazis together.

SECOND

7

BLACK MAMBA

5:45 A.M.
HLUHLUWE-UMFOLOZI PRESERVE
ZULULAND, SOUTH AFRICA

Khamisi Taylor stood in front of the head warden's desk. Stiff-backed, he waited while Warden Gerald Kellogg finished reading his preliminary report on the past day's tragedy.

The only sound was the creak of an overhead fan, slowly churning.

Khamisi wore a borrowed set of clothes, the pants too long, the shirt too tight. But they were dry. After spending all day and night in the tepid water hole, shoulder deep in the muddy pan, arms aching while he held the rifle at the ready, he appreciated the warm clothes and solid footing.

He also appreciated the daylight. Through the back office window, dawn painted the sky a dusty rose. The world reappeared out of the shadows.

He had survived. He was alive.

But he had yet to fully accept that.

In his skull, the calls of the *ukufa* still echoed.

Closer at hand, the head warden, Gerald Kellogg, rubbed absently at his bushy auburn mustache as he continued to read. The morning sunlight gleamed off his bald pate, giving it an oily pink sheen. He finally looked up, staring over a pair of half-moon reading glasses perched on his nose.

"And is this the report you intend for me to file, Mr. Taylor?" Warden Kellogg ran a finger along one line on the yellow paper. " 'An unknown apex predator.' Is that all you can say about what killed and dragged off Dr. Fairfield?"

"Sir, I didn't get a clear look at the animal. It was something large and white-furred. As I reported."

"A lioness perhaps," Kellogg said.

"No, sir . . . it was no lion."

"How can you be sure? Didn't you just say you didn't see it?"

"Yes, sir . . . what I meant, sir . . . was that what I saw did not match any known predators of the lowveld."

"Then what was it?"

Khamisi remained silent. He knew better than to mention the *ukufa*. In the brightness of an ordinary day, whispers of monsters would only provoke derision. The superstitious tribesman.

"So some creature attacked and dragged off Dr. Fairfield, something you never saw clearly enough to identify . . ."

Khamisi nodded slowly.

" . . . yet still you ran and hid in the water hole?" Gerald Kellogg crumpled up the report. "How do you think that reflects on our service here? One of our own wardens allows a sixty-year-old woman to be killed while he ran and hid. Tucked tail without even knowing what was out there."

"Sir. That's not a fair—"

"Fair?" The warden's voice boomed, loud enough to be heard in the outer room, where the entire staff had been called in due to the emergency. "How *fair* is it that I have to contact Dr. Fairfield's next of kin and tell them their mother or grandmother was attacked and eaten while one of my wardens—one of my *armed* wardens—ran and hid?"

"There was nothing I could do."

"Except save your own . . . skin."

Khamisi heard the unspoken word purposefully left out.

Save your *black* skin.

Gerald Kellogg had not been thrilled to hire Khamisi. The warden's family had ties to the old Afrikaner government, and he had risen through the ranks because of his connections and ties. He still belonged to the Oldavi country club, exclusively white, where even after the fall of apartheid much economic power was still brokered. Though new laws had been passed, barriers broken in government, unions formed, business was still business in South Africa. The De Beerses still owned their diamond mines. The Waalenbergs still owned most everything else.

Change would be slow.

Khamisi's position was a small step, one he meant to keep open for the next generation. So he kept his voice calm. "I'm sure once investigators canvass the site, they'll support my course of action."

"Will they, now, Mr. Taylor? I sent a dozen men out there, an hour after the search-and-rescue helicopter found you after midnight wallowing in the muddy water. They reported in fifteen minutes ago. They found the rhino carcass, almost stripped by jackals and hyenas. No sign of the calf that you reported. And more importantly, no sign of Dr. Fairfield."

Khamisi shook his head, searching for a way past these accusations. He flashed back to his long vigil in the water hole. The day seemed never ending, but the night had been worse. With the loss of the sun, Khamisi had waited to be attacked. Instead, he had heard the yip-yip-yip of hyenas and the bark of jackals descend into the valley, accompanied by the furious growls and cries of scuffling scavengers.

The presence of the scavengers had made Khamisi almost believe it was safe to attempt a run for the Jeep. If the usual jackals and hyenas had returned, then perhaps the *ukufa* had left.

Still, he hadn't moved.

Fresh in his mind had been the ambush that had waylaid Dr. Fairfield.

"Surely there were other tracks," he said.

"There were."

Khamisi brightened. If he had proof . . .

"They were lion tracks," Warden Kellogg said. "Two adult females. Just like I said earlier."

"Lions?"

"Yes. I believe we have a few pictures of these strange creatures around here somewhere. Maybe you'd better study them so you can identify them in the future. What with all the free time you'll have."

"Sir?"

"You're suspended, Mr. Taylor."

Khamisi could not keep the shock from his face. He knew if it had been any other warden . . . any other *white* warden . . . that there would be more leniency, more trust. But not when he was wearing a tribesman's skin. He knew better than to argue. It would only make matters worse.

"Without pay, Mr. Taylor. Until a full inquiry is completed."

A full inquiry. Khamisi knew how that would end.

"And I've been told by the local constabulary to inform you that you are not to leave the immediate area. There is also the matter of criminal negligence to rule out."

Khamisi closed his eyes.

Despite the rising sun, the nightmare refused to end.

Ten minutes later, Gerald Kellogg still sat at his desk, his office now empty. He ran a sweating palm over the top of his head, like shining an apple. The sour set to his lips refused to relax. The night had been interminable, so many fires to put out. And there were still a thousand details to attend to: dealing with the media, attending to the biologist's family, including Dr. Fairfield's partner.

Kellogg shook his head at this last problem. Dr. Paula Kane would prove the biggest thorn in the coming day. He knew the term "partnership" between the two older women went beyond research. It was Dr. Paula Kane who had pressed for the search-and-rescue helicopter last night after Dr. Fairfield hadn't returned home from the day trip into the bush.

Woken in the middle of the night, Gerald had urged caution. It was not uncommon for researchers to bivouac overnight. What got him out of bed was when he learned *where* Dr. Fairfield had been headed with one of his wardens. To the park's northwestern border. Not far from the Waalenbergs' private estate and preserve.

A search near there required his immediate supervision.

It had been a hectic night, necessitating fast footwork and coordination, but everything was almost over, the genie returned to its proverbial bottle.

Except for one last item to attend to.

There was no reason to put it off any longer.

He picked up the phone and dialed the private number. He waited for the line to pick up, tapping a pen on a notepad.

"Report," came a terse response as the connection was made.

"I just finished my interview with him."

"And?"

"He saw nothing . . . nothing clearly."

"What does that mean?"

"Claims to have caught glimpses. Nothing he could identify."

A long stretch of silence followed.

Gerald grew nervous. "His report will be edited. Lions. That will be the conclusion. We'll shoot a few for good measure and end the matter in another day or so. The man, meanwhile, has been suspended."

"Very good. You know what you must do."

Kellogg argued against it. "He's been suspended. He won't dare rock the boat. I've scared him good. I don't think—"

"Exactly. Don't think. You have your orders. Make it look like an accident."

The line clicked off.

Kellogg settled the phone receiver in its cradle. The room stifled despite the chug of the air-conditioning and the slowly turning fan. Nothing could truly withstand the blistering savanna heat as the day warmed up.

But it wasn't the temperature that rolled a bead of sweat down his forehead.

You have your orders.

And he knew well enough not to disobey.

He glanced down to the notepad on his desk. He had absently doodled as he spoke on the phone, a reflection of how uneasy the man on the other end of the line made him feel.

Gerald hurriedly scribbled over it, tore the sheet off, and ripped the page into tiny strips. No evidence. Ever. That was the rule. And he had his orders.

Make it look like an accident.

4:50 A.M.
37,000 FEET ABOVE GERMANY

"We'll be landing in another hour," Monk said. "Maybe you should try taking another nap."

Gray stretched. The low hum of the Challenger 600 jet had lulled him, but his mind still ticked through the past day's events, trying to piece the puzzle together. He had the Darwin Bible open in front of him.

"How's Fiona?" he asked.

Monk nodded back to the sofa near the rear of the plane. Fiona was sprawled out under a blanket. "Crashed finally. Knocked her down with some pain meds. Kid doesn't shut up."

She had been talking nonstop since the pair arrived at the Copenhagen airport. Gray had alerted Monk by telephone, and he had arranged a private car to whisk them safely to the waiting jet, already refueling. Logan smoothed out all diplomatic and visa issues.

Still, Gray had not breathed easily until the Challenger was wheels up and into the air.

"Her bullet wound?"

Monk shrugged and collapsed into a neighboring chair. "Scratch really. Okay, a really deep nasty scratch. Will hurt like hell the next few days. But some antiseptic, liquid skin sealant, and a bandage wrap, and she'll be right as rain in a couple more days. Ready to rip more people off."

Monk patted his jacket, making sure his wallet was still there.

"She only stole it as a way to say hello," Gray said. He hid a tired smile. Grette Neal had explained the same to him yesterday. God, was it only yesterday?

While Monk had ministered to Fiona, Gray had reported to Logan. The temporary director was not happy to hear about his escapades following the auction . . . an auction

Gray had been forbidden to attend. Still, the damage was done. Luckily he still had the flash drive containing all the participants' pictures, including the ice-blond pair. He had forwarded it all to Logan, along with faxed copies of some of the pages from the Bible and his notes. He had even sent his drawing of the cloverleaf tattoo he had spotted on the night's assailants. Some unknown blond assassin squad.

Logan and Kat would work at their end to ascertain who was behind all this. Logan had already made inquiries with the Copenhagen authorities. They reported no deaths at the park. It seemed the body of the assassin they had clotheslined had disappeared. So the aftermath of their flight from Tivoli Gardens proved no worse than bruises and scrapes among the jostled visitors. No serious injuries . . . except to a parade float.

He watched Monk check the pocket of his jeans.

"Ring still there?" Gray asked, needling his friend.

"She didn't have to steal that, too."

Gray had to give Fiona credit. Fast fingers.

"So you going to tell me about that ring box?" Gray asked, closing the Darwin Bible.

"I wanted to surprise you with it . . ."

"Monk, I didn't know you cared that much."

"Oh, shut up. I meant I wanted to tell you about it in my own time, not . . . not because Ms. Copperfield over there pulled it out of a hat."

Gray leaned back, facing Monk, arms crossed. "So you're going to pop the question. I don't know . . . Mrs. *Kat* Kokkalis. She'll never go for it."

"I didn't think so either. I bought the damn thing two months ago. Haven't found the moment to ask her."

"More like, you hadn't found the *courage*."

"Well, maybe that, too."

Gray reached over and patted Monk on the knee. "She loves you, Monk. Quit worrying."

Monk grinned like a schoolboy at him. Not a good look for him. Still, Gray recognized the depth of feeling in his eyes. Along with a shimmer of genuine fear. Monk rubbed at the joint where his prosthetic hand met the stump of his wrist. Despite his bravado, the man had been shaken by last year's mutilation. Kat's attention had gone a long way toward healing him, more than any of the doctors. Still, a deep vein of insecurity remained.

Monk opened the small black velvet box and stared at the three-carat engagement ring. "Maybe I should have gotten a bigger diamond . . . especially now."

"What do you mean?"

Monk glanced over at him. The new expression shone from his face . . . a trembling hope was the best way to describe it. "Kat's pregnant."

Gray sat up, surprised. "What? How?"

"I think you know *how*," Monk said.

"Christ . . . congratulations," he blurted out, still recovering. The last came out somewhat as a question. "I mean . . . you are keeping the baby."

Monk raised one eyebrow.

"Of course," Gray said, shaking his head at his stupidity.

"It's still early," Monk said. "Kat doesn't want anyone to know . . . she said it was okay to tell you."

Gray nodded, taking time to assimilate the news. He tried to picture Monk as a father and was surprised how easy that was to imagine.

"My God, that's just great."

Monk snapped the ring box closed. "So what about you?"

Gray frowned. "What about me?"

"You and Rachel. What did she say when you called her about your escapades in Tivoli Gardens?"

Gray's brow crinkled.

Monk's eyes widened. "Gray . . ."

"What?"

"You didn't call her, did you?"

"I didn't think—"

"She's with the carabinieri. So you know she heard about any possible terrorist attack in Copenhagen. Especially some nut job yelling 'Bomb!' in a crowded park and joyriding in a parade float. She has to know *you* were involved."

Monk was right. He should have called her right away.

"Grayson Pierce, what am I going to do with you?" Monk shook his head sadly. "When are you going to cut that girl free?"

"What are you talking about?"

"C'mon. I'm happy you and Rachel have hit it off, but where's it really going?"

Gray bristled. "Not that it's any of your business, but that's what we were planning on discussing here, before all hell broke loose."

"Lucky break for you."

"You know, just because you have a two-month-old engagement ring in your pocket does not make you a relationship expert."

Monk held up both palms. "All right . . . backing off . . . I was just saying . . ."

Gray was not letting him off the hook that easily. "What?"

"You don't really want a relationship."

He blinked at the frontal assault. "What are you talking about? Rachel and I have been bending over backward to make this work. I love Rachel. You know that."

"I know you do. I never said otherwise. You just don't want a *real* relationship with her." Monk ticked off three items on his fingers. "That means *wife,* a *mortgage,* and *kids.*"

Gray just shook his head.

"All you're doing with Rachel is enjoying a prolonged first date."

Gray sought some retort, but Monk was hitting too close to home. He remembered how it took overcoming a certain awkwardness each time he and Rachel met, a buffer that had to be crossed before a deeper intimacy could be re-established. Like a first date.

"How long have I known you?" Monk asked.

Gray waved the question away.

"And during that time how many serious girlfriends have you had?" Monk formed his fist into a big zero. "And look who you pick for your first serious relationship."

"Rachel's wonderful."

"She is. And I think it's great that you're finally open-ing up more. But man, talk about setting up impossible barriers."

"What barriers?"

"How about the goddamn Atlantic for one. Standing between you and a full relationship." Monk waggled three fingers at him.

Wife, mortgage, kids.

"You're not ready," Monk said. "I mean, I mention Kat's pregnant and you should've seen your face. Scared the crap out of you. And it's *my* kid."

Gray's heart beat heavily in his throat. He found himself breathing harder. Punched in the gut.

Monk sighed. "You have issues, my man. Maybe some-thing you need to work through with your pops. I don't know."

Gray was saved from responding by a chime over the jet's intercom.

The pilot reported, "We're approximately thirty minutes out. We'll be beginning our descent soon."

Gray glanced out the window. The sun rose to the east.

"Maybe I'll try to catch a little downtime," Gray muttered to the window. "Until we land."

"Sounds good."

Gray turned to Monk. He opened his mouth to respond in some way to Monk's words, but he resorted to the truth instead. "I do love Rachel."

Monk reclined his seat and rolled over to his side with a grunt. "I know. That's what makes it so hard."

7:05 A.M.
HLUHLUWE-UMFOLOZI PRESERVE

Khamisi Taylor sipped the tea in the small parlor. Though it was steeped well and sweetened with honey, he tasted none of it.

"And there's no chance Marcia could be alive?" Paula Kane asked.

Khamisi shook his head. He did not shrink from the reality. That was not why he had come here after his dressing-down by the head warden. He had wanted to retreat to his one-bedroom home at the edge of the preserve, where a row of squat houses were leased to the wardens on duty. Khamisi wondered how long he would be able to remain at the house if his suspension turned into a full dismissal.

Still, he had not returned directly home. Instead he had driven halfway across the park to another settlement of transient housing, a small enclave where park researchers resided for as long as their grant money lasted.

Khamisi had been to this particular whitewashed two-story Colonial home many times, with its giant shady acacia trees, tiny garden, and small courtyard where a smattering of chickens roamed. The two residents here never seemed to run out of grants. In fact, the last time Khamisi had been here was to celebrate the women's tenth anniversary here at the park. Among the scientific community, they had become as much of a fixture at Hluhluwe-Umfolozi as the big five trophy animals.

But now they were one.

Dr. Paula Kane sat on a tiny divan across the low table from Khamisi. Tears filled her eyes, but her cheeks remained dry.

"It's all right," she said. Her eyes wandered to a wall of photos, a panorama of a happy life. He knew the pair had been together since graduate school at Oxford so many years ago. "I hadn't held out much hope."

She was a small woman, slight of figure, with salt-and-pepper dark hair, cut square to her shoulder. Though he knew she was somewhere in her late fifties, she appeared a decade younger. She had always retained a certain hard beauty, exuding a confidence that surpassed any camouflaging makeup. But this morning, she appeared faded, a ghost of herself, something vital gone. It looked like she'd slept in her khaki pants and loose white blouse.

Khamisi had no words to ease the pain etched in every line of her body, only his sympathy. "I'm sorry."

Paula's eyes returned to him. "I know you did everything you could. I've heard the rumblings out there. A white woman dies, but a black man lives. It will not sit well with certain types out here."

Khamisi knew she was referring to the head warden. Paula and Marcia had butted heads with the man many times. She knew the warden's ties and memberships as well as any other. While apartheid might have been crushed in the cities and townships, out in the bush, the myth of the Great White Hunter still reigned supreme.

"Her death was not your fault," Paula said, reading something in his face.

He turned away. He appreciated her understanding, but at the same time, the warden's accusations had stoked his own guilt. Rationally, he knew he had done all he could to protect Dr. Fairfield. But he had come out of the bush. She had not. Those were the facts.

Khamisi stood. He didn't want to intrude any longer. He had come to pay his respects and to tell Dr. Kane in person what had transpired. He had done that.

"I should be going," he said.

Paula stood and accompanied him to the screen door. She stopped him with a touch before he left. "What do you think it was?" she asked.

He turned to her.

"What killed her?" Paula asked.

Khamisi stared out at the morning sunlight, too bright to speak of monsters. He had also been forbidden to discuss it. His job was on the line.

He glanced down to Paula and told her the truth.

"It was no lion."

"Then what—?"

"I'm going to find out."

He pushed through the screen door and climbed down the steps. His small rusted pickup sat baking in the sun. He crossed to it, climbed into its stifling interior, and headed back home.

For the hundredth time that morning, the prior day's terror unfolded. He barely heard the rumble of his engine over the echo of the *ukufa*'s hunting screams. Not a lion. He would never believe that.

He reached the line of stilted houses, makeshift and without air-conditioning. The homes comprised staff housing here at the park. He braked with a cloud of red dust beside his front yard gate.

Exhausted, he would rest for a few hours.

Then he would seek the truth.

He already knew *where* he wanted to begin his investigation.

But that would have to wait.

As he approached his front yard fence, Khamisi noted that the gate hung ajar. He always made sure he latched it before leaving for the day. Then again, when the disappearances had been reported last night, someone might have come here to check if he was at home.

Still, the edge to Khamisi's senses had never dulled . . . not since the moment he heard that first cry in the jungle. In fact, he doubted his senses would ever relax.

He slipped through the gate. He noted his front door seemed secure. He spotted mail sprouting from his mailbox, untouched. He mounted the steps, one at a time.

He climbed, wishing he had at least a sidearm.

Floorboards creaked. The sound had come not from under his own feet—but from inside his house.

All of Khamisi's senses urged him to run.

Not again. Not this time.

He reached the porch, stood to the side, and tested the door latch.

Unlocked.

He unhitched the latch and pushed the door open. Near the back of the house, another floorboard rubbed.

"Who's there?" he called out.

8:52 A.M.
HIMALAYAS

"Come see this."

Painter startled awake, instantly alert. A dagger of a headache stabbed between his eyes. He rolled off the bed, fully clothed. He had not realized he had fallen asleep. He and Lisa had returned to their room a couple of hours ago, under guard. Anna had needed to attend to matters and arrange for some items Painter had requested.

"How long have I been out?" he asked, the headache slowly fading.

"Sorry. I didn't know you were asleep." Lisa sat cross-legged by the table before the fireplace. She had sheets of paper scattered on the top. "Couldn't have been more than fifteen . . . twenty minutes. I wanted you to see this."

Painter stood. The room bobbled for a breath, then settled back into place. Not good. He crossed over to Lisa and sank beside her.

He noted her camera resting on some of the papers. Lisa had requested the Nikon be returned as the first act of cooperation from their captors.

She slid a sheet of paper over to him. "Look."

Lisa had drawn a line of symbols across the paper. Painter recognized them as the runes that Lama Khemsar had scrawled on his wall. She must have copied it from the digital photo. Painter saw that each symbol had a corresponding letter under it.

ᛉᚷᛖᛈ I ᛚᛐᛗᚲᚲᚷᚲᛗ

S C H W A R Z E S O N N E

"It was a simple replacement code. Each rune representing a letter of the alphabet. Took some trial and error."

"Schwarze Sonne," he read aloud.

"Black Sun. The name of the project here."

"So Lama Khemsar knew about all this." Painter shook his head. "The old Buddhist did have ties here."

"And plainly it traumatized him." Lisa took the paper from him. "The madness must have awakened old wounds. Brought them back to life."

"Or maybe the lama was cooperating all along, maintaining the monastery as some guard post of the castle here."

"If so, look what that cooperation gained him," Lisa said pointedly. "Is that an example of the reward we'll get for our cooperation?"

"We have no choice. It's the only way to stay alive. To stay necessary."

"And after that? When we're no longer *necessary*?"

Painter offered no delusions. "They'll kill us. Our cooperation is only buying us some time."

Painter noted she didn't flinch from the truth but seemed to take strength from it. A resolve stiffened her shoulders.

"So what do we do first?" she asked.

"Acknowledge the first step in any conflict."

"And that is?"

"Know thy enemy."

"I think I know *too* much about Anna and her crew as it is."

"No. I meant discovering who was behind the bombing here. The saboteur . . . and whoever employed him. Something larger is going on here. Those first few acts of sabotage—messing with the safety controls of the Bell, the first illnesses—they were meant to draw us. Raise some smoke. Lure us here with the rumors of strange illnesses."

"But why would they do that?"

"To make sure Anna's group was discovered and shut down. Don't you find it strange that the Bell, the heart of the technology, was only destroyed after we arrived here? What might that suggest?"

"While they wanted Anna's project shut down, they also didn't want the heart of the technology falling into anyone else's hands."

Painter nodded. "And maybe something even more dire. All this might be misdirection. A bit of sleight of hand. Look over here, while the real trick is pulled off out of sight. But who is the mysterious magician in the wings? What is his purpose, his intent? That's what we must find out."

"And the electronic equipment you requisitioned from Anna?"

"Perhaps a way to help us sniff out the mole here. If we can trap this saboteur, we might have some of our answers, find out who is really pulling all the strings out here."

A knock on the door startled them both.

Painter stood up as the bar was removed and the door swung open.

Anna strode in with Gunther at her side. The guard had cleaned up since the last time Painter had seen him. It was a sign of the man's menace that no other guards followed them inside. He did not even have a gun.

"I thought you might like to join us for breakfast," Anna said. "By the time we're finished, the equipment you requested should be here."

"All of it? How? From where?"

"Kathmandu. We have a sheltered helipad on the other side of the mountain."

"Really? And you've never been discovered?"

Anna shrugged. "It's simply a matter of folding our flights in with the dozens of daily sightseeing tours and mountaineering teams. The pilot should be back within the hour."

Painter nodded. He planned on putting that hour to the best of uses.

Gathering intel.

Every problem had its solution. At least he hoped so.

They set out from their room. The hallways beyond were unusually crowded. Word had spread. Everyone seemed busy or angry or casting hard glances at them . . . as if Painter and Lisa were somehow to blame for the sabotage here. But no one approached too closely. Gunther's heavy tread cleared a path. Their captor had become their protector.

They finally reached Anna's study.

A long table had been set up before the fire, heaping

platters upon it. Sausages, dark breads, steaming stews, porridges, aged cheeses, an assortment of blackberries, plums, and melons.

"Is there an army coming to join us?" Painter asked.

"Constant fuel is most important in cold climates, both for the home and the heart," Anna said, ever the good German.

They took their seats. Food was passed. Just one big happy family.

"If there's any hope for a cure," Lisa said, "we'll have to know more about this Bell of yours. Its history . . . how it works . . ."

Anna, sullen after the walk, brightened. What researcher didn't enjoy discussing their discoveries?

"It started out as an experiment as an energy generator," she began. "A new engine. The Bell got its name from its bell-shaped outer containment jar, a ceramic vessel the size of a hundred-gallon drum, lined by lead. Inside were two metal cylinders, one inside the other, that would be spun in opposite directions."

Anna pantomimed with her hands.

"Lubricating it all and filling the Bell was a mercurylike liquid metal. What was called Xerum 525."

Painter recalled the name. "That's the substance you said you couldn't duplicate."

Anna nodded. "We've tried for decades, trying to reverse engineer the liquid metal. Aspects of its composition defy testing. We know it contains thorium and beryllium peroxides, but that's about it. All we know for sure is that Xerum 525 was a by-product of Nazi research into zero point energy. It was produced at another lab, one destroyed just after the war."

"And you've not found a way to manufacture more?" Painter asked.

Anna shook her head.

"But what did the Bell actually do?" Lisa asked.

"As I said before, it was purely an experiment. Most likely another attempt to tap into the infinite power of zero point. Though once the Nazi researchers turned it on, strange effects were noted. The Bell emitted a pale glow. Electrical equipment in a huge radius short-circuited. Deaths were reported. During a series of follow-up experiments, they refined the device and built shielding. Experiments were done deep within an abandoned mine. No further deaths occurred, but villagers a kilometer away from the mine reported insomnia, vertigo, and muscle spasms. Something was being radiated by the Bell. Interest grew."

"As a potential weapon?" Painter guessed.

"I can't say. Many of the records were destroyed by the head researcher. But we do know the original team exposed all sorts of biologics to the Bell: ferns, molds, eggs, meat, milk. And an entire spectrum of animal life. Invertebrates and vertebrates. Cockroaches, snails, chameleons, toads, and of course mice and rats."

"And what about the top of the food chain?" Painter asked. "Humans."

Anna nodded. "I'm afraid so. Morality is often the first casualty to progress."

"So what happened during these experiments?" Lisa asked. She had lost all interest in her plate of food. Not in distaste for the subject matter but wide-eyed interest.

Anna seemed to sense a commonality here and turned her attention to Lisa. "Again the effects were inexplicable. The chlorophyll in plants disappeared, turning the plants white. Within hours they would decompose into a greasy sludge. In animals, blood would gel in veins. A crystalline substance would form within tissues, destroying cells from the inside out."

"Let me guess," Painter said. "Only the cockroaches were unaffected."

Lisa frowned at him, then returned to Anna. "Do you have any idea what caused those effects?"

"We can only conjecture. Even now. We believe the Bell, as it spins, creates a strong electromagnetic vortex. The presence of Xerum 525, a by-product of earlier zero point research, when exposed to this vortex, generates an aura of strange quantum energies."

Painter put it together in his head. "So the Xerum 525 is the *fuel* source, and the Bell is the *engine*."

Anna nodded.

"Turning the Bell into a Mixmaster," a new voice grumbled.

All eyes turned to Gunther. He had a mouthful of sausage. It was the first time he had shown any interest in the conversation.

"A crude but accurate description," Anna concurred. "Imagine the nature of zero point as a bowl of cake batter. The spinning Bell is like a beater that dips into it and sucks quantum energy outward, into our existence, splattering with all manner of strange subatomic particles. The earliest experiments were attempts to manipulate the speed of this mixer and so control the splatter."

"To make less of a mess."

"And along with it, to lessen the degenerative side effects. And they succeeded. Adverse effects waned, and something remarkable took their place."

Painter knew they were coming to the heart of the matter.

Anna leaned forward. "Rather than *degeneration* of biologic tissues, the Nazi scientists began noting *enhancements*. Accelerated growth in molds. Gigantism in ferns. Faster reflexes in mice, and higher intelligence in rats. The consistency of the results could not be attributed to random mutations alone. And it appeared that the higher the order of animal, the more benefit was derived from exposure."

"So human test subjects went next," Painter said.

"Keep a historical perspective, Mr. Crowe. The Nazis were convinced that they would give rise to the next super-race. And here was a tool to do it in a generation. Morality held no benefit. There was a larger imperative."

"To create a master race. To rule the world."

"So the Nazis believed. To that end, they invested much effort in advancing research into the Bell. But before it could be completed, they ran out of time. Germany fell. The Bell was evacuated so the research could be continued in secret. It was the last great hope for the Third Reich. A chance for the Aryan race to be born anew. To arise and rule the world."

"And Himmler chose this place," Painter said. "Deep in the Himalayas. What madness." He shook his head.

"Oftentimes, it is *madness* more than *genius* that moves the world forward. Who else but the mad would reach so far, stretching for the impossible? And in so doing, prove the impossible possible."

"And sometimes it merely invents the most efficient means of genocide."

Anna sighed.

Lisa brought the discussion back in line. "What became of the human studies?" She kept her tone clinical.

Anna recognized a more collegial dining partner. "In adults, the effects were still detrimental. Especially at higher settings. But the research did not stop there. When a *fetus* was exposed in utero, one in six children born of such exposure showed remarkable improvements. Alterations in the gene for myostatin produced children with more well-developed muscles. Other enhancements arose, too. Keener eyesight, improved hand-eye coordination, and amazing IQ scores."

"Superchildren," Painter said.

"But sadly such children seldom lived past the age of

two," Anna said. "Eventually they would begin to degenerate, going pale. Crystals formed in tissues. Fingers and toes necrosed and fell away."

"Interesting," Lisa said. "Sounds like the same side effects as the first series of tests."

Painter glanced at her. Did she just say *interesting*? Lisa's gaze was fixed on Anna with fascination. How could she remain so clinical? Then he noted Lisa's left knee bobbing up and down under the table. He touched her knee and calmed it. She trembled under his touch. Outwardly, her face continued to remain passive. Painter realized all of Lisa's *interest* was feigned. She was bottling up her anger and horror, allowing him to play good cop, bad cop. Her cooperative attitude allowed him to pepper their interrogation with a few harder questions, all the better to gain the answers he needed.

Painter squeezed her knee, acknowledging her effort.

Lisa continued her act. "You mentioned one out of six babies showed these short-lived improvements. What about the other five?"

Anna nodded. "Stillborn. Fatal mutations. Deaths of the mothers. Mortality was high."

"And who were all these mothers?" Painter asked, voicing the outrage for both of them. "Not volunteers, I'm assuming."

"Don't judge too harshly, Mr. Crowe. Do you know the level of infant mortality in your own country? It is worse than some third world countries. What benefit do those deaths gain?"

Oh, dear God, she can't be serious. It was a ludicrous comparison.

"The Nazis had their imperative," Anna said. "They were at least consistent."

Painter sought some words to blast her, but anger trapped his tongue.

Lisa spoke up instead. Her hand found his atop her knee and clutched tightly. "I'm assuming that these scientists sought some ways to further fine-tune the Bell, to eradicate these side effects."

"Of course. But by the end of the war, not much more progress was made. There is only one anecdotal report of a full success. A supposedly perfect child. Prior to this, all the children born under the Bell bore slight imperfections. Patches of pigment loss, organ asymmetry, different colored eyes." Anna glanced to Gunther, then back again. "But this child appeared unblemished. Even crude genetic analysis of the boy's genome tested flawless. But the technique employed to achieve this result remained unknown. The head researcher performed this last experiment in secret. When my grandfather came to evacuate the Bell, the head researcher objected and destroyed all of his personal lab notes. The child died shortly thereafter."

"From side effects?"

"No, the head researcher's daughter drowned herself and the baby."

"Why?"

Anna shook her head. "My grandfather refused to talk about it. As I said, the story was anecdotal."

"What was this researcher's name?" Painter asked.

"I don't recall. I can look it up, if you'd like."

Painter shrugged. If only he had access to Sigma's computers. He sensed there was more to her grandfather's story.

"And after the evacuation?" Lisa asked. "The research continued here?"

"Yes. Though isolated, we continued to keep a finger on the scientific community at large. After the war, Nazi scientists had spread to the winds, many into deep black projects around the world. Europe. Soviet Union. South America.

The United States. They were our ears and eyes abroad, filtering data to us. Some still believed in the cause. Others were blackmailed with their pasts."

"So you kept current."

A nod. "Over the next two decades, great leaps were made. Superchildren were born who lived longer. They were raised like princes here. Given the title *Ritter des Sonnekönig*. Knights of the Sun King. To note their births from the Black Sun project."

"How very Wagnerian," Painter scoffed.

"Perhaps. My grandfather liked tradition. But I'll have you know all experimental subjects here at *Granitschloß* were volunteers."

"But was this a moral choice? Or was it because you didn't have any Jews handy in the Himalayas?"

Anna frowned, not even dignifying his remark with a comment. She continued, "While the progress was solid, decrepitude continued to plague the *Sonnekönige*. The onset of symptoms still generally occurred at about two years, but the symptoms were milder. What was an acute degeneration became a chronic one. And with the increased longevity, a new symptom arose: mental deterioration. Acute paranoia, schizophrenia, psychosis."

Lisa spoke up. "These last symptoms . . . they sound like what happened to the monks at the monastery."

Anna nodded. "It's all a matter of degree and age of exposure. Children exposed in utero to a controlled level of the Bell's quantum radiation showed enhancements, followed by a lifelong chronic degeneration. While adults, like Painter and me, exposed to *moderate* amounts of uncontrolled radiation were struck by a more acute form of the same degeneration, a more rapid decline. But the monks, exposed to a *high* level of the radiation, progressed immediately into the mental degenerative state."

"And the *Sonnekönige*?" Painter said.

"Like us, there was no cure for their disease. In fact, while the Bell holds promise of helping us, the *Sonnekönige* are immune to the Bell. It seems their exposure so young makes them resistant to any further manipulation by the Bell—for better or worse."

"So when they went mad . . . ?" Painter pictured rampaging supermen throughout the castle.

"Such a condition threatened our security. The human tests were eventually halted."

Painter could not hide his surprise. "You abandoned the research?"

"Not exactly. Human testing was already an inefficient means of experimentation. It took too long to judge results. New models were employed. Modified strains of mice, fetal tissue grown in vitro, stem cells. With the human genome mapped, DNA testing became a faster method with which to judge progress. Our pace accelerated. I suspect if we restarted the *Sonnekönige* project, we'd see much better results today."

"So then why haven't you tried again?"

Anna shrugged. "We're still seeing dementia in our mice. That's worrisome. But mostly, we've declined human studies because our interests over the last decade have turned more clinical. We don't see ourselves as harbingers of a new master race. We are indeed no longer Nazis. We believe our work can benefit mankind as a whole, once perfected."

"So why not come out now?" Lisa asked.

"And be bound by the laws of nations and the ignorant? Science is not a democratic process. Such arbitrary restraints of morality would only slow our progress tenfold. That is not acceptable."

Painter forced himself not to snort. It seemed *some* Nazi philosophies still flourished here.

"What became of the *Sonnekönige*?" Lisa asked.

"Most tragic. While many died of degenerative conditions, many more had to be euthanized when their minds deteriorated. Still, a handful have survived. Like Klaus, who you've met."

Painter pictured the giant guardsman from earlier. He remembered the man's palsied limb and stricken face, signs of degeneration. Painter's attention drifted over to Gunther. The man met his gaze, face unreadable. One blue eye, one dead white. Another of the *Sonnekönige*.

"Gunther was the last to be born here."

Anna pointed to her shoulder and signaled to the large man.

Frown lines deepened, but Gunther reached and rolled the loose edge of his sleeve to expose his upper arm. He revealed a black tattoo.

"The symbol of the *Sonnekönige*," Anna said. "A mark of pride, duty, and accomplishment."

Gunther pulled down his sleeve, hiding it away.

Painter flashed back to the sled ride last night, to the snide comment directed at Gunther by one of the guards. What was the word again? *Leprakönig*. Leper King. Plainly there remained little respect for the former Knights of the Sun King. Gunther was the last of his kind, slowly degenerating into oblivion. Who would mourn him?

Anna's eyes lingered on Gunther before focusing back on them.

Maybe there would be one mourner.

Lisa spoke up. She still held Painter's hand. "One thing you've yet to make clear. The Bell. How is it bringing about

these changes? You said they were too consistent to be mutations generated by random chance."

Anna nodded. "Indeed. Our research has not been limited
to the *effects* of the Bell. Much of our studies have focused
on *how* it works."

"Have you made much progress?" Painter asked.

"Of course. In fact, we are certain we understand the basic
tenets of its functioning."

Painter blinked his surprise. "Really?"

Anna's brow crinkled. "I thought it was obvious." She
glanced between Painter and Lisa. "The Bell controls
evolution."

7:35 A.M.
HLUHLUWE-UMFOLOZI PRESERVE

"Who's there?" Khamisi repeated, standing at the threshold to his house. Someone lurked inside, back in the rear
bedroom.

Or maybe it was some animal.

Monkeys were always breaking into homes, sometimes
larger animals did.

Still, he refused to enter. He strained to see, but all the
curtains had been drawn. After the ride here in the blinding
sun, the gloom of his home was as dark as any jungle.

Standing on the porch, Khamisi reached through the door
for the light switch. His fingers fumbled. He found and
flicked the switch. A single lamp ignited, illuminating the
sparsely furnished front room and a galley kitchen. But the
light did nothing to show who or what waited in the back
bedroom.

He heard a scuffle of something back there.

"Who—?"

A sharp sting to the side of his neck cut off his words. Startled, he fell forward into the room. His hand slapped at the bite. His fingers found something feathered imbedded there.

He pulled it out and stared at it, uncomprehending for a breath.

A dart.

He used the same to tranquilize large animals.

But this one was different.

It fell from his fingers.

The moment of incomprehension was all it took for the toxin to reach his brain. The world tipped on its side. Khamisi fought for balance—and failed.

The plank floor rushed toward his face.

He managed to catch himself slightly, but still he struck hard, cracking his head. Pinpoints of light shattered out into a closing darkness. His head lolled. From his angle, he spotted a stretch of rope on the planks. He focused harder. *Not rope*.

Snake. Ten feet long.

He recognized it on sight.

Black mamba.

It was dead, cut in half. A machete lay nearby. *His* machete.

Coldness numbed his limbs as the hard truth struck him.

The poisoned dart.

It hadn't been like those he employed in the field. This dart had *two* needles. Like fangs.

His eyes glazed upon the dead snake.

Staged.

Death by snakebite.

From the back bedroom, floorboards creaked. He had just enough strength left to turn his head. A dark figure stood in the doorway now, illuminated by the lamplight, studying him, expressionless.

No.
It made no sense.
Why?
He would have no answer.
Darkness folded over him, taking him away.

8

MIXED BLOOD

"You're staying here," Gray said. He stood in the center of the Challenger's main cabin, fists on his hips, not budging.

"Bollocks," Fiona retorted. A step away, she made her stand.

To the side, Monk leaned against the open jet doorway, arms crossed, much too amused.

"I still haven't told you the address," Fiona argued. "You can spend the next month searching door to door throughout the city, or I can go with you and take you to the place. Your choice, mate."

Gray's face heated. Why hadn't he teased the address from the girl when she was still weak and vulnerable? He shook his head. *Weak* and *vulnerable* never described Fiona.

"So what's it going to be?"

"Looks like we have a tagalong," Monk said.

Gray refused to relent. Maybe if he scared her, reminded her of her close call in Tivoli Gardens. "What about your gunshot wound?"

Fiona's nose flared. "What about it? Good as new. That liquid bandage. Patched me right up."

"She can even swim with it," Monk said. "Waterproof."

Gray glared at his partner. "That's not the point."

"Then what is the point?" Fiona pressed.

Gray focused back at her. He didn't want to be responsible for the girl any longer. And he certainly didn't have time to be babysitting her.

"He's afraid you'll get hurt again," Monk said with a shrug.

Gray sighed. "Fiona, just tell us the address."

"Once we're in the car," she said. "Then I'll tell you. I'm not staying cooped up in here."

"Day's wasting," Monk said. "And it looks like we might get wet."

The sky was blue and morning bright, but dark clouds stacked to the north. A storm was rolling in.

"Fine." Gray waved his partner out the door. He could at least keep an eye on Fiona.

The trio climbed down the jet steps. They had already cleared customs, and a rented BMW waited for them. Monk carried a black backpack over one shoulder, Gray a matching one. He glanced over to Fiona. She had one, too. Where—?

"There was an extra one," Monk explained. "Don't worry. There're no guns or flash grenades in hers. At least, I don't think so."

Gray shook his head and continued across the tarmac toward the parking garage. Besides the backpack, they were all similarly dressed: black jeans, sneakers, sweaters. Tourist haute couture. At least Fiona had customized her clothes with a few buttons. One caught his eye. It read: STRANGERS HAVE THE BEST CANDY.

As Gray entered the parking garage, he surreptitiously checked his weapons one last time. He patted the 9mm Glock holstered under his sweater and fingered the hilt of a carbonized dagger sheathed at his left wrist. He had additional armaments in the backpack: flash grenades, packets of C4 explosive, extra clips.

He was not going anywhere unprepared this time.

They finally reached their ride. A midnight blue BMW 525i.

Fiona strode toward the driver's door.

Gray cut her off. "Funny."

Monk strode around the far side of the car and called, "Shotgun!"

Fiona ducked, searching around.

Gray steadied her and guided her toward the rear door. "He was only claiming the front seat."

Fiona scowled across the car at Monk. "Wanker."

"Sorry. Don't be so jumpy, kid."

They all climbed into the sedan. Gray started the engine and glanced back to Fiona. "Well? Where to?"

Monk already had a map pulled out.

Fiona leaned forward and reached over Monk's shoulder. She traced a finger along the map.

"Out of town. Twenty kilometers southwest. We have to go to the village of Büren in Alme Valley."

"What's the address there?"

Fiona leaned back. "Funny," she said, repeating his own word from a moment ago.

He met her gaze in the rearview mirror. She wore a disgusted look at his last lame attempt to coerce the information from her.

Couldn't blame a guy for trying.

She waved for him to head out.

With no choice, he obeyed.

On the far side of the parking garage, two figures sat in a white Mercedes roadster. The man lowered the binoculars and donned a pair of Italian sunglasses. He nodded to his twin sister beside him. She spoke into the satellite phone, whispering in Dutch.

Her other hand held his. He massaged his thumb across her tattoo.

She squeezed his fingers.

Glancing down, he noted where she had chewed one of her fingernails to a ragged nub. The imperfection was as glaring as a broken nose.

She noted his attention and tried to hide her nail, embarrassed.

There was no reason for shame. He understood the consternation and heartache that resulted in the chewed nail. They had lost Hans, one of their older brothers, last night.

Killed by the driver of the car that had just left.

Fury narrowed his vision as he watched the BMW slide out of the parking garage. The GPS transponder they'd planted would track the vehicle.

"Understood," his sister said into the phone. "As expected, they've followed the book's trail here. Undoubtedly, they will be headed to the Hirszfeld estate in Büren. We'll leave the jet under surveillance. All is prepared."

As she listened, she caught her twin brother's eye.

"Yes," she said both to the phone and her brother, "we will not fail. The Darwin Bible will be ours."

He nodded, agreeing. He slipped his hand from hers, twisted the key, and started the ignition.

"Good-bye, Grandfather," his sister said.

Lowering the phone, she reached over and shifted a single lock of his blond hair that had fallen out of place. She combed it in place with her fingers, then smoothed it out.

Perfect.

Always perfect.

He kissed the tips of her fingers as she pulled back.

Love and a promise.

They would have their revenge.

Mourning would come later.

He drifted their polar white Mercedes out of its parking place to begin the hunt.

11:08 A.M.
HIMALAYAS

The soldering gun's tip flared fiery crimson. Painter steadied the tool. His hand shook, but it was not fear that trembled his fingers. The headache continued to pound behind his right eye. He had taken a fistful of Tylenol, along with two tabs of phenobarbital, an anticonvulsant. None of the drugs would stave off the eventual debilitation and madness, but according to Anna, they would buy him more functional hours.

How long did he have?

Less than three days, maybe even shorter before he was incapacitated.

He fought to block out this concern. Worry and despair could debilitate him just as quickly as the disease. As his grandfather said in that sage Pequot Indian manner of his, *Wringin' your hands only stops you from rollin' up your sleeves.*

Taking this to heart, Painter concentrated on soldering the cable connection to an exposed ground wire. The wiring ran throughout the entire subterranean castle and out to its various antennas. Including the satellite uplink dish hidden somewhere near the top of the mountain.

Once done, Painter leaned back and waited for the new solder to cool. He sat at a bench with an array of tools and parts neatly aligned, like a surgeon. His workspace was flanked by two open laptops.

Both supplied by Gunther. The man who had slaughtered the monks. Murdered Ang Gelu. Painter still felt a well of fury whenever near the man.

Like now.

The large guard stood at his shoulder, watching his every move. They were alone in a maintenance room. Painter considered putting the soldering gun through the man's eye. But what then? They were miles from civilization, and a death sentence hung over his head. Cooperation was their only means of survival. To that end, Lisa remained with Anna in her study, continuing her own line of investigation into a cure.

Painter and Gunther pursued another angle.

Hunting down the saboteur.

According to Gunther, the bomb that had destroyed the Bell had been set by hand. And since no one had left the grounds since the explosion, the saboteur was likely still in the castle.

If they could apprehend the subject, perhaps more could be learned.

So a bit of bait had been distributed through word of mouth.

All that was left was to set the trap to go along with it.

One laptop was plugged into the castle's networked communications systems. Painter had already piggybacked into the system, using passwords supplied by Gunther. He had sent out a series of compressed code packets intended to monitor the system for all outgoing communication. If the saboteur tried to communicate to the outside world, he would be discovered, his location pinned down.

But Painter did not expect the saboteur to be so ham-fisted. He or she had survived and operated in secret for a long time. That implied cunning—and a means of communication independent of the castle's main communication network.

So Painter had built something new.

The saboteur must have obtained a private portable satellite phone, one employed in secret to communicate with his superiors. But such a phone needed a clear line-of-sight path between the unit's antenna and the geosynchronous orbiting satellite. Unfortunately there were too many niches, windows, and service hatches where the saboteur could accomplish this, too many to guard without raising suspicions.

So an alternative was needed.

Painter checked the signal amplifier he had attached to the ground wire. It was a device he had engineered himself back at Sigma. His expertise as a Sigma operative, before assuming the directorship, had been on surveillance and microengineering. This was his arena.

The amplifier linked the ground wire to the second laptop.

"Should be ready," Painter said, his headache finally waning a bit.

"Turn it on."

Painter switched on the battery power source, set the amplitude of signal, and adjusted the pulse rate. The laptop would do the rest. It would monitor for any pickups. It was crude at best, not capable of eavesdropping. It could only gain a general signal-location of an illicit transmission, accurate to within a thirty-yard radius. It should be enough.

Painter fine-tuned his equipment. "All set. Now all we have to do is wait for the bastard to call out."

Gunther nodded.

"That is if the saboteur takes the bait," Painter added.

A half hour ago, they had spread a rumor that a cache of Xerum 525 had survived the explosion, locked in a lead-lined secret vault. It gave the entire castle's populace hope. If there was some of the irreplaceable fuel, then maybe a new Bell could be fabricated. Anna even had researchers assembling another Bell out of spare parts. If not a cure for the progressive disease, the Bell offered the chance to buy more time. For all of them.

But hope was not the purpose of the ruse.

Word had to reach the saboteur. He needed to be convinced his plan had failed. That the Bell could be rebuilt after all. To seek guidance from his superiors, he would have to place a call out.

And when that happened, Painter would be ready.

In the meantime, Painter turned to Gunther. "What's it like to be a superman?" he asked. "A Knight of the Black Sun."

Gunther shrugged. The extent of his communication seemed to be grunts, frowns, and a few monosyllabic responses.

"I mean, do you feel superior? Stronger, faster, able to leap buildings in a single bound."

Gunther just stared at him.

Painter sighed, trying a new tack to get the guy talking, strike up some sort of rapport. "What does *Leprakönig* mean? I heard people using that word when you're around."

Painter damn well knew what it meant, but it got the response he needed. Gunther glanced away, but Painter noted the fire in his eyes. Silence stretched. He wasn't sure the man was going to speak.

"Leper King," Gunther finally growled.

Now it was Painter's turn to remain silent. He let the weight hang in the small room. Gunther finally folded.

"When perfection is sought, none wish to look upon failure. If the madness does not claim us, the disease is horrible to witness. Better to be shut away. Out of sight."

"Exiled. Like lepers."

Painter tried to imagine what it would be like to be raised as the *last* of the *Sonnekönige,* knowing your doomed fate at a young age. Once a revered line of princes, now a shunned and shambling line of lepers.

"Yet you still help here," Painter said. "Still serve."

"It was what I was born for. I know my duty."

Painter wondered if that had been drilled into them or somehow genetically wired. He studied the man. Somehow he knew it went beyond that. But what?

"Why do you even care what happens to us all?" Painter asked.

"I believe in the work here. What I suffer will one day help spare others from the same fate."

"And the search for the cure now? It doesn't have anything to do with prolonging your own life."

Gunther's eyes flashed. *"Ich bin nicht krank."*

"What do you mean you're not sick?"

"The *Sonnekönige* were born under the Bell," Gunther said pointedly.

Understanding struck Painter. He remembered Anna's description of the castle's supermen, how they were resistant to any further manipulation by the Bell. *For better or worse.*

"You're immune," he said.

Gunther turned away.

Painter let the implication sink in. So it wasn't self-preservation that drove Gunther to help.

Then what—?

Painter suddenly remembered the way Anna had looked across the table at Gunther earlier. With warm affection. The man had not discouraged it. Plainly he had another reason for continuing to cooperate despite the lack of respect from the others.

"You love Anna," Painter mumbled aloud.

"Of course I do," Gunther snapped back. "She's my sister."

Holed up in Anna's study, Lisa stood by the wall where a light box hung. Normally such boxes illuminated a patient's X-ray films, but presently Lisa had snugged two acetate sheets in place, striped with black lines. They were archived chromosome maps from research into the Bell's mutational effects, before shots and after shots of fetal DNA, collected by amniocentesis. The *after* shots had circles where the Bell had transformed certain chromosomes. Notations in German were written beside them.

Anna had translated them and had gone off to fetch more books.

At the light box, Lisa ran a finger down the mutational changes, searching for any pattern. She had reviewed several of the case studies. There seemed no rhyme or reason to the mutations.

With no answers, Lisa returned to the dining table, now piled high with books and bound reams of scientific data, a trail of human experimentation going back decades.

The hearth fire crackled behind her. She had to restrain an urge to chuck the research into the flames. Still, even if Anna hadn't been present, Lisa probably wouldn't have. She had come to Nepal to study physiologic effects at high altitudes. Though a medical doctor, she was a researcher at heart.

Like Anna.

No . . . not exactly like Anna.

Lisa nudged aside a research monograph resting on the table. *Teratogenesis in the Embryonic Blastoderm*. The document related to aborted monstrosities that resulted from exposure to the Bell's irradiation. What the black stripes on acetate had delineated with clinical detachment, the photographs in the book revealed with horrifying detail: limbless embryos, Cyclopean fetuses, hydrocephalic stillborn children.

No, she was definitely not Anna.

Anger built again in Lisa's chest.

Anna clattered down the iron ladder that led to the second tier of her research library, another load of books tucked under one arm. The Germans certainly were not holding

back. And why would they? It was in all their best interest
to discover a cure to the quantum disease. Anna believed it
to be a futile effort, confident that all possibilities had been
explored over the past decades, but it hadn't taken much
persuasion to get her to cooperate.

Lisa had noted how the woman's hands shook with a
barely detectable palsy. Anna kept rubbing her palms, trying to hide it. The remainder of the castle suffered more
openly. The tension in the air all morning had been pal-
pable. Lisa had witnessed a few yelling matches and one
fistfight. She had also heard of two suicides in the castle
over the past several hours. With the Bell gone and little
hope of a cure, the place was coming apart at the seams.
What if the madness set in before she and Painter could
figure out a solution?

She pushed that thought aside. She would not give up.
Whatever the reason for the current cooperation, Lisa intended to use it to her best advantage.

Lisa nodded to Anna as she approached. "Okay, I think
I have a layman's grasp on the larger picture here. But you
raised something earlier that's been nagging at me."

Dropping the books to the table, Anna settled into a seat.
"What is that?"

"You mentioned that you believed the Bell controlled
evolution." Lisa waved her hand across the breadth of
books and manuscripts on the table. "But what I see here
is just some mutagenic radiation that you've tied to a eugenics program. Building a better human being through
genetic manipulation. Were you just being grandiose
when you used the word *evolution*?"

Anna shook her head, taking no offense. "How do *you*
define evolution, Dr. Cummings?"

"The usual Darwinian way, I suppose."

"And that is?"

Lisa frowned. "A gradual process of biological change . . .

where a single-celled organism spread and diversified into the present-day range of living organisms."

"And God has no hand in this at all?"

Lisa was taken aback by her question. "Like in creationism?"

Anna shrugged, eyes fixed on her. "Or intelligent design."

"You can't be serious? Next you'll be telling me how evolution is just a theory."

"Don't be silly. I'm not a layman who associates *theory* with a 'hunch' or 'guess.' Nothing in science reaches the level of theory without a vast pool of facts and tested hypotheses behind it."

"So then you accept Darwin's theory of evolution?"

"Certainly. Without a doubt. It's supported across all disciplines of science."

"Then why were you talking about—"

"One does not necessarily rule the other out."

Lisa cocked up one eyebrow. "Intelligent design *and* evolution?"

Anna nodded. "But let's back up so I'm not misunderstood. Let's first dismiss the ravings of the Flat Earth Creationists who doubt the world is even a globe, or even the strict biblical literalists who believe the planet is at best ten thousand years old. Let's jump ahead to the main arguments of those who advocate intelligent design."

Lisa shook her head. An ex-Nazi stumping for pseudoscience. What was going on?

Anna cleared her throat. "Admittedly, I will contend that most arguments for intelligent design are fallacious. Misinterpreting the Second Law of Thermodynamics, building statistical models that don't withstand review, misrepresenting radiometric dating of rocks. The list goes on and on. None of it valid, but it does throw up lots of misleading smoke."

Lisa nodded. It was one of the main reasons she had concern for the current drive to have pseudoscience presented alongside evolution in high school biology classes. It was a multidisciplinary quagmire that your average Ph.D. would have difficulty sorting through, let alone a high school student.

Anna, though, was not done with her side of the argument. "That all said, there is one concern proposed by the intelligent design camp that bears consideration."

"And what is that?"

"The randomness of mutations. Pure chance could not produce so many beneficial mutations over time. How many birth defects do you know that have produced beneficial changes?"

Lisa had heard that argument before. *Life evolved too fast to be pure chance.* She was not falling for it.

"Evolution is not pure chance," Lisa countered. "Natural selection, or environmental pressure, weeds out detrimental changes and only allows better-suited organisms to pass on their genes."

"Survival of the fittest?"

"Or fit *enough.* Changes don't have to be perfect. Just good enough to have an advantage. And over the vast scope of hundreds of millions of years, these small advantages or changes accumulate into the variety we see today."

"Over hundreds of millions of years? Granted, that is indeed a vast gulf of time, but does it still allow enough room for the full scope of evolutionary change? And what about those occasional spurts of evolution, where vast changes occurred rapidly?"

"I presume you're referring to the Cambrian explosion?" Lisa asked. It was one of the mainstays of intelligent design. The Cambrian Period encompassed a relatively short period of time. Fifteen million years. But during that time a vast explosion of new life appeared: sponges, snails, jellyfish, and trilobites. Seemingly out of the blue. Too fast a pace for antievolutionists.

"*Nein*. The fossil record has plenty of evidence that this 'sudden appearance' of invertebrates was not so *sudden*. There were abundant Precambrian sponges and wormlike metazoans. Even the diversity of shapes during this time could be justified by the appearance in the genetic code of Hox genes."

"Hox genes?"

"A set of four to six control genes appeared in the genetic code just prior to the Cambrian Period. They proved to be control switches for embryonic development, defining up and down, right and left, top and bottom, basic bodily form. Fruit flies, frogs, humans, all have the exact same Hox genes. You can snip a Hox gene from a fly, replace it into a frog's DNA, and it functions just fine. And as these genes are the fundamental master switches for embryonic development, it only takes minuscule changes in any of them to create massively new body shapes."

Though unsure where this was all leading, the depth of the woman's knowledge on the subject surprised Lisa. It rivaled her own. If Anna were a colleague at a conference, Lisa thought she might actually enjoy the debate. In fact, she kept having to remind herself to whom she was talking.

"So the rise of Hox genes just prior to the Cambrian Period might explain that dramatic explosion of forms. But," Anna countered, "Hox genes do *not* explain other moments of rapid—almost *purposeful*—evolution."

"Like what?" The discussion was becoming more interesting by the moment.

"Like the peppered moths. Are you familiar with the story?"

Lisa nodded. Now Anna was bringing up one of the mainstays on the other side of the camp. Peppered moths lived on birches and were speckled white, to blend in with the bark and avoid being eaten by birds. But when a coal plant opened in the Manchester region and blackened the trees with soot, the white moths found themselves exposed and easy targets for the birds. But in just a few generations, the population changed its predominant color to a solid black, to camouflage against the soot-covered trees.

"If mutations were random," Anna argued, "it seems amazingly lucky *black* showed up when it did. If it was purely a random event, then where were the red moths, the green moths, the purple ones? Or even the two-headed ones?"

Lisa had to force herself not to roll her eyes. "I could say the other colored moths were eaten, too. And the two-headed ones died off. But you're misunderstanding the example. The change in color of these moths was *not* from mutation. The species already had a black gene. A few black moths were born each generation, but they were mostly eaten, maintaining the general population as white. But once the trees blackened, then the few black moths had an advantage and filled the population as the white moths were consumed. That was the point of the example. Environments *can* influence a population. But it wasn't a mutational event. The black gene was already present."

Anna was smiling at her.

Lisa realized the woman had been testing her knowledge. She sat straighter, both angry and conversely more intrigued.

"Very good," Anna said. "Then let me bring up a more recent event. One that occurred in a controlled laboratory setting. A researcher produced a strain of E. coli bacteria that could not digest lactose. Then he spread a thriving population onto a growth plate where the only food source was lactose. What would science say should happen?"

Lisa shrugged. "Unable to digest the lactose, the bacteria would starve and die."

"And that's exactly what happened to ninety-eight percent

of the bacteria. But *two* percent continued to thrive just fine. They had spontaneously mutated a gene to digest lactose. In one generation. I find that astonishing, *ja*? That goes against all probability of randomness. Of all the genes in an E. coli's DNA and the rarity of mutation, why did two percent of the population all mutate the one gene necessary to survive? It *defies* randomness."

Lisa had to contend that it was strange. "Maybe there was laboratory contamination."

"The experiment has been repeated. With similar results."

Lisa remained unconvinced.

"I see the doubt in your eyes. So let's look elsewhere for another example of the impossibility of randomness in gene mutation."

"Where's that?"

"Back to the beginning of life. Back to the primordial soup. Where the engine of evolution first switched on."

Lisa recalled Anna making some mention before about the story of the Bell stretching back to the origin of life. Was this where Anna was leading now? Lisa pricked her ears a bit more, ready to hear where this might lead.

"Let's turn the clock back," Anna said. "Back before the first cell. Remember Darwin's tenet: what exists had to arise from a simpler, less complex form. So before the single cell, what was there? How far can we reduce life and still call it life? Is DNA alive? Is a chromosome? How about a protein or an enzyme? Where is the line between chemistry and life?"

"Okay, that *is* an intriguing question," Lisa conceded.

"Then I'll ask another. How did life make the leap from a chemical primordial soup to the first cell?"

Lisa knew that answer. "Earth's early atmosphere was full of hydrogen, methane, and water. Add a few jolts of energy, say from a lightning strike, and these gases can form simple organic compounds. These then cooked up in the proverbial primordial soup and eventually formed a molecule that could replicate."

"Which was proven in the lab," Anna agreed, nodding. "A bottle full of primordial gases produced a slurry of amino acids, the building blocks of proteins."

"And life started."

"Ah, you are so eager to jump ahead," Anna teased. "We've only formed *amino acids*. Building blocks. How do we go from a few amino acids to that first fully replicating protein?"

"Mix enough amino acids together and eventually they'll chain up into the right combination."

"By random chance?"

A nod.

"That's where we come to the root of the problem, Dr. Cummings. I might concede with you that Darwin's evolution played a significant role *after* the first self-replicating protein formed. But do you know how many amino acids must link up in order to form this first replicating protein?"

"No."

"A minimum of thirty-two amino acids. That's the smallest protein that holds the capacity to replicate. The odds of this protein forming by random chance are astronomically thin. Ten to the power of forty-one."

Lisa shrugged at this number. Despite her feelings for the woman, a grudging respect began to grow.

"Let's put these odds in perspective," Anna said. "If you took *all* the protein found in *all* the rain forests of the world and dissolved it *all* down into an amino acid soup, it would still remain vastly improbable for a thirty-two-amino-acid chain to form. In fact, it would take *five thousand times* that amount to form one of these chains. Five thousand rain forests. So again, how do we go from a slurry of amino acids to that first replicator, the first bit of life?"

Lisa shook her head.

Anna crossed her arms, satisfied. "That's an evolutionary gap even Darwin has a hard time leaping."

"Still," Lisa countered, refusing to concede, "to fill this gap with the Hand of God is not science. Because we don't have an answer yet to fill this gap, it doesn't mean it has a supernatural cause."

"I'm not saying it's supernatural. And who says I don't have an answer to fill this gap?"

Lisa gaped at her. "What answer?"

"Something we discovered decades ago through our study of the Bell. Something that today's researchers are only beginning to explore in earnest."

"What's that?" Lisa found herself sitting straighter, forgoing any attempt to hide her interest in anything associated with the Bell.

"We call it *quantum* evolution."

Lisa recalled the history of the Bell and the Nazi research into the strange and fuzzy world of subatomic particles and quantum physics. "What does any of this have to do with evolution?"

"Not only does this new field of quantum evolution offer the strongest support for intelligent design," Anna said, "but it also answers the fundamental question of who the *designer* is."

"You're kidding. Who? God?"

"*Nein.*" Anna stared her in the eye. "Us."

Before Anna could explain further, an old radio wired to the wall sputtered with static and a familiar voice rasped through. It was Gunther.

"We have a trace on the saboteur. We're ready to move."

7:37 A.M.
BÜREN, GERMANY

Gray steered the BMW around an old farm truck, its bed piled high with hay. He slipped into fifth gear and raced through the last hairpin turn. Cresting the hill, he had a panoramic view of the valley ahead.

"Alme Valley," Monk said beside him. He clutched tight to a handhold above the door.

Gray slowed, downshifting.

Monk glared at him. "I see Rachel has been giving you Italian driving lessons."

"When in Rome . . ."

"We're not in Rome."

Plainly they were not. As they crested the ridge, a wide river valley stretched ahead, a green swath of meadows, forests, and tilled fields. Across the valley, a picture-postcard German hamlet huddled in the lowlands, a township of peaked red-tile roofs and stone houses set amid narrow, twisted streets.

But all eyes fixed upon the massive castle perched on the far ridge, nestled in the forest, overlooking the town. Towers jutted high, topped by fluttering flags. While hulking and massive, like many of the fortified structures along the larger Rhine River, the castle also had a fairy-tale quality to it, a place of enchanted princesses and knights on white stallions.

"If Dracula had been gay," Monk said, "that would so be his castle."

Gray knew what he meant. There was something vaguely sinister about the place, but it might just be the lowering sky to the north. They'd be lucky to reach the lowland village before the storm struck.

"Where to now?" Gray asked.

A crumpling sound rose from the backseat as Fiona

checked the map. She had confiscated it from Monk and assumed the role of navigator, since she still withheld their destination.

She leaned forward and pointed to the river. "You have to cross that bridge."

"Are you sure?"

"Yes, I'm sure. I know how to read a map."

Gray headed down into the valley, avoiding a long line of bicyclists outfitted in a motley display of racing jerseys. He sped the BMW along the winding road to the valley floor and entered the outskirts of the village.

It appeared to be from another century. A German Brigadoon. Everywhere tulips filled window boxes, and each peaked roof supported high gables. Off to the sides, cobbled streets stretched out from the main thorough-fare. They passed a square lined by outdoor cafés, beer gardens, and a central bandstand, where Gray was sure a polka band played every night.

Then they were trundling across the bridge and soon found themselves back in the meadows and small farmsteads.

"Take the next left!" Fiona yelled.

Gray had to brake sharply and twist the BMW around a sharp turn. "A little warning next time."

The road grew narrower, lined by tall hedgerows. Asphalt turned to cobbles. The BMW shuddered over the uneven surface. Soon weeds were sprouting among the cobbles. Iron gates appeared ahead, spanning the narrow road, waiting open.

Gray slowed. "Where are we?"

"This is the place," Fiona said. "Where the Darwin Bible came from. The Hirszfeld estate."

Gray edged the BMW through the gates. Rain began pelting down from the darkening skies. At first lightly . . . then more forcefully.

"Just in time," Monk said.

Beyond the gates, a wide courtyard opened, framed on

two sides by the wings of a small country cottage estate. The main house, directly ahead, stood only two stories high, but its slate-tiled roof rose in steep pitches, giving the home a bit of majesty.

A shatter of lightning crackled overhead, drawing the eye.

The castle they'd noted earlier rose directly atop the wooded ridge behind the estate. It seemed to loom over the cottage.

"Oy!" a call snapped out.

Gray's attention flicked back.

A bicyclist who had been trotting his bike out of the rain had almost got himself run over. The youth, dressed in a yellow soccer jersey and biker's shorts, slapped the BMW's hood with the palm of his hand.

"Watch where you're going, mate!" He flipped Gray off.

Fiona already had the back window rolled down, head sticking out. "Sod off, you prat! Why don't you watch where you're running around in those poncey shorts of yours!"

Monk shook his head. "Looks like Fiona's got a date for later."

Gray pulled the car into a slot near the main house. There was only one other car, but Gray noted a line of mountain and racing bikes chained up in racks. A cluster of bedraggled young men and women stood under one awning, backpacks resting on the ground. He heard them speaking as he cut the engine. Spanish. The place had to be a youth hostel. Or at least it was now. He could practically smell the patchouli and hemp.

Was this the right place?

Even if it was, Gray doubted he'd find anything of value here. But they had come this far. "Wait here," he said. "Monk, stay with—"

The back door popped open, and Fiona climbed out.

"Next time," Monk said, reaching for his door, "choose the model with child locks for the back."

"C'mon." Gray headed out after her.

Backpack over her shoulder, Fiona strode toward the front door of the main house.

He caught up with her at the porch steps and grabbed her elbow. "We stick together. No running off."

She faced him, equally angry. "Exactly. We stick together. No running off. That means no leaving me in airplanes or cars." She twisted out of his grip and pulled open the door.

A chime announced their arrival.

A clerk glanced up from a mahogany reception desk just inside the door. An early morning fire glowed in the hearth, chasing away the chill. The entrance hall was box-beamed and tiled in slate. Muted murals that looked centuries old decorated the walls. But the place showed signs of disrepair: crumbling plaster, dust in the rafters, frayed and faded rugs on the floor. The place had seen better days.

The clerk nodded to them, a hale young man in a rugby shirt and green slacks. In his late teens or early twenties, he looked like some blond collegiate freshman from an Abercrombie & Fitch advertisement.

"Guten morgen," the clerk said, greeting Gray as he stepped to the counter.

Monk scanned the hall as thunder rumbled down the valley. "Nothing *guten* about this morning," he mumbled.

"Ah, Americans," the clerk said, hearing Monk's gripe. There was a slight chill to his tone.

Gray cleared his throat. "We were wondering if this is the old Hirszfeld estate?"

The clerk's eyes widened slightly. *"Ja, aber* . . . it's been the Burgschloß Hostel for going on two decades. When my father, Johann Hirszfeld, inherited the place."

So they were at the right place. He glanced at Fiona, who lifted her eyebrows at him as if asking *What?* She was busy searching through her backpack. He prayed Monk was correct: that there were no flash grenades in there.

Gray turned his attention back to the clerk. "I was wondering if I might speak to your father."

"Concerning . . . ?" The chill was back, along with a certain wariness.

Fiona bumped him aside. "Concerning this." She slapped a familiar book on the reception counter. It was the Darwin Bible.

Oh, God . . . he had left the book under guard on the jet.

Apparently not well enough.

"Fiona," Gray said in a warning tone.

"It's mine," she said out of the side of her mouth.

The clerk picked up the book and flipped through it. There was no sign of recognition. "A Bible? We don't allow proselytizing here at the hostel." He closed the book and slid it back toward Fiona. "Besides, my father is Jewish."

With the cat out of the bag, Gray proceeded more directly. "The Bible belonged to Charles Darwin. We believe it was once a part of your family's library. We were wondering if we could ask your father more about it."

The clerk eyed the Bible with less derision. "The library was sold off before my father took over this place," he said slowly. "I never did get to see it. I've heard from neighbors that it had been in the family going back centuries."

The clerk stepped around the reception desk and led the way past the hearth to an arched opening into a small neighboring hall. One wall was lined by tall thin windows, giving the room a cloistered feel. The opposite wall held a cold hearth large enough to walk into upright. The room was filled with rows of tables and benches, but it was empty, except for an older woman in a smock who swept the floor.

"This was the old family library and study. Now it's the hostel's dining hall. My father refused to sell the estate, but there were back taxes. I suppose that was why the library was sold half a century ago. My father had to auction off most of the original furnishings. Each generation, a bit of history vanishes."

"A shame," Gray said.

The clerk nodded and turned away. "Let me call my father. See if he's willing to talk to you."

A few moments later, the clerk waved to them and guided them to wide-set double doors. He unlocked the way and held the door. It led to the private section of the estate.

The clerk introduced himself as Ryan Hirszfeld as he marched them to the back of the house and out into a glass-and-bronze conservatory. Potted ferns and colorful bromeliads lined the walls. Stepped shelves climbed one windowed side, crowded with a mix of specimen plants, some looking like weeds. At the back, a lone palm tree rose, its crown brushing against the glass roof, some fronds yellowing in neglect. There was an old, overgrown feel to the place, unkempt and untended. The feeling was enhanced by the drizzle of water leaking through a cracked pane, trailing into a bucket.

The sunroom was far from sunny.

In the center of the conservatory, a frail man sat in a wheelchair, a blanket over his lap, staring out toward the back of the property. Rainwater sluiced across all the surfaces, making the world beyond appear insubstantial and unreal.

Ryan went to him, almost shyly. *"Vater. Hier sind die Leute mit der Bibel."*

"Auf Englisch, Ryan . . . *auf Englisch."* The man hauled on one wheel and the chair turned to face them. His skin looked paper thin. His voice wheezed. Suffering from emphysema, Gray guessed.

Ryan, the son, wore a pained expression. Gray wondered if he was even aware of it.

"I am Johann Hirszfeld," the old man said. "So you've come to inquire about the old library. Certainly has been a lot of interest lately. Not a word for decades. Now twice in one year."

Gray remembered Fiona's story of the mysterious elderly gentleman who had visited Grette's bookshop and searched through their files. He must have seen the bill of lading and followed the same path here.

"Ryan says you have one of the books."

"The Darwin Bible," Gray said.

The old man held out his hands. Fiona stepped forward and placed it in his palms. He settled it to his lap. "Haven't seen this since I was a boy," he wheezed. He glanced up at his son. "*Danke,* Ryan. You should see to the front desk."

Ryan nodded, stepping back reluctantly, then turned and left.

Johann waited for his son to shut the conservatory door, then sighed, his eyes returning to the Bible. He opened the front cover, checking the Darwin family tree inside. "This was one of my family's most cherished possessions. The Bible was a gift to my great-grandfather in 1901 from the British Royal Society. He had been a distinguished botanist at the turn of the century."

Gray heard the melancholy in the man's voice.

"Our family has a long tradition of scientific study and accomplishments. Nothing along the lines of Herr Darwin, but we've made a few footnotes." His eyes drifted back to the rain and watery property. "That's long over. Now I guess we'll have to be known as hoteliers."

"About the Bible," Gray said. "Can you tell me anything else about it? Was the library always kept here?"

"*Natürlich.* Some books were taken out into the field when one or another of my relatives went abroad for research. But this book only left the household once. I only know that because I was here when it was returned. Mailed back by my grandfather. Caused a stir here."

"Why's that?"

"I thought you might ask. That's why I sent Ryan out. Best he not know."

"Ask about what?"

"My grandfather Hugo worked for the Nazis. As did his daughter, my aunt Tola. The two of them were inseparable. I learned later, whispered scandalously among the relatives, that they were involved in some secret research project. Both were noted and distinguished biologists."

"What sort of research?" Monk asked.

"No one ever knew. Both my grandfather and Aunt Tola died at the end of the war. But a month before that, a crate arrived from my grandfather. It contained the part of the library he had taken with him. Maybe he knew he was doomed and wanted to preserve the books. Five books actually." The man tapped the Bible. "This was one of them. Though what he might want with the Bible as a research tool, no one could tell me."

"Maybe a piece of home," Fiona said, softly.

Johann seemed finally to see the young girl. He slowly nodded. "Maybe. Perhaps some connection to his own father. Some symbolic stamp of approval for what he was doing." The old man shook his head. "Working for the Nazis. Horrible business."

Gray remembered something Ryan had said. "Wait. But you're Jewish, aren't you?"

"Yes. But you have to understand, my great-grandmother, Hugo's mother, was German, with deep local family roots. Which included connections within the Nazi party. Even when Hitler's pogrom began, our family was spared. We were classified as *Mischlinge,* mixed blood. Enough German to avoid a death sentence. But to prove that loyalty, my grandfather and aunt found themselves recruited by the Nazis. They were gathering scientists like squirrels after nuts."

"So they were forced," Gray said.

Johann stared out into the storm. "It was complicated times. My grandfather held some strange beliefs."

"Like what?"

Johann seemed not to hear the question. He opened the Bible and flipped through the pages. Gray noted the hand-inked marks. He stepped forward and pointed to a few of the hand-drawn hash marks.

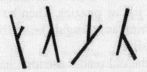

"We were wondering what those were," Gray said.

"Are you familiar with the Thule Society?" the old man asked, seeming not to hear his question.

Gray shook his head.

"They were an extreme German nationalistic group. My grandfather was a member, initiated when he was twenty-two. His mother's family had ties with the founding members. They believed deeply in the *Übermensch* philosophy."

"*Übermensch*. Supermen."

"Correct. The society was named after a mythical land of Thule, some remnant of the lost kingdom of Atlantis, a land of some superrace."

Monk made a dismissive noise.

"As I said," Johann wheezed, "my grandfather held a few strange beliefs. But he was not in the minority at the time. Especially here locally. It was in these forests that the ancient Germanic Teuton tribes held off the Roman legions, defining the boundary between Germany and the Roman Empire. The Thule Society believed that these Teutonic warriors were descendants of this lost superrace."

Gray understood the appeal of the myth. If these ancient German warriors were supermen, then their descendants—

modern Germans—still carried the genetic heritage. "It was the beginning of the Aryan philosophy."

"Their beliefs were also mixed up with much mysticism and occult trappings. I never understood it all. But according to my family, my grandfather was unusually inquisitive. Always searching up strange things, investigating historical mysteries. In his spare time, he was ever keen about sharpening his mind. Memorization tricks, jigsaw puzzles. Always with the jigsaw puzzles. Then he discovered some of the occult stories and sought the truth behind them. It became an obsession."

As he spoke, the old man's attention had returned to the Bible. He riffled through the pages. He finally reached the end and searched the inside back cover. *"Das ist merkwürdig."*

Merkwürdig. Strange.

Gray stepped closer, looking over the man's shoulder. "What?"

The old man ran a bony finger down the inside cover. He flipped to the front, then back again. "The Darwin family tree. It wasn't just written on the inside of the front . . . but also on the back. I was only a boy at the time, but I remember that clearly."

Johann held up the book. "The family tree at the back is gone."

"Let me see." Gray took the book. He examined the inside of the end cover more closely. Fiona and Monk flanked him.

He ran a finger along the binding, then examined the back cover closely.

"Look here," he said. "It looks like someone sliced free the back flyleaf page of the Bible and glued it over the inside of the back cover. *Over* the original pastedown." Gray glanced to Fiona. "Would Grette have done that?"

"Not a chance. She would rather rip apart the *Mona Lisa*."

If not Grette . . .

Gray glanced to Johann.

"I'm sure no one in my family would've done that. The library was sold only a few years after the war. After it was mailed back here, I doubt anyone touched the Bible."

That left only Hugo Hirszfeld.

"Knife," Gray said and crossed to a garden table.

Monk reached to his pack and unhooked a Swiss Army knife. He opened it and passed it to Gray. Using the tip, Gray razored the edges of the back sheet, then teased a corner up. The thick flyleaf lifted easily. Only the edges had been glued.

Johann wheeled his chair to join them. He had to push up with his arms to see over the table's edge. Gray did not hide what he was doing. He might need the man's cooperation for whatever was exposed.

He removed the flyleaf and revealed the original pasteboard of the cover. Neatly written upon it was the other half of the Darwin family tree. Johann had been correct. But that was not all that was there now.

"Horrible," Johann said. "Why would Grandfather do that? Deface the Bible so?"

Superimposed over the family tree, inked across the entire page in black, dug deep into the backboard of the Bible, was a strange symbol.

In the same ink, a single line in German had been penned below it.

Gott, verzeihen mir.

Gray translated.

God, forgive me.

Monk pointed to the symbol. "What is that?"

"A rune," Johann said, scowling and dropping back into his seat. "More of my grandfather's madness."

Gray turned to him.

Johann explained. "The Thule Society believed in rune magic. Ancient power and rites associated with the Nordic symbols. As the Nazis took to heart the Thule's philosophy of supermen, they also absorbed the mysticism about runes."

Gray was familiar with the Nazi symbology and its ties to runes, but what did it mean here?

"Do you know the significance of this particular symbol?" Gray asked.

"No. It's not a subject a German Jew would find of interest. Not after the war." Johann turned his wheelchair and stared out at the storm. Thunder rumbled, sounding far away and close at the same time. "But I know who might be able to help you. A curator at the museum up there."

Gray closed the Bible and joined Johann. "What museum?"

A crackle of lightning lit the conservatory. Johann pointed upward. Gray craned. In the fading light, veiled in rain, rose the massive castle.

"Historisches Museum des Hochstifts Paderborn," Johann said. "It is open today. Inside the castle." The old man scowled at his neighbor. "They'll certainly know what the symbol means."

"Why's that?" Gray asked.

Johann stared at him as though he were a simpleton. "Who better? That is Wewelsburg Castle." When Gray didn't respond, the old man continued with a sigh. "Himmler's Black Camelot. The stronghold of the Nazi SS."

"So it *was* Dracula's castle," Monk mumbled.

Johann continued, "Back in the seventeenth century, witch trials were held up there, thousands of women tortured and executed. Himmler only added to its blood debt. Twelve hundred Jews from the Niederhagen concentration camp died during Himmler's reconstruction of the castle. A cursed place. Should be torn down."

"But the museum there," Gray asked, directing Johann away from his growing anger. The man's wheezing had worsened. "They would know about the rune?"

A nod. "Heinrich Himmler was a member of the Thule Society, steeped in rune lore. In fact, it was how my grandfather was brought to his attention. They shared an obsession with runes."

Gray sensed a convergence of ties and events, all centered on this occult Thule Society. But what? He needed more information. A trip to the castle museum was doubly warranted.

Johann wheeled himself away from Gray, dismissing him. "It was because of such common interests with my grandfather that Himmler granted our family, a family of *Mischlinge,* the pardon. We were spared the camps."

Because of Himmler.

Gray understood the root of the man's anger . . . and why he had asked his son to leave the room. It was a family burden best left undiscovered. Johann stared out into the storm.

Gray collected the Bible and waved everyone out. *"Danke,"* he called back to the old man.

Johann did not acknowledge him, lost in the past.

Gray and the others were soon out on the front porch again. The rain continued to pour out of low skies. The courtyard was deserted. There would be no biking or hiking today.

"Let's go," Gray said and headed into the rain.

"Perfect day to storm a castle," Monk said sarcastically.

As they hurried across the courtyard, Gray noted a new car parked next to theirs. Empty. Engine steaming in the cold rain. Must have just arrived.

An ice-white Mercedes.

9

SABOTEUR

12:32 P.M.
HIMALAYAS

"Where is the signal coming from?" Anna asked.

The woman had rushed into the maintenance room, responding immediately to Gunther's call. She had arrived alone, claiming Lisa had wanted to remain behind in the library to follow up on some research. Painter thought it more likely that Anna still wanted to keep them apart.

Just as well that Lisa was out of harm's way.

Especially if they were truly on the track of the saboteur.

Leaning closer to the laptop screen, Painter massaged the tips of his fingers. A persistent tingling itched behind his nails. He stopped rubbing long enough to point at the three-dimensional schematic of the castle.

"Best estimate is this region," Painter said, tapping the screen. He had been surprised to see how extensively the castle spread into the mountain. It hollowed right through the peak. The signal came from the far side. "But it's not a pinpoint. The saboteur would need a clear line of sight to use his satellite phone."

Anna straightened. "The helipad is there."

Gunther nodded with a grunt.

On the screen, the overlay of pulsing lines suddenly collapsed. "He's ended the call," Painter said. "We'll have to move fast."

Anna turned to Gunther. "Contact Klaus. Have his men close off the helipad. Now."

Gunther swung to a phone receiver on the wall and started the lockdown. The plan had been to search everyone in the signal vicinity, discover who had an illicit sat-phone in their possession.

Anna returned to Painter. "Thank you for your help. We'll search from here."

"I may be of further help." Painter had been busy typing on the laptop. He memorized the number that appeared on the screen, then detached his hand-built signal amplifier from the castle's ground wire. He straightened. "But I'll need one of your portable satellite phones."

"I can't leave you here with a phone," Anna said, knuckling her temple and wincing. Headache.

"You don't have to leave me. I'm going with you to the helipad."

Gunther stepped forward, his usual frown deepening.

Anna waved him back. "We don't have time to argue." But something silent passed between the large man and his sister. A warning for the big man to keep an eye on Painter.

Anna led the way out.

Painter followed, still rubbing his fingers. The nails had begun to burn. He studied them for the first time, expecting the nail beds to be inflamed, but instead, his fingernails were oddly blanched, bled of color.

Frostbite?

Gunther passed him one of the castle's phones, noted Painter's attention, and shook his head. He held out a hand. Painter didn't understand—then noted the man was missing the fingernails on his last three fingers.

Gunther lowered his arm and marched after Anna.

Painter clenched and unclenched his hands. So the tingling burn wasn't frostbite. The quantum disease was advancing. He recalled Anna's list of debilitations in the Bell's test subjects: loss of fingers, ears, toes. Not unlike leprosy.

How much time?

As they headed toward the far side of the mountain, Painter studied Gunther. The man had lived his whole life with a sword hanging over his head. Chronic and progressive wasting, followed by madness. Painter was headed for the *Reader's Digest* version of the same condition. He could not deny it terrified him—not so much the debilitation as the loss of his mind.

How long did he have?

Gunther must have sensed his reverie. "I will not let this happen to Anna," he growled under his breath to Painter. "I will do anything to stop it."

Painter was again reminded that the pair were brother and sister. Only after learning this did Painter see subtle similarities of feature: curve of lip, sculpt of chin, identical frown lines. Family. But the similarities ended there. Anna's dark hair, emerald rich eyes contrasted sharply with her brother's washed-out appearance. Only Gunther had been born under the Bell, one child sacrificed, a tithing in blood, and the last of the *Sonnekönige*.

As they crossed hallways and descended stairs, Painter worked the back cover off the portable phone. He pocketed it, loosened the battery, and jury-rigged his amplifier to the antenna wire behind the battery. The broadcast would only be a single burst, seconds long, but it should do the job.

"What is that?" Gunther asked.

"A GPS sniffer. The amplifier recorded the chip-specs from the saboteur's phone during the call. I may be able to use it to hunt him down if he's close."

Gunther grunted, buying the lie.

So far so good.

The stairs emptied into a wide passageway, large enough to trundle a tank through. Old steel tracks ran along the floor and headed straight through the heart of the mountain. The helipad was located at the other end, remote from the main castle. They mounted a flatbed car. Gunther released the hand brake and engaged the electric motor with the press of a floor pedal. There were no seats, only rails. Painter held on as they zipped down the passage, lit intermittently by overhead lamps.

"So you have your own subway system," Painter said.

"For moving goods," Anna replied, wincing, her brows furrowed tight in pain. She had taken two pills on the way here. Pain relievers?

They passed a series of storage rooms piled high with barrels, boxes, and crates, apparently flown in and warehoused. In another minute, they reached the terminal end of the passageway. The air had grown more heated, steamy, smelling vaguely sulfurous. A deep sonorous thrum vibrated through the stone and up Painter's legs as he climbed off the train cart. He knew from his peek at the castle schematics that the geothermal plant was located in the nether regions of this area.

But they were headed up, not down.

A ramp continued from here, wide enough to accommodate a Humvee. They climbed up into a cavernous space. Light streamed through an open set of steel doors in the roof. It looked like the warehouse of a commercial airfield: cranes, forklifts, heavy equipment. And in the center rested a pair of A-Star Ecuriel helicopters, one black, one white, both shaped like angry hornets, made for high-altitude flying.

Klaus, the hulking *Sonnekönige* guard, noted their entrance and marched up to them, favoring his weak side. He ignored everyone except Anna. "All is secure," he said in crisp German.

He nodded to a line of men and women off to the side. A

good dozen stood under the watchful eyes of a phalanx of armed guards.

"No one slipped past you?" Anna asked.

"*Nein.* We were ready."

Anna had positioned four *Sonnekönige* in each main quadrant of the castle, ready to lock down whichever region Painter pinpointed with his device. But what if he had made a mistake? The commotion here would surely alert the saboteur. He or she would go even deeper into hiding. This was their one chance.

Anna knew it, too. She moved stiffly as she crossed the space. "Have you found—?"

She stumbled a step, weaving a bit. Gunther caught her arm, steadying her, his face worried.

"I'm fine," she whispered to him and continued on her own.

"We've searched everyone," Klaus said, doing his best to ignore her misstep. "We've found no phone or device. We were about to start searching the helipad."

Anna's frown deepened. It was what they had feared. Rather than carrying the phone, the saboteur might easily have stashed it somewhere after the call.

Or then again, Painter might have miscalculated.

In which case, he would have to redeem himself.

Painter stepped to Anna's side. He lifted his makeshift device. "I might be able to accelerate the search for the phone."

She eyed him suspiciously, but their choices were few. She nodded.

Gunther kept to his shoulder.

Painter lifted the satellite phone, turned it on, and punched in the number he had memorized. Nine digits. Nothing happened. Eyes were fixed on him.

He scrunched in concentration and punched them in again.

Still nothing.

Had he got the number wrong?

"Was ist los?" Anna asked.

Painter stared at the line of digits on the phone's small screen. He read through them again and saw his error. "I mixed up the last two numbers. Transposed them."

He shook his head and typed them in again, concentrating hard, going slow. He finally entered the right sequence. Anna met his eyes when he glanced up. His error was more than stress. She knew it, too. Keypad punching was often used as a test of mental acuity.

And this had only been a simple telephone number.

But an important one.

Painter's signal net had acquired the saboteur's sat-phone number. He pressed the transmit button and glanced up.

After a millisecond, a phone rang in the chamber, trilling loudly.

All eyes turned.

To Klaus.

The *Sonnekönig* backed up a step.

"Your saboteur . . . ," Painter said.

Klaus opened his mouth, ready to deny—but instead he yanked out his handgun, his face going hard.

Gunther reacted a second faster, his MK23 pistol already in hand.

A blast of muzzle fire.

Klaus's weapon flew from his fingertips with a ricocheted spark.

Gunther lunged forward, pressing his pistol's smoking barrel against Klaus's cheek. Cold flesh sizzled, branded by the hot muzzle. Klaus didn't even wince. They needed the saboteur alive, to answer questions. Gunther asked the foremost one.

"Warum?" he growled. Why?

Klaus glared out of his one good eye. The other's lid

drooped along with his half-paralyzed face, turning his sneer into something more dreadful. He spat on the ground. "To put an end to the humiliating reign of the *Leprakönige*."

A long-suppressed hatred shone from his twisted face. Painter could only imagine the years of anger smoldering in the man's bones, years of ridicule while his body deteriorated. Once a prince, now a leper. But Painter sensed it was more than mere revenge. Someone had turned the man into a mole.

But who?

"Brother," Klaus said to Gunther, "it doesn't have to be this way. A life of the living dead. There is a cure." A keening edge of hope and pleading entered the man's voice. "We can be kings among men again."

So there was the man's forty pieces of silver.

Promise of a cure.

Gunther was not swayed. "I am not your brother," he answered from deep in his chest. "And I was *never* a king."

Painter sensed the true difference between these two *Sonnekönige*. Klaus was a decade older. As such, he had grown up as a prince here, only to have it all taken away. Gunther, on the other hand, had been born at the end of the test run, when the reality of the debilitation and madness had become known. He had always been a leper, knowing no other life.

And there was another critical difference between them.

"You sentenced Anna to death with your betrayal," Gunther said. "I will make you and anyone who supported you suffer for it."

Klaus did not retreat but became more earnest. "She can be cured, too. It can be arranged."

Gunther's eyes narrowed.

Klaus sensed the hesitation, the hope in his adversary. Not for himself, but his sister. "She doesn't have to die."

Painter remembered Gunther's words earlier. *I will not let this happen to Anna. I will do anything to stop it.* Did that include betraying everyone else? Even defying his sister's wishes?

"Who promised you this cure?" Anna asked in a hard voice.

Klaus laughed gutturally. "Men far greater than the sniveling things you have become here. It is only right that you should be cast aside. You have served your purpose. But no longer."

A loud *pop* exploded in Painter's hands. The satellite phone he'd used to expose the saboteur shattered as the battery detonated, short-circuited by his amplifier. Fingers stinging, he dropped the smoking remains of the sat-phone and glanced skyward, toward the helipad bay doors. He prayed the amplifier had lasted long enough.

He was not the only one distracted. All eyes had swung toward him when the phone blew up. Including Gunther's.

Using the momentary inattention, Klaus freed a hunting knife and leaped at the other *Sonnekönig*. Gunther fired, catching his attacker in the gut with the large slug. Still, Klaus's blade grazed through the meat of Gunther's shoulder as he fell.

Gasping, Gunther twisted and threw Klaus to the floor.

The man crashed hard, sprawled out. Still, he managed to roll up on his side, his good arm clutching his belly. Blood poured heavily out of the stomach wound. Klaus coughed. More blood. Bright red. Arterial. Gunther's wild shot had struck something vital.

Anna hurried to Gunther's side to check his wound. He brushed her back, keeping his pistol trained on Klaus. Blood soaked through Gunther's sleeve and dripped to the stone.

Klaus merely laughed, a grating of rocks. "You will all die! Strangled when the knot tightens!"

He coughed again, convulsive. Blood spread in a pool. With a final trembling sneer, he slumped to the floor face-down. Gunther lowered his gun. Klaus needed no further guarding. One last breath and the large man lay still.

Dead.

Gunther allowed Anna to use an oily scrap of rag from a pile nearby to tie off his wound until it could be better tended.

Painter circled Klaus's body, nagged by something. Others in the room had gathered around, talking among themselves in voices both fearful and hopeful. They had all heard the mention of a cure.

Anna joined him. "I'll have one of our technicians examine his satellite phone. Maybe it can lead us to whoever orchestrated the sabotage."

"Not enough time," Painter mumbled, tuning everything else out. He concentrated on what bothered him. It was like grasping at threads just out of reach.

As he paced, he ran through what clues Klaus had offered.

. . . *we can be kings among men again.*

. . . *you have served your purpose. But no longer.*

A headache flared as Painter attempted to piece things together.

Klaus must have been recruited as a double agent . . . in a game of industrial espionage. For someone carrying on parallel research. And now the work at the castle here had become superfluous, and steps had been put into motion to eliminate the competition.

"Could he have spoken truthfully?" Gunther asked.

Painter remembered the large man's hesitation a moment before, baited by an offer of a cure, for himself and his sister. It had all died with Klaus.

But they weren't giving up.

Anna had dropped to a knee. She removed a small phone from Klaus's pocket. "We'll have to work quickly."

"Can you help?" Gunther asked Painter, nodding to the phone.

Their only hope lay in finding out who had picked up the other line.

"If you could trace the call . . . ," Anna said, standing up.

Painter shook his head, not in denial. He pressed the heels of his hands against his eyes. His head pounded, rounding up to a full migraine. But even that wasn't what had him shaking his head.

Close . . . whatever nagged him was so close . . .

Anna stepped near to him, touched his elbow. "It is to all our best interest to—"

"I know," he snapped. "Now shut up! Let me think."

Anna's hand dropped from his arm.

His outburst silenced the room. He fought to drag up what his mind kept hidden. It was like transposing the numbers on the sat-phone. The sharp edge to his mental acuity was dulling.

"The sat-phone . . . something about the sat-phone . . . ," he whispered, pressing back the migraine by sheer will. "But what?"

Anna spoke softly. "What do you mean?"

Then it struck him. How could he have been so blind?

Painter lowered his arms and opened his eyes. "Klaus knew the castle was under electronic surveillance. So why did he make the call at all? Expose himself? Why take that risk?"

Cold terror washed over him. He swung to Anna. "The rumor. The one about having a cache of Xerum 525 still left. Were we the only ones who knew the rumor was false? That there really isn't any more of the liquid metal?"

The others in the room gasped at his revelation. A few voices rose in anger. Much hope had been seeded by the rumor, inflaming some optimism that a second Bell could be built. Now it was dashed.

But certainly someone else had believed the rumor, too.

"Only Gunther knew the truth," Anna said, confirming his worst fear.

Painter stared out across the helipad. He pictured the

castle schematic in his head. He now knew *why* Klaus had made the call . . . and *why* he made it from here. The bastard thought he could hide in plain sight afterward, so confident he hadn't even disposed of the phone. He had chosen this spot specifically.

"Anna, when you spread the rumor, where did you say you had the Xerum 525 locked up? How had it avoided being destroyed in the explosion?"

"I claimed it was locked up in a vault."

"What vault?"

"Away from the explosion site. The one in my study. Why?"

All the way on the other side of the castle.

"We've been played," Painter said. "Klaus called from here, knowing the castle was being monitored. He *meant* to lure us here. To pull our attention away from your study, from the secret vault, from the supposed last cache of Xerum 525."

Anna shook her head, not understanding.

"Klaus's call was a *decoy*. The real goal all along was the fabled last batch of Xerum 525."

Anna's eyes grew wide.

Gunther understood now, too. "There must be a second saboteur."

"While we're distracted here, he's going after the Xerum 525."

"My study," Anna said, turning to Painter.

It finally struck him, what had been nagging him the most, making him heartsick and nauseated. It burst forth with a white-hot stab of blinding pain. Someone stood in the direct path of the saboteur.

Lisa searched the upper story of the library. She had climbed the wrought-iron ladder to the rickety iron balcony and now circled the room. She kept one hand on the balcony railing.

She had spent the past hour gathering books and papers on quantum mechanics. She even found the original treatise of Max Planck, the father of quantum theory, a theory that defined a bewildering world of elemental particles, a world where energy could be broken down into small packets, called quanta, and where elemental matter behaved like both particles *and* waves.

It all made her head ache.

What did any of this have to do with evolution?

She sensed any cure lay in discovering that answer.

Reaching out, she tilted a book from the shelf, studying the binding. She squinted at the faded lettering.

Was this the right volume?

A commotion at the door drew her attention around. She knew the exit was guarded. What now? Was Anna returning already? Had they found the saboteur? Lisa turned back toward the ladder. She hoped Painter was with Anna. She didn't like being apart from him. And maybe he could make heads or tails of these strange theories of matter and energy.

She reached the ladder and turned to step down on the first rung.

A sharp scream, quickly silenced, froze her in place.

It came from right outside the door.

Reacting on instinct, Lisa lunged back up and spread herself flat on the wrought-iron balcony. The open floor grating offered little cover. She slid close to the stacks, into the shadows, away from the wall sconces on this level.

As she lay still, the door across the room opened and closed. A figure slipped into the room. A woman. In a snow-white parka. But it wasn't Anna. The woman tossed back her hood and pulled down a scarf. She had long white hair and was as pale as a ghost.

Friend or foe?

Lisa kept hidden until she knew more.

There was something too confident about the woman. The way her eyes searched the room. She half turned. A spray of blood marred the side of her jacket. In her other hand, she held a curved katana, a short Japanese saber. Blood dripped from the blade.

The woman danced into the room, turning in a slow circle.

Hunting.

Lisa dared not breathe. She prayed the shadows kept her hidden up here. The library's few lamps lit the lower level, as did the hearth fire. It crackled and shone with a few flames. But the upper balcony remained gloomy.

Would it be enough to hide her?

Lisa watched the intruder make another circle, standing in the middle of the room, bloodied katana held at the ready.

Seemingly satisfied, the ice-blond woman strode quickly toward Anna's desk. She ignored the clutter on top and stepped behind the wide table. Reaching to a tapestry on the wall, she pulled it back and exposed a large black cast-iron wall safe.

Hooking the tapestry aside, she knelt and inspected the combination lock, the handle, the edges of the door.

With the woman's concentration so focused, Lisa allowed herself to breathe. Whatever thievery was afoot, so be it. Let the woman abscond with whatever she came for and be gone. If the burglar had slain the guards, maybe Lisa could turn it to her advantage. If she could reach a phone . . . the intrusion might actually turn out for the best.

A loud clatter startled her.

A few yards away, a heavy book had fallen from its shelf and landed splayed open on the wrought-iron balcony. Pages still fluttered from the impact. Lisa recognized the book she had half pulled out a moment ago. Forgotten until now, gravity had done the rest, slowly tugging the book free.

Below, the woman retreated to the center of the room.

A pistol had appeared in her other hand, as if out of thin air, pointed up.

Lisa had nowhere to hide.

9:18 A.M.
BÜREN, GERMANY

Gray pulled open the door to the team's BMW. He began to duck inside when a shout rose behind him. He turned toward the entrance to the hostel. Ryan Hirszfeld hurried toward them, hunched under an umbrella. Thunder echoed, and rain lashed across the parking lot of the cottage estate.

"Get inside," Gray ordered Monk and Fiona, waving to the sedan.

He faced Ryan as the young man reached his side.

"Are you heading to the castle . . . to Wewelsburg?" he asked, lifting the umbrella to shelter them both.

"Yes, we are. Why?"

"Might I hop a ride with you?"

"I don't think—"

Ryan cut him off. "You were asking about my great-grandfather . . . Hugo. I may have more information for you. It'll only cost you a ride up the hill."

Gray hesitated. The young man must have eavesdropped on their earlier conversation with Johann, his father. What could Ryan know that his father didn't? Still, the man stared at him with earnest eyes.

Turning, Gray popped the back door and held it open.

"*Danke.*" Ryan folded the umbrella and ducked into the back with Fiona.

Gray climbed behind the wheel. In moments, they were bumping down the driveway out of the estate.

"Shouldn't you be home watching the store?" Monk asked, half turned in the passenger seat to address Ryan.

"Alicia will cover the front desk for me," Ryan said. "The storm will keep everyone close to the fire."

Gray studied the young man in the rearview mirror. He looked suddenly uncomfortable under Monk's and Fiona's scrutiny.

"What did you want to tell us?" Gray asked.

Ryan's eyes met his in the mirror. He swallowed and nodded. "My father thinks I know nothing about my great-grandfather Hugo. Thinks it best be buried in the past, *ja*? But it's still whispered about. Same with Aunt Tola."

Gray understood. Family secrets had a way of surfacing, no matter how deeply you tried to bury them. Curiosity had plainly been instilled in Ryan about his ancestors and their role during the war. It practically shone from the man's eyes.

"You've been doing your own investigation into the past?" Gray said.

Ryan nodded. "For three years now. But the trail goes back further. To when the Berlin Wall came down. When the Soviet Union dissolved."

"I don't understand," Gray said.

"Do you remember when Russia declassified the older Soviet files?"

"I suppose. But what about them?"

"Well, back when Wewelsburg was reconstructed—"

"Wait a sec." Fiona stirred. She'd been sitting with her arms crossed, as if disgruntled by the intrusion of the stranger. But Gray had caught the few sidelong glances she gave the man, sizing him up. He wondered if the man still had his wallet. "Reconstructed? They rebuilt that ugly place?" she asked.

Ryan nodded as the castle came into view on the ridge-line. Gray signaled and turned onto Burgstrasse, the road that headed up toward the castle. "Himmler had it blown up near the end of the war. Only the North Tower was untouched. After the war, it was rebuilt. Part museum, part youth hostel. Still bothers my father."

Gray could understand why.

"It was finished in 1979," Ryan continued. "The museum directors over the years have petitioned former Allied governments for documents and such related to the castle."

"Including Russia," Monk said.

"*Natürlich*. Once records were decommissioned, the current director sent archivists over to Russia. Three years ago, they returned with truckloads of declassified documents related to the Russian campaign in the area. The archivists had also left here with a long list of names to search for in the Russian files. Including my great-grandfather, Hugo Hirszfeld."

"Why him?"

"He was intimately involved in the Thule Society rituals at the castle. He was well known locally for his knowledge of runes, which decorate the castle. He even corresponded with Karl Wiligut, Himmler's personal astrologer."

Gray pictured the three-pronged mark in the Bible but remained silent.

"The archivists returned with several boxes specifically about my great-grandfather. My father was informed but refused to participate in any way."

"But you snuck up there?" Monk said.

"I wanted to know more about him," Ryan said. "Figure out why . . . what happened . . ." He shook his head.

The past had a way of grabbing hold and not letting go.

"And what did you learn?" Gray asked.

"Not much. One box contained papers from the Nazi research lab where my great-grandfather worked. He was given the rank of *Oberarbeitsleiter*. Head of the project." This last was said with a tone both shamed and defiant. "But whatever they were working on must not have been declassified. Most of the papers were personal correspondence. With friends, with family."

"And you read through them all?"

A slow nod. "Enough to get the feeling my great-grandfather had begun to have doubts about his work. Yet he couldn't leave."

"Or he would've been shot," Fiona said.

Ryan shook his head, a forlorn expression waxing for a breath. "I think it was more the project itself . . . he couldn't let it go. Not completely. It was like he was repulsed but drawn at the same time."

Gray sensed Ryan's personal pursuit into the past was tinged with the same tidal push and pull.

Monk tilted his head and cracked his neck with a loud *pop*. "What does any of this have to do with the Darwin Bible?" he asked, bringing the subject back around to the beginning.

"I found one note," Ryan answered. "Addressed to my great-aunt Tola. It mentions the crate of books my great-grandfather sent back to the estate. I remember it because of his rather strange remarks about it."

"What did he say?"

"The letter is up at the museum. I thought you might like to have a copy of it . . . to go along with the Bible."

"You don't remember what it said?"

Ryan scrunched his brow. "Only a couple lines. '*Perfection can be found hidden in my books, dear Tola. The truth is too beautiful to let die and too monstrous to set free.*'"

Silence settled in the car.

"He died two months later."

Gray contemplated the words. *Hidden in my books*. The five books Hugo had mailed back home before he died. Had he done it to keep some secret safe? To preserve what was *too beautiful to let die and too monstrous to set free*?

Gray fixed Ryan with a stare in the rearview mirror. "Did you tell anyone else about what you found?"

"No, but the old gentleman and his niece and nephew . . . the ones who came earlier this year to speak to my father about the books. They had already been here, searching through my great-grandfather's papers in the archives. I think they must have read the same note and come to inquire further with my father."

"These folks . . . the niece and nephew. What did they look like?"

"White hair. Tall. Athletic. Good stock, as my grandfather would say."

Gray shared a glance with Monk.

Fiona cleared her throat. She pointed to the back of her hand. "Did they have a mark . . . a tattoo here?"

Ryan slowly nodded. "I think so. Shortly after they arrived, my father sent me away. Like with you today. Mustn't speak in front of the children." Ryan tried to smile, but he plainly sensed the tension in the car. His eyes darted around. "Do you know them?"

"Fellow competitors," Gray said. "Collectors like us."

Ryan's expression remained guarded, disbelieving, but he didn't inquire further.

Gray again pictured the hand-drawn rune hidden in the Bible. Did the other four books contain similar cryptic symbols? Did it tie back to Hugo's research with the Nazis? Was that what this was all about? It seemed unlikely these assassins would just show up here and start sifting through records . . . not unless they were searching for something specific.

But what?

Monk still faced backward. But he swung around and settled into his seat. He spoke low, under his breath. "You know we're being followed, right?"

Gray only nodded.

A quarter mile back, slowly climbing the switchbacks behind them, a car followed in the rain. The same one he had spotted earlier parked back at the hostel. A pearl white Mercedes roadster. Maybe they were just fellow tourists, out on a sightseeing excursion to the castle.

Right.

"Perhaps you shouldn't follow so close, Isaak."

"They've already spotted us, Ischke." He nodded past the rainswept windshield to the BMW a quarter mile ahead. "Note how his turns are more restrained, less enthusiastically sharp and tight. He knows."

"Is that something we want? To alert them?"

Isaak tilted his head toward his sister. "The hunt is always the best when the prey is spooked."

"I don't think Hans would agree." Her manner darkened with grief.

He reached a finger and touched the back of her hand, sharing her sadness and apologizing. He knew how sensitive she could be.

"There is no other road down from the ridge," he assured her. "Except for the one we are on. All is ready at the castle. All we have to do is flush them into the trap. If they are looking over their shoulder at us, they are less likely to see what's in front of them."

She inhaled her agreement and understanding.

"It's time we cleared up all these tattered loose ends. Then we can go home."

"Home," she echoed with a contented sigh.

"We're almost done. We must always remember the goal, Ischke. Hans's sacrifice will not be in vain, his spilt blood will herald a new dawn, a better world."

"So Grandfather says."

"And you know it's true."

He tilted his head toward her. Her lips thinned into a weary smile.

"Careful of the blood, sweet Ischke."

His sister glanced down to the long steel blade of the dagger. She had been absently wiping it clean with a white chamois. A crimson drop had almost fallen onto the knee of her white pants. One loose end severed. A few more to go.

"Thank you, Isaak."

1:22 P.M.
HIMALAYAS

Lisa stared at the raised pistol.

"Wer ist dort? Zeigen Sie sich!" the blond woman called up to her.

Though Lisa didn't speak German, she understood the gist. She rose into view slowly. Hands up. "I don't speak German," she called down.

The woman eyed her, so focused in intent that Lisa swore she could feel it like a laser across her body.

"You're one of the Americans," the woman said in crisp English. "Come down. Slowly."

The pistol didn't waver.

With no cover on the open balcony grating, Lisa had no choice. She stepped to the ladder, turned her back, and climbed down. With every rung, she expected to hear a blast of a pistol. Her shoulders tensed. But she reached the ground safely.

Lisa turned, arms still held a bit out to the side.

The woman stepped toward her. Lisa stepped back. She sensed a good portion of the woman's restraint in not immediately shooting her was due to the noise it might generate. Except for the single short cry, she had dispatched the outer guards with barely a sound, employing the sword.

The assassin still held the bloody katana in her other hand.

Maybe Lisa would've been safer staying atop the balcony, making the woman fire at her like a duck in a shooting gallery. Maybe the gunfire would have drawn others in time. She had been foolish to put herself within sword reach of the intruder. But panic had clouded Lisa's judgment. It was hard to refuse someone when they had a gun pointed at your face.

"The Xerum 525," the woman said. "Is it in the safe?"

Lisa weighed her answer for a heartbeat. Truth or lie? There seemed little choice. "Anna took it," she answered. She waved vaguely toward the door.

"Where?"

She remembered Painter's earlier lesson after they had been captured. Be necessary. Be useful. "I don't know the castle well enough to describe it. But I know how to get there. I . . . can take you." Lisa's voice faltered. She needed to be more convincing. And how better than to barter as though her lie had value? "I'll take you *only* if you promise to help me get out of here."

The enemy of my enemy is my friend.

Would the woman fall for it? She was stunningly beautiful: svelte, unblemished skin, generous lips, but her glacial blue eyes glinted with cold calculation and intelligence.

She scared Lisa witless.

There was something unearthly about her.

"Then you will show me," the woman said and holstered her pistol. She kept the katana in hand.

Lisa would've preferred it the other way around.

The sword pointed at the door.

Lisa was to go first. She circled toward the door, keeping some distance. Perhaps she could make a break for it out in the halls. It would be her only hope. She would have to watch for a moment, some distraction, a hesitation, and then just run like hell.

A brush of air, the flicker of flame in the hearth, was her only warning.

Lisa turned—and the woman was already there, a step away, having glided swiftly and silently from behind. Impossibly fast. Their eyes met. Lisa knew in the heartbeat before the sword fell that the woman had not believed her for a moment.

It had all been a trap to drop Lisa's guard.

It would be her last mistake.

The world froze . . . caught in a flash of fine Japanese silver as it plunged toward Lisa's heart.

9:30 A.M.
WEWELSBURG, GERMANY

Gray slid the BMW into a parking place beside a blue Wolters tour bus. The large German vehicle hid the sedan from direct view of the street. The arched entryway to the castle courtyard stood directly ahead.

"Stay in the car," he ordered the others. He twisted around. "That means you, young lady."

Fiona made an obscene gesture, but she stayed buckled.

"Monk, get behind the wheel. Keep the engine running."

"Got it."

Ryan stared at him wide-eyed. *"Was ist los?"*

"Nothing's *los*," Monk answered. "But keep your head down just in case."

Gray opened the door. A gust of rain slapped against him, sounding like machine-gun fire as it struck the flank of the neighboring bus. Thunder rumbled in the distance.

"Ryan, may I borrow your umbrella?"

The young man nodded and passed it forward.

Gray climbed out. He shook out the umbrella and hurried to the far side of the bus. He took up a post near the rear door, sheltering against the rain. He hoped to appear like just another tour employee. He kept himself shielded by the umbrella while he watched the road.

Headlights appeared out of the gloom, climbing the last switchback.

The white two-seater roadster appeared a moment later. It slid up to the parking lot and, without slowing, passed it. He watched the taillights recede into the rain, heading toward the tiny hamlet of Wewelsburg that nestled against the flank of the castle. The car disappeared around a corner.

Gray waited a full five minutes, circling behind the bus and signaling the all clear to Monk. Monk cut the engine. Finally satisfied that the Mercedes was not returning, Gray waved the others out.

"Paranoid much?" Fiona asked as she passed and headed to the arch.

"It's not paranoia if they're really out to get you," Monk called after her. He turned to Gray. "Are they really out to get us?"

Gray stared into the storm. He didn't like coincidences, but he couldn't stop moving forward just because he was spooked. "Stick with Fiona and Ryan. Let's talk to this director, get a copy of old Hugo's letter to his daughter, and get the hell out of here."

Monk eyed the hulking mass of tower and turret. Rain poured over the gray stone and sluiced from green gutters. Only a few of the windows on the lower floors shone with signs of life. The vast bulk was dark and oppressive.

"Just so we're clear," he grumbled, "if I see one friggin' black bat, I'm out of here."

1:31 P.M.
HIMALAYAS

Lisa watched the sword plunge toward her chest. It all happened between heartbeats. Time thickened and slowed. This was how she was going to die.

Then a tinkle of glass shattered the stillness . . . followed by the soft crack of a gunshot, sounding impossibly far away. Near at hand, the assassin's throat blossomed with a fountain of blood and bone, head thrown back.

But even then, the assassin's death stroke completed its arc.

The sword struck Lisa in the chest, pierced skin, and collided into her sternum. But there was no weight behind it. Limp fingers released the katana's hilt. The heel of a dying hand knocked it down before further damage could be inflicted.

Lisa stumbled back, released from the spell.

The length of Japanese steel pirouetted and struck the floor with the sound of a perfectly tuned bell. The body of the assassin followed next, thudding heavily beside it.

Lisa retreated, disbelieving, numb, senseless.

More tinkling of glass.

Words reached her as if from underwater.

"Are you okay? Lisa . . ."

She stared up. Across the library. The single library window. Frosted and glazed before, its pane shattered away under the butt of a rifle. A face appeared in the opening, framed by shards of broken glass.

Painter.

Beyond his shoulder, a storm blew, swirling snow and icemelt. Something large, heavy, and dark descended out of the sky. A helicopter. A rope and harness dangled below it.

Lisa trembled and sank to her knees.

"We'll be right there," he promised.

Five minutes later, Painter stood over the body of the assassin. The second saboteur. Anna was on one knee, searching the woman. Off to the side, Lisa sat in a chair by the hearth, her sweater off, her shirt open, exposing her bra and a bloody cut below it. Assisted by Gunther, Lisa had already cleaned the wound and now applied a series of butterfly bandages to seal the inch-long slice. She had been lucky. Her bra's underwire had helped block the blade from penetrating deeper, saving her life. Talk about offering additional support.

"No papers, no identification," Anna said, turning to him. Her gaze fell heavily onto Painter. "We needed the saboteur alive."

He had no excuse. "I aimed for her shoulder."

He shook his head in frustration. A debilitating bout of vertigo had paralyzed him after his descent in the rope harness. But they had no time to spare, barely making it here from the far side of the mountain. They would've never made it on foot through the castle. The helicopter had been their only chance, hopping over the shoulder of the mountain and dropping someone down on a harness.

Anna was no good with a gun, and Gunther was piloting the helo.

That left only Painter.

So despite the vertigo and double vision, Painter had crawled to the castle and aimed as best he could through the window. He'd had to act fast as he saw the woman rush Lisa, sword poised.

So he had taken his shot.

And though it may have cost them everything—even the knowledge of the true puppetmaster who manipulated these saboteurs—Painter did not regret his choice. He had seen the horror on Lisa's face. Vertigo be damned, he had fired. His head still pounded now. A new fear rose.

What if he had struck Lisa . . . ? How long until he was more of a liability than an asset? He shoved this thought aside.

Quit wringing your hands and roll up your sleeves.

"What about any distinguishing marks?" Painter asked, getting back into the game.

"Only this." Anna turned over the woman's wrist and exposed the back of the assassin's hand. "Do you recognize it?"

A black tattoo marred her perfect white skin. Four entwined loops.

"Looks Celtic, but it means nothing to me."

"Nor me." Anna sat back, dropping the corpse's hand.

Painter noted something else and knelt down closer. He turned the hand over again, still warm. The woman's pinkie fingernail was missing, the bed scarred. A tiny blemish, but a significant one.

Anna took the hand from him. She rubbed the nail bed. "Dry . . ." A deep furrow formed between her brows. Her eyes met his.

"Does that mean what I think it means?" he asked.

Anna's gaze shifted to the woman's face. "But I'd have to do a retinal scan for sure. Look for petechia around the optic nerve."

Painter didn't need any further evidence. He had seen how fast the assassin had moved across the room, preternaturally agile. "She's one of the *Sonnekönige*."

Lisa and Gunther joined them.

"Not one of ours," Anna said. "She's way too young. Too perfect. Whoever created her employed our latest techniques, those that we finessed over the past decades from our in vitro studies. They've advanced them into human subjects."

"Could someone have created them here, behind your back . . . after hours?"

Anna shook her head. "It takes an enormous amount of energy to activate the Bell. We would know."

"Then that only means one thing."

"She was created somewhere else." Anna rose to her feet. "Someone else has an operable Bell."

Painter remained where he was, examining the nail and tattoo. "And that someone means to shut you down now," he mumbled.

Silence settled over the room.

In the quiet, Painter heard a tiny chime, barely audible. It came from the woman. He realized he had heard it a few times, but there had been so much commotion, so much speculation, it had not fully registered.

He pulled up her parka sleeve.

A digital watch with a thick leather band, a full two inches in width, was secured to her wrist. Painter studied its red face. A holographic hand swept fully around, marking off the seconds. A digital readout glowed.

01:32

Seconds subtracted with every sweep.

Just over a minute.

Painter unstrapped the watch and checked the inside of the band. Two silver contact points were wired in place. Heartbeat monitor. And somewhere inside the watch must be a microtransmitter.

"What are you doing?" Anna asked.

"Did you search her for any explosives?"

"She's clean," Anna said. "Why?"

Painter stood and spoke rapidly. "She's wired with a monitor. When her heartbeat stopped, a transmission must've been sent out." He glanced to the watch in his hand. "This is just a timer."

He held it out toward them.

01:05

"Klaus and this woman had full access to your facilities for who knows how long. Plenty of time to jury-rig a fail-safe." Painter held up the watch. "Something tells me we don't want to be here when this reaches zero."

The second hand swept around, and a small chime sounded as the count dropped below a minute.

00:59

"We must get out of here. Now!"

10

BLACK CAMELOT

9:32 A.M.
WEWELSBURG, GERMANY

"The SS started out as the personal bodyguard for Hitler," the docent said in French, leading a group of sodden tourists through the heart of the Wewelsburg museum. "In fact, the term SS is derived from the German word *Schutzstaffel,* which means 'guard detachment.' Only later did they become Himmler's Black Order."

Gray stepped aside as the tour group passed. While waiting for the museum director, he had eavesdropped on enough of the tour to gain the gist of the castle's history. How Himmler had leased the castle for only one Reichsmark, then spent a quarter billion rebuilding the castle into his personal Camelot, a small price compared to the cost in human blood and suffering.

Gray stood beside a display case with a striped prison uniform from the Niederhagen concentration camp.

Thunder rumbled from beyond the walls, rattling the old windows.

As the tour group drifted away, the docent's voice faded into the babble of the few other visitors, all seeking shelter against the storm.

Monk stood with Fiona. Ryan had gone to fetch the director. Monk leaned down to examine one of the infamous *Toten Kopf* rings on display, a silver band granted to SS officers. It was engraved with runes, along with a skull and crossbones. A gruesome piece of art, ripe with symbolism and power.

Other exhibits stretched across the small hall: miniature models, photographs of daily life, SS paraphernalia, even a strange little teapot that once belonged to Himmler. A sun-shaped rune decorated the pot.

"Here comes the director," Monk said, stepping closer. He nodded to a squat gentleman who strode out a private door. Ryan accompanied him.

The museum director appeared to be in his late fifties, salt-and-pepper hair, rumpled black suit. As he approached, he removed a pair of eyeglasses and held out his other hand toward Gray.

"Dr. Dieter Ulmstrom," the man said. "Director of the Historisches Museum des Hochstifts Paderborn. *Wilkommen.*"

The man's harried look belied his welcome.

He continued, "Young Ryan here has explained how you've come to investigate some runes found in an old book. How intriguing."

Again the man appeared more hassled than *intrigued*.

"We won't keep you long," Gray said. "We were wondering if you could help us identify a particular rune and its significance."

"Certainly. If there is one thing a museum director at Wewelsburg must be fluent with, it is rune lore."

Gray waved to Fiona for the Darwin Bible. She already had it out.

Flipping open the back cover, Gray held the book out.

Lips pursing, Dr. Ulmstrom replaced his glasses and looked closer. He studied the rune scoured in ink by Hugo Hirszfeld on the back pasteboard.

"May I examine the book, *bitte*?"

After a moment's hesitation, Gray relented.

The director flipped through the pages, pausing at some of the chicken-scratched marks inside. "A Bible . . . how strange . . ."

"The symbol at the back," Gray pressed.

"Of course. It is the *Mensch* rune."

"*Mensch*," Gray said. "As in the German word for 'man.'"

"*Ja*. Note the form. Like a decapitated stick figure." The director drifted back to the earlier pages. "Ryan's great-grandfather seemed very fixated on symbols associated with the All-Father."

"What do you mean?" Gray asked.

Ulmstrom pointed to one of the scratches on the inner pages of the Bible.

"This is the rune for *k*," the director said, "also called *cen* in Anglo-Saxon. It's an earlier rune for 'man,' only two upraised arms, a cruder portrayal. And on this other page is the rune's mirror image." He flipped a few pages and pointed to another.

"The two symbols are sort of like two sides of the same coin. Yin and yang. Male and female. Light and dark."

Gray nodded. It reminded him of his discussions with Ang Gelu when he had studied with the Buddhist monk, how all societies seemed to be transfixed by this duality. This reverie tweaked his concern about Painter Crowe. There'd been no word yet from Nepal.

Monk redirected the talk. "These runes? What do they all have to do with this All-Father guy?"

"All three are related. Symbolically. The big rune, the *Mensch* rune, is often considered to represent the Norse god Thor, a bringer of life, a higher state of being. What we all strive to become."

Gray's mind puzzled through to the answer, picturing it in his head. "And these two earlier runes, the *k* runes, they form the two halves of the *Mensch* rune."

"Huh?" Monk grunted.

"Like this," Fiona said, understanding. Using her finger, she drew in the dust atop a display case. "You push the two-armed runes together to form the *Mensch* rune. Like a jigsaw."

$$ \mathsf{Y} \mathsf{Y} = \mathsf{Y} $$

"*Sehr gut,*" the director said. He tapped the first two runes. "These represent the common man—in all his duality—joining together to form the All-Father, a supreme being." Ulmstrom handed the Bible back to Gray and shook his head. "These runes certainly seemed to obsess Ryan's great-grandfather."

Gray stared at the symbol on the back cover. "Ryan, Hugo was a biologist, correct?"

Ryan stirred. He seemed dismayed by all this. "*Ja*. As was my great-aunt Tola."

Gray nodded slowly. The Nazis were always interested in the myth of the superman, the All-Father from which the Aryan race supposedly descended. All these scribblings, were they just Hugo's declaration of his belief in this Nazi dogma? Gray didn't think so. He remembered Ryan's description of his great-grandfather's notes, the scientist's growing disillusionment—and then the cryptic note to his daughter, a hint of a secret, one *too beautiful to let die and too monstrous to set free*.

From one biologist to another.

He sensed it was all tied together: runes, the All-Father, some long-abandoned research. Whatever the secret was, it seemed it was worth killing over.

Ulmstrom continued, "The *Mensch* rune was also of particular interest to the Nazis. They even renamed it the *leben-rune*."

"The life rune?" Gray asked, focusing his attention back.

"*Ja*. They used it to represent the *Lebensborn* program."

"What's that?" Monk asked.

Gray answered. "A Nazi breeding program. Farms to produce more blond, blue-eyed children."

The director nodded. "But like the duality of the *k* rune, the *leben-rune* also has its mirror image." He motioned for Gray to turn the Bible upside down, upending the symbol. "Reversed, the *leben-rune* becomes its opposite. The *toten-rune*."

Monk frowned at Gray.

He translated. "The rune of death."

1:37 P.M.
HIMALAYAS

Death ticked down.

0:55

Painter stood with the dead assassin's wrist timer in his hand. "No time to make it out on foot. Never get clear of the blast zone."

"Then what—?" Anna asked.

"The helicopter," Painter said and pointed toward the window. The A-Star helicopter they'd used to hop here still sat outside the castle, engine warm.

"The others." Anna headed to the phone, ready to raise the alarm.

"Keine Zeit," Gunther barked, stopping her.

The man unhitched his assault rifle, a Russian A-91 Bullpup. With his other hand, he yanked out a grenade cartridge from his waistband and jammed it into the rifle's 40mm launcher.

"Hier!" He strode in large steps to Anna's massive desk. *"Schnell!"*

He pointed the rifle at arm's length toward the room's barred window.

Painter grabbed Lisa's hand and ran for shelter, Anna on their heels. Gunther waited until they were close enough and fired. A jet of gas blasted from the rock-steady weapon.

They all leaped behind the desk.

Gunther grabbed his sister around the waist and bodily rolled her under him. The grenade exploded deafeningly. Painter felt his ears pop. Lisa clamped her hands over her ears. The concussion shoved the desk a full foot. Bits of rock and glass pelted the front of the desk. Rock dust and smoke choked over them.

Gunther hauled Anna to her feet. They wasted no words. Across the library, a ragged hole had been blasted through to the outside. Books—shredded and aflame—dotted the floor and had been blown out into the courtyard.

They ran for the exit.

The helicopter sat beyond the mountain overhang. A good forty yards. Bounding through the jumbled blast zone, they sprinted for the helicopter.

Painter still clutched the wrist timer. He didn't check it until they were at the helicopter. Gunther had reached the chopper first and ripped open the rear door. Painter helped Anna and Lisa inside, then dove in after them.

Gunther was already in the pilot's seat. Belts snapped into place. Painter glanced at the timer. Not that it would do any good. Either they'd get clear or they wouldn't.

He stared at the number. His head pounded, stabbing his eyes with pain. He could barely make out the digital readout.

00:09

No time left.

Gunther had the engine roaring. Painter glanced up. The rotors had begun to spin . . . slowly, too slowly. He glanced out a side window. The helo perched at the top of a steep snowy slope, freshly corniced from last night's storm. The sky beyond was shredded with clouds, and icy mists clung to cliffs and valleys.

From the front seat, Gunther swore under his breath. The bird refused to climb into the thin air, not without top rotor speed.

00:03

They'd never make it.

Painter reached for Lisa's hand.

He gripped it tightly—then suddenly the world lifted and crashed back down. A distant hollow boom sounded. They all held their breath, ready to be blasted off the mountain. But nothing else happened. Maybe it wouldn't be so bad after all.

Then the cornice upon which they were perched broke away. The A-Star tilted down nose first. Rotors churned uselessly overhead. The entire snowy slope slipped in one sheet, sliding away, as if shrugged off the mountain, taking the helicopter with it.

They were headed for the cliff's edge. Snow tumbled over it in a churning torrent.

The ground bumped again . . . another explosion . . .

The helo bucked but refused to get airborne.

Gunther wrestled with the controls, choking the throttle.

The cliff rushed toward them. The snow could be heard beyond the roar of the helicopter, growling like Class V rapids.

Lisa pressed against Painter's side, her hand white-knuckled around his fingers. On her other side, Anna sat ramrod straight, face blank, eyes fixed forward.

In front, Gunther went deathly silent as they were carried over the cliff.

Shoved off the edge, they tipped sideways, snow falling away under them, behind them. Dropping fast, the craft jittered, yawing back and forth. Cliffs of rock rose in all directions.

No one made a sound. The rotors screamed for all of them.

Then just like that, the craft found air. With no more jolt than an elevator coming to a stop, the A-star steadied. Gunther grunted at the controls . . . slowly, slowly, spiraling the craft upward.

Ahead, the last of the avalanche tumbled over the cliff face.

The helo climbed enough to survey the damage to the castle. Smoke choked out all the façade's windows. The front doors had been blown off. Over the shoulder of the mountain, a thick black column rose into the sky, coming from the helipad on the far side.

Anna sagged, palms on the side window. "Almost a hundred and fifty men and women."

"Maybe some got out," Lisa said dully, unblinking.

They spotted no movement.

Only smoke.

Anna pointed toward the castle. *"Wir sollten suchen—"*

But there would be no search, no rescue.

Ever.

A blinding white flash, like a crack of lightning, blazed from all the windows. Beyond the shoulder, a sodium-arc sunrise. No noise. Like heat lightning. It burned into the retina, shutting off all sight.

Blinded, Painter felt the helo lurch up as Gunther yanked on the collective. A noise intruded, a vast grating rumble of rock. Impossibly loud. Not just an avalanche. It sounded tectonic, a grinding of continental plates.

The helo trembled in the air, a fly in a paint shaker.

Sight returned painfully.

Painter pressed against the window and stared below.

"My God . . . ," he uttered in awe.

Rock dust obscured most of the view, but it could not hide the scope of the destruction. The entire side of the mountain had buckled in on itself. The shoulder of granite that had overhung the castle had collapsed, as if all beneath it—the castle and a good section of mountain—had simply vanished.

"Unmöglich," Anna mumbled, stunned.

"What?"

"Such annihilation . . . it had to be a ZPE bomb." Her eyes had gone glassy.

Painter waited for her to explain.

She did after another shuddering breath. "ZPE. Zero point energy. Einstein's formulas led to the first nuclear bomb, tapping into the energies of a few uranium atoms. But that's nothing compared to the potential power hidden within

Planck's quantum theories. Such bombs would tap into the very energies birthed during the big bang."

Silence settled throughout the cabin.

Anna shook her head. "Experiments with the fuel source for the Bell—the Xerum 525—hinted at the possible use of zero point energy as a weapon. But we never pursued that avenue with any real intent."

"But somebody else did," Painter said. He pictured the dead, ice blond assassin.

Anna turned to Painter, her face etched with horror and utter violation. "We have to stop them."

"But who? Who are they?"

Lisa stirred. "I think we may find out." She pointed out the starboard side.

Over the edge of a neighboring peak, a trio of helicopters appeared, camouflaged in white against the glaciered peaks. They spread out and swept toward the lone A-Star.

Painter knew enough of aerial combat to recognize the pattern.

Attack formation.

9:32 A.M.
WEWELSBURG, GERMANY

"The North Tower is this way," Dr. Ulmstrom said.

The museum director led Gray, Monk, and Fiona out the back of the main hall. Ryan had left a moment earlier with a slim woman dressed in tweed, a museum archivist. They were off to make copies of Hugo Hirszfeld's letter and anything else pertaining to his great-grandfather's research. Gray sensed he was close to discerning some answers, but he needed more information.

To that end, he had agreed to the director's personal tour of Himmler's castle. It was here where Hugo had begun his connection with the Nazis. Gray sensed that to move forward he would need as much background as possible—and who better to supply that information than the museum curator?

"To truly understand the Nazis," Ulmstrom said, leading the way, "you have to stop considering them as a political party. They called themselves Nationalsozialistische Deutsche Arbeiterpartei—the National Socialist German Workers' Party—but in reality, they were really a cult."

"A cult?" Gray asked.

"They bore all the trappings, *ja*? A spiritual leader who could not be questioned, disciples who wore matching clothes, rituals and blood oaths performed in secret, and most important of all, the creation of a potent totem to worship. The *Hakenkreuz*. The Broken Cross, also called the swastika. A symbol to supplant the crucifix and the Star of David."

"Hari krishnas on steroids," Monk mumbled.

"Do not joke. The Nazis understood the inherent power of ideas. A power greater than any gun or rocket. They used it to subjugate and brainwash an entire nation."

Lightning cracked, brightening the hall behind them. Thunder followed on its heels, booming, felt in the gut. The lights flickered.

They all stopped in the hall.

"One squeaking bat," Monk whispered. "Even a small one . . ."

The lights flared brighter, then steadied. They continued onward. The short hall ended at a barred glass door. A larger room lay beyond.

"The *Obergruppenführersaal*." Ulmstrom pulled out a weighty set of keys and unlocked the door. "The inner sanctum to the castle. This is restricted from regular visitors, but I think you might appreciate it."

He held the door for them to enter.

They trailed inside. Rain pelted against the ring of windows that surrounded the circular chamber.

"Himmler built this room to mirror King Arthur's in Camelot. He even had a massive oaken round table placed in the middle of the room and gathered his twelve leading officers of his Black Order for meetings and rituals here."

"What's this Black Order?" Monk asked.

"It was another name for Himmler's SS. But more accurately, the *Schwarze Auftrag*—the Black Order—was a name given to Himmler's inner circle, a secret cabal that traced its roots back to the occult Thule Society."

Gray's attention focused. The Thule Society again. Himmler was a member of the group, so was Ryan's great-grandfather. He pondered the connection. An inner cabal of occultists and scientists who believed that a master race once ruled the world—and would again.

The director continued his tour. "Himmler believed this room and its tower to be the spiritual and geographic center of the new Aryan world."

"Why here?" Gray asked.

Ulmstrom shrugged and walked to the middle of the room. "This region is where the Teutons defeated the Romans, a pivotal battle in Germanic history."

Gray had heard a similar story from Ryan's father.

"But the reasons may be multiple. Legends are ripe here. Nearby stands an old Stonehenge-like set of prehistoric monoliths, called Externsteine. Some claim the roots of the Norse World Tree, Yggdrasil, lie below it. And then, of course, there were the witches."

"The ones killed here," Gray said.

"Himmler believed, and perhaps rightly so, that the women were slain because they were pagans, practicing Nordic rites and rituals. In his eyes, the fact that their blood was spilt at this castle only succeeded in consecrating these grounds."

"So then it's like the real estate agents say," Monk mumbled. "It's all about location, location, location."

Ulmstrom frowned but continued. "Whatever the reason, here is the ultimate purpose of Wewelsburg." He pointed down to the floor.

In the gloom, a pattern had been done in dark green tiles against a white background. It looked like a sun, radiating twelve lightning bolts.

"The *Schwarze Sonne*. The Black Sun." Ulmstrom stalked around its circumference. "This symbol also has roots in many myths. But to the Nazis it represented the land from which the All-Father descended. A land that went by many names. Thule, Hyperborea, Agartha. Ultimately the symbol represents the sun under which the Aryan race would be reborn."

"Returning again to the All-Father," Gray said, picturing the *Mensch* rune.

"That was the ultimate goal of the Nazis . . . or at least for Himmler and his Black Order. To advance the German people back to their godlike status. It was why Himmler chose this symbol to represent his Black Order."

Gray began to sense what research Hugo might have been involved with. A biologist with roots at Wewelsburg. Could he have been involved with a twisted form of the *Lebensborn* project, some type of eugenics program? But why would people kill over such a program today? What had Hugo discovered that he felt needed to be kept so secret, burying it in code in his family's books?

Gray remembered Ryan's recitation of his great-grandfather's letter to his daughter, shortly before his death. He hinted at a secret that was *too beautiful to let die and too monstrous to set free*. What had he discovered? What had he wanted kept secret from his Nazi superiors?

Lightning crackled again, shining through all the windows. The symbol of the Black Sun shone brilliantly. Electric lights trembled as the thunder reverberated throughout the hilltop castle. Not the best place to be in an electrical storm.

Confirming this, the lights flared again—then went dark.

Blackout.

Still, enough murky illumination came through the windows to see.

Voices shouted in the distance.

A loud clang rang out closer at hand.

All eyes turned.

The door to the chamber had slammed closed. Gray reached for the butt of his gun, holstered under his sweater.

"Security lockdown," Ulmstrom assured them. "Nothing to fear. Back-up generators should—"

Lights flickered, then ignited again.

Ulmstrom nodded. "Ah, there we go. *Es tut mir leid,*" he apologized. "This way."

He led them back through the security door, but rather than heading toward the main hall, he aimed for a set of stairs to the side. Apparently the tour was not over.

"I think you might find this next chamber of particular interest as you'll see the *Mensch* rune from the Bible depicted there."

Footsteps approached down the hall, coming fast.

Gray turned, realizing his hand still rested on his gun. But there was no need to unholster it. Ryan hurried toward them, a stuffed manila envelope clutched in his hand.

He joined them, slightly out of breath. His eyes darted a

bit, plainly spooked by the brief blackout. *"Ich glaube . . ."* He cleared his throat. "I have all the paperwork, including the letter to my great-aunt Tola."

Monk took the envelope. "Now we can get our butts out of here."

Maybe they should. Gray glanced to Dr. Ulmstrom. He stood at the head of stairs leading down.

The curator stepped toward them. "If you're in a hurry . . ."

"No, *bitte*. What were you saying about the *Mensch* rune?" It would be foolish to leave without exploring this fully.

Ulmstrom lifted an arm and motioned toward the stairs. "Below lies the only chamber in the entire castle where the *Mensch* rune can be found. Of course, the rune's presence only makes sense considering . . ."

"Considering what?"

Ulmstrom sighed, checked his watch. "Come. I'll have to make this quick anyway." He turned and strode to the staircase and headed down.

Gray waved Fiona and Ryan to follow. Monk rolled his eyes at Gray as he passed. "Spooky castle . . . time to go . . ."

Gray understood Monk's itchiness to leave. He felt it, too. First the false alarm with the Mercedes, then the blackout. But nothing untoward had happened. And Gray hated to pass up a chance to learn more about the Bible's rune and its history here.

Ulmstrom's voice carried up to Gray. The others had reached the landing below. "This chamber lies immediately below the *Obergruppenführersaal*."

Gray joined them while the curator unlocked a matching door to the one above, also barred and sealed with thick glass. He held it open for them, then stepped in after them.

Beyond lay another circular chamber. This one windowless, lit gloomily by a few wall sconces. Twelve granite columns circled the space, holding up a domed roof. In the center of the ceiling, a twisted swastika symbol had been painted.

"This is the castle's crypt," Ulmstrom said. "Note the well in the center of the room. It is where the coat of arms of fallen SS officers would be burned ceremonially."

Gray had already spotted the stone well, directly below the swastika in the ceiling.

"If you stand near the well, and look at the walls, you'll see the *Mensch* runes depicted here."

Gray stepped closer and followed his directions. At the cardinal points, the runes had been engraved in the stone walls. Now Gray understood Ulmstrom's remark. *The rune's presence only makes sense considering . . .*

The *Mensch* runes were all upside down.

Toten-runes.

Death runes.

A loud clang, a match to the one a moment ago, resounded across the chamber. Only this time there had been no blackout. Gray swung around, realizing his mistake. Curiosity had lessened his guard. Dr. Ulmstrom had never moved far from the door.

The curator now stood outside it, clicking the lock.

He called through the thick glass, doubtless bulletproof. "Now you'll understand the true meaning of the *toten-rune.*"

A loud pop sounded next. All the lamps went dark. With no windows, the chamber sank into complete darkness.

In the shocked silence, a new sound intruded: a fierce hissing.

But it came from no snake or serpent.

Gray tasted it on the back of his tongue.

Gas.

1:49 P.M.
HIMALAYAS

The trio of helicopters fanned out for an attack run.

Painter studied the approach of the choppers through a set of binoculars. He had unbelted and crawled into the copilot seat. He recognized the enemy crafts: Eurocopter Tigers, medium-weight, outfitted with air-to-air gun pods and missiles.

"Do you have any weapons equipped on the helo?" Painter asked Gunther.

He shook his head. *"Nein."*

Gunther worked the rudder pedals to bring them around, swinging away from their adversaries. Pitching the helo forward, he accelerated away. It was their only real counter-measure: speed.

The A-Star, lighter and unburdened of armaments, was quicker and more maneuverable. But even that advantage had its limitations.

Painter knew the direction in which Gunther was headed now, forced by the others. Painter had thoroughly studied the region's terrain maps. The Chinese border lay only thirty miles away.

If the attack choppers didn't eliminate them, invading Chinese airspace would. And with the current tensions between the Nepalese government and the Maoist rebels, the border was closely watched. They were literally between a rock and a hard place.

Anna yelled from the backseat, head craned to watch their rear. "Missile launch!"

Even before her warning ended, a screaming streak of smoke and fire shot past their port side, missing by mere yards. The missile slammed into the ice-encrusted ridgeline ahead. Fire and rock shot high. A large chunk of cliff broke off and slid away, like a glacier calving.

Gunther tipped their helo on its side and sped clear of the rain of debris.

He darted their craft down and raced between two ridges of rock. They were temporarily out of the direct line of fire.

"If we put down," Anna said. "Fast. Flee on foot."

Painter shook his head, shouting to be heard above the engine. "I know these Tigers. They have infrared. Our heat signatures would just give us away. Then there'd be no escaping their guns or rockets."

"Then what do we do?"

Painter's head still spasmed with white-hot bursts. His vision had constricted to a laser focus.

Lisa answered, leaning forward from the backseat, her eyes on the compass. "Everest," she said.

"What?"

She nodded to the compass. "We're heading right toward Everest. What if we landed over there, got lost in the mass of climbers."

Painter considered her plan. *To hide in plain sight.*

"The storm's backlogged the mountain," she continued loudly. "Some two hundred people were waiting to ascend when I left. Including some Nepalese soldiers. Might even be more after the monastery burned down."

Lisa glanced over to Anna. Painter read her expression. They were fighting for their lives alongside the very enemy who had burned down that monastery. But a greater adversary threatened all. While Anna had made brutal, unforgivable choices, this other faction had triggered the necessity for her actions, setting in motion the chain of events that led them all here.

And Painter knew it wouldn't stop here. This was just the beginning, a feint meant to misdirect. Something monstrous was afoot. Anna's words echoed in his pounding head.

We must stop them.

Lisa finished, "With so many satellite phones and video feeds broadcasting from Base Camp, they'd dare not attack."

"Or so we hope," Painter said. "If they don't back off, we'd be jeopardizing many lives."

Lisa leaned back, digesting his words. Painter knew her brother was among those at Base Camp. She met his eyes.

"It's too important," she said, coming to the same conclusion he had a moment ago. "We have to risk it. Word must get out!"

Painter glanced around the cabin.

Anna said, "It will be shorter to go *over* the shoulder of Everest to get to the other side, rather than taking the longer route *around*." She pointed to the wall of mountain ahead of them.

"So we head for the Base Camp?" Painter said.

They were all in agreement.

Others were not.

A helicopter roared over the ridgeline, its skids passing directly over their rotors. The intruder seemed startled to come across them. The Tiger twisted and climbed in a surprised pirouette.

But they'd been found.

Painter prayed the others were spread out in a wide search pattern—then again, one Tiger was enough.

Their unarmed A-Star shot out of the trough into a wider couloir, a bowl-shaped gully full of snow and ice. No cover. The Tiger's pilot responded quickly, plunging toward them.

Gunther throttled up the engine speed and increased the blade pitch, attempting a full-out sprint. They might outrun the heavier Tiger, but not its missiles.

To punctuate this, the diving Tiger opened fire with its gun pods, spitting flames, and chewing through the snow.

"Forget outrunning the bastard!" Painter yelled and jerked his thumb straight up. "Take the race that way."

Gunther glanced at him, heavy brows knit tight.

"He's heavier," Painter explained, motioning with his hands. "We can climb to a higher elevation. Where he can't follow."

Gunther nodded and pulled back on the collective, turning forward motion into vertical. Like riding an express elevator, the helo shot upward.

The Tiger was taken aback by the sudden change of direction and took an extra moment to follow, spiraling up after them.

Painter watched the altimeter. The world record for elevation reached by a helicopter had been set by a stripped-down A-Star. It had landed on the summit of Everest. They didn't need to climb that far. The armament-heavy Tiger was already petering out as they went above the twenty-two-thousand-foot mark, its rotors churning uselessly in the rarefied air, making it difficult to maintain yaw and roll, confounding an attack pitch in which to employ its missiles.

For now, their craft continued to sail upward into safety.

But they could not stay up here forever.

What went up eventually had to come down.

And like a circling shark, the attack helicopter waited below. All it had to do was track them. Painter spotted the two other Tigers winging in their direction, called into the hunt, a pack closing in on its wounded prey.

"Get above the chopper," Painter said, pantomiming with one palm over the other.

Gunther's frown never wavered, but he obeyed.

Painter twisted around to Anna and Lisa. "Both of you, look out your side windows. Let me know when that Tiger is directly below us."

Nods answered him.

Painter turned his attention to the lever in front of him.

"Just about there!" Lisa called from her side.

"Now!" Anna responded a second later.

Painter yanked on the lever. It controlled the winch assembly on the undercarriage of the chopper. The rope and harness had lowered Painter earlier when he'd been pursuing the assassin. But he wasn't lowering the harness now. The emergency lever he gripped was used to jettison the assembly if it should be jammed. He cranked it fully back and felt the *pop* of the release.

Painter pressed his face to the window.

Gunther banked them around, pitching for a better view.

The winch assembly tumbled end over end, unreeling its harness in a wide tangled mess.

It struck the Tiger below, smashing into its rotors. The effect was as destructive as any depth charge. The blades tore apart, flying in all directions. The chopper itself twisted like a spun top, flipping sideways and falling away.

With no time to spare, Painter pointed toward their only neighbor at this elevation. The white summit of Everest rose ahead, shrouded in clouds.

They had to reach Base Camp on its lower slopes—but below, the skies were not safe.

Two more helicopters, angry as hornets, raced toward them.

And Painter was out of winches.

Lisa watched the other helicopters swoop toward them, growing from gnats to hawks. It was now a race.

Pitching the chopper steeply, Gunther dove out of the rarefied ether. He aimed for the gap between Mount Everest and its sister peak, Mount Lhotse. A shouldered ridgeline— the famous south col—connected Lhotse to Everest. They needed to get over its edge and put the mountain between them and the others. On the far side, Base Camp lay at the foot of the col.

If they could reach it . . .

She pictured her brother, his goofy smile, the cowlick at the back of his head that he was perpetually trying to smooth down. What were they thinking, bringing this war to Base Camp, to her brother?

In front of her, Painter was bent with Gunther. The engine's roar ate their words. She had to place her trust in Painter. He would not jeopardize anyone's life needlessly.

The col rose toward them. The world expanded outward as they dove toward the mountain pass. Everest filled the starboard side, a plume of snow blowing from its tip. Lhotse, the fourth highest peak in the world, was a wall to the left.

Gunther steepened their angle. Lisa clutched her seat harness. She felt like she might tumble out the front windshield. The world ahead became a sheet of ice and snow.

A whistling scream cut through the roar.

"Missile!" Anna screamed.

Gunther yanked on the stick. The nose of the chopper shot up and yawed to the right. The missile sailed under their skids and streaked into the eastern ridge of the col. Fire blasted upward. Gunther banked them clear of the eruption, dipping the nose down again.

Pressing her cheek against the side window, Lisa glanced to the rear. The two choppers had closed the distance, angling toward them. Then a wall of ice cut off the view.

"We're over the ridge!" Painter yelled. "Hang tight!"

Lisa swung back around. The helicopter plunged down the vertiginous slope of the south col. Snow and ice raced under them. Ahead, a darker scar appeared. Base Camp.

They aimed for it, as if intending to crash headlong into the tent city.

The camp swelled below them, growing with each second, prayer flags flapping, individual tents discernable now.

"We're going to land hard!" Painter yelled.

Gunther didn't slow.

Lisa found a prayer rising to her lips or maybe a mantra. "Oh God . . . oh God . . . oh God . . ."

At the last moment, Gunther pulled up, fighting the controls. Winds fought him. The helicopter continued falling, rotors now shrieking.

The world beyond was a Tilt-A-Whirl.

Thrown about, Lisa clenched the armrests.

Then the skids slammed hard to the ground, slightly nose down, throwing Lisa forward. The seat harness held her. Rotor wash churned up snow in a flurried burst, but the chopper rocked back onto its skids, level and even.

"Everybody out!" Painter yelled as Gunther throttled down.

Hatches popped, and they tumbled out.

Painter appeared at Lisa's side, taking her arm in his. Anna and Gunther followed. A mass of people converged toward them. Lisa glanced up to the ridge. Smoke rose behind the col from the missile attack. Everyone at camp must have heard it, emptying tents.

Voices in a slur of languages assaulted them.

Lisa, half-deafened by the helicopter, felt distant from it all.

Then one voice reached her.

"Lisa!"

She turned. A familiar shape in black snowpants and a gray thermal shirt shoved through the crowd, elbowing and pushing.

"Josh!"

Painter allowed her to divert the group in his direction. Then Lisa was in her brother's arms, hugging tight. He smelled vaguely of yaks. She had never smelled anything better.

Gunther grunted behind them. *"Pass auf!"*

A warning.

Cries arose around them. Attention shifted in a spreading tide. Arms pointed.

Lisa freed herself from her brother.

A pair of attack helicopters hovered at the top of the col, stirring the smoke from the missile impact. They hung in place, predatory, lethal.

Go away, Lisa prayed, willing it with all her strength. *Just go away.*

"Who are they?" a new voice grated.

Lisa didn't need to turn to recognize Boston Bob, a mistake from her past. His accent and perpetual whining undercurrent identified him plainly enough. Always intrusive, he must have followed Josh. She ignored him.

But Josh must have felt her tense when the helicopters appeared. "Lisa . . . ?"

She shook her head, eyes fixed to the skies. She needed her full concentration to will them away.

But to no avail.

In unison, both helicopters tipped out of their hovers and dove down the slope toward them. Spats of fire lit their noses. Snow and ice blasted up in parallel lines of death, chewing down the slope, aiming straight for Base Camp.

"No . . . ," Lisa moaned.

Boston Bob yelled, backing away, "What the hell did you do?"

The crowd, stunned and frozen for a breath, suddenly erupted in screams and shouts, breaking apart and fleeing in all directions.

Painter grabbed Lisa's other arm. He tugged her away, hauling Josh, too. They retreated, but there was nowhere to hide.

"A radio!" Painter yelled at Josh. "Where's a radio?"

Her brother stared mutely at the sky.

Lisa shook her brother's arm, drawing his eyes down. "Josh, we need to find a radio." She understood Painter's focus. If nothing else, word of what had happened must reach the outside world.

Her brother coughed, collected himself, and pointed. "This way . . . they set up an emergency communication net after the rebel attack at the monastery." He hurried out toward a large red tent.

Lisa noted Boston Bob kept up with them, checking over his shoulder, sensing the authority radiating from Painter and Gunther. Or maybe it was the assault rifle Gunther carried. The German had slammed another grenade into the weapon's launcher. He was ready to make a last stand, guard them while they attempted to radio out.

But before they could reach the tent, Painter yelled, "Get down!"

He yanked Lisa to the ground. Everyone followed his example, though Josh had to pull Boston Bob off his legs.

A strange new scream suddenly echoed off the mountains.

Painter's gaze searched the skies.

"What—?" Lisa asked.

"Wait," Painter said with a confused frown.

Then over the shoulder of Mount Lhotse, a pair of military jets shot into view, streaking on twin contrails. Fire flared from under their wings.

Missiles.

Oh, no!

But the base wasn't the target. The jets shot overhead, streaking away, booming as they passed and sailing straight up into the ether.

The pair of attack helicopters, already three-quarters of the way down the slope, exploded as the jets' heat-seeking missiles crashed into them. Fiery ruins slammed into the slope, blasting snow and flames. Debris rained, but none of it reached the camp.

Painter gained his feet, then helped Lisa up.

The others followed.

Boston Bob shoved forward, bullying up to Lisa. "What

the hell was all that? What shit did you bring down on our heads?"

Lisa turned away. Whatever had possessed her back in Seattle to sleep with him? It was as if that had been a different woman.

"Don't turn your back on me, you bitch!"

Lisa swung around, fingers clenched—but there was no need. Painter was already there. His arm pistoned and smashed into the man's face. Lisa had heard the term "cold-cocked" but never had witnessed it. Boston Bob fell back, stiff as a board, and crashed to the ground. He did not get up, splayed out, nose broken, out cold.

Painter shook his hand, wincing.

Josh gaped, then grinned. "Oh, man, I've been wanting to do that for a solid week."

Before more could be said, a sandy-haired man stepped out of the red communication tent. He wore a military uniform. A *United States* military uniform. He stepped to their group, his eyes settling on Painter.

"Director Crowe?" the man asked in a Georgian drawl, his arm out.

Painter accepted the handshake, grimacing at the pressure on his bruised knuckles.

"Logan Gregory sends his best wishes, sir." The man nodded to the blasted ruins smoking on the slope.

"Better late than never," Painter said.

"We have him on the horn for you. If you'll follow me."

Painter accompanied the Air Force officer, Major Brooks, into the communication tent. Lisa tried to follow with Anna and Gunther. Major Brooks held up an arm, blocking them.

"I'll be right back," Painter assured them. "Hold fast."

Ducking, he entered the tent. Inside stood an array of

equipment. A communication officer stepped back from a satellite telecommunication station. Painter took his place, picking up the receiver.

"Logan?"

The voice came through clear. "Director Crowe, it's wonderful to hear you're okay."

"I think I have you to thank for that."

"We got your SOS."

Painter nodded. So his message had gotten out, sent by burst transmission from his jury-rigged amplifier back at the castle. Luckily the GPS signal had broadcast before the overloaded amplifier had exploded. Apparently it had been enough to track.

"It took some fast footwork to get surveillance up and coordinate with the Royal Nepalese military," Logan explained. "Still, it was close, too close."

Logan must have been monitoring the entire situation via satellite, possibly from the time they'd fled the castle. But details could wait. Painter had more important concerns.

"Logan, before I fully debrief, I need you to get started on a search. I'm going to fax you a symbol, a tattoo." Painter mimed writing on a pad to Major Brooks. Supplies were brought to him. He quickly drew the symbol he had seen on the assassin's hand. It was all they had to go on.

"Get started immediately," Painter continued. "See if you can find out if any terrorist organization, political party, drug cartel, even Boy Scout troop, might be associated with this symbol."

"I'll get right on it."

Finishing a rough approximation of the cloverleaf tattoo, Painter passed it to the communication officer, who stepped to a fax machine and fed the sheet into it.

While the transmission was sent, Painter gave a thumbnail version of what happened. He was grateful Logan didn't interrupt with too many questions.

"Did the fax arrive there yet?" Painter asked after a few minutes.

"Just in my hands now."

"Perfect. The search . . . give it top priority."

A long pause followed. Dead air. Painter thought maybe they'd lost their signal, then Logan spoke, tentative, confused. "Sir . . ."

"What is it?"

"I know this symbol. Grayson Pierce sent it to me eight hours ago."

"What?"

Logan explained about the events in Copenhagen. Painter struggled to wrap his mind around it. With the adrenaline from the chase dissipating, the pounding in his head confounded his attention and focus. He fought against it, putting pieces together. The same assassins were after Gray, *Sonnekönige* born under a foreign Bell. But what were they doing in Europe? What was so important about a bunch of books? Gray was currently off in Germany investigating the trail further, seeing what he might uncover.

Painter closed his eyes. It only made his headache worse. The attacks in Europe only further confirmed his fear that something global was afoot. Something major was stirring, about to come to fruition.

But what?

There was only one place to start, a single clue. "The symbol has to be significant. We must find out who it belongs to."

Logan spoke crisply. "I may have that answer."

"What? Already?"

"I've had eight hours, sir."

Right. Of course. Painter shook his head. He glanced down to the pen in his hand, then noted something odd. He turned his hand. The nail on his fourth finger was gone, ripped away, possibly when he'd punched the asshole a moment ago. There was no blood, just pale, dry flesh, numb and cold.

Painter understood the significance.

Time was running out.

Logan explained what he had learned. Painter interrupted him. "Have you passed this intel to Gray?"

"Not yet, sir. We're having trouble reaching him at the moment."

Painter frowned, dismissing his own health concerns. "Get word to him," he said firmly. "However you can. Gray has no idea what he's up against."

9:50 A.M.
WEWELSBURG, GERMANY

Light flared in the crypt as Monk clicked on a flashlight.

Gray found his own flashlight and pulled it free of his pack. He turned it on, pointing it up. Tiny vents ran along the edges of the dome. A greenish gas poured forth, heavier than air, spilling in smoky waterfalls from all the vents.

They were too high and too many to plug.

Fiona drifted closer to him. Ryan stood on the other side of the well, arms clutched around himself, disbelieving his eyes.

Movement drew Gray's attention back to Monk.

He had pulled out his 9mm Glock and aimed it at the glass door.

"No!" Gray called out.

Too late. Monk fired.

The pistol blast echoed, accompanied by a sharp *ping* as the bullet ricocheted off the glass and struck one of the steel vents with a fiery spark. At least the gas didn't appear to be flammable. The spark could have killed them all.

Monk seemed to realize the same. "Bulletproof," he said sourly.

The curator affirmed this. "We had to install extra security. Too many neo-Nazis trying to break in." The reflection of their lights off the glass hid his position.

"Bastard," Monk mumbled.

The gas began to fill the lower spaces. It smelled sweetly musty but tasted acrid. Not cyanide, at least. That had a bitter almond scent.

"Keep standing," Gray said. "Heads high. Get in the center of the room, away from the vents."

They gathered around the ceremonial pit. Fiona's hand found his. She clasped it tightly. She lifted her other hand. "I nicked his wallet, if that makes any difference."

Monk saw what she held. "Great. You couldn't steal his keys?"

Ryan called out in German. "My . . . my father knows we're up here! He'll call the *Politzei*!"

Gray had to give the young man credit. He was trying his best.

A new voice responded, faceless behind the reflective glass. "I'm afraid your father will not be calling anyone . . . ever again." The words were not spoken in threat, merely a statement.

Ryan fell back a step, as if physically struck. His eyes flicked to Gray, then back to the door.

Gray recognized the voice. As did Fiona. Her fingers had clenched hard in his grip. It was the tattooed buyer from the auction house.

"There will be none of your tricks this time," the man said. "No escape."

Gray's head began to feel woozy. His body grew lighter, growing weightless. He shook his head to clear the cobwebs. The man was correct. There would be no escape. But that didn't mean they were defenseless.

Knowledge was power.

Gray turned to Monk. "Get your lighter out of your pack," he ordered.

As Monk obeyed, Gray dropped his own backpack and yanked out his notebook. He threw it into the pit.

"Monk, toss in Ryan's copies." Gray held out his hand. "Fiona, the Bible, please."

They both obeyed.

"Light the pit," Gray said.

Monk flicked his lighter and ignited one of Ryan's recently copied sheets. He dropped it into the pit. In seconds, a smattering of flame and smoke rose, consuming all. The rising smoke even seemed to drive back the poison momentarily . . . or so Gray hoped. His head swam drunkenly.

Beyond the doors, voices murmured, too low to make out.

Gray held up the Darwin Bible. "Only we know what secret is hidden in this Bible!" he called out.

The white-blond assassin, still faceless behind the glass, answered, vaguely amused. "Dr. Ulmstrom discerned all we needed to know. The *Mensch* rune. The Bible is worthless to us now."

"Is it?" Gray held the book up, shining his light on it. "We only showed Ulmstrom what Hugo Hirszfeld wrote on the *back* pasteboard of the Bible. But not what was scrawled on the *front*!"

A moment of silence, then voices again drew back into furtive murmurs. Gray thought he heard a woman's voice, perhaps the blond man's pale twin.

A clear *nein* arose in Ulmstrom's voice, defensive.

Fiona stumbled next to him, her knees giving way. Monk caught her, holding her head above the rising pool of poisonous gas. But even he wobbled on his feet.

Gray could wait no longer.

He clicked off his flashlight for dramatic effect and dropped the Bible into the fire pit. He was still Roman Catholic enough to feel a twinge of misgiving, burning a Bible. The old pages took to flame immediately, flaring up to their knees. A fresh curl of smoke plumed upward.

Gray took a deep breath, putting as much conviction as possible in his voice, needing to sell it. "If we die, so does the secret of the Darwin Bible!"

He waited, praying his ruse would work.

One second . . . two . . .

The gas rose under them. Each breath gagged now.

Ryan suddenly collapsed, as if someone had cut the strings holding him up. Monk reached for his arm but went down on a knee, burdened by Fiona. He never rose again. He slumped, cradling Fiona with him.

Gray stared toward the black door. Monk's flashlight rolled from his limp fingers, spinning. Was anyone even out there? Had anyone believed him?

He would never know.

As the world drowned from sight, Gray fell back into darkness.

5:50 P.M.
HLUHLUWE-UMFOLOZI PRESERVE

Thousands of miles away, another man woke.

The world returned in a miasma of pain and color. His eyes flickered open to something fluttering over his face, the wings of a bird. His ears filled with a chanting.

"He wakes," another said in Zulu.

"Khamisi . . ." This time a woman's voice.

It took a moment for the waking man to reconnect the name to himself. It fit uneasily. A groan reached his ears. In his own voice.

"Help him sit up," the woman said. She also spoke Zulu, but her accent was British, familiar.

Khamisi felt himself tugged up into a weak slouch, propped by pillows. His sight stabilized. The room, a mud brick hut, was dark, but painful lances of light pierced around shaded windows and the edges of a rug shielding the hut's door. The roof was decorated with colorful gourds, twists of hides, and strings of feathers. The odor of the room cloyed with strange scents. Something was snapped under his nose. It reeked of ammonia and shoved his head back.

He flailed out a bit. He saw his right arm trailed an IV line, attached to a hanging bag of yellowish fluid. His arms were caught.

On one side, the bare-chested shaman wearing a crown of feathers held his shoulder steady. He had been the one chanting and waving a desiccated vulture wing over his face, to ward away death's scavengers.

On the other, Dr. Paula Kane held his arm, placing it back down on the blanket. He was naked beneath it. Sweat had soaked the cloth to his skin.

"Where . . . what . . . ?" his voice croaked.

"Water," Paula ordered.

The third person in the room obeyed, a crooked-backed elder of the Zulu. He passed a dented canteen.

"Can you hold it?" Paula asked.

Khamisi nodded, strength feebly returning. He took the canteen and sipped the tepid water, loosening his pasty tongue and his memories. The elder who brought the canteen . . . he had been in Khamisi's house.

His heart suddenly beat faster. His other hand, trailing the IV line, rose to his neck. A bandage lay there. He remembered it all. The fanged dart. The black mamba. The staged snake attack.

"What happened?"

The old man filled in the blank spaces. Khamisi recognized him as the elder who had first reported seeing an *ukufa* in the park five months ago. Back then, his claims had been dismissed, even by Khamisi.

"I heard what happened to Missus Doctor." He nodded to Paula in sympathy and sorrow. "And I heard what you say you saw. People talk. I come by your home, to speak to you. But you not home. So I wait. Others come, so I hide. They chop a snake. Mamba. Bad magic. I stay hiding."

Khamisi closed his eyes, remembering. He had then come home, been darted, left for dead. But his attackers hadn't known about the man hiding in the back.

"I come out," the elder continued. "I call others. In secret, we take you away."

Paula Kane finished the story. "We brought you here," she said. "The poison almost killed you, but medicine—both modern and ancient—saved you. It was a close call."

Khamisi glanced from the IV bottle to the shaman.

"Thank you."

"Do you feel strong enough to walk?" Paula asked. "You should get your limbs moving. The poison hits the circulatory system like a load of bricks."

Assisted by the shaman, Khamisi stood up, modestly keeping his soaked blanket around his waist. He was walked to the door. While taking his first steps he felt as weak as a babe, but a frail strength quickly suffused his limbs.

The rug over the door was pulled back.

Light and the day's heat flowed inside, blinding and blistering.

Midafternoon, he guessed. The sun sank in the west.

Shielding his eyes, he stepped out.

He recognized the tiny Zulu village. It stood at the edge of the Hluhluwe-Umfolozi reserve. Not far from where they'd found the rhino, where Dr. Fairfield had been attacked.

Khamisi glanced at Paula Kane. She stood with her arms crossed, her face exhausted.

"It was the head warden," Khamisi said. He had no doubts. "He wanted to silence me."

"About how Marcia died. What you saw."

He nodded.

"What did you—?"

Her words were cut off as a twin-engine helicopter sped past overhead, low and loud. Rotor wash thrashed bushes and tree limbs. Rugs flapped from doorways, as if trying to wave away the interloper.

The heavy aircraft raced away, passing low over the savanna.

Khamisi watched it. It was no tourist junket.

Beside him, Paula had raised a pair of Bushnell binoculars, following the aircraft. It drifted farther away, then settled for a landing. Khamisi stepped out farther to watch.

Paula passed him the binoculars. "There've been flights in and out of there all day."

Khamisi lifted the glasses. The world magnified and zoomed. He saw the twin-engine drop behind a barrier of ten-foot-high black fencing. It marked the boundary of the Waalenberg private estate. The helicopter vanished behind it.

"Something has them all stirred up," Paula said.

The tiny hairs on the back of Khamisi's neck quivered.

He twisted the focus, fixing more sharply on the fencing. The old main gates, rarely used, stood closed. He recognized the old family crest, done in silver filigree across the gates. The Waalenberg Crown and Cross.

THIRD

THIRD

II
DEMON IN THE MACHINE

12:33 A.M.
AIRBORNE OVER THE INDIAN OCEAN

"Captain Bryant and I will do our best to investigate the Waalenbergs here in Washington," Logan Gregory said over the phone.

Painter wore an earpiece that dangled a microphone. He needed his hands free as he sifted through the mountain of paperwork that Logan had faxed to their staging area in Kathmandu. It contained everything about the Waalenbergs: family history, financial reports, international ties, even gossip and innuendo.

On top of the pile rested a grainy photograph: a man and a woman climbing out of a limousine. Gray Pierce had taken the picture from a hotel suite across the street, prior to the start of an auction. The digital surveillance had confirmed Logan's assessment. The tattoo was tied to the Waalenberg clan. The two in the photo were Isaak and Ischke Waalenberg, twins, the youngest heirs to the family fortune, a fortune that rivaled most countries' gross national product.

But more importantly, Painter recognized the wan complexions and white hair. The pair were more than heirs. They were *Sonnekönige*. Like Gunther, like the assassin back at the mountain castle.

Painter glanced to the front of the Gulfstream's cabin.

Gunther slept, sprawled across a sofa, legs dangling over the end. His sister, Anna, sat in a nearby chair, facing a pile of research as daunting as Painter's. The two were guarded over by Major Brooks and a pair of armed U.S. Rangers. Roles were now reversed. The captors had become the prisoners. But despite the shift in power, nothing had really changed between them. Anna needed Painter's connections and logistical support; Painter needed Anna's knowledge of the Bell and the science behind it. As Anna had stated earlier, "Once this is over, then we'll settle matters of legality and responsibility."

Logan cut into his reverie. "Kat and I have an appointment set for the morning with the South African embassy. We'll see if they can't help shed some light on this reclusive family."

And *reclusive* was putting it mildly. The Waalengbergs were the Kennedys of South Africa: rich, ruthless, with their own estate the size of Rhode Island outside of Johannesburg. Though the family owned vast tracts elsewhere, the Waalenberg family seldom strayed far from their main estate.

Painter picked up the grainy digital photo.

A family of *Sonnekönige*.

As time ran short, there could be only one place a second Bell could be hidden. Somewhere on that estate.

"A British operative will meet you when you touch down in Johannesburg. MI5 has had their eye on the Waalenbergs for years—tracking unusual transactions—but they've been unable to penetrate their wall of privacy and secrecy."

Not surprising, since the Waalenbergs practically own the country, Painter thought.

"They'll offer ground support and local expertise," Logan finished. "I'll have more details by the time you touch down in three hours."

"Very good." Painter stared at the picture. "And what about Gray and Monk?"

"They've dropped off the map. We found their car parked at the airport in Frankfurt."

Frankfurt? That made no sense. The city was a major international airline hub, but Gray already had access to a government jet, faster than any commercial airline. "And no word at all?"

"No, sir. We're listening on all channels."

The news was definitely disconcerting.

Rubbing at a needling headache that even codeine couldn't touch, Painter concentrated on the drone of the plane as it sailed through the dark skies. What had happened to Gray? The options were few: he'd gone into hiding, been captured, or killed. Where was he?

"Turn over every stone, Logan."

"It's under way. Hopefully by the time you reach Johannesburg, I'll have more news on that matter, too."

"Do you ever sleep, Logan?"

"There's a Starbucks on the corner, sir. Make that *every* corner." A tired amusement flavored his words. "But what about you, sir?"

He had taken a power nap back in Kathmandu while all the preparations had been made and fires put out—literally and politically—in Nepal. They had been delayed too long in Kathmandu.

"I'm holding up fine, Logan. No worries."

Right.

As Painter signed off, his thumb rubbed absently over the pale pebbly flesh that was the nail bed to his fourth finger. All his other fingers tingled—and now his toes. Logan had attempted to convince him to fly back to Washington, have tests run at Johns Hopkins, but Painter had trusted that Anna's group was well ahead of the curve on this particular illness. *Damaged at the quantum level.*

No conventional treatment would help. To slow down the disease, they needed another functioning Bell. According to Anna, periodic treatment with the Bell's radiation under controlled situations could buy them years instead of days. *And maybe down the line, even a complete cure,* Anna concluded hopefully.

But first they needed another Bell.

And more information.

A voice behind his shoulder startled him. "I think we should talk to Anna," Lisa said, as if reading his mind.

Painter turned. He thought Lisa had been asleep in back. She had cleaned up, showered, and now leaned against his seat back, dressed in khaki slacks and a cream-colored blouse.

Her eyes searched his face, clinical, judging. "You look like crap," she said.

"Such a good bedside manner," he said, standing and stretching.

The plane tilted and darkened. Lisa grabbed his elbow, steadying him. The world brightened and stabilized. It hadn't been the plane, just his head.

"Promise me you'll get some more sleep before we land," she said, squeezing his elbow in a demanding pinch.

"If there's time—*owww!*"

She had a grip like iron.

"Okay, I promise," he relented.

Her grip relaxed. She nodded to Anna. The woman was hunched over a stack of invoices, going over bills of lading for the Waalenberg estate. She was looking for any telltale signs that the Waalenbergs had been bringing in supplies consistent with the operation of a functioning Bell.

"I want to know more about how that Bell works," Lisa said. "The fundamental theories behind it. If the disease causes quantum damage, we must understand how and why. She and Gunther are the only survivors from *Granitschloß.*

I doubt Gunther has been instructed on the finer points of the Bell's theories."

Painter nodded. "More guard dog than scientist."

As if confirming this, a loud snore rumbled from the man.

"All the remaining knowledge of the Bell is in Anna's head. If her mind should go . . ."

They'd lose it all.

"We need to secure the information before that happens," Painter agreed.

Lisa's eyes met his. She did not hide her thoughts. They were plain on her face. He remembered her climbing on board the plane in Kathmandu. Exhausted, frayed to a ragged edge, she had not hesitated to come along. She understood. Like now.

It wasn't just Anna's mind and memory that were at risk.

Painter was also in danger.

Only one person had been following this trail from the beginning, one person with the medical and scientific mind to follow it all, a mind free of impending dementia. Back at the castle, Lisa and Anna had shared long conversations alone. Also on her own, Lisa had explored the depths of Anna's research library. Who knew what tiny fact might prove to be the critical one, the difference between success and failure?

Lisa had understood.

It had taken no discussion in Kathmandu.

She had simply climbed on board.

Lisa's hand slipped from his elbow and slid to his hand. She gave his fingers a squeeze and nodded to Anna. "Let's go pick her brain."

"To understand how the Bell works," Anna explained, "you must first understand quantum theory."

Lisa studied the German woman. Her pupils were dilated

from the codeine. She was taking too much. Anna's fingers shook with fine tremors. She clutched her reading glasses in both hands, as if they were an anchor. They had retreated to the back of the jet. Gunther still slept under guard in the front.

"I don't think we have time for the full Ph.D. program," Painter said.

"*Natürlich*. Only three principles need to be understood." Anna let go of her glasses long enough to hold up one finger. "First, we must understand that once matter is broken down to the subatomic level—the world of electrons, protons, and neutrons—then the classical laws of the universe begin to erode. Max Planck discovered that electrons, protons, and neutrons act as both particles *and* waves. Which seems strange and contradictory. Particles have distinct orbits and paths, while waves are more diffuse, less distinct, lacking any specific coordinates."

"And these subatomic particles act like both?" Lisa asked.

"They have the *potential* to be either a wave or a particle," Anna said. "Which brings us to our next point. The Heisenberg Uncertainty Principle."

Lisa was already familiar with it and had read further about it back in Anna's laboratory. "Heisenberg basically states that nothing is certain until it is observed," she said. "But I don't understand what that has to do with electrons, protons, and neutrons."

"The best example of Heisenberg's principle is Schrödinger's cat," Anna responded. "Put a cat in a sealed box hooked to a device that may or may not poison the cat at any moment. Purely random odds. Dead or alive. Heisenberg tells us that in that situation, with the box closed, that the cat is *potentially* both dead *and* alive. Only once someone opens the box and looks inside does reality choose one state or the other. Dead *or* alive."

"Sounds more philosophical than scientific," Lisa said.

"Perhaps when you're talking about a cat. But it has been proven true at the subatomic level."

"Proven? How?" Painter asked. He had sat quietly up until now, letting Lisa direct the questioning. She sensed he knew much of this already but wanted Lisa to get all the information she needed.

"In the classic double-slit test," Anna said. "Which brings us to point number three." She picked up two pieces of paper and drew two slits on one and held them up on end, one behind the other.

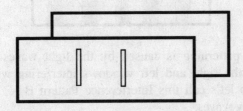

"What I'm about to tell you is going to seem strange and against common sense. . . . Suppose this piece of paper were a concrete wall and the slits were two windows. If you took a gun and sprayed bullets at both slits, you'd get a certain pattern on the wall on the far side. Like this."

She took the second piece of paper and punched dots on it.

"Call this Diffraction Pattern A. The way bullets or particles would pass through these slits."

Lisa nodded. "Okay."

"Next, instead of bullets, let's shine a big spotlight on the wall, with light passing through both slits. Because light travels in waves, we would get a different pattern on the far wall."

She shaded a pattern of light and dark bands across a new piece of paper.

"This patterning is caused by the light waves passing through the right and left windows interfering with each other. So let's call this Interference Pattern B . . . what is caused by waves."

"Got it," Lisa said, not sure where this was going.

Anna held up the two patterns. "Now take an electron gun and shoot a single line of electrons at the double slits. What pattern would you get?"

"Since you're shooting electrons like bullets, I'd guess Diffraction Pattern A." Lisa pointed to the first picture.

"Actually, in laboratory tests you get the second. Interference Pattern B."

Lisa thought about this. "The wave pattern. So then the electrons must be shooting out of the gun—not like bullets—but like *light* out of a flashlight, traveling in waves and creating Pattern B."

"Correct."

"So electrons move like waves."

"Yes. *But* only when no one actually witnesses the electrons passing through the slits."

"I don't understand."

"In another experiment, scientists placed a little clicker at one of the slits. It beeped whenever it sensed an electron passing through the slit, measuring or observing the passage of an electron past the detector. What was the pattern on the other side when the device was turned on?"

"It shouldn't change, should it?"

"In the larger world, you're correct. But *not* at the subatomic world. Once the device was switched on, it immediately changed into Diffraction Pattern A."

"So the simple act of measuring changed the pattern?"

"Just as Heisenberg predicted. Though it may seem impossible, it's true. Verified over and over again. Electrons exist in a constant state of both wave and particle until something measures the electron. That very act of measuring the electron *forces* it to collapse into one reality or the other."

Lisa tried to picture a subatomic world where everything was held in a constant state of *potential*. It made no sense.

"If subatomic particles make up atoms," Lisa asked, "and atoms make up the world we know, touch, and feel, where is the line between the phantom world of quantum mechanics and our world of real objects?"

"Again, the only way to *collapse* potential is to have something measure it. Such measuring tools are constantly present in the environment. It can be one particle bumping into another, a photon of light hitting something. Constantly the environment is *measuring* the subatomic world, collapsing potential into hard reality. Look at your hands, for example. At the quantum level, the subatomic particles that make up your atoms operate according to fuzzy quantum rules, but expand outward, into the world of billions of atoms that make up your fingernail. Those atoms are bumping, jostling, and interacting—measuring one another—forcing potential into one fixed reality."

"Okay . . ."

Anna must have heard the skepticism in her voice.

"I know it's bizarre, but I've barely scratched the surface of the fuzzy world of quantum theory. I'm skipping over such concepts as nonlocality, time tunneling, and multiple universes."

Painter nodded. "Gets pretty weird out there."

"But all you need to understand are those three points," Anna said, ticking them off on her fingers. "Subatomic particles exist in a quantum state of potential. It takes a measuring tool to collapse that potential. And it is the *environment* that constantly performs those measurements to fix our reality."

Lisa lifted her hand, acquiescing for the moment. "But what does that have to do with the Bell? Back at the library, you mentioned something called *quantum evolution*."

"Exactly," Anna said. "What is DNA? Nothing but a protein machine, *ja*? Producing all the basic building blocks of cells, of bodies."

"At its simplest."

"Then go even simpler. Is DNA not merely genetic codes locked in chemical bonds? And what breaks these bonds, turning genes on and off?"

Lisa switched back to basic chemistry. "The movement of electrons and protons."

"And these subatomic particles obey which rules: the classical or the quantum?"

"The quantum."

"So if a proton could be in two places—A or B—turning a gene on or off—which place would it be found?"

Lisa squinted. "If it has the potential to be in both places, then it *is* in both places. The gene is both on *and* off. Until something measures it."

"And what measures it?"

"The environment."

"And the environment of a gene is . . . ?"

Lisa's eyes slowly widened. "The DNA molecule itself."

A nod and a smile. "At its most fundamental level, the living cell acts as its own quantum-measuring device. And it is this constant cellular measurement that is the true engine of evolution. It explains how mutations are *not* random. Why evolution occurs at a pace faster than attributable by random chance."

"Wait," Lisa said. "You'll have to back that one up."

"Consider an example, then. Remember those bacteria that could not digest lactose—how when they were starved, offered only lactose, they mutated at a miraculous pace to develop an enzyme that could digest lactose. Against astronomical odds." Anna lifted an eyebrow. "Can you explain it now? Using the three quantum principles? Especially if I tell you that the beneficial mutation required only a single proton to move from one place to another."

Lisa was willing to try. "Okay, if the proton could be in both places, then quantum theory says the proton *was* in both places. So the gene was both mutated *and* not mutated. Held in the potential between both."

Anna nodded. "Go on."

"Then the cell, acting as a quantum-measuring tool, would force the DNA to collapse on one side of the fence or the other. To mutate or not to mutate. And because the cell is living and influenced by its environment, it tilted the scale, defying randomness to produce the beneficial mutation."

"What scientists now call adaptive mutation. The environment influenced the cell, the cell influenced the DNA, and the mutation occurred that benefited the cell. All driven by the mechanics of the quantum world."

Lisa began to conceive an inkling of where this was heading. Anna had used the term "intelligent design" in their previous discussion. The woman had even answered the question of *who* she thought was behind that intelligence.

Us.

Lisa now understood. It is *our* own cells that are directing evolution, responding to the environment and collapsing potential in DNA to better fit that environment. Darwinian natural selection then kicked in to preserve these modifications.

"But even more importantly," Anna said, her voice beginning to catch and rasp a bit, "quantum mechanics explains how life's *first* spark started. Remember the improbability of that first replicating protein forming out of the primordial soup? In the quantum world, randomness is taken out of the equation. The first replicating protein formed because it was order out of chaos. Its ability to measure and collapse quantum potential superseded the randomness of merely bumping and jostling that had been going on in the primordial soup. Life started because it was a *better* quantum-measuring tool."

"And God had nothing to do with it?" Lisa said, repeating a question Anna had first asked her . . . what seemed like decades ago.

Anna lifted a palm to her forehead, fingers shaking. Her eyes tweaked. She stared out the window with a pained expression. Her voice was almost too soft to hear. "I didn't say that either . . . you're looking at it the wrong way, in the wrong direction."

Lisa let that drop. She recognized that Anna was growing too exhausted to continue. They all needed more sleep. But there was one question that had to be asked.

"The Bell?" Lisa asked. "What does it do?"

Anna lowered her hand and stared first at Painter, then at Lisa. "The Bell is the *ultimate* quantum-measuring device."

Lisa held her breath, considering what Anna was saying.

Something fiery shone through Anna's exhaustion. It was difficult to read: pride, justification, faith . . . but also a fair amount of fear.

"The Bell's field—if it could be mastered—holds the

ability not only to *evolve* DNA to its more perfect form, but also to take mankind with it."

"And what about us?" Painter said, stirring. From his expression, he was plainly unmoved by her ardor. "You and me? How is what is happening to us perfection?"

The fire died in Anna's eyes, quenched by exhaustion and defeat. "Because as much as the Bell holds the potential to evolve, the reverse also lurks within its quantum waves."

"The reverse?"

"The disease that's inflicted our cells." Anna glanced away. "It's not just degeneration . . . it's *devolution*."

Painter stared at her, stunned.

Her words dropped to a hoarse whisper. "Our bodies are heading back to the primordial ooze from which we came."

5:05 A.M.
SOUTH AFRICA

The monkeys woke him.

Monkeys?

The strangeness shocked him, snapping him from a groggy somnolence to an instant alertness. Gray shoved up. Memory crackled up next as he tried to comprehend his surroundings.

He was alive.

In a cell.

He remembered the flow of gas, the Wewelsburg museum, the lie. He had burned the Darwin Bible, claiming it contained a secret only his group knew about. He had hoped caution would outweigh revenge. Apparently it had. He was alive. But where were the others? Monk, Fiona, and Ryan?

Gray searched his cell. It was utilitarian. A cot, a toilet, an open shower stall. No windows. The door was inch-thick bars. It opened into a hallway lit by overhead fluorescent lighting. Gray took a moment to inspect himself. Someone had stripped him naked, but a neat pile of clothes had been folded atop a chair bolted to the foot of the bed.

He tossed aside the blanket and stood up. The world tilted, but a few breaths steadied it. An edge of nausea continued. His lungs felt coarse and heavy. The aftereffects of the poisoning.

Gray also noted a deep ache in his thigh. He fingered a fist-size bruise on his flank. He felt some scabbed needle pricks. There was also a Band-Aid stuck to the back of his left hand. From an IV? Apparently someone had treated him, saving his life.

Distantly he heard another spat of howls and screamed calls.

Wild monkeys.

It wasn't a caged sound.

More like the natural world awakening.

But what world? The air smelled drier, warmer, scented muskier. He was in a much more temperate climate. Maybe somewhere in Africa. How long had he been out? They had left him no wristwatch to check the time of day, let alone *which* day it was. But he sensed no more than a day had passed. The thickening of stubble on his chin belied any long nap.

He stepped to the doorway and reached for the piled clothes.

His motion drew someone's attention.

Directly across the hall, Monk stepped to the barred door on the far cell. Gray felt a surge of relief at finding his partner alive. "Thank God . . . ," he whispered.

"You okay?"

"Groggy . . . wearing off though."

Monk was already dressed, wearing the same white jumpsuit that had been left for him. Gray climbed into his.

Monk lifted up his left arm, baring his stumped wrist

and the titanium bio-contact implants that normally linked Monk's prosthesis to his arm. "Bastards even took my god-damn hand."

Monk's missing prosthesis was the least of their worries. In fact, it might be to their advantage. But first things first . . .

"Fiona and Ryan?"

"No clue. They may be in another cell here . . . or somewhere else entirely."

Or dead, Gray added silently.

"What now, boss?" Monk asked.

"Not much choice. We wait for our captors to make the first move. They want the information we have. We'll see what we can buy with that knowledge."

Monk nodded. He knew Gray had been bluffing back at the castle, but the ruse had to be maintained. The cellblock was likely under surveillance.

Proving this, a door clanged open at the end of the hall.

Many footsteps approached. A group.

They came into view: a troop of guards dressed in green and black camouflage uniforms, led by the tall, pale blond man, the buyer from the auction. He was dapperly fashioned as usual: in black twill pants and pressed linen shirt, with white leather loafers and a white cashmere cardigan. He looked like he was dressed for a garden party.

Ten guards accompanied him. They split into two groups, crossing to each cell. Gray and Monk were marched out, barefoot, with their arms secured in plastic ties behind their backs.

The leader stepped in front of them.

His blue eyes were ice upon Gray.

"Good morning," he said stiffly and a bit staged, as if he were sensitive to the cameras in the halls, knew he was being watched. "My grandfather requests an audience with you."

Despite the civility, a black anger etched each word, an

unspoken promise of pain. The man had been denied his kill before and now merely bided his time. Still, what was the real source of his fury? His brother's death . . . or the fact that Gray had outfoxed him at the castle? Either way, behind all the cultured dress and mannerisms lurked something feral.

"This way," he said and turned away.

He again led the group down the hall, Gray and Monk in tow. As they proceeded, Gray searched the cells to either side. Empty. No sign of Fiona or Ryan. Were they still alive?

The hall ended at three steps that led up to a massive steel exterior door.

It stood open, guarded.

Gray stepped out of the sterile cellblock and into a dark and verdant wonderland. A jungle canopy climbed high all around, trailing thorny vines and flowering orchids. The dense leafy foliage hid the sky. Still Gray knew it must be very early in the morning, well before sunrise. Ahead, black Victorian-era iron lampposts marked paths that trailed off into a wild jungle. Birds twittered and squawked. Insects droned. Farther up in the canopy, a single hidden monkey announced them with a staccato, coughing call. His outburst woke a flame-feathered bird and set it to wing through the lower branches.

"Africa," Monk mumbled under his breath. "Sub-Saharan at least. Maybe equatorial."

Gray agreed. He estimated that it must be the morning of the next day. He'd lost eighteen to twenty hours. That could put them anywhere in Africa.

But where?

The guards escorted them along a gravel pathway. Gray heard the soft measured step of something large pushing through the undergrowth a few yards off the trail. But even so close, its shape could not be discerned. The forest offered plenty of cover if they could make a run for it.

But the chance never arose. The path ended after only fifty yards. A few more steps and the jungle fell away around them.

The forest opened into a stretch of manicured and lamplit greensward, a garden of dancing waters and flowing springs. Ponds and creeks trickled. Waterfalls burbled. A long-horned antelope lifted its head at their appearance, froze for a heartbeat, then took flight, bounding away into the forest cover.

The sky, clear above, twinkled with stars, but to the east, a pale rosy glow hinted at the approach of morning, maybe an hour off.

Closer at hand, another sight drew Gray's eye and fully captured his attention.

Across the gardens rose a six-story mansion of stacked fieldstone and exposed exotic woods. It reminded him of The Ahwahnee lodge in Yosemite, but this was much more massive, Wagnerian in scope. A woodland Versailles. It had to cover ten acres, rising in gables and tiers, balconies and balustrades. To the left, a glass-enclosed conservatory protruded, lit from within, blazing in the predawn darkness like a rising sun.

The wealth here was staggering.

They headed toward the manor house, across a stone path that split the water garden and arched over a few of the ponds and creeks. A two-meter-long snake slithered across one of the stone bridges. It was not identifiable until it reared up and fanned open its hood.

King cobra.

The snake guarded the bridge until the white-blond man broke off a long reed from a creekbed and shooed it away like an unruly cat. The snake hissed, fangs bared, but it backed down and sashayed off the planks and slid into the dark waters.

They continued on, unfazed. Gray's neck slowly craned as they approached the manor house.

He spotted another eccentricity about the construction. Spreading outward from the upper stories were forest-top pathways—wood-slatted suspended bridges—allowing household guests to step out of the upper-story levels and into the very jungle canopy itself. These paths were also strung with lamps. They cast a constellation through the dark jungle. Gray turned in a circle as he walked. They glowed all around.

"Heads up," Monk mumbled, nodding to the left.

Up on the canopy trail, a guard marched slowly into view, limned against one of the lamps, rifle on his shoulder. Gray glanced to Monk. Where there was one, there must be more. An entire army could be hidden up in the canopy. Escape seemed less and less likely.

At last they reached a set of steps that led up to a wide porch of polished zebra wood. A woman waited, a twin to their escort and as nattily attired. The man stepped forward and kissed each of her cheeks.

He spoke to her in Dutch. While not fluent with the language, Gray was familiar enough to catch the gist.

"Are the others prepared, Ischke?" he asked.

"We just wait word from *grootvader*." She nodded to the illuminated conservatory at the far end of the porch. "Then the hunt can begin."

Gray struggled for any clue to their meaning, but he was too much in the dark.

With a heavy sigh, the blond man turned back to them, fingering a stray lock of hair back in place. "My grandfather will see you in the solarium," their guide said, biting off each word. He headed down the length of the porch toward it. "You will speak to him civilly and with respect, or I will personally see you suffer for every word of disrespect."

"Isaak . . . ," the woman called to him.

He stopped and turned. "*Ja,* Ischke?"

She spoke in Dutch again. "*De jongen en het meisje?* Should we bring them out now?"

A nod answered her, followed by a final order in Dutch.

As Gray translated this last bit, he had to be tugged to move. He glanced over a shoulder at the woman. She vanished inside the house.

De jongen en het meisje.

The boy and the girl.

It had to be Ryan and Fiona.

The two were still alive. Gray took some consolation in the revelation—but Isaak's last words chilled and terrified him.

Bloody them up first.

5:18 A.M.
AIRBORNE OVER AFRICA

Painter sat with a pen in hand. The only noise in the plane was the occasional snore from Gunther. The man seemed oblivious to the danger into which they were flying. Then again, Gunther did not have the same time constraints as Anna and Painter. Though all three were headed toward the same place—*devolution*—Anna and Painter were in the fast lane.

Unable to sleep, Painter had used the time to review the history of the Waalenberg clan, gaining as much intel on the family as possible.

To know your enemy.

The Waalenbergs had first reached Africa by way of Algiers in 1617. They proudly traced their family history back to the infamous Barbary pirates along the North African coast. The first Waalenberg was a quartermaster for the famous pirate Sleyman Reis De Veenboer, who operated an entire Dutch fleet of corsairs and galleys out of Algiers.

Eventually, rich upon spoils from the slave trade, the Waalenbergs had moved south, settling into the large Dutch colony at the Cape of Good Hope. But their piracy didn't

end there. It just went aground. They gained a powerful
stranglehold on the immigrant Dutch population, so that
when gold was discovered in the lands they settled, the
Waalenbergs profited the most. And the gold found was not
a small amount. The Witwatersrand Reef, a low mountain
range near Johannesburg, was the source of forty percent
of all the world's gold. Though not as ostentatious as the
famous diamond mines of the De Beerses, the gold of the
"Reef" was still one of the world's most valuable store-
houses of wealth.

It was upon such wealth that the family set up a dynasty
that transcended the First and Second Boer Wars, and all
the political machinations that became South Africa today.
They were one of the richest families on the planet—though
for the past generations, the Waalenbergs had grown ever
more reclusive, especially under the auspices of their current
patriarch, Sir Baldric Waalenberg. And as they disappeared
from the public's eye, rumors grew around the family: of
atrocities, perversions, drug addictions, inbreeding. Yet
still the Waalenbergs grew richer, with stakes in diamonds,
oil, petrochemicals, pharmaceuticals. They put the *multi* in
multinational.

Could this family truly be behind the events at *Granitschloß*?

They were certainly powerful enough and had ample
resources. And the tattoo Painter had found on the blond
assassin definitely bore a resemblance to the "Cross" of the
Waalenberg crest. And then there were the twins, Isaak and
Ischke Waalenberg. What was their purpose in Europe?

So many unanswered questions.

Painter flipped a page and tapped his pen on the Waalenberg crest.

Something about the symbol . . .

As with the history of the Waalenbergs, Logan had forwarded information about the symbol. It traced back to the

Celts, another Nordic tribe. Emblematic of the sun, the symbol was often found emblazoned on Celtic shields, earning it the name of *shield knot*.

Painter's hand paused.

Shield knot.

Words filled his head, spoken by Klaus as he died, a curse cast at them.

You will all die! Strangled when the knot tightens!

Painter had thought Klaus had been making a reference to a tightening *noose*. But what if he had been referring instead to the symbol?

When the knot tightens . . .

Painter turned over a fax sheet. He sketched while staring at the Waalenberg crest. He drew the symbol as if someone had cinched the knot more tightly, drawing the loops together, like tying a shoelace.

"What are you doing?" Lisa materialized at his shoulder.

Startled again, he scooted his pen across the paper, almost tearing it.

"Good God, woman, will you please stop sneaking up on me like that!"

Yawning, she settled on the arm of his chair, perching there. She patted him on the shoulder. "Such a delicate disposition." Her hand remained there as she leaned closer. "Really. What were you drawing?"

Painter suddenly was too conscious of her right breast next to his cheek.

He cleared his throat and returned to his sketch. "Just playing with the symbol we found on the assassin. Another of my operatives saw it on a pair of *Sonnekönige* in Europe. Twin grandchildren of Sir Baldric Waalenberg. It must be important. Perhaps a clue we've overlooked."

"Or maybe the old bastard just likes branding his offspring, like cattle. They're certainly breeding them as such."

Painter nodded. "Then there was something Klaus said.

Something about tightening a knot. Like an unspoken secret."

He finished the sketch with a few more careful strokes, cinching it down.

He put one beside the other.

The original and the tightened.

Painter studied both drawings and realized the implication.

Lisa must have noted the slight intake in his breath. "What?" she asked, leaning even closer.

He pointed his pen at the second sketch. "No wonder Klaus was swayed to their side. And possibly why the Waalenbergs had become so reclusive these past few generations."

"I don't understand."

"We're not dealing with a new enemy here. We're dealing with the *same* one." Painter shaded the center of the cinched-down shield knot, revealing its secret heart.

Lisa gasped. "A swastika."

Painter glanced to the slumbering giant and his sister.

He sighed. "More Nazis."

6:04 A.M.
SOUTH AFRICA

The glass conservatory had to be as old as the original house. Its paned windows were leaded and swirled, as if melted under the African sun and set into a black iron framework that reminded Gray of a spiderweb. Condensation on the inside of the glass blurred the view to the dark jungle outside.

After first stepping inside, Gray was struck by the moisture. The humidity in the chamber had to be pressing the 100 percent mark. His thin cotton jumpsuit sagged against him.

But the solarium was not for his comfort. It sheltered a wild profusion of greenery, potted and shelved, climbing in tiers, hanging from baskets held by black chains. The air was perfumed by hundreds of blossoms. A small fountain of bamboo and stone tinkled quietly in the center of the room. It was a handsome garden, but Gray wondered who needed a hothouse when you already lived in Africa.

The answer appeared ahead.

A white-haired gentleman stood on a second tier with a tiny pair of snip scissors in one hand and tweezing forceps in the other. With the skill of a surgeon, he leaned over a small bonsai tree—a flowering plum—and clipped a tiny branch. He straightened with a satisfied sigh.

The tree appeared ancient, twisted, and was bound in copper wire. It hung heavy with blossoms, each one perfectly symmetrical, balanced and in harmony.

"She is two hundred and twenty-two years old," the old man said, admiring his handiwork. His accent was thick, Heidi's grandfather in a waistcoat. "She was already old when given to me by Emperor Hirohito himself in 1941."

He set down his tools and turned. He wore a white apron over a navy suit with a red tie. He held out a hand toward his grandson. "Isaak, *te'vreden* . . ."

The young man hurried forward and helped the elder down from the second tier. This earned him a fatherly pat on the shoulder. The old man shed his apron, retrieved a black cane, and leaned heavily upon it. Gray noted the prominent crest upon the cane's silver crown. A filigreed capital *W* surmounted the familiar cloverleaf symbol, the same icon tattooed on the twins, Ischke and Isaak.

"I am Sir Baldric Waalenberg," the patriarch said softly, eyeing Gray and Monk. "If you'll please join me in the salon, we have much to talk about."

Swinging around, he tapped his way toward the back of the solarium.

The old man had to be in his late eighties, but besides the need for a cane, he showed little debilitation. He still had a thick mane of silver-white hair, parted in the middle, and cut a bit rakishly to the shoulder. A pair of eyeglasses hung from a silver chain around his neck, one lens of which was outfitted with what looked like a jeweler's magnifying loupe.

As they crossed the slate floor, Gray noted that the conservatory's flora consisted of organized sections: bonsai trees and shrubs, a fern garden, and last, a section that was dense with orchids.

The patriarch noted his attention. "I've been breeding *Phalaenopsis* for the past six decades." He paused by a tall stalk bearing midnight purple blossoms, the hue of a ripe bruise.

"Pretty," Monk said, but his sarcasm was plain.

Isaak glared at Monk.

The old man seemed oblivious. "Yet still, the *black* orchid escapes me. The Holy Grail of orchid breeding. I've come so very close. But under magnification, there is either banding or more purpling than a solid ebony."

He absently fingered the jeweler's loupe.

Gray now understood the difference between the jungle outside and the hothouse. Nature wasn't enjoyed here. It was something to master. Under the dome of the conservatory, nature was snipped, strangled, and bred, its growth stunted with copper bonsai wire, its very pollination orchestrated by hand.

At the back of the solarium, they passed through a stained-glass door and reached a seating area of rattan and mahogany woods, a small salon dug into the side of the main house. On the far side, a double set of swinging doors, muffled with insulating strips, led into the interior of the mansion.

Baldric Waalenberg settled into a wingback chair.

Isaak crossed to a desk, complete with an HP computer and wall-mounted LCD monitor. A blackboard stood next to it.

Prominently chalked across its surface was a line of symbols. All of them runes, Gray saw, noting the last was the *Mensch* rune from the Darwin Bible.

ᚠ ᛁ ᚷ ᛗ ᛦ

Gray counted and memorized them discreetly. Five symbols. Five books. Here was the complete set of Hugo Hirszfeld's runes. But what did they mean? What secret was *too beautiful to let die and too monstrous to set free*?

The old man folded his hands in his lap and nodded to Isaak.

He tapped a key, and a high-definition image filled the LCD monitor.

A tall cage hung suspended above the jungle floor. It was sectioned into two halves. A small figure huddled within each side.

Gray took a step forward, but a guard restrained him at rifle point. On the screen, one of the figures looked up, face bright, illuminated by an overhead spotlight.

Fiona.

And in the other half of the cage, Ryan.

Fiona had her left hand bandaged, rolled up in the hem of her shirt. The cloth was stained dark. Ryan held his right hand tucked under his armpit, putting on pressure. *Bloody them up first*. The bitch must have cut their hands. Gray prayed that was all it was. A dark fury hollowed out his chest. His vision sharpened as his heart hammered.

"Now we will talk, *ja*?" the old man said with a warm grin. "Like gentlemen."

Gray faced him, but he kept one eye on the screen. So much for gentility. "What do you want to know?" he asked coldly.

"The Bible. What else did you find within its pages?"

"And you'll let them free?"

"And I want my goddamn hand back!" Monk blurted out.

Gray glanced from Monk to the old man.

Baldric nodded to Isaak, who in turn waved to one of the guards and barked an order in Dutch. The guard turned on a heel and shoved through the double doors, entering the manor house's interior.

"There is no need for further nastiness. If you cooperate, you have my word you will all be kept well."

Gray saw no advantage in holding out, especially as he held nothing of value except lies. He shifted sideways and displayed his bound wrists. "I'll have to show you what we found. I can't accurately describe it. It's another symbol, like these others."

Another nod, and in a moment, Gray was free. He rubbed his wrists and approached the blackboard. Several rifles were dead-leveled upon him.

He had to draw something that would be convincing, but he was not all that familiar with runes. Gray remembered Himmler's teapot, the one back at the museum. A runic symbol had decorated the pottery. It should be cryptic enough, convincing enough. And by throwing a proverbial wrench in the works, it might also delay these folks from solving the mystery here.

He picked up a piece of chalk and sketched the symbol on the pot.

Baldric leaned forward, eyes pinched. "A sun wheel, interesting."

Gray stood by the board, chalk in hand, like a student awaiting a teacher's verdict on a math problem.

"And this is all you found in the Darwin Bible?" Baldric asked.

From the corner of his eye, Gray noted a slight smirk on Isaak's face.

Something was wrong.

Baldric waited for Gray to answer.

"Let them go first," Gray demanded, nodding to the monitor.

The old man locked gazes with Gray. Despite his dissembling attitude, Gray recognized a savage intelligence and a hint of hard cruelty. The old man enjoyed all this immensely.

But finally Baldric broke their standoff, glancing over to his grandson and nodding again.

"Wie eerst?" Isaak asked. Who first?

Gray tensed. Something was definitely wrong.

Baldric answered in English, his eyes again fixed on Gray,

wanting to fully enjoy the entertainment. "The boy, I think. We'll save the girl for later."

Isaak tabbed a command on the keyboard.

On the screen, the bottom of the trapdoor fell open underneath Ryan. He silently screamed, flailing as he fell. He crashed hard into the tall grasses below. He stood quickly, searching around, terrified. The boy was plainly aware of a danger to which Gray was blind, perhaps something drawn by their dripping blood.

Ischke's earlier words replayed in Gray's head.

We just wait word from grootvader . . . *Then the hunt can begin.*

What hunt?

Baldric motioned to Isaak, miming turning a knob.

Isaak tapped a key, and sound rose from speakers. Screams and shouts echoed out.

Fiona's voice rang clear. "Run, Ryan! Get up in a tree!"

The boy danced once more in a circle, then ran, limping, out of the frame. Worse still, Gray heard laughter. From guards out of camera view.

Then a new scream stretched out from the speakers.

Feral and full of bloodlust.

The cry shivered the hairs all over Gray's body, standing them on end.

Baldric made a slashing motion across his neck and the audio was muted.

"It is not only orchids we breed here, Commander Pierce," Baldric said, dropping all pretense of civility.

"You gave us your word," Gray said.

"If you cooperated!" Baldric stood, rising smoothly. He waved an arm dismissively to the blackboard. "Do you think us fools? We knew all along that there was nothing else in the Darwin Bible. We have what we need already. This was all a test, a demonstration. We brought you here for other reasons. Other questions that need answering."

Gray reeled from what he was hearing, realization dawning. "The gas . . ."

"Only meant to incapacitate. Never kill. Your little sham was amusing though, I'll grant you that. Now it is time to move on."

Baldric stepped closer to the mounted screen. "You are protective of this little one, are you not? This fiery little slip of a girl. *Zeer goed.* I will show you what awaits her in the forest."

A nod, a tapped key, and an image filled a side window on the monitor.

Gray's eyes widened in horror.

Baldric spoke. "We wish to know more about a certain accomplice of yours. But I wanted to be sure we are done with games now, *ja*? Or do you need another demonstration?"

Gray continued to stare at the image on the screen, defeated. "Who? Who do you want to know about?"

Baldric stepped closer. "Your boss. Painter Crowe."

12

UKUFA

RICHARDS BAY, SOUTH AFRICA

Lisa watched Painter's legs tremble as they climbed the steps
to the local office of British Telecom International. They had
come here to meet a UK operative who would aid in logistical and ground support for any assault on the Waalenberg
estate. The firm was only a short taxi ride from the airport at
Richards Bay, a major port along the southern coast of South
Africa. It lay only an hour's drive from the estate.

Painter clutched the handrail, leaving a moist handprint.
She caught his elbow and assisted him up the last step.

"I've got it," he said with a bit of a snap.

She didn't respond to his anger, knowing it bubbled up
from an internalized anxiety. He was also in a lot of pain.
He'd been popping codeine like M&M's. He limped toward
the door to the telecom firm.

Lisa had hoped the downtime on the plane would have
helped him regain some strength, but if anything, the half
day spent in the air had only advanced his debilitation . . .
his *devolution,* if Anna was to be believed.

The German woman and Gunther remained at the airport,
under guard. Not that any sentry was necessary. Anna had

spent the last hour of the trip vomiting in the jet's bathroom. When they had left, Gunther had been cradling Anna on the couch, a damp washcloth over her brow. Her left eye had turned bloodshot and seemed painfully bruised. Lisa had given her an antiemetic for the nausea and a shot of morphine.

Though Lisa hadn't voiced it aloud, she estimated Anna and Painter had at best another day before they were too far gone for any hope of a treatment.

Major Brooks, their only escort, opened the door ahead for them. His eyes scanned the streets below, ever vigilant, but few people were about at this early morning hour.

Painter walked stiff-limbed through the door, struggling to hide his limp.

Lisa followed. In a few minutes, they were ushered past the reception area, through a large gray maze of cubicles and offices, and into a conference room.

It was empty. Its wall of windows at the back overlooked the lagoon of Richards Bay. To the north stretched an industrial port of cranes and container ships. To the south, divided by a seawall, spread a section of the original lagoon, now a conservation area and park, home to crocodiles, sharks, hippos, pelicans, cormorants, and the ever-present flamingos.

The rising sun turned the waters below into a fiery mirror.

As they waited, tea and scones were brought into the room and spread out on the table. Painter had already settled into a seat. Lisa joined him. Major Brooks remained standing, not far from the door.

Though she didn't ask, Painter read something in her expression. "I'm fine."

"No, you're not," she countered softly. The empty room intimidated her for some reason.

He smiled at her, his eyes sparkling. Despite his outward degeneration, the man himself remained sharp. She had noted a very slight slurring to his speech, but it could just be the drugs. Would his mind be the last to go?

Beneath the table, her hand reached for his, a reflexive gesture.

He took it.

She didn't want him to go. The strength of her emotion overwhelmed her, surprising her. She had barely gotten to know him. She wanted to know more. His favorite food, what made him belly laugh, how he danced, what he would whisper when he said good night. She didn't want it all to go away.

Her fingers squeezed, as if her will alone could hold him here.

At that moment, the door to the room opened again. The UK operative had finally arrived.

Lisa turned, surprised at who walked in. She had been picturing some James Bond clone, some clean-cut and Armani-suited spy. Instead, a middle-aged woman, dressed in a wrinkled khaki safari suit, entered the room. She carried a hat crumpled in one hand. Her face was mildly pancaked in red dust, except around her eyes, where sunglasses must have sat. It gave her a startled appearance, despite the weary set to her shoulders and a certain sadness in her eyes.

"I'm Dr. Paula Kane," she said, nodding to Major Brooks as she entered, then stepping over to join them. "We don't have much time to coordinate."

Painter stood over the table. An array of satellite photos was spread out over the table. "How old are these shots?" he asked.

"Taken at dusk last night," Paula Kane said.

The woman had already explained her role here. After graduating with a Ph.D. in biology, she had been recruited by British intelligence and posted in South Africa. She and a partner ran a series of research projects while secretly monitoring and watching the Waalenberg estate. They had been spying upon the family for close to a decade, until a tragedy less than two days ago. Her partner had been killed under strange circumstances. *Lion attack* was the official explanation. But the woman had looked little convinced as she offered this explanation.

"We did an infrared pass after midnight," Paula continued, "but there was a glitch. We lost the image."

Painter stared at the layout of the massive estate, over a hundred thousand acres. A small landing strip was visible, cut through a swath of jungle. Outbuildings dotted a landscape of forested highlands, vast grassy savannas, and dense jungle. In the center of the densest section of forest squatted a castle of stone and wood. The Waalenberg main residence.

"And we can't get a better view of the lay of the land around the mansion?"

Paula Kane shook her head. "The jungle in the area is Afromontane forest, ancient woodlands. Only a few such forests remain in South Africa. The Waalenbergs picked this location for their estate both because of its remoteness and to capture this gigantic forest for themselves. The bones of this forest are trees forty meters high, layered into distinct strata and canopies. The biodiversity within its bower is denser than any rain forest or Congo jungle."

"And it offers a perfect insulating cover," Painter said.

"What goes on beneath that canopy is known only to the Waalenbergs. But we do know the engineering of the manor house is only the tip of an iceberg. A vast underground complex lies beneath the estate."

"How deep?" Painter asked, eyeing Lisa. If they were experimenting with the Bell here, they would want it buried away.

"We don't know. Not for sure. But the Waalenbergs made their fortune in gold mining."

"At the Witwatersrand Reef."

Paula glanced up at him. "Correct. I see you've been doing your homework." She turned her attention back to the satellite photos. "The same expertise at mine engineering was used to construct a subterranean complex beneath their mansion. We know the mining engineer, Bertrand Culbert, was consulted in the construction of the manor's *foundations,* but he died shortly thereafter."

"Let me guess. Under mysterious circumstances."

"Trampled by a water buffalo. But his death was not the first, nor the last associated with the Waalenbergs." Her eyes flared with pain, plainly reminded of her partner. "Rumors abound of people vanishing in the area."

"Yet no one has served a search warrant on the estate."

"You have to understand the volatility of South African politics. Regimes may change, but gold has always ruled here. The Waalenbergs are untouchable. Gold protects them better than any moat or personal army."

"And what about you?" Painter asked. "What's MI5's interest here?"

"Our interest goes back a considerable way, I'm afraid. British intelligence has had their eye on the Waalenbergs since the end of World War II."

Painter settled back down into his chair, tiring. One of his eyes was having trouble focusing. He rubbed at it. Too conscious of Lisa studying him, he turned his attention to Paula. He had not voiced his discovery of the Nazi symbol buried within the center of the Waalenberg crest, but apparently MI5 was already aware of the connection.

"We knew the Waalenbergs were major financial backers of the Ahnenerbe Forschungs und Lehrgemeinshaft, the Nazis' Ancestral Heritage and Teaching Society. Are you familiar with the group?"

He shook his head, triggering a spasm. His headaches of

late had spread to his neck and shot pain down his spine. He rode the agony, teeth clenched.

"The Ancestral Heritage Society was a research group, under Heinrich Himmler. They were conducting projects seeking out the roots of the Aryan race. They were also responsible for some of the most heinous atrocities committed in concentration camps and other secret facilities. Basically they were mad scientists with guns."

Painter held back a wince—but this time it was more *psychic* than physical. He had heard Sigma described in similar terms. *Scientists with guns.* Was that their true enemy here? A Nazi version of Sigma?

Lisa stirred. "What was the Waalenbergs' interest in this line of research?"

"We're not entirely sure. But there were many Nazi sympathizers in South Africa during the war. We know the current patriarch, Sir Baldric Waalenberg, also had interests in eugenics, and he participated in scientific conferences in Germany and Austria before hostilities broke out. But after the war, he disappeared into seclusion, taking his entire family with him."

"Licking his wounds?" Painter asked.

"We don't believe so. After the war, Allied forces scoured the German countryside, searching for secret Nazi technology." Paula shrugged. "Including our own British forces."

Painter nodded. He had already heard about that pillaging and looting from Anna.

"But the Nazis were good at spiriting away much of their technology, employing a scorched-earth policy. Executing scientists, bombing facilities. Our forces came upon one such site in Bavaria minutes late. We discovered a scientist, shot in the head in a ditch, yet still alive. Before he died, he revealed some clues as to what had been going on. Research into a new energy source, one discovered through quantum experimentation. They'd had some breakthrough. A fuel source of extraordinary power."

Painter shared a glance with Lisa, remembering Anna's discussion about zero point energy.

"Whatever was discovered, the secret was smuggled out, escaped through rat runs set up by the Nazis. Little is known except the name of the substance and *where* the trail ended."

"At the Waalenberg estate?" Lisa guessed.

Paula nodded.

"And the name of the substance?" Painter asked, though he already knew the answer, putting it together in his head. "Was it called Xerum 525?"

Paula glanced to him sharply, straightening with a frown. "How did you know?"

"The Bell's fuel source," Lisa mumbled to him.

But to Painter, it only made sense. It was time to come clean with Dr. Paula Kane. Painter stood.

"There's someone you need to meet."

Anna's reaction was no less intense. "So the secret to manufacturing Xerum 525 wasn't destroyed? *Unglaublich!*"

They were all gathered back at the Richards Bay airport, huddled in a hangar while a pair of dusty Isuzu Trooper trucks were being loaded with weapons and equipment.

Lisa ran an inventory check through a medical kit while overseeing the discussion between Painter, Anna, and Paula. Gunther stood at Lisa's side. His brow was deeply furrowed with worry as he watched his sister. Anna seemed steadier after the medicine Lisa had given her.

But for how long?

"While the Bell had been evacuated to the north with your grandfather," Painter explained to Anna, "the secrets of Xerum 525 must have been shipped south. Dividing two parts of one experiment. At some point, word must have reached the Waalenbergs of the Bell's survival. Baldric Waalenberg—as a financial backer for the Ancestral Heritage Society—must have known about *Granitschloß*."

Paula agreed. "The society was the group that backed Himmler's expeditions into the Himalayas."

"And once discovered, it would have been easy for Baldric to infiltrate spies into *Granitschloß*."

Anna's face had grown paler—and not from illness. "The bastard has been using us! All along!"

Painter nodded. He had already explained the gist of it to Lisa and Paula on the ride back to the hangar. Baldric Waalenberg had been orchestrating everything, pulling strings from afar. Not one to waste talent or reinvent the wheel, he had allowed the *Granitschloß* scientists, experts in the Bell, to continue their research, while all the time, his spies siphoned the information back out to Africa.

"Afterward, Baldric must have built his own Bell," Painter said, "experimenting in secret, producing his own *Sonnekönige*, refining them through the advanced techniques discovered by your scientists. It was the perfect setup. Without another source of Xerum 525, *Granitschloß* was vulnerable, unwittingly under the thumb of Baldric Waalenberg. At any moment, he could pull the rug out from under them."

"Which he did," Anna spat out.

"But why?" Paula asked. "If this secret orchestration was working so well?"

Painter shrugged. "Maybe it was because Anna's group was drifting further and further away from the Nazi ideal of Aryan supremacy."

Anna pressed a palm against her forehead, as if that would ward against what she was learning. "And there were rumblings . . . among some of the scientists . . . of going mainstream, of joining the scientific community and sharing our research."

"But I don't think it was just that," Painter said. "Something more is afoot. Something larger. Something that suddenly made *Granitschloß* obsolete."

"I believe you might be correct," Paula said. "For the past four months, there has been a sudden increase in activity at the estate. Something stirred them up."

"They must have come to some breakthrough on their own," Anna said with a worried expression.

Gunther finally spoke up, gruff, a grinding of boulders. *"Genug!"* He'd had enough and struggled with English in his frustration. "The bastard has Bell . . . has *Xerum* . . . we find it. We use it." He waved an arm to his sister. "Enough talk!"

Lisa found herself heartily agreeing, siding with the giant. "We must find a way inside." And soon, she added to herself.

"It would take an army to storm the place." Painter turned to Paula. "Can we expect any help from the South African government?"

She shook her head. "Not a chance. The Waalenbergs have greased too many palms. We're going to have to find a more covert infiltration."

"The satellite photos didn't help much," Painter said.

"So we go low tech," Paula said and led them toward the waiting Isuzu Troopers. "I have a man already on the ground out there."

6:28 A.M.

Khamisi lay flat on his belly. Though dawn had come, the first rays of the sun only cast deeper shadows along the floor of the jungle. He wore camouflage fatigues and had his large double-bore rifle, his .465 Nitro Holland & Holland Royal, strapped to his back. In his hand, he carried a traditional Zulu short spear, an assegai.

Behind him lay two other Zulu scouts: Tau, the grandson of the elder who had rescued Khamisi from the attack, and his best friend, Njongo. They also carried firearms, along with short and long spears. They were more traditionally attired in pelts, skin daubed with paint, and otter-skin headbands.

The trio had spent the night mapping the forest around the mansion, discerning an approach that avoided the elevated walkways and the guards that patrolled them. They had used game trails that burrowed through the underbrush and skirted along with a small herd of impala, keeping hidden in the shadows. Khamisi had stopped at several points to rig ropes, linking walkway to ground, camouflaged as vines, along with a few other surprises.

With his duty done, he and the scouts had been heading out to where a stream flowed under the wildlife fencing that circled the estate.

Then a moment ago, he had heard the feral scream.

Hoo eeee OOOO.

It ended with a screeched yowl.

Khamisi froze. His very bones remembered the call.

Ukufa.

Paula Kane had been right. She had believed the creatures came from the Waalenberg estate. Whether escaped or purposefully planted to ambush Khamisi and Marcia, she didn't know. Either way, they were loose now, hunting.

But who?

The call had come a distance to the left.

It wasn't hunting them. The creatures were too skilled hunters. They would not give away their presence so soon. Something else had drawn them, stirred up their bloodlust.

Then he heard a voice shout out in German, a sobbed cry for help.

It was closer.

His bones still vibrating from the call, Khamisi wanted to run, to flee far and fast. It was a primal reaction.

Tau mumbled in Zulu behind him, urging the same.

Khamisi instead turned in the direction of the pleading cry. He had lost Marcia to the creatures. He remembered his own terror, neck deep in the water hole, waiting for dawn. He could not ignore this other.

Rolling to Tau, Khamisi passed on the maps he had drawn. "Get back to camp. Get these to Dr. Kane."

"Khamisi . . . brother . . . no, come away." Tau's eyes were huge with his own fear. His grandfather must have told him stories of the *ukufa,* the myths come to life. Khamisi had to give the man and his friend credit. No one else had volunteered to enter the estate. Superstitions ran high.

But now faced with the reality, Tau had no intention of remaining.

And Khamisi couldn't blame him. He remembered his own terror when he'd been with Marcia. Instead of holding his ground, he had fled, run, allowed the doctor to be killed.

"Go," Khamisi ordered. He nodded toward the distant fence line. The maps had to get out.

Tau and Njongo hesitated for a breath. Then Tau nodded, and the pair rose up in a low crouch and vanished into the jungle. Khamisi couldn't even hear their footfalls.

The jungle had fallen into a dread silence, heavy and as dense as the forest itself. Khamisi set out in the direction of the cries—both man and creature.

After another full minute, another yowl burst out of the jungle like a flight of startled birds. It ended in a series of yipping cackles. Khamisi paused, struck by something familiar in this last eerie bit.

Before he could consider it further, a soft sobbing drew his attention.

It came from directly ahead.

Khamisi used the muzzle of his double-bore rifle to part some leaves. A small glade opened in the jungle ahead, where a tree had fallen recently and cleared a part of the forest. The hole in the canopy allowed a shaft of morning sunlight to pierce to the floor. It made the surrounding jungle even darker with shadows.

Across the glade, movement drew his eye. A young man—no more than a boy—low in a tree, struggled to reach another branch, to climb higher. He couldn't reach. He couldn't get a grip with his right hand. Even from here, Khamisi saw the trail of blood soaked down the boy's sleeve as he vainly struggled.

Then the boy suddenly sank to his knees, hugging the bole, attempting to hide.

And the reason for the boy's sudden terror stepped into view.

Khamisi froze as the creature stalked into the glade, under the tree. It was massive, belying its silent tread out of the forest. It was larger than a full-grown male lion, but it was no lion. Its shaggy fur was albino white, its eyes a hyper-reflective red. Its back sloped from thickset high shoulders to a lower rear end. Its muscled neck supported a large, muzzled head topped by a pair of wide batlike belled ears. These swiveled, focused on the tree.

Lifting its head, it sniffed upward, drawn by the blood.

Lips rippled back from a maw of ripping teeth.

It howled again, ending again in a hair-raising series of cackling whoops.

Then it began to climb.

Khamisi knew what he faced.

Ukufa.

Death.

But as monstrous as it appeared, Khamisi knew its true name.

6:30 A.M.

"Species *Crocuta crocuta*," Baldric Waalenberg said, stepping to the LCD monitor. He had noted Gray's continued focus upon the creature on the screen, overlaying the video feed of Fiona in the cage.

Gray studied the massive bearlike creature, frozen, facing the camera, growling, mouth wide, baring white gums and yellowed fangs. It had to weigh three hundred pounds. It guarded the macerated remains of some antelope.

"The spotted hyena," Baldric continued. "The species is the second-largest carnivore in Africa, capable of dropping a bull wildebeest all by itself."

Gray frowned. The creature on the monitor was no ordinary hyena. It massed three to four times the normal size. And the pale fur. Some combination of gigantism and albinism. A mutated monstrosity.

"What did you do to it?" he asked, unable to keep the disgust from his voice. He also wanted to keep the man talking, buying time. He matched gazes with Monk, then returned his attention to the old man.

"We made the creature better, stronger." Baldric glanced to his grandson. Isaak continued to watch the play dispassionately. "Did we not, Isaak?"

"*Ja, grootvader.*"

"Prehistoric cave pictures in Europe show the great ancestor of today's hyena. The giant hyena. We've found a way to return *Crocuta* to its former glory." Baldric spoke with the same scientific dispassion as when he had discussed breeding black orchids. "Even enhanced the species' intelligence by incorporating human stem cells into its cerebral cortex. Fascinating results."

Gray had read of similar experiments done with mice. At Stanford, scientists had produced mice whose brains were one percent human. What the hell was going on here?

Baldric stepped to the blackboard with the five runic symbols. He tapped the board with the cane. "We have a series of Cray XT3 supercomputers working on Hugo's code. Once solved, this will allow us to do the same with mankind. To bring about the next evolution of man. Out of Africa again, man will rise anew, putting an end to the mud races and racial mixing, a purity will supersede all. It only waits to be unlocked from our corrupted genetic code and purified."

Gray heard echoes of the Nazis' *Übermensch* philosophy, the superman myth. The old man was mad. He had to be. But Gray noted the lucidity of his gaze. And on the screen lay proof of some monstrous success toward that end.

Gray's attention shifted to Isaak as he tapped a key and the mutated hyena vanished. Insight flashed through him. The albinism in the hyena. Isaak and his twin sister. The other white-blond assassins. Children all. Baldric hadn't been experimenting only with orchids and hyenas.

"Now let us return to the matter of Painter Crowe," the old man said. He waved a hand toward the screen. "Now that you understand what awaits the young *meisje* in the cage if you don't answer our questions truthfully. No more games."

Gray studied the screen, the girl in the cage. He could not let anything happen to Fiona. If nothing else, he needed to buy her time. The girl had been pulled into all of this because of his own clumsy inquiries in Copenhagen. She was his responsibility. And more than that, he liked the girl, respected her, even when she was being a pain in the ass. Gray knew what he had to do.

He faced Baldric.

"What do you want to know?"

"Unlike you, Painter Crowe has proven more of an adversary than we had anticipated. He has vanished after escaping our ambush. You're going to help us find out where he's gone."

"How?"

"By contacting Sigma command. We have a scrambled, untraceable line. You're going to break communication silence and find out what Sigma knows about the Black Sun project and where Painter Crowe has gone into hiding. And any hint of treachery . . ." Baldric nodded to the monitor.

Gray now understood the strident lesson here. They wanted Gray to understand fully, strangling any hope of deception. Save Fiona or betray Sigma?

The decision was momentarily postponed as one of the guards returned with another of Gray's demands.

"My hand!" Monk called out, noting the prosthesis carried by the guard. He struggled, his elbows still bound behind his back.

Baldric waved the guard forward. "Give the prosthesis to Isaak."

Isaak spoke up, speaking Dutch. "Did the lab clear it of any hidden weapons?"

The man nodded. "*Ja,* sir. All clear."

Still Isaak inspected the prosthetic hand. It was a marvel of DARPA engineering, incorporating direct peripheral nerve control through the titanium wrist contact points. It also was engineered with advanced mechanics and actuators that allowed precise movements and sensory input.

Monk stared at Gray.

Gray noted Monk's left fingers had finished tapping a code on the contact points of his right wrist's stump.

Gray nodded, stepping closer to Monk.

There was one other feature of DARPA's electronic prosthesis.

It was *wireless*.

A radioed signal passed between Monk and his prosthetic hand.

In response, the disembodied prosthetic clenched in Isaak's grip.

Fingers formed a fist.

Except for a raised middle finger.

"Screw you," Monk mumbled.

Gray grabbed Monk's elbow and yanked him toward the double doors that led into the main house.

The explosion was not large—no more than an extra loud and brilliant flash grenade. The charge had been blended directly into the plastic sleeve of the outer hand, impossible to detect. And while it wasn't much, it proved enough of a distraction. Cries of surprise and pain erupted from the guards. Gray and Monk slammed through the double doors, fled down the hall, and took the first turn. Out of direct sight, they pounded across polished hardwood floors.

Alarms immediately erupted, clanging and urgent.

They needed an escape route ASAP.

Gray noted wide stairs leading up. He guided Monk to them.

"Where we going?" Monk asked.

"Up, up, up . . ." Gray said as they fled, taking two steps at a time. Security would expect them to make a break for the nearest door or window. He knew another way out. In his head, a schematic of the manor house revolved. He had studied the estate closely as they were marched over here. Gray concentrated, trusting his sense of direction and position in space.

"This way." He hauled Monk off a landing and down another corridor. They were on the sixth floor. Alarms continued.

"Where—?" Monk began again.

"High ground," Gray answered and pointed toward the end of the corridor where a door awaited. "To the walkway in the canopy."

But it wouldn't be that easy.

As if someone had overheard their plan, an inner metal shutter began lowering over the exit door. An automated lockdown.

"Hurry!" Gray yelled.

The shutter trundled quickly, already three-quarters closed.

Gray sped faster, leaving Monk behind. He grabbed a hall chair as he ran past it and flung it ahead. It landed on the hardwood floor and skittered across the polished surface. Gray chased after it. The chair struck the closed outer door as the inner metal shutter clamped down atop it. Gears ground. A red light flared above the doorway. Malfunction. Gray was sure some warning bulb was already flaring in the mansion's main security nest.

As he reached the door, the wooden chair legs splintered and cracked, crushed beneath the grinding shutter.

Monk ran up, out of breath, arms still clamped behind his back.

Gray ducked under the chair and reached for the knob on the exit door. It was a strain with the shutter blocking the way.

His fingers clamped on the knob and twisted.

Locked.

"Goddamn it!" he swore.

More of the chair cracked. Behind them, the tromp of boots echoed, coming fast up the stairs. Voices barked orders.

Gray twisted around. "Brace me!" he said to Monk. He would have to kick the far door open.

On his back, legs pistoned up and ready, Gray leaned against Monk's shoulder for leverage.

Then the exit door simply popped open ahead of him, revealing a pair of legs in camouflaged khakis. One of the walkway patrols must have noted the malfunction and come to investigate.

Gray aimed for the man's shins and kicked out.

Caught by surprise, the man's legs went out from under him. He hit his head with a clang against the shutter and landed hard on the planks. Gray dove out and clocked the man again with his heel. His body went slack.

Monk followed, rolling to Gray, but not before kicking the trapped chair free of the shutter. The metal security gate continued its descent and slammed closed.

Gray relieved the guard of his weapons. He used a knife to slice away Monk's bindings and passed him the man's sidearm, an HK Mark 23 semiautomatic pistol. Gray confiscated the rifle.

Weapons in hand, they fled down the canopy bridge to the first crossroads. It divided just as the bridge reached the jungle. They checked both directions. So far it was all clear.

"We're going to have to split up," Gray said. "Better our chances. You have to get help, get to a phone, contact Logan."

"What about you?"

Gray didn't answer. He didn't have to.

"Gray . . . she may already be dead."

"We don't know that."

Monk searched his face. He had seen the monster on the computer screen. He knew Gray had no choice.

Monk nodded.

Without another word, they fled in opposite directions.

6:34 A.M.

Khamisi reached the canopy walkway, scaling up a tree on the opposite side of the glade. He moved swiftly and silently.

Below, the *ukufa* still circled the tree, guarding its trapped prey. The loud *bang* a moment ago had startled the *ukufa*. It had dropped from the tree, wary and cautious. It stalked around the tree again, ears high. Alarms and klaxons echoed out from the manor house.

The commotion also concerned Khamisi.

Had Tau and Njongo been discovered?

Or maybe their camouflaged base camp outside the estate

grounds had been found? Their rallying point was disguised as a Zulu hunting campsite, one of the many such nomadic camps. Had someone realized it was more than that?

Whatever the cause of the alarm, the noise at least had made the giant hyena monster—the *ukufa*—more guarded. Khamisi used its distraction to reach one of the overhead bridges. He rolled onto the planks, freeing his rifle. Anxiety kept his senses sharp. Terror, however, had shed from him. Khamisi had noted the creature's ambling gait, the soft rattling growl, a few sharp nervous cackles escalating into whoops.

Normal hyena behavior.

Though monstrous in size, it was not something mythic or supernatural.

Khamisi took strength in its flesh.

On the bridge, he hurried along the planks to where it crossed near the boy's tree. He unhooked a coil of rope from his pack.

Bending over the walkway's steel cabling, he spotted the boy. He whistled sharply, a bird call. The boy's attention had remained focused below. The sudden noise above his head made him flinch. But he glanced up and spotted Khamisi.

"I'm going to get you out of there," he called out in low tones, using English, hoping the boy understood.

Below, something else heard Khamisi, too.

The *ukufa* stared up at the bridge. Red eyes locked onto Khamisi's. Lids lowered as it studied the man on the bridge. Teeth bared. Khamisi read a calculating attention in its focus.

Was this the creature that had ambushed Marcia?

Khamisi would have liked nothing better than to unload both barrels into its smiling face, but the noise of the large-bore rifle would draw too much attention. The estate was already on full alert. So instead, he placed the rifle at his feet. He would need both arms and shoulders.

"Boy!" Khamisi said. "I'm going to toss you a rope. Snug it around your waist." He mimed what to do. "I'll pull you up."

The boy nodded, eyes wide, face swollen from crying and fear.

Leaning over the edge, Khamisi swung the coil of rope and tossed it toward the boy. The rope unfurled, crashing through the leaves. It failed to reach the boy, nesting up in the branches above.

"You'll have to climb to it!"

The boy needed no goading. With a chance to escape, his effort at climbing grew more determined. He scrambled and kicked and got himself up to the next branch. He tied the rope around his waist, shaking it loose from the branches. He showed some skill with the rope. Good.

Khamisi pulled in the slack, bracing it around one of the steel cable posts supporting the bridge. "I'm going to start pulling you up! You're going to swing out."

"Hurry!" the boy called out, too sharply and too loudly.

Khamisi pivoted on a hip and saw the *ukufa* had noted the boy's renewed movement. It drew the monster like a cat after a mouse. It had mounted the tree and was climbing up, digging in its claws.

With no time to waste, Khamisi began wheeling the rope up, arm over arm. He felt the boy's weight burden the rope as he was lifted free of his perch. Bending to check, he spotted the boy swinging back and forth like a pendulum.

The *ukufa* did, too, eyes tracking the arc. It continued its climb. Khamisi read its intent. It was planning to leap and snag the boy, like bait on a line.

Khamisi hauled faster. The boy continued to swing.

"Wie zijn u?" a voice suddenly barked behind him.

Startled, he almost let go of the rope. He craned over a shoulder.

A tall, lithe woman stood on the walkway, dressed in black, feral-eyed. Her hair was blond but shaved close to the scalp. One of the senior Waalenberg children. She must have just stepped onto this section and discovered him. She had a knife already in one hand. Khamisi dared not let go of the rope.

Not good.

Below, the boy cried out.

Khamisi and the woman glanced down.

The *ukufa* had reached the boy's former perch and bunched up for its leap. Behind Khamisi, the woman laughed, a match to the cackle of the creature below. The planks creaked as she stepped toward his back, knife in hand.

They were both trapped.

6:38 A.M.

Gray knelt at the crossroads. The elevated walkway split into three paths. The left led back to the manor house. The center walkway skirted the forest's edge and overlooked the central gardens. The path to the right simply headed straight off into the heart of the jungle.

Which way?

Crouched, Gray studied the slant of shadows, comparing it to the pattern he had studied on the LCD monitor. The length and direction of the shadows had offered a general clue to the position of the rising sun in respect to the location of Fiona's imprisonment. But that still left a large swath of estate to cover.

Feet pounded on the walkway, shaking it slightly.

More guards.

He had encountered two groups already.

Gray shouldered his rifle, rolled to the edge of the walkway, and dropped off its edge. He hung by his arms to the cabling and worked hand over hand to the leafy shelter of a tree branch. A moment later, a trio of guards clattered by overhead, bouncing the walkway. Gray clung tightly, jiggled about.

Once they were past, he used the tree branch to scoot back onto the path. Hooking and swinging his leg over, he noticed a rhythmic vibration in the cable in his hand. More guards?

Flat on his belly on the planks, he leaned an ear against the cable, listening like an Indian tracker on a trail. There was a distinct rhythm to the vibration, audible, like a plucked string of a steel guitar. Three fast twangs, three slow, three fast again. And it repeated.

Morse code.

S.O.S.

Someone was knocking out a signal on the cable.

Gray crouched and sidled back to the branching of the walkway. He felt the other support cables. Only one vibrated. It led off along the path to the right, the one headed into the depths of the jungle.

Could it be . . . ?

With no better clue, Gray set off down the right path. He kept pace near the walkway's edge, attempting to keep his tread silent and the bridge from swaying. The path continued to diverge. Gray paused at each crossing to find the cable vibrating in code and followed its trail.

Gray was so focused on the path, that when he ducked under the heavy frond of a palm leaf he suddenly found himself staring at a guard only four yards away. Brown-haired, midtwenties, typical Hitler youth. The guard leaned on the cable handrail, facing Gray's direction. His gun was already rising, as he'd been alerted by the shuffle of the palm tree.

Gray didn't have time to get his rifle up. Instead, still moving, he slammed his weight to the side—not in an attempt to dodge the coming slug. The guard couldn't miss at this range.

Gray struck the cabled handrail, jarring it.

The guard, braced against it, bobbled. The muzzle of his rifle jittered too high. Gray closed the gap in two steps, getting under the rifleman's guard, the pilfered dagger already in his hand.

Gray used the man's imbalance to silence his scream, planting the dagger through the man's wind box, severing his larynx. A twist and the carotid spurted. He'd be dead in seconds. Gray caught his body and heaved it over the rail. He felt no remorse, remembering the guards laughing as Ryan had dropped into the monster's den. How many others had died that way? The body fell in a shushing whisper of leaves, then crashed into the grassy underbrush.

Crouched low, Gray listened. Had anyone heard the guard's fall?

Off to the left, surprisingly near, a woman shouted in accented English. "Stop kicking the bars! Or we'll drop you now!"

Gray recognized the voice. *Ischke.* Isaak's twin sister.

A more familiar voice responded to the woman. "Sod off, you bony-assed prat!"

Fiona.

She was alive.

Despite the danger, Gray grinned—both in relief and respect.

Staying low, he snuck down to the end of the walkway. It dead-ended at a circular path that edged an open glade. The one from the video. The cage was suspended from the elevated walkway.

Fiona kicked the cage's bars. *Three fast, three slow, three fast.* Her face was a mask of determination. Gray felt the vibration under his feet now, transmitted along the cage's support cables.

Good girl.

She must have heard the alarms from the manor house. Perhaps guessed it might be Gray and sought to signal him. Either that . . . or she was just damned pissed. And the pattern was just an annoying coincidence.

Gray spotted three guards at the two-, three-, and nine-o'clock positions. Ischke, still dazzling in her black and white outfit, stood on the far side—at twelve o'clock—both hands on the inside rail, staring down at Fiona.

"A bullet through your knee might quiet you down," she called to the girl, placing a palm on a holstered pistol.

Fiona paused in midkick, mumbled something under her breath, then lowered her foot.

Gray calculated the odds. He had one rifle against three guards, all armed, and Ischke with her pistol. Not good.

A spat of static sounded from across the glade. Garbled words followed.

Ischke unhooked her radio and lifted it to her lips. *"Ja?"*

She listened for half a minute, asked another question that Gray couldn't make out, then signed off. Lowering the radio, she spoke to the guards.

"New orders!" she barked to the others in Dutch. "We kill the girl now."

6:40 A.M.

The *ukufa* let out a trebling series of yips, ready to leap at the dangling boy. Khamisi sensed the approach of the woman at his back. Hands on the rope, he couldn't go for any of his weapons.

"Who are you?" the woman asked again, knife threatening.

Khamisi did the only thing he could.

Bending his knees, he threw himself over the cabled railing. He clenched hard to the rope as he tumbled. Overhead, the line whistled around the steel support post. As Khamisi fell earthward, he caught a glimpse of the boy being dragged skyward, flailing with a long scream of surprise.

The *ukufa* leaped at its fleeing prey, but Khamisi's falling weight zipped the boy straight up to the walkway, banging him hard against it.

The sudden stop ripped the rope from Khamisi's grip.

He fell, landing on his back in the grass. Overhead, the boy clung to the underside of the walkway. The woman stared down at Khamisi, eyes wide.

Something large crashed to the ground a few meters from him.

Khamisi sat up.

The *ukufa* bounded to its feet, throwing ropes of saliva, furious, growling.

Its red gaze fell heavily upon the only prey in sight.

Khamisi.

His hands were empty. His rifle still rested on the planks above.

The creature yowled in bloodlust and anger. It leaped at him, intending to tear out his throat.

Khamisi fell to his back, lifting his only weapon. The Zulu assegai. The short spear was still strapped to his thigh. As the *ukufa* dropped onto him, Khamisi shoved the blade up. His father had once taught him how to use the weapon. Like all Zulu boys. Before they left for Australia. With an instinct that crossed deep into the past of his ancestors, Khamisi slipped the blade under the creature's ribs—one of flesh, not myth—and drove it deep as the hyena's weight fell atop him.

The *ukufa* screamed. Pain and momentum carried it over Khamisi and yanked the spear's handle from his fingers. Khamisi rolled clear, weaponless now. The *ukufa* thrashed in the grass, corkscrewing the impaled blade inside it. It screamed one last time, jerking hard, then went limp.

Dead.

An angry cry above drew his eye.

The woman on the bridge had found Khamisi's rifle and had it pointed at him. The blast sounded like a grenade. A bush exploded at his heels, gouting up soil. Khamisi shoved back. Overhead, the woman shifted the rifle, fixing him more surely in its sights.

The second blast sounded oddly sharper.

Khamisi twisted away—but found himself unscathed.

He glanced up in time to see the woman topple over the cable, her chest a bloody ruin.

A new figure stepped into view on the walkway.

A muscular man with a shaved head. He had a pistol held out, steadied on the stump of a wrist. He leaned over the cable and spotted the boy, still dangling by his hands.

"Ryan . . ."

The boy sobbed with relief. "Get me out of here."

"That's the plan . . ." His gaze found Khamisi. "That is, if that guy down there knows the way out of here. I'm so friggin' lost."

6:44 A.M.

The pair of gunshots echoed through the forest.

A small flock of green parrots took wing from canopy roosts, squawking in protest, flapping across the glade.

Gray crouched.

Had Monk been found?

Ischke must have thought the same, her head craned in the direction of the gunfire. She waved to the guards. "Check it out!"

She raised her radio again.

The guards, rifles in hand, pounded around the circular elevated walk, all coming in Gray's direction. Caught off guard, Gray dropped and rolled, hugging his rifle to his chest. He flung himself off the planks. The closest guard would be in view in mere seconds. Like before, he snatched the planks' support cable, but in his haste, off balance, he barely caught a purchase with one hand. His body swung. The rifle slipped from his shoulder, dropping away.

Twisting and reaching, he snagged the leather strap with one finger. He silently sighed in relief.

Guards suddenly battered past overhead, boots hammering, jigging and bouncing his perch.

The rifle's leather strap popped off Gray's finger. Gravity disarmed him. The weapon fell, spearing into the underbrush. Gray grabbed another handhold and hung there. At least the rifle hadn't gone off when it hit the ground.

The guards' footfalls echoed away.

He heard Ischke talking on her radio.

Now what?

He had a knife against her pistol. He didn't question her compunction to use it or her marksmanship.

The only real advantage he had was surprise.

And that was severely overrated.

Hand over hand, Gray traversed the underside of the walkway and reached the circular concourse. He continued along the underside, keeping to the outer edge, out of direct view of the Waalenberg woman. He had to move slowly or his swaying weight would alert Ischke. He timed his movements to the occasional breeze that ruffled the canopy.

But his appearance did not go unnoticed.

Fiona crouched in her cage, putting as many bars as she could between her and Ischke. Plainly she had understood Ischke's earlier words in Dutch. *We kill the girl now.* Though the gunfire had momentarily distracted the blond twin, eventually her attention would return to Fiona.

From her low vantage, Fiona spotted Gray, a white-jumpsuited gorilla scaling the underside of the walkway, half-hidden by the foliage. She jerked in surprise, almost standing, then forced herself to stay low. Her eyes tracked him, their gazes met.

Despite her noisy bravado, Gray read the terror in her

face. The girl looked so much smaller in the cage. She hugged her arms around her chest, attempting to hold herself together. Hardened as she was by the streets, he sensed her only defense against a complete panicked breakdown was her prickly blustering. It sustained her—barely.

Blocking with her body, she signaled him. She pointed down and slightly shook her head, eyes wide in fear, alerting him.

It wasn't safe below.

He searched the thick grasses and bushes of the glade. Shadows lay thick. He saw nothing, but he trusted Fiona's warning.

Don't fall.

Gray estimated how far he'd come. He was about at the eight o'clock position along the circular walkway. Ischke stood at the twelve o'clock. He still had a distance to traverse, and his arms were tiring, his fingers aching. He had to move faster. Stopping and starting were killing him. But he feared going any faster would draw Ischke's attention.

Fiona must have realized the same. She stood and began kicking the bars again, rattling her cage, swaying it with her weight. The motion allowed Gray to increase his pace.

Unfortunately her effort also drew Ischke's wrath.

The woman lowered her radio and yelled at Fiona. "Enough of your foolishness, child!"

Fiona still clutched the bars and kicked.

Gray hurried past the nine o'clock position.

Ischke stepped to the inner rail, half in view. Luckily her focus was fully on Fiona. The woman pulled a device out of the pocket of her sweater. She used her teeth to extend the antenna. She pointed it at Fiona. "It is time you met Skuld, named after the Norse goddess of fate."

A button was pressed.

Almost directly under Gray's toes, something howled in anger and pain. It thrashed out of the shadowed eaves of the jungle and stalked into the grassy clearing. One of the mutated hyenas. Its hulked mass had to tip three hundred pounds, all muscle and teeth. It growled low, hackles high on its sloped back. Lips snarled back as it barked and snapped at the empty air, sniffing up at the cage.

Gray realized the monster must have been stalking him all along from below. He suspected what was coming.

He hurried, swinging past the ten-o'clock spot.

Ischke called to Fiona, enjoying the terror, prolonging the cruelty. "A chip in Skuld's brain allows us to stimulate its bloodlust, its appetite." She tweaked the button again. The hyena howled, leaped at the cage, flinging ropes of drool, driven into a ravening bloodlust.

So that was how the Waalenbergs controlled their monsters.

Radio implants.

Subverting nature again to their will.

"It's time we sated poor Skuld's hunger," Ischke said.

Gray would never make it in time. Still, he rushed.

Eleven o'clock.

So close.

But too late.

Ischke pressed another button. Gray heard a distinct *clink* as the trapdoor in Fiona's cage unlatched.

Oh, no.

Gray paused in midswing. He watched the trapdoor fall open beneath Fiona. She fell toward the slathering beast below.

Gray prepared to drop after her, to protect her.

But Fiona had learned from Ryan's demise. She was prepared. As she fell, she caught the lower bars of her cage and hung there. The creature, Skuld, leaped for her legs. She tucked up and hauled with her arms.

The beast missed and crashed back to the underbrush with a yowl of frustration.

Climbing up, Fiona now clung to the outside of the cage like a spider monkey.

Ischke laughed with dark delight. "*Zeer goed, meisje.* Such resourcefulness! *Grootvader* might have even considered your genes for his stock. But alas you'll have to satisfy Skuld instead."

From below, Gray watched Ischke raise her pistol again.

He swung beneath her, staring up between the planks.

"Now to end this," Ischke muttered in Dutch.

Indeed.

Gray pulled with his arms, kicked back his legs—then swung forward and over, like a gymnast on a high bar. His heels struck Ischke in the belly as she leaned on the rail, steadying her aim at Fiona.

As his heels connected, her pistol blasted.

Gray heard the ring of slug on iron.

Missed.

Ischke was knocked back as Gray followed through and crashed to the planks. He rolled up, knife in hand. Ischke was down on one knee. Her pistol lay between them.

They both lunged for it.

Ischke, even with the wind kicked out of her, proved incredibly fast, like a striking snake. Her fingers reached the pistol first, snatching it up.

Gray had a knife.

He jammed his blade through her wrist and into the planks. She screamed in surprise, dropping the pistol. Gray tried to grab it, but the hilt bounced off the planks as Ischke thrashed. It flew past the walkway's edge.

The momentary distraction was long enough for Ischke to yank her wrist free from the planks. She pivoted off her other wrist and kicked out at Gray's head.

He lunged back, but her shin struck his shoulder as hard as the bumper of a speeding car. Gray rolled with it, bruised to the bone. Damn, she was strong.

Before he could get up, she leaped at him, swinging her arm at his face, trying to use the tip of the blade impaled through her wrist to blind him. He barely caught her elbow, twisted it, and carried them both to the walkway's edge.

He didn't stop.

Locked together, their bodies fell off the walkway.

But Gray hooked his left knee around one of the walkway's support posts. His body jerked to a stop, swinging by his leg, wrenching his knee. Ischke peeled off of him and dropped away.

Upside down, he watched the woman snap through some branches and crash hard into the grassy sward.

Gray hauled himself back up to the walkway, sprawling flat.

With disbelief, he saw Ischke climb to her feet below. She limped a step to steady herself, ankle painfully twisted.

A clatter to Gray's side startled him.

Fiona landed on the planks, swinging over from one of the cage's suspension wires.

During the fight, the girl must have crabbed her way atop the cage, then used the wires to reach the walkway. She hurried to him, shaking her left hand and wincing. Fresh blood flowed from where Ischke had cut her.

Gray searched again below.

The woman stared up at him. Murder in her eyes.

But she wasn't alone in the clearing.

Behind her, Skuld raced toward the woman, the hyena's muzzle low to the ground, a shark in the grass, scenting blood.

How fitting, Gray thought.

But the woman merely raised her uninjured arm toward the beast. The massive hyena ground to a stop, lifted its nose, dripping drool, and rubbed against her palm like a savage pit bull greeting its abusive master. It mewled and lowered to its belly.

Ischke never broke eye contact with Gray.

She limped forward.

Gray stared below.

Steps from the woman, Ischke's pistol rested in plain view.

Gray climbed up, gaining his feet. He grabbed Fiona's shoulder and shoved her forward. "Run!"

She needed no further goading. They raced around the arc of the walkway. The girl flew on fear and adrenaline. They reached the exit.

Fiona made the corner, hanging on to one of the support posts to keep her footing. Gray followed her example. As he swung clear, a ringing spark off the support post accompanied a pistol blast.

Ischke had found her gun.

Spurred on, they ran faster along the straight path, putting distance between them and the limping shooter. In a minute, approaching a crisscross of paths, Gray suspected they might be safe. Caution overcame panic.

He slowed Fiona by the same crossroads he had stopped at before. Paths led in all directions. Which way? By now, there was a good chance Ischke had raised an alarm—unless the fall had broken her radio, but he couldn't count on that. He had to assume guards were already congregating between here and the outside world.

And what about Monk? What did the gunplay that drew off Ischke's guards portend? Was he alive, dead, recaptured? There were too many unknown variables. Gray needed a place to hole up and hide, to let his trail cool.

But where?

He eyed the one path that bridged back to the manor house.

No one would expect to look for them over there. Plus the place had phones. If he could get to an outside line . . . maybe even find out more about whatever the hell was really going on there . . .

But it was a pipe dream. The place was locked up tight, a fortress.

Fiona noted his attention.

She tugged on his arm and pulled something from her pocket. It looked like a couple of playing cards on a chain. She held them up.

Not playing cards.

Key cards.

"I nicked them from that ice bitch," Fiona said, half spitting. "Teach her to slice me."

Gray took the cards and examined them. He remembered Monk scolding Fiona for not stealing the museum director's keys when they were trapped in Himmler's crypt. It seemed the girl had taken Monk's lesson to heart.

With narrowed eyes, Gray again studied the manor house.

Thanks to his little pickpocket, he now held the keys to the castle.

But what to do?

13

XERUM 525

10:34 A.M.
HLUHLUWE-UMFOLOZI PRESERVE
ZULULAND, SOUTH AFRICA

Painter sat in the mud-stone and woven-grass hut, cross-legged around a series of maps and schematics. The air smelled of dung and dust. But the small Zulu encampment served as the perfect staging spot, only ten minutes from the Waalenberg estate.

Periodically, security helicopters buzzed the camp, rising from the estate, wary and watchful of their borders, but Paula Kane had the site well orchestrated. From the air, none could tell that the small sandy village was anything but a way station for the nomadic tribes of Zulu that eked out a living in the area. Nobody would suspect the council under way in one of the ramshackle huts.

The group had gathered to strategize and pool resources.

Across from Painter, Anna and Gunther sat together. Lisa kept near Painter's elbow—as she had since arriving in Africa, her face stoic but her eyes worried. Near the back, Major Brooks stood in the shadows, ever vigilant, palm resting on his holstered pistol.

They were all attentive on the final debriefing from

Khamisi, a former game warden here. At his side, leaning forward, head to head, was the most surprising addition to the gathering.

Monk Kokkalis.

To Painter's shock, Monk had wandered into the encampment with an exhausted and shell-shocked young man, both led by Khamisi. The young man was recuperating in another hut, kept safely out of harm's way, but Monk had spent the last hour relating his story, answering questions, and filling in blanks.

Anna stared at the set of runes Monk had finished drawing. Her eyes were bloodshot. She reached out a trembling hand toward the paper. "These are all the runes found in the books of Hugo Hirszfeld?"

Monk nodded. "And that old fart was convinced they were damn important, critical to some next stage in his plan."

Anna's gaze rose to Painter. "Dr. Hugo Hirszfeld was the overseer for the original Black Sun project. Do you remember how I told you he was convinced he had solved the riddle of the Bell? Performed one last experiment, one done in secret, attended only by himself. A private experiment that supposedly produced a perfect child, one uncorrupted of taint or devolution. A perfect Knight of the Sun. But his method . . . how he did it . . . no one knew."

"And the letter he wrote his daughter," Painter said, "whatever he discovered frightened him. *A truth . . . too beautiful to let die and too monstrous to set free.* To that end, he hid the secret in this runic code."

Anna sighed wearily. "And Baldric Waalenberg was confident enough that he could solve the code, gain the lost knowledge for himself, that he destroyed the *Granitschloß.*"

"I think it was more than just that you were no longer needed," Painter said. "I think you were right before. Your group was a growing threat with talk of coming out of hiding, going mainstream. And with perfection so close, the culmination of the Aryan dream, he could not risk your continuing presence."

Anna shifted the paper with Monk's sketched runes toward her. "If Hugo was right, deciphering his code could prove critical to treating our own condition. The Bell already holds the ability to *slow* down our disease—but if we could solve this riddle, it may offer a true *cure*."

Lisa inserted a bit of reality into the discussion. "But before any of that can happen, we must gain access to the Waalenberg Bell. Then we can worry about cures."

"And what about Gray?" Monk asked. "And the girl?"

Painter kept his face tight. "There is no telling where he is. Hiding, captured, dead. For the moment, Commander Pierce is on his own."

Monk's face soured. "I can sneak back in. Use the map Khamisi has of the grounds."

"No. Now is not the time to divide forces." Painter rubbed at a needling headache behind his right ear. Noises echoed. Nausea welled.

Monk stared at him.

He waved away the man's concern. But something in Monk's focus suggested that it wasn't just his boss's *physical* failings that worried him. Was Painter making the right choices? How was his mental status? The doubt touched a chord in himself. How clear *was* his thinking?

Lisa's hand drifted to his knee, as if sensing his consternation.

"I'm fine," he mumbled—as much to himself as to her.

Further inquiry was interrupted by the room's rug door being shoved open. Sunlight and heat wafted inside. Paula Kane ducked into the dark interior. A Zulu elder followed her in full ceremonial regalia: plumes, feathers, leopard skin decorated with colorful beadwork. Though in his midsixties, his face was unlined, seemingly carved of stone, his head shaved. He carried a wooden staff topped with feathers, but he also bore an antique firearm, looking more ceremonial than functional.

Painter recognized the weapon as he stood up. An old smoothbore English "Brown Bess," a flintlock from the Napoleonic Wars.

Paula Kane introduced the visitor. "Mosi D'Gana. Zulu chief."

The elder spoke in crisp English. "All is ready."

"Thank you for your assistance," Painter said formally.

Mosi nodded his head slightly, acknowledging the words. "But it is not for you we lend our spears. We owe the Voortrekkers for Blood River."

Painter frowned, but Paula Kane filled in the details. "When the English drove the Dutch Boers out of Cape Town, they began a major trek into the interior. Friction escalated between the arriving immigrants and the native tribes. The Xhosa, the Pondo, the Swazi, and the Zulus. In 1838, along a tributary of the Buffalo River, the Zulus were betrayed, thousands killed, their homelands lost. It was a slaughter. The river became known as Blood River. The Voortrekker conspirator of that murderous assault was Piet Waalenberg."

Mosi lifted his old weapon and held it out to Painter. "We do not forget."

Painter did not doubt that this very gun had been involved in that infamous battle. He accepted the weapon, knowing a pact had been forged with the passing of the flintlock.

Mosi settled to the ground, dropping smoothly into a cross-legged position. "We have much to plan."

Paula nodded to Khamisi and held open the rug flap. "Khamisi, your truck is ready. Tau and Njongo are already waiting." She checked her watch. "You'll have to hurry."

The former game warden stood. Each had their own duty to perform before nightfall.

Painter met Monk's gaze. He again read the worry in the man's eyes. But not for Painter—for Gray. Sundown was eight hours away. But there was nothing they could do until then.

Gray was on his own.

12:05 P.M.

"Keep your head down," Gray whispered to Fiona.

They strode toward the guard at the end of the hall. Gray wore one of the camouflage uniforms, from jackboots to black cap, the brim pulled low over his eyes. The guard who had lent Gray the outfit was unconscious, gagged, and hog-tied in a closet of one of the upper bedrooms.

He had also borrowed the guard's radio, clipped to his belt and trailing an earpiece. The chatter on the line was all in Dutch, making it hard to discern, but it kept them abreast of events.

Walking in Gray's shadow, Fiona wore a maid's outfit, borrowed from the same closet. It was a bit large, but it was better to hide her shape and age. Most of the house staff were natives in various shades of dark skin, typical of an Afrikaner household. Fiona's mocha-brown complexion, her Pakistani heritage, fit well enough. She also hid her straight hair under a bonnet. She could pass as native if no one looked *too* closely. To complete the act, she walked in tiny submissive steps, shoulders slumped, head down.

So far, their disguises had not even been tested.

Word had spread that Gray and Fiona had been spotted in the jungle. With the manor house shuttered down, only a skeleton patrol kept post inside the mansion. Most of the security forces were searching the forests, outbuildings, and borders.

Unfortunately, security was not so thin here as to leave

an outside phone line open. Shortly after using Ischke's key card to gain entry back inside the mansion, Gray had tested a few house phones. Access required passing through a coded security net. Any attempt to gain an outside line would only expose them.

So their options were few.

They could hide. But to what end? Who knew when or if Monk would make it to civilization? So a more proactive role was needed. The plan was to first gain a schematic of the mansion. That meant penetrating the security nest on the main floor. Their only weapons were a sidearm carried by Gray and a hand Taser in Fiona's pocket.

Ahead, at the end of the hall, a sentry manned the upper balcony, guarding over the main entryway with an automatic rifle. Gray strode up to the man. He was tall, stocky, and his heavy-lidded eyes made him look piggish and mean. Gray nodded and continued toward the stairs. Fiona followed at his heels.

All went well.

Then the man said something in Dutch. The words were beyond Gray, but they had a lurid ring to them, ending in a guttural low laugh.

Half turning, Gray saw the guard reach to Fiona's bottom and give it a firm pinch. Another hand went for her elbow.

Wrong thing to do.

Fiona swung to the man. "Piss off, you wanker."

Her skirt brushed the man's knee. A blue spark burned through her pocket and zapped the man's thigh. His body arched back, a strangled noise gargled forth.

Gray caught him as he fell back, still convulsing in his arms. Gray dragged him off the landing and into a side room. He dropped him to the floor, pistol-whipped him unconscious, and began gagging him and tying him up.

"Why did you do that?" Gray asked.

Fiona stepped behind Gray and pinched his butt, hard and sharp.

"Hey!" He stood and swung around.

"How do you like it?" Fiona fumed.

Point taken. Still he cautioned, "I can't keep tying up these bastards."

Fiona stood with her arms crossed. Her eyes, though angry, were also scared. He couldn't blame her for her jumpiness. He wiped some cold sweat from his brow. Maybe they had better just hide and hope for the best.

Gray's radio crackled. He listened hard. Had their attack by the staircase been noted? He translated through the garble. ". . . *ge'vangene* . . . bringing in the main door . . ."

More followed, but Gray barely heard much past the word *ge'vangene*.

Prisoner.

That could only mean one thing.

"They caught Monk . . . ," he whispered, going cold.

Fiona uncrossed her arms, face concerned.

"C'mon," he said and headed toward the door. He had relieved the downed guard of his Taser and shouldered the man's rifle.

Gray led the way back to the stairs. He whispered his plan to Fiona as they hurried down the stairs to the main entrance hall. The lower floor was empty, as was the foyer ahead.

They crossed the polished floor decorated with woven rugs in African motifs. Their footsteps echoed. To either side, stuffed trophies mounted the walls: the head of an endangered black rhino, a massive lion with a moth-eaten mane, a row of antelopes with various racks of horns.

Gray crossed toward the foyer. Fiona pulled a feather duster from an apron pocket, a part of her disguise. She crossed to one side of the door. Gray took a post, rifle in hand, on the other.

They didn't have long to wait, barely getting into position in time.

How many guards would be accompanying Monk?

At least he was alive.

The metal shutter over the main entrance began to rise, clattering upward. Gray leaned down to count legs. He held up two fingers toward Fiona. Two guards were accompanying a prisoner in a white jumpsuit.

Gray stepped into view as the gate trundled fully up.

The guards saw nothing but one of their own, a sentry with a rifle manning the door. They entered with the prisoner in tow. Neither noticed Gray palming a Taser or Fiona coming up from the other side.

The attack was over in moments.

Two guards convulsed on the rug, heels drumming. Gray kicked each in the side of the head, probably harder than he should have. But anger fueled through him.

The prisoner was not Monk.

"Who are you?" he asked the startled captive as he quickly dragged the first guard toward a neighboring supply closet.

The gray-haired woman used her free arm to help Fiona with the second man. She was stronger than she appeared. Her left arm was bandaged and secured across her chest in a tight sling. The left side of her face was savaged with jagged scratches, sutured and raw. Something had attacked and mauled her. Despite her recent injuries, her eyes met Gray's, fiery and determined.

"My name is Dr. Marcia Fairfield."

12:25 P.M.

The Jeep trundled down the empty lane.

Behind the wheel, Warden Gerald Kellogg mopped his sweating brow. He had a bottle of Birkenhead Premium Lager propped between his legs.

Despite the hectic morning, Kellogg refused to break routine. There was nothing else he could do anyway. Security at the Waalenberg estate had passed on the sketchy details. An escape. Kellogg had already alerted the park rangers and posted men at all the gates. He passed on pictures, faxed over from the Waalenberg estate. Poachers was the cover. Armed and dangerous.

Until word of a sighting reached Kellogg's office, he had nothing to keep him from his usual two-hour lunch at home. Tuesday meant roasted game hen and sweet potatoes. He drove his Jeep across the cattle guard and into the main drive, lined by short hedges. Ahead, a two-story beadboard Colonial sat on a full acre of manicured property, a perk of his position. It had a staff of ten to maintain the grounds and household, which included only himself. He was in no hurry to marry.

Why buy the cow and all that . . .

Plus his tastes leaned toward unripened fruit.

He had a new girl in the house, little Aina, eleven years old, from Nigeria, black as pitch, just like he liked them, better to hide the bruising. Not that there was anyone to question him. He had a manservant, Mxali, a Swazi brute, recruited from prison, who ran his household with discipline and terror. Any problems were dealt with swiftly, both at home and when needed elsewhere. And the Waalenbergs were only too happy to help any troublemakers disappear. What became of them once they were dropped off by helicopter at the Waalenberg estate, Gerald would prefer not to know. But he had heard rumors.

Despite the midday heat, he shivered.

Best not to ask too many questions.

He parked his car in the shade under a leafy acacia tree, climbed out, and strode down the gravel path to the side door that led to the kitchen. A pair of gardeners hoed the flower bed. They kept their eyes down as Gerald passed, as they were taught.

The smell of roasting hens and garlic whetted his appetite. His nose and stomach drew him up the three wooden steps to the open screen door. He entered the kitchen, belly growling.

To the left, the stove door was open. The cook knelt on the planks, head in the oven. Kellogg frowned at the odd tableau. It took him a moment to realize it wasn't the cook.

"Mxali . . . ?"

Kellogg finally noted the underlying smell of seared flesh behind the garlic. Something protruded from the man's arm. A feathered dart. Mxali's weapon of choice. Usually poisoned.

Something was dreadfully wrong.

Kellogg backed away, turning to the door.

The two gardeners had dropped their hoes and had rifles pointed at his wide belly. It was not uncommon for small marauding bands, filth from the black townships, to raid farms and outlying homes. Kellogg held up his arms, skin going cold with terror.

A creak of a board drew him around, half ducking.

A dark figure stepped out of the shadows of the next room.

Kellogg gasped as he recognized the intruder—and the hatred in his eyes.

Not marauders. Even worse.

A ghost.

"Khamisi . . ."

12:30 P.M.

"So what exactly is wrong with him?" Monk asked, thumbing where Painter had disappeared into one of the neighboring huts with Dr. Paula Kane's satellite phone. The director was coordinating with Logan Gregory.

Under the shadowy eaves of another hut, he shared a log with Dr. Lisa Cummings. The medical doctor was quite the looker, even when covered with dust and a bit haunted around the eyes.

She turned her attention to Monk. "His cells are denaturing, dissolving from the inside out. That's according to Anna Sporrenberg. She's studied the deleterious effects of the Bell's radiation extensively in the past. It causes multisystem organ failure. Her brother, Gunther, suffers from a chronic version of it, too. But his rate of decline is slowed by his enhanced healing and immunity. Anna and Painter, exposed as adults to an overdose of the radiation, have no such innate protection."

She went into more details, knowing Monk shared a background in medicine: low platelet counts, rising bilirubin levels, edema, muscle tenderness with bouts of rigidity around the neck and shoulders, bone infarctions, hepatosplenomegaly, audible murmurs in the heartbeat, and strange calcification of distal extremities and vitreous humor of the eyes.

But ultimately it all came down to one question.

"How long do they have?" Monk asked.

Lisa sighed and stared back toward the hut into which Painter had vanished. "No more than a day. Even if a cure could be found today, I fear there might still be permanent and sustained damage."

"Did you note his slurring . . . how he dropped words? Is that all the drugs . . . or . . . or . . . ?"

Lisa glanced back to him, her eyes more sharply pained. "It's more than the drugs."

Monk sensed this was the first time she admitted this to herself. It was stated with dread and hopelessness. He also saw how much she suffered for it. Her reaction was more than just a concerned doctor or a worried friend. She cared for Painter and plainly struggled to hold her emotions in check, to guard her heart.

Painter appeared in the doorway. He waved Monk over. "I have Kat on the horn."

Monk rose quickly, checked the sky for choppers, and crossed to Painter. He accepted the satellite phone, covered the mouthpiece, and nodded to Dr. Cummings. "Boss, I think the woman could use some company."

Painter rolled his eyes. They were bloodshot, splotchy with hemorrhages in the sclera. He shaded his sore eyes and crossed toward the woman.

Monk watched from the doorway and lifted the phone. "Hey, babe."

"Don't *babe* me. What the hell are you doing in Africa?"

Monk smiled. Kat's scolding was as welcome as lemonade in the desert. Besides, her question was rhetorical. She had surely been debriefed.

"I thought this was supposed to be a babysitting assignment?" she continued.

Monk merely waited, letting her vent.

"When you get home, I'm locking you . . ."

She continued for another long, scrambled minute.

Finally, Monk got a word in edgewise. "I miss you, too."

A blustering sound subsided into a sigh. "I heard Gray is still missing."

"He'll be fine," he assured her, while hoping the same.

"Find him, Monk. Do whatever it takes."

Monk appreciated her understanding. He intended to do just that. She asked for no promise of caution. She knew him too well. Still, he heard the tears in her next words.

"I love you."

That was caution enough for any man.

"I love you, too." He lowered his voice and slightly turned away. "*Both* of you."

"Come home."

"Try to stop me."

Kat sighed again. "Logan is paging me. I must sign off.

We've a meeting scheduled for zero seven hundred with an attaché at the South African embassy. We'll do what we can to put pressure on from here."

"Give 'em hell, babe."

"We will. Bye, Monk."

"Kat, I—" But the line had disconnected. Damn.

Monk lowered the phone and stared at Lisa and Painter. The two leaned together, talking, but Monk sensed it was more the need to be close than any real communication. He stared down at the phone. At least Kat was safe and sound.

12:37 P.M.

"They were taking me to an internment cell down below," Dr. Marcia Fairfield said. "For further questioning. Something must be worrying them."

The three of them were back up in the room on the first-floor landing. The guard who had manhandled Fiona still lay unconscious on the floor, blood dribbling from his nostrils.

Dr. Fairfield had quickly related her story, how she was ambushed in the field, attacked by the Waalenbergs' pets, dragged away. The Waalenbergs had learned through channels about a possible role she had with UK intelligence. So they staged her kidnapping as a fatal lion attack. Her wounds certainly still looked swollen and raw. "I was able to convince them that my companion, a game warden, had been killed. It was all I could do. Hope he made it back to civilization."

"But what are the Waalenbergs hiding?" Gray asked. "What are they doing?"

The woman shook her head. "Some macabre version of a genetic Manhattan Project. That's as much as I can tell. But I think there is some other scheme in the works. A sideline project. Maybe even an attack. I overheard one of my guards talking. Something about a serum of some sort. Serum 525, I heard them say. I also heard Washington, D.C., mentioned in the same context."

Gray frowned. "Did you hear of any timetable?"

"Not exactly. But from their laughter I got the impression whatever was going to happen would be soon. Very soon."

Gray paced a few steps, knuckling his chin. *This serum . . . maybe it's a biowarfare agent . . . a pathogen, a virus . . .* He shook his head. He needed more information—and quickly.

"We have to get into those basement labs," he mumbled. "Find out what's going on."

"They were taking me to that internment area," Dr. Fairfield said.

He nodded, understanding. "If I pose as one of your guards, that might be our ticket down there."

"We'd have to hurry," Marcia said. "As it is, they must be wondering what's keeping me."

Gray turned to Fiona, ready for an argument. It would be safest if she stayed hidden in the room, out of sight. It would be hard to justify her presence alongside a prisoner and a guard. It would only arouse suspicion and attention.

"I know! No place for a maid," Fiona said, surprising him yet again. She nudged the guard on the floor with her toe. "I'll keep Casanova here company until you get back."

Despite her brave words, her eyes shone with fear.

"We won't be gone long," he promised.

"You'd better not be."

With the matter settled, Gray grabbed his rifle, waved Dr. Fairfield toward the door, and said, "Let's go."

In short order, Gray marched Marcia at gunpoint into the central elevator. No one accosted them. A card reader restricted access to the subterranean levels. He swiped Ischke's second key card. The lighted buttons for the sublevels changed from red to green.

"Any idea where to start?" Gray asked.

Marcia reached out. "The greater the treasure, the deeper it's buried." She pressed the bottommost number. Seven levels down. The elevator began to descend.

As Gray watched the floors count down, Marcia's words nagged.

An attack. Possibly in Washington.

But what type of attack?

6:41 A.M. EST
WASHINGTON, D.C.

Embassy Row was only two miles from the National Mall. Their driver turned onto Massachusetts Avenue and headed toward the South African embassy. Kat rode with Logan in the backseat, comparing final notes. The sun had just risen, and the embassy appeared ahead.

Its four stories of Indiana limestone shone brilliantly in the morning sunlight, highlighting its gables and dormers typical of the Cape Dutch style. The driver pulled up to the residence wing of the embassy. The ambassador had agreed to meet them in his private study at this early hour. It seemed any issues concerning the Waalenbergs were best dealt with out of the public's eye.

Which was fine with Kat.

She had a pistol in an ankle holster.

Kat climbed out and waited for Logan. Four fluted pilasters supported a carved parapet with the South African coat of arms. Beneath it, a doorman noted their arrival and opened the glazed front door.

As second in command, Logan led the way. Kat kept a step or two behind, watching the street, wary. With as much money as the Waalenbergs wielded, she did not trust who might be in their private employ . . . and that included the ambassador, John Hourigan.

The entrance hall opened wide around them. A secretary in a neat navy business suit ushered them across the hall. "Ambassador Hourigan will be down momentarily. I'm to take you to his study. Can I bring you any tea or coffee?"

Logan and Kat declined.

They were soon ensconced in a richly paneled room. The furniture—desks, bookcases, occasional tables—was constructed of the same wood. Stinkwood, native to South Africa, so rare it was no longer available for commercial export.

Logan took a seat by the desk. Kat remained standing.

They didn't have long to wait.

The doors opened again, and a tall, thin man with sandy-blond hair entered. He wore a navy suit but carried his jacket over one arm. Kat suspected the casual approach was pure artifice, meant to make his manner appear more amiable and cooperative. Like meeting here in his private residence.

She wasn't buying it.

As Logan made introductions, Kat surveyed the room. With a background in the intelligence services, she imagined the conversation here would be taped. She studied the room, guessing where the surveillance equipment was hidden.

Ambassador Hourigan finally settled to his seat. "You've come to inquire about the Waalenberg estate . . . or so I was informed. How may I be of service?"

"We believe someone in their employ may have been involved in a kidnapping in Germany."

His eyes widened too perfectly. "I'm shocked to hear such allegations. But I've heard nothing about this from the German BKA, Interpol, or Europol."

"Our sources are concrete," Logan insisted. "All we ask is cooperation with your Scorpions to follow up locally."

Kat watched the man feign an intensely pensive expression. The Scorpions were the South African equivalent of the FBI. Cooperation seemed unlikely. The best Logan sought here was to keep such organizations out of Sigma's way. While they could not negotiate cooperation against such a political powerhouse as the Waalenbergs, they might place enough pressure to keep any policing authorities from helping them. A small concession, but a meaningful one.

Kat continued standing, watching the slow dance these two men performed, each trying to gain the best advantage.

"I assure you that the Waalenbergs hold the international community and governing bodies in the utmost respect. The family has supported relief efforts, multinational charity organizations, and nonprofit trusts throughout the world. In fact in their latest act of generosity, they've endowed all South African embassies and chanceries around the globe with a golden centennial bell, marking the hundred-year anniversary of the first gold coin minted in South Africa."

"That is all well and good, but it doesn't—"

Kat cut Logan off, speaking for the first time. "Did you say gold *bell*?"

Hourigan's eyes met hers. "Yes, gifts from Sir Baldric Waalenberg himself. One hundred gold-plated centennial bells bearing the South African coat of arms. Ours is being installed in the residence hall on the fourth floor."

Logan met Kat's eyes.

Kat spoke. "Would it be possible to see it?"

The strange tack of the conversation unsettled the ambassador, but he failed to come up with a good reason to deny it, and Kat imagined he hoped it would be a way to even gain an upper hand in the quiet war of diplomacy going on here.

"I would be delighted to show you." He stood up and checked his watch. "I'm afraid we'll have to move smartly. I do have a breakfast meeting I must not be late to."

As Kat had imagined, Hourigan was using the tour as an excuse to end the conversation early, to wheedle out of any firm commitment. Logan stared hard at her. She hoped she was right.

They were led to an elevator and taken to the top floor of the building. They passed hallways decorated in artwork and South African native crafts. Then, a large hall opened; it appeared more museum than living space. There were display cabinets, long tables, and massive chests with hand-beaten brass fixtures. A wall of windows overlooked the rear yard and gardens. But in a corner hung a giant gold bell. It looked as if it had recently been uncrated, as bits of the straw stuffing were still scattered on the floor. The bell itself stood a full meter tall and half again as wide at the mouth. The coat of arms had been stamped on it.

Kat stepped closer. A thick power cable ran from its top and coiled to the floor.

The ambassador noted her attention. "It's automated to ring at set times of the day. Quite a marvel of engineering. If you look up inside the bell, it's a marvel of gears, like a fine Rolex."

Kat turned to Logan. He had paled. Like Kat, he had studied the sketches Anna Sporrenberg had made of the original Bell. This was an exact duplicate done in gold. Both had also read of the detrimental effects that could be radiated from the device. Madness and death. Kat stared out the upper-story window. From this height, she could just make out the white dome of the Capitol.

The ambassador's earlier words now horrified.

A hundred golden bells . . . endowed around the globe.

"It took a special technician to install it," the ambassador continued, though now a slightly bored lilt entered his voice, winding the meeting toward its end. "I believe he's around here somewhere."

The room's door closed behind them, slamming slightly. All three turned.

"Ah, here he is," Hourigan said upon turning. His voice died when he spotted the submachine gun held by the newcomer. His hair was white-blond. Even from across the room, Kat spotted a dark tattoo on the hand supporting the gun.

Kat dove for her ankle holster.

Without a word, the assassin opened fire, spraying bullets.

Glass shattered, and wood splintered.

Behind her, beaten by ricocheting rounds, the golden bell rang and rang.

12:44 P.M.
SOUTH AFRICA

The elevator doors opened on the seventh sublevel. Gray stepped out, rifle in hand. He searched both directions along a gray hallway. Unlike the rich woods and fine craftsmanship used in the main manor house, this sublevel was lit by fluorescents and maintained a rigid sterility in its decor: bleached linoleum floors, gray walls, low roof. Smooth steel doors with glowing electronic locks lined one side of the hall. The other doors appeared more ordinary.

Gray placed his palm against one.

The panel vibrated. He heard a rhythmic hum.

Power plant? Must be massive.

Marcia stepped to his side. "I think we've come down too far," she whispered. "This feels more storage and utility."

Gray agreed. Still . . .

He crossed to one of the locked steel doors. "Begs the question, what're they storing?"

The sign on the door read: EMBRYONAAL.

"Embryonic lab," Marcia translated.

She crossed to join him, eyes guarded, wincing slightly as she moved her bandaged and splinted arm.

Gray raised Ischke's card again and swiped it. The indicator glowed green and a magnetic lock released. Gray pushed the door. He had shouldered his rifle and now had his pistol out.

The overhead fluorescents flickered then came on steady.

The room was a long hall, a good forty meters. Gray noted how chilly the air was in here, crisper, filtered. A flush line of floor-to-ceiling stainless-steel freezers covered one side. Compressors hummed. On the other side were steel carts, tanks of liquid nitrogen, and a large microscope table wired to a micro-dissection table.

It appeared to be some form of a cryonics lab.

At a central workstation, a Hewlett-Packard computer idled. The screensaver spun on the LCD monitor. A silver symbol rotated against a black background. A familiar symbol. Gray had seen it depicted on the floor of Wewelsburg castle.

"The Black Sun," Gray mumbled.

Marcia glanced at him.

Gray pointed to the spinning sun. "The symbol represents Himmler's Black Order, a cabal of Thule Society occultists and scientists obsessed with the superman philosophy. Baldric must've been a member, too."

Gray sensed they had come full circle. From Ryan's great-grandfather to here. He nodded to the computer. "Look for a main directory. See what you can find out."

While Marcia aimed for the workstation, Gray crossed to one of the freezers. He pulled it open. Frigid air welled out. Inside were drawers, indexed and numbered. Behind him, he heard Marcia tapping at the computer. Gray edged one drawer open. Neatly arranged in clips were a score of tiny glass straws filled with a yellow liquid.

"Frozen embryos," Marcia said behind him.

He closed the drawer and looked down the length of the hall at the number of giant freezers. If Marcia was correct, there had to be thousands of embryos stored here.

She spoke, drawing him over. "The computer is a database, logging genomes and genealogy." She glanced over to him. "Both human and animal. Mammalian species. Look at this."

Strange notations filled the screen.

NUCLEOTIDE VERANDERING (DNA)
[*CROCUTA CROCUTA*]
Thu Nov 6 14:56:25 GMT

Schema V.1.16

VERANDERING	CODE RANGSCHIKKEN
Loci A.0. Transversie	
A.0.2. Dipyrimidine to	ATGGTTACGCGCTCATG
Dithymidine (c[CT]>TT)	GAATTCTCGCTCATGGA
	ATTCTCGCTCGTCAACT
Loci A.3. Gedeeltelijk	
A.3.3.4. Dinucleotide (transcriptie)	CTAGAAATTACGCTCTTA
	CGCTTCTCGCTTGTTAC
	GCGCTCA
Loci B.5.	
B.5.1.3. Cryptische plaatsactivering	GTTACGCGCTCGCGCTCA
	TGGAATTCTCGC TCATG

Loci B.7.

B.7.5.1. Pentanucleotide	ATGGTTACGCGCTCCGC
(g[TACAGATTC] verminderde	TGGAATTCTCGCTCATG
stabiliteit)	GAATTCTCGCTC

"They appear to be a list of mutational changes," Marcia said. "Defined down to the level of polynucleotides."

Gray tapped the name near the top. *"Crocuta crocuta,"* he read. "The spotted hyena. I've seen the end result of that research. Baldric Waalenberg mentioned how he was perfecting the species, even incorporating human stem cells in their brains."

Marcia brightened and tapped back to a main directory. "That explains the name of the entire database. *Hersenschim.* Which translates to 'chimera.' A biologic term for an organism with genetic material from more than one species, whether from grafting like in plants or insertion of foreign cells into an embryo." She tapped one-handed at the computer, focused. "But to what end?"

Straightening, Gray glanced down the length of the embryonic lab. Was all this any different from Baldric's manipulation of orchids and bonsai trees? Just another way to control nature, to manipulate and design it according to his own definition of perfection.

"Hmm . . . ," Marcia mumbled. "Strange."

Gray turned back to her. "What?"

"As I said, there are human embryos here." She glanced over a shoulder to Gray. "According to the cross-referenced genealogy, all of these embryos are genetically tied to the Waalenbergs."

No surprise there. Gray had noted the similarities in the Waalenberg offspring. Their patriarch had been tweaking the family lineage for generations.

But apparently that wasn't the strange part.

Marcia continued, "Each of the Waalenberg embryos in turn is referenced to stem cell lines that are then tracked to *Crocuta crocuta*."

"The hyenas?"

Marcia nodded.

Understanding and horror grew. "Are you saying he's been planting his *own* children's stem cells into those monsters?" Gray could not hide his shock. Did the man's atrocities, his conceit, never end?

"That's not all," Marcia said.

Gray felt a sickening jolt in his gut, knowing what she was going to say next.

Marcia pointed to a complicated chart on the screen. "According to this, stem cells from the hyenas are cross-referenced back to the next generation of human embryos."

"Dear God . . ."

Gray pictured Ischke holding out her hand and stopping the charging hyena. It was more than just master and dog. It was family. Baldric had been implanting cells from his mutated hyenas back into his children, cross-pollinating like his orchids.

"But even *that's* not the worst . . . ," Marcia began, pale and disturbed to her core. "The Waalenbergs have been—"

Gray cut her off. He had heard enough. They had more to search. "We should keep moving."

Marcia glanced to the computer with reluctance, but she nodded and stood. They left the monster lab and continued down the hall. The next door was marked FOETUSSEN. A fetal lab. Gray continued down the hall without stopping. He had no desire to see what horrors lay inside there.

"How are they achieving these results?" Marcia asked. "The mutations, the successful chimeras . . . ? They must have some way of controlling their genetic manipulations."

"Possibly," he mumbled. "But it's not perfected—not yet."

Gray remembered Hugo Hirszfeld's work, the code he hid in runes. He now understood Baldric's obsession with it. A promise of perfection. *Too beautiful to let die and too monstrous to set free.*

And certainly the concerns of the monstrous didn't scare Baldric. In fact, he bred the monstrous into his own family. And now that he had Hugo's code, what was Baldric's next step? Especially with Sigma breathing down his neck. No wonder Baldric wanted so desperately to know about Painter Crowe.

They reached another door. The room beyond must be huge, as it was spaced a distance from the fetal lab. Gray noted the name on the door.

XERUM 525.

He matched gazes with Marcia.

"Not *serum*," Gray said.

"Xerum," Marcia read, shaking her head in a lack of understanding.

Gray used his stolen card. The green light flashed, the lock released, and he pushed inside. The room's lights flickered on. The air here smelled vaguely corrosive with a hint of ozone. The floor and walls were dark.

"Lead," Marcia said, touching the walls.

Gray didn't like the sound of that, but he had to know more. The cavernous space looked like a storage facility for hazardous wastes. Shelves stretched deep into the room. Stacked on them were yellow ten-gallon drums with the number 525 stamped on them.

Gray remembered his concern about a biowarfare agent. Or did the drums hold some type of fissionable material, nuclear waste? Was that the reason the room was lead-lined?

Marcia showed little concern. She crossed to the shelves. Each shelf spot bore a label, marking each drum. "Albania," she read, then stepped to the next one. "Argentina."

Other countries were named, in alphabetical order.

Gray stared across the shelves. There had to be a hundred drums at least.

Marcia glanced to him. He understood the sudden concern in her eyes.

Oh, no . . .

Gray hurried into the room, searching the shelves, stopping periodically to read a label: BELGIUM . . . FINLAND . . . GREECE . . .

He ran on.

At last he reached the spot he was looking for.

UNITED STATES.

He recalled what Marcia had overheard, something about Washington, D.C. A possible attack. Gray stared down the rows of drums. From all the countries named here, it wasn't just Washington under threat. At least not yet. Gray remembered Baldric's concern about Painter, about Sigma. They were his most immediate threat.

To compensate, Baldric must have moved up his timetable.

Above the label marked UNITED STATES, the shelf was empty.

The corresponding drum of Xerum 525 was gone.

7:45 A.M. EST
GEORGETOWN UNIVERSITY HOSPITAL
WASHINGTON, D.C.

"ETA on MedSTAR?" the radio dispatcher asked. He sat before the hospital's touch-screen program, wireless headset in place.

The helicopter crackled back, "En route. Two minutes out."

"The ER is asking for an update." Everyone had heard about the shootout on Embassy Row. Homeland Security protocols were in effect. Calls and alarms were being raised throughout the city. Confusion reigned at the moment.

"Embassy medical personnel pronounced two on the spot. Two of their own. South African nationals, including the ambassador. But two Americans are also down."

"Status?"

"One dead . . . one critical."

14

MENAGERIE

1:55 P.M.
SOUTH AFRICA

Fiona listened at the doorway, Taser in hand. Voices approached the first-floor landing. Terror strangled her. Whatever reserve of adrenaline had been sustaining her for the past twenty-four hours was reaching its end. Her hands shook, her breathing remained shallow and rapid.

The gagged and bound guard, the one who'd grabbed her, lay sprawled behind her. She'd had to shock him again when the bloke had begun to moan.

The voices approached her hiding spot.

Fiona tensed.

Where was Gray? He had been gone almost an hour.

Two people approached her door. She recognized one of their voices. It was the blond bitch who had sliced her palm. Ischke Waalenberg. She and her companion spoke Dutch, but Fiona was fluent in the language.

". . . key cards," Ischke said angrily. "I must have lost mine when I fell."

"Well, dear *zuster,* you are home and safe now."

Zuster. Sister. So her companion was her brother.

"We'll change the codes as a precaution," he added.

"And no one has found the two Americans or the girl?"

"We have all the borders of the estate under double guard. We're confident that they're still on the grounds. We'll find them. And *grootvader* has a surprise."

"What sort of surprise?"

"Insurance that no one leaves the estate alive. Remember he did take DNA samples from them when they first arrived."

Ischke laughed, chilling Fiona's blood. The voices wandered away.

"Come." The brother's voice faded down the stairs as they descended toward the main floor. "*Grootvader* wants us all downstairs."

Their voices trailed to a stop near the bottom of the staircase. With her ear pressed to the door, Fiona could make out no other words, but it sounded like an argument over some matter. But she had heard enough.

No one leaves the estate alive.

What were they planning? Ischke's icy laugh still rang in her head, mirthless and satisfied. Whatever was being plotted, they seemed certain of its outcome. But what did their DNA samples have to do with it?

Fiona knew there was only one way to find out. She had no idea when Gray would return and feared time was running out for all of them. They would need to know what the danger was . . . if they were to avoid it.

That meant only one thing.

She pocketed her Taser and took out her feather duster. She twisted the dead bolt and unlocked the door. For this hunt, she needed all the skills from the street. She pulled open the door and slipped out of the room. Pausing, her back to the door, she pushed it closed with her rear end. She had never felt so alone, so purely frightened. Reconsidering, she rested her hand on the doorknob. She closed her eyes and steadied herself, offering up a prayer, not to God, but to someone who had taught her how courage came in many forms, including sacrifice.

"Mutti . . . ," she prayed.

She missed her foster mother, Grette Neal. Old secrets from the past had killed the woman, and now new secrets threatened Fiona and the others. For any hope of survival, she needed to be as brave and selfless as Mutti.

The voices below drifted away down the staircase.

Fiona sidled closer, feather duster raised in defense. She peered over the first-landing balcony, just enough to spot the white-blond heads of the twins. Their words reached her again.

"Don't keep *grootvader* waiting," the brother said.

"I'll be right down. I just want to check on Skuld. Make sure she is back in her kennel. She was quite aroused, and I fear she might harm herself in her frustration."

"The same might be said of you, my sweet *zuster*."

Fiona took a step closer. The brother touched his sister's cheek, creepily intimate.

Ischke leaned into his touch, then pulled away. "I won't be long."

Her brother nodded and stepped toward the central lift. "I will let *grootvader* know." He pressed a button and the doors opened.

Ischke headed off in a different direction, toward the back of the manor.

Fiona hurried to follow. She clutched the Taser in her pocket. If she could get the bitch alone, make her talk . . .

Flying down the steps, Fiona slowed near the bottom, resuming a more subdued pace. Ischke was headed down a central hall that seemed to run straight through the heart of the manor house.

Fiona followed from a distance, head lowered, feather duster folded in her arms like a nun with a Bible. She took tiny steps, a nondescript mouse of a servant. Ischke descended a set of five stairs, passing a pair of sentries, and followed along another hallway to the left.

Fiona approached the pair of guards. She increased her pace, appearing like a servant late to some obscure duty. Still, she stayed deeply bowed, half-buried in her oversize maid outfit.

She reached the short stairs.

The guards ignored her, plainly on their best behavior after the mistress of the house had just passed them. Fiona skipped down the five steps. Once in the lower hall, Fiona found it empty.

She stopped.

Ischke was gone.

A mix of relief and terror suffused through her in equal parts.

Should I return to the room? Hope for the best?

She remembered Ischke's cold laughter—then the woman's voice barked sharply, close, coming from a double set of decorative iron-and-glass doors to the right.

Something had pissed Ischke off.

Fiona hurried forward. She listened at the door.

"The meat must be bloody! Fresh!" Ischke hollered. "Or I'll put you in there with her."

Mumbled apologies. Footsteps ran away.

Fiona leaned closer, her ear to the glass.

A mistake.

The door shoved open, striking her in the side of the head. Ischke stormed through, running straight into Fiona.

Ischke swore, elbowing her aside.

Fiona reacted instinctively, relying on old skills. She untangled herself and bunched into a ball, dropping to a knee, cowering—it didn't take much acting.

"Watch where you're going!" Ischke fumed.

"Ja, maitresse," she fawned, bowing deeper.

"Get out of my way!"

Fiona panicked. Where was she supposed to go? Finding Fiona at the door, Ischke would wonder what she had been doing crouched there. The woman's body still held the door open. Fiona scraped her way, bowing through the open doorway, out of Ischke's way.

Fiona's hand went to her hidden Taser, but it took her a moment to drop what she had just stolen from Ischke's sweater pocket. She had not meant to steal it, just reflexes. Stupid. Now the delay cost her everything. Before she could free her Taser, Ischke swore and strode away. The heavy iron-and-glass door swung shut with a clang between them.

Fiona cringed, cursing herself. What now? She would have to wait a few moments before leaving. Suspicions would be too aroused if she were spotted on Ischke's trail again. Besides, she knew where Ischke was headed. Back to the lift. Unfortunately, Fiona didn't know the house well enough to take an alternate route to the main hall, to attempt an ambush.

Tears threatened, a mix of fear and frustration.

She had bollixed the whole deal.

Despairing, she finally took note of the chamber ahead. It was brightly lit, with natural sunlight streaming through a geodesic glass roof. It was some type of inner circular courtyard. Giant palms rose from the central floor and crowned toward the glass roof. All around, massive colonnades supported the high roof and set off deep cloisters around the room. Three lofty halls, arched and as high as the central courtyard, branched off like chapels off a church's nave, forming a cross.

But this hall was no place of worship.

The smell struck her first. Musky, fetid, the reek of a charnel house. Cries and ululating moans echoed across the cavernous space. Curiosity drew her a step forward. Three stairs led down to the main floor, empty of staff. The man whom she had heard run off after being scolded by Ischke was nowhere in sight.

From her post, she searched the room.

Fitted into each of the sunken cloisters around the edges of the giant courtyard were massive cages, sealed in front by iron-and-glass grates, like the entry door. Behind the bars, she spotted hulking shapes, some curled in slumber, others pacing, one hunkered over a knob of leg bone, gnawing. The hyena creatures.

But that wasn't all.

In other cages, she spotted additional monstrosities. A gorilla sat sullen near the front of one cage, staring straight at Fiona with an unnerving intelligence. Worse yet, some mutation had stripped the beast of its fur. Wrinkled elephantine skin hung from its body.

In another, a lion paced back and forth. It was furred, but it grew out bleached and patchy and was presently fouled with feces and gore. It panted, eyes red-rimmed. Fangs protruded, saber-toothed and sickled.

All around were twisted forms: a striped antelope with corkscrewing horns, a pair of skeletally tall jackals, an albino warthog plated like an armadillo. Gruesome and sad at the same time. The jackals caged together wailed and yipped, moving woodenly, crippled.

Still, pity did little to hold back the terror of seeing the giant hyenas. Her eyes fixed on the one gnawing a thigh bone of some massive animal. Water buffalo or wildebeest. A bit of meat and black fur still waited to be worried from the bone. Fiona could not help imagining that it could have been her. If Gray hadn't rescued her . . .

She shivered.

Tensing its massive jaws, the giant hyena cracked the leg bone, snapping it like a gunshot.

Fiona jumped, awakened again.

She retreated to the door. She had waited long enough. With her mission a failure, she would sneak back to her hiding place with her tail tucked between her legs.

She grabbed the door and yanked on it.

Locked.

2:30 P.M.

Gray stared at the row of heavy steel levers, heart pounding in his throat. It had taken him too long to find the master circuit switches for the electrical board. He could sense the power flowing through the giant cabling in the room, an electromagnetic force felt at the base of the neck.

He had already wasted too much time.

After discovering one of the drums of Xerum 525 was missing, one intended for the United States, urgency weighed heavily upon Gray. He had abandoned any attempt to reconnoiter the remainder of the subbasement. Right now, it was more important to get a warning off to Washington.

Marcia had reported seeing an emergency shortwave radio in the security block when she had been taken from her cell. She knew whom to call, a partner of hers, Dr. Paula Kane, who could pass on the warning. Still, they both knew that to go for the radio was probably a suicide mission. But what choice did they have?

At least Fiona was safely ensconced away.

"What are you waiting for?" Marcia asked. She had cut free her sling and changed into a laboratory smock from one of the storage lockers. In the dark, she might pass for one of the lab's researchers.

Marcia stood at his back, clutching an emergency flashlight.

Gray raised a hand to the first lever.

They had already located the fire stairs for the subbasement. The stairs should lead back to the main house. But to get outside and reach the security block, they needed an additional means of distraction, extra insurance.

The answer had come a few moments ago. Gray had been leaning against one of the hallway doors. He noted the vibration and hum of the level's power plant. If they could fry the main board—create more chaos, possibly blind their captors for a spell—they'd have a better chance of making it to that radio.

"Ready?" Gray asked.

Marcia flicked on her flashlight. She met his gaze, took a deep breath, and nodded. "Let's do it."

"Lights out," Gray said and yanked the first lever.

Then the next and the next.

2:35 P.M.

Fiona watched the lamps around the courtyard flicker and die.

Oh, God . . .

Fiona stood in the center of the courtyard, near a small fountain. Moments ago, she had slipped from her post by the locked main door and had crept halfway across the central courtyard. She had gone in search of another exit. Surely there had to be one.

She froze now.

A momentary silence spread across the room, as if the animals sensed some primary change, a loss of the perpetual subsonic hum of power. Or maybe it was merely a sense of power shifting *to* them.

A door creaked open behind her.

Fiona slowly turned.

One of the iron-and-glass cages nudged open, nosed by

one of the hyena monsters. The blackout had demagnetized the locks. The beast crept out of its cage. Blood dripped from its muzzle. It had been the one gnawing the thigh bone. A low growl flowed from it.

Somewhere behind her, Fiona heard a cackling yip as some silent communication passed through the menagerie's predators. Other doors creaked on iron hinges.

Fiona remained fixed by the fountain. Even the water pump had died, silencing the waters, as if fearful of drawing attention to itself.

Somewhere down one of the arched side chapels, a bright scream echoed forth. Human. Fiona imagined it was the zookeeper whom Ischke had scolded. It seemed his charges would get their bloody meal after all. Footsteps ran in her direction. Then a new scream erupted, pained and garbled amid a yowl of yips and cries.

Fiona shut her ears against the last cry, followed by the sound of feeding.

Her full attention remained on the first escapee.

The bloody-muzzled hyena approached. Fiona recognized the creature from the shadow of spotting on its flank, barely discernible, white on white. It was the same beast from the jungle.

Ischke's pet.

Skuld.

It had been denied its caged treat before.

But no longer.

2:40 P.M.

"Help us . . . *bitte!*" Gunther rushed into the hut, followed by Major Brooks.

Lisa stood up, lowering her stethoscope from Painter's chest. She had been monitoring a systolic murmur. In just the past half day, it had changed from an early-peaking murmur to a late one, suggesting a rapidly progressing stenosis of the man's aortic valve. Mild angina had worsened to bouts of syncope, swooning faints if Painter overexerted. She had never seen such a rapid degeneration. She suspected calcification around his heart valve. Such odd mineralized deposits had begun appearing throughout Painter's body, even in the fluids of his eye.

Lying flat on his back, Painter pushed to his elbows with a wince. "What's wrong?" he asked Gunther.

Major Brooks answered with a worried southern drawl. "It's his sister, sir. She's having some type of fit . . . a seizure."

Lisa grabbed the med kit. Painter tried to stand but had to be assisted by Lisa on his second attempt. "Just stay here," she warned.

"I can manage," he answered, showing his irritation.

Lisa didn't have time to argue. She let go of his arm. He teetered. She hurried to Gunther. "Let's go."

Brooks waited, unsure whether to follow or lend an arm to Painter.

The major was waved off.

Painter hobbled after them.

Lisa ran out of the hut and crossed to the neighboring one. The day's heat struck her like stepping into an oven. The air hung motionless, burning, impossible to breathe. The sun blinded. But in a moment, Lisa was ducking into the cooler darkness of the next room.

Anna lay on a grass mat, half on her side, body arched, muscles contracted. Lisa hurried to her. She had already established an intravenous catheter in her forearm. Painter had the same. It was easier to administer drugs and fluids.

Lisa quickly dropped to a knee and grabbed up a syringe premeasured with diazepam. She gave the entire dose in one bolus IV. In seconds, Anna relaxed, dropping back to the floor. Her eyes fluttered open and consciousness returned, groggy but attentive.

Painter arrived. Monk appeared in tow with him.

"How is she?" Painter asked.

"How do you think?" Lisa asked, exasperated.

Gunther helped his sister sit up. Her face was ashen, covered in a sheen of sweat. Painter was destined for the same in the next hour. Though both were exposed, Painter's larger bulk seemed to be sustaining him a bit more heartily. But their survival was down to hours.

Lisa stared up at the shaft of sunlight spearing into the room from a slit window. Twilight was too far off.

Monk spoke into the worried silence. "I spoke to Khamisi. He reports that every light in the damn mansion just went out." He wore a tentative grin, as if unsure any good news was welcome. "I'm guessing it's Gray's handiwork."

Painter frowned. It was his only expression lately. "We don't know that."

"And we don't know it isn't." Monk wiped a hand across the top of his shaved head. "Sir, I think we need to consider moving up the timetable. Khamisi says—"

"Khamisi is not running this op," Painter said, coughing harshly.

Monk met Lisa's eyes. The two of them had held a private discussion twenty minutes ago. It was one of the reasons Monk had made the call to Khamisi. Certain expediencies had to be verified. Monk nodded to her.

She slipped a second syringe from her pocket, stepped to Painter's side.

"Let me flush your catheter," Lisa said. "There's blood in it."

Painter held up his arm. It trembled.

Lisa supported his wrist and injected her dose. Monk stepped beside Painter and caught him as his legs went out from under him.

"What—?" Painter's head lolled back.

Monk shouldered him under one arm. "It's for your own good, sir."

Painter frowned at Lisa. His other arm swung at her—whether to hit her or express some shock at her betrayal, Lisa doubted he even knew. The sedative swooned him away.

Major Brooks watched, his mouth hanging open.

Monk shrugged at the Air Force man. "Never seen a mutiny before?"

Brooks collected himself. "All I can say, sir . . . about bloody time."

Monk nodded. "Khamisi is on his way in with the package. ETA three minutes. He and Dr. Kane will take over ground support here."

Lisa turned to Gunther. "Can you carry your sister?"

As proof, he scooped her up and stood.

"What are you all doing?" Anna asked weakly.

"You two are not going to last until nightfall," Lisa said. "We're going to make a run for the Bell."

"How . . . ?"

"Don't worry that pretty little head of yours," Monk said and hobbled out with Painter, supported by Major Brooks. "We've got it covered."

Monk again met Lisa's eyes. She read his expression.

It may be too late already.

2:41 P.M.

Gray led the way up the stairs, pistol in hand. He and Marcia moved as silently as possible. She kept a palm over her flashlight's lamp, keeping any illumination to a minimum. Just enough to see where they were going. With the elevators incapacitated, he feared running into a stray guard on the stairs.

Though he was disguised as a guard, one leading a researcher out of the darkened basement, he'd still rather avoid any unnecessary encounters.

They crossed past the sixth sublevel, dark like the one below.

Gray continued, increasing his pace, balancing caution against the fear secondary generators would kick in at some point. Climbing around the next landing, a glow appeared ahead.

Holding up a hand, he stopped Marcia behind him.

The light didn't move. It remained stationary.

Not a wandering guard. Probably an emergency lamp.

Still . . .

"Stay here," he whispered to Marcia.

She nodded.

Gray continued ahead, pistol raised and ready. He climbed the steps. At the next landing, light seeped through a half-open doorway. As Gray approached, he heard voices. Farther up the stairs, it remained dark. So why was there light and power here? This level must be on a separate circuit.

Voices echoed down the corridor.

Familiar voices. Isaak and Baldric.

They were out of direct sight, hidden deeper in the room. He glanced below and saw Marcia's face limned in the light washing down the stairs. He waved her up to his landing.

She had heard the voices, too.

Isaak and Baldric seemed unconcerned about the loss of electricity. With power here, did they even know the rest of the manor was blacked out? Gray held his curiosity in check. He had to warn Washington.

Words reached him. "The Bell will kill all of them," Baldric said.

Gray paused. Were they talking about Washington? If so, what were their plans? If he knew more . . .

Gray held up two fingers to Marcia. Two minutes. If he wasn't back, she was to head up on her own. He had left her his second pistol. If he could see this *Bell*, it might be the difference between saving lives and losing them.

He held up the two fingers again.

Marcia nodded. It would be up to her if Gray was caught.

He squeezed into the opening, not budging the door, afraid a squeak of hinges would alert the two inside. The same gray fluorescent-lit hall stretched ahead. But it ended a short distance away at a double set of steel doors, opposite where the darkened elevator opened on this floor.

One of the double doors stood open.

Gray moved quickly, staying on the balls of his feet. He reached the doors and hugged the wall. He dropped to a knee and peered past the edge of the door.

The chamber beyond was low-roofed but cavernous, encompassing this entire sublevel. Here was the heart of the laboratory. Banks of computers lined one wall. Monitors glowed with scrolling numbers and code. The computers probably warranted the separate circuit, their own power supply.

The room's occupants, so focused on the task at hand, hadn't noted the loss of power elsewhere. But surely they would be alerted any minute.

Baldric and Isaak, grandfather and grandson, were bent over a station. A thirty-inch flat-screen monitor on the wall flashed rapidly through a series of runes, one after the other. It was the five from Hugo's books.

"The code remains unbroken," Isaak said. "Is it wise to move the Bell program global while we still have this riddle unsolved?"

"It will be solved!" Baldric slammed a fist on the table.

"It is only a matter of time. Besides, we are close enough to perfection. Like with you and your sister. You will live long. Fifty years. The deterioration will not weaken you until your last decade. It is time for us to move forward."

Isaak looked little convinced.

Baldric straightened. He lifted an arm and waved it toward the ceiling. "See what delays have wrought. Our attempt to distract international attention to the Himalayas has backfired."

"Because we underestimated Anna Sporrenberg."

"And Sigma," Baldric added. "But no matter. Governments now breathe down our necks. Gold will buy us only so much protection. We must act now. First Washington, then the world. And in that chaos, there will be plenty of time to break the code. Perfection will be ours."

"And out of Africa, a new world will arise," Isaak said in rote, as if it were a prayer drilled into him at a young age, cemented in his genetic code.

"Pure and cleansed of corruption," Baldric added, ending the litany. But his words were equally dispassionate. It was as if all this were no more than another step in his breeding program, a scientific exercise.

Baldric teetered straighter on his cane. Gray noted how enfeebled the man really appeared, with no audience but his grandson. Gray wondered if the accelerated timetable wasn't fueled more by Baldric's own impending mortality than by any true necessity. Were they all unwitting pawns in Baldric's desire to move forward in his plan? Had Baldric orchestrated this scenario on purpose—consciously or unconsciously—to justify acting now, during his lifetime?

Isaak spoke again. He had shifted over to another workstation. "We've green lights across the board. The Bell is powered up and ready for activation. We'll now be able to cleanse the estate of the escaped prisoners."

Gray stiffened. What was this all about?

Baldric turned his back on the flashing runic code and focused toward the room's center. "Prepare for activation."

Gray shifted to see farther into the room.

In its center rested a massive shell, composed of some type of ceramic or metallic compound. It was shaped like an upended bell and stood as tall as Gray. He doubted he could hug his arms halfway around its circumference.

Motors sounded, chugging and echoing, and an inner metal sleeve lowered from the ceiling, encased in a clockwork of gears. It dropped into the larger outer shell. At the same time, a neighboring yellow tank opened a gasket and a stream of purplish metallic liquid flowed into the heart of the Bell.

Lubricant? Fuel source?

Gray had no idea, but he noted the numbers stamped on the side of the tank: 525. It was the mysterious Xerum.

"Raise the blast shield," Baldric ordered. He had to yell to be heard above the clanking gears of the motor assembly. He motioned to the floor with his cane.

The level here was covered by the same gray tile, except for a dull black circular section, thirty yards across, surrounding the Bell. A raised border edged it, a foot thick, like the ring in a circus. The ceiling above was a mirror of the floor, except the roof had an indented border.

It was all lead.

Gray realized the outer floor ring must rise on pistons and insert into the ceiling, forming an entire cylinder locked around the Bell.

"What's wrong?" Baldric yelled again, turning to Isaak at his station.

Isaak toggled a switch back and forth. "We're getting no power to the blast shield motors!"

Gray glanced to his toes. The motors must be on the level below. The *darkened* level. A phone rang inside the room, chiming stridently, competing with the motors. Gray could guess who was calling. Security had finally discovered where the masters of the house were hidden.

Time to go.

Gray straightened and turned.

A pipe swung down and struck his wrist, knocking the pistol from his hand. The wielder swung at his head. Gray barely ducked in time.

Ischke stalked toward him. Behind her, the doors to the darkened elevator stood open, pried apart. The woman must have been trapped in the elevator when the power went out, then climbed down here. Masked by the noise from the Bell's motors, Gray had not heard the doors being pried open behind him.

Ischke raised her pipe, plainly skilled in the art of staff fighting.

Gray fixed his eyes on her and retreated into the Bell's chamber. He refused to glance toward the fire stairs. He prayed Marcia had already left, was en route to reach the shortwave radio and raise the alarm in Washington.

Ischke, her clothes stained with oil, her face smudged, followed Gray inside the Bell chamber.

Baldric spoke behind Gray. "*Wat is dit?* It seems little Ischke has trapped the mouse who has chewed through the wiring."

Gray turned.

Unarmed. Out of options.

"Generators are coming back online," Isaak said, his manner bored, unimpressed by the intrusion.

A grind of motors rumbled under Gray's feet. The blast shield began to rise from the floor.

"Now to exterminate the other rats," Baldric said.

2:45 P.M.

Monk yelled to be heard over the helicopter's rotors. Sand and dust swirled around them in the rotor wash's whirlwind. "You know how to fly this bird?"

Gunther nodded, grabbing the chopper's stick.

Monk clapped the large man on the shoulder. He would have to trust the Nazi. Monk could not fly the bird himself, not one-handed. Still, with the giant's allegiance now centered on his sister's survival, Monk thought it was a safe bet.

Anna sat in the back with Lisa. Painter slumped between them, head hanging. He had only been lightly sedated. Painter mumbled occasionally, nonsensically, warning about some impending sandstorm, lost in past fears.

Ducking his head under the blades, Monk circled around the helicopter. On the far side, Khamisi stood beside Mosi D'Gana, the Zulu chieftain. They clasped each other's forearms.

Mosi had shed his ceremonial gear and now wore khaki fatigues, cap, and an automatic rifle over one shoulder. A holstered pistol hung from a black belt. But he had not totally abandoned his heritage. A short spear with a wicked blade was strapped to his back.

"You have the command," Mosi said formally to Khamisi as Monk approached.

"My honor, sir."

Mosi nodded and let go of Khamisi's arm. "I've heard good things about you, Fat Boy."

Monk joined them. Fat Boy?

Khamisi's eyes widened, a mix of shame and honor shining in them. He nodded back and stepped away. Mosi climbed into the helicopter. He would be joining the first-wave assault. Monk had no choice. He owed the chieftain.

Khamisi crossed to Paula Kane. The pair would be coordinating the ground assault.

Monk searched beyond the swirling plume of sand and dust. The forces had gathered quickly, coming in on foot, on horseback, on rusted motorcycles and beat-up trucks. Mosi had spread the word. And like his great ancestor Shaka Zulu, he gathered an army. Men and women. In traditional pelts, in worn fatigues, in Levi's. And more were still coming.

It would be up to them to keep the Waalenberg army occupied, to secure the estate if possible. How would the Zulus fare against the superiorly armed and experienced security forces of the estate? Would it be Bloody River all over again?

There was only one way to find out.

Monk pulled himself into the crowded rear compartment. Mosi settled into a seat next to Major Brooks. They sat on the bench facing Anna, Lisa, and Painter. One other newcomer, a half-naked Zulu warrior named Tau, was also strapped in the back. He half twisted to keep a short spear thrust at the throat of the chopper's copilot.

Head Warden Gerald Kellogg sat next to Gunther, bound and gagged. One eye was swollen and purpling.

Monk tapped Gunther on the shoulder, and waved a finger to get the bird in the air. With a nod of acknowledgment, Gunther pulled on the collective, and the chopper leaped into the air with a roar of the engines.

The ground dropped away. The estate stretched out ahead of them. Monk had been informed that the estate was equipped with surface-to-air missiles. Weaponless, the slow-moving commercial chopper would be a flying bull's-eye.

That would not be good.

Monk leaned forward.

"Time to earn your keep, warden."

Monk grinned wickedly. He knew it was not a pretty sight, but it came in handy now.

Kellogg blanched.

Satisfied, Monk reached forward and lifted the radio's mouthpiece to the warden's lips. "Connect us to the security band."

Khamisi had already obtained the codes. Hence Kellogg's black eye.

"Stick to the script," Monk warned, still grinning.

Kellogg leaned a bit farther away.

Was his smile really *that* awful?

To reinforce the threat, Tau pressed the point of his spear into the soft flesh of the man's neck.

Static squelched from the radio, and Kellogg passed on the message as instructed. "We've recaptured one of your prisoners," the warden told base security. "Monk Kokkalis. We're flying him over to the rooftop helipad."

Gunther monitored security's response over his headphones.

"Roger that. Over and out," Kellogg said.

Gunther yelled a bit. "We've been given the all clear. Here we go."

He nosed the helicopter forward and sped toward the estate. Ahead, the mansion came into view. It looked even more massive from the air.

Swinging around and settling into his seat, Monk faced Lisa. Beside her, Anna leaned against the window, eyes squeezed closed in pain. Painter hung in his straps and groaned. The sedative was wearing thin.

Lisa helped settle him back.

Monk noted that she held Painter's hand—and had all along.

Her face found Monk's.

Fear shone bright in her eyes.

But not for herself.

"Is the broadcast rod raised?" Baldric asked.

Isaak nodded at his console.

"Ready the Bell for activation."

Baldric turned to Gray. "We've fed your companions' DNA codes into the Bell. It will modify its output to denature and selectively destroy any matching DNA while remaining harmless to all others. Our version of a final solution."

Gray pictured Fiona hidden up in her room. And Monk was being flown in right now.

"There's no need to kill them," Gray said. "You've recaptured my partner. Leave the others alone."

"If I've learned nothing in these past days, I've learned it's best to leave no loose strings." Baldric nodded to Isaak. "Activate the Bell."

"Wait!" Gray yelled, stepping forward.

Ischke had retrieved his pistol and warned him away with it.

Baldric glanced back, bored and impatient.

Gray had only one card to play. "I know how to break Hugo's code."

Surprise softened Baldric's stern demeanor. He lifted a delaying hand toward Isaak. "You do? You can succeed where a series of Cray computers has so far failed?"

Doubt rang in the man's voice.

Gray knew he had to offer Baldric something, anything to stop him from switching the Bell on and irradiating his friends. He pointed to the monitor, repetitively cycling through the runes. The computer shuffled and sought a combination that offered some mnemonic cipher.

"You'll fail on your own," Gray promised.

"And why's that?"

Gray licked his dry lips, scared, but he had to stay focused. He knew with certainty that the computer would fail because he had already solved the riddle of the runes. He didn't understand the answer, but he knew he was right, especially considering Hugo Hirszfeld's Jewish heritage.

Still, how much could he give away? He had to bargain to the best of his ability, balancing between the truth and the answer.

"You have the wrong rune from the Darwin Bible," Gray said truthfully. "And there are *six*, not just *five*, runes."

Baldric sighed. Disbelief deepened the lines around his mouth. "Like the sun wheel you drew before, I suppose?" He turned back toward Isaak.

"No!" Gray called out firmly. "Let me show you!"

He searched around and spotted a marker on one of the computer stations. He pointed and waved for it. "Pass me that."

Brows pinched, Baldric nodded to Isaak.

The marker was tossed at him.

Gray caught it and knelt on the floor. He drew on the gray linoleum tiles with the black marker. "The rune from the Darwin Bible."

He drew it.

"The *Mensch* rune," Baldric said.

Gray tapped it. "It represents man's higher state, the godlike plane hidden in all of us, our perfected selves."

"So?"

"This was Hugo's goal. The end result sought. Yes?"

Baldric slowly nodded.

"Hugo would not have incorporated the *result* into his code. His code leads to this." He tapped the rune harder. "This doesn't belong in the code."

Slowly understanding dawned . . . as did the old man's belief. "The other runes in the Darwin Bible . . ."

Gray drew on the floor, illustrating his point.

$$\Psi\mathsf{f} = \Upsilon$$

"These two runes make up the third." He circled the two double-pronged runes. "These represent mankind at his most basic, what leads to the higher state. As such, it is these two runes that must be incorporated into the code."

Gray wrote the original series of runes. "This is the wrong sequence."

$$\Gamma\mathsf{I}\mathsf{X}\mathsf{M}\Upsilon$$

He crossed them out and inscribed the correct set, splitting the last rune.

$$\Gamma\mathsf{I}\mathsf{X}\mathsf{M}\Upsilon\mathsf{f}$$

Baldric stepped closer. "And this is the correct series? What must be deciphered?"

Gray answered truthfully. "Yes."

Baldric nodded, eyes squinting as he considered this revelation. "I believe you are right, Commander Pierce."

Gray stood.

"*Dank u*," Baldric said and turned back to Isaak. "Activate the Bell. Kill his friends."

3:07 P.M.

Lisa helped lift Painter out of the helicopter as the rotors wound down. The Zulu warrior Tau shouldered his other side. The sedative she had given Painter was short-acting. It would wear off in another few minutes.

Gunther supported Anna, her eyes glazed. The woman had dosed herself with another numbing injection of morphine. But she had begun coughing up bloody sputum.

Ahead of them, Monk and Mosi D'Gana stood over the dead bodies of a trio of helipad sentries. Security had been caught off guard, expecting to be accepting a prisoner. It had only taken a short spat from a pair of pistols equipped with silencers to commandeer the helipad.

Monk switched places with Tau. "Stay here. Guard the chopper. Keep an eye on the prisoner."

Warden Kellogg had been pulled from the helicopter and dumped on the roof. He was gagged, his hands cuffed behind his back, his ankles tied. He wasn't going anywhere.

Monk waved Major Brooks and Mosi D'Gana to take the lead. They had all reviewed the house schematics from Paula Kane and calculated the best route to the subbasement level. It was a ways to go. The helipad was situated near the back of the mansion.

Brooks and Mosi led them toward the rooftop door to the manor house, assault rifles held at shoulders. The pair moved as if they'd worked together before, synchronized, efficient. Gunther also carried a pistol in his fist and a stubby-nosed assault rifle across his back. Bristling with armament, they reached the door.

Brooks dashed forward. Key cards stolen from the dead guards unlocked the way below. Brooks and Mosi disappeared inside, scouting ahead. The others hung back.

Monk checked his watch. Timing was everything.

A short whistling rose from below.

"Down we go," Monk said.

They hurried through the door and found a short stairwell leading to the sixth floor. Brooks stood at the landing. Another guard sprawled on the stairs, his neck sliced open, his life's blood pumping away. Mosi crouched at the next landing, bloodied knife in hand.

They continued down, around and around the stairs. They encountered no other guards. As they'd hoped, most of the estate's forces were directed outward. The massing of Zulu tribesmen had to be drawing a majority of their attention.

Monk checked his watch again.

Reaching the second floor, they exited the stairs and aimed down a long corridor of polished wood. It was shadowy and dark. The wall sconces flickered, as if the electrical system was still fritzing after the blackout . . . or something was drawing off a lot of power.

Lisa also noted a rankness to the air.

The corridor dead-ended into a cross passage. Brooks scouted to the right, the direction they needed to go. He came slamming back around, flattening against the wall.

"Go back . . . back . . ."

A fierce and challenging growl erupted around the corner. A series of cackles followed . . . and excited yips. A single screeched scream drowned it all away.

"Ukufa," Mosi said, waving them back.

"Run!" Brooks said. "We'll try to scare them off, then catch up."

Monk tugged Lisa and Painter away.

"What are . . . ?" Lisa asked, words strangling.

"Someone's loosed the dogs on us," Monk said.

Gunther stumbled along with Anna. The giant carried his sister, her feet uselessly scuffling the floor.

A burst of gunfire erupted behind them.

Yips and ululations changed into cries of pain and anger. They ran faster.

More blasts echoed, sounding almost frantic.

"Damn it!" Brooks swore loudly.

Lisa glanced over a shoulder.

Brooks and Mosi abandoned their post and pounded down the corridor, arms pointing back, firing.

"Go, go, go . . . ," Brooks yelled. "Too goddamn many!"

Three massive white-furred creatures ripped around the corner behind the men, heads low to the ground, jaws slathering, hackles bristling. Claws dug into the wood floors as they raced in a serpentine pattern, almost anticipating the bullets, avoiding kill shots. All three bled from wounds but seemed more goaded than weakened from their injuries.

Lisa turned back around in time to see a pair of the same beasts stalk out of rooms to either side at the end of the corridor, cutting off escape.

An ambush.

Gunther's massive pistol went off like a cannon, deafening. His shot missed the lead creature as it shifted out of position like a flicker of shadow.

Monk raised his own gun, pulling to a stop.

Lisa's momentum carried her forward. She went down on a knee, pulling Painter's limp form with her. He crashed, waking slightly with the impact.

"Where—?" he asked groggily.

Lisa pulled him lower as the hall filled with gunfire.

A sharp scream arose behind her.

She jerked around. A heavily muscled form lunged out of a neighboring doorway and slammed Major Brooks into the wall.

Lisa scrabbled away with a cry.

Mosi dove to the man's aid, a spear above his head, a howl on his lips.

Lisa hugged Painter.

The creatures were everywhere.

Movement caught Lisa's eye. Another beast rose from behind a door to the left, creaking the hinges. Its muzzle was bloody with fresh gore. Crimson eyes glowed in the dark room. She flashed back to the madness of the first Buddhist monk she had seen, ravening, wild, but still operating with cunning and intelligence.

It was the same here.

As the monster stalked toward her, its lips snarled back with a growl of triumph.

15

HORNS OF THE BULL

3:10 P.M.
SOUTH AFRICA

Khamisi lay in a gully covered by a camouflaged tarp.

"Three minutes," Dr. Paula Kane said next to him, also on her belly.

The two studied the black fence line through binoculars.

Khamisi had his forces spread out along the border of the park. Some Zulu tribesmen wandered in plain sight, switching cows along old paths. A group of elders in traditional beads, plumes, and feathers stood wrapped in shoulder blankets. Back at the village, drums and singing had begun, loud and bright. The gathering at the way station had been staged as a wedding ceremony.

Motorcycles, ATV bikes, and trucks had been parked haphazardly around the area. Some of the younger warriors, even women, skulked around the vehicles, a few couples clasped in amorous embraces, others lifted carved wooden cups, shouting in feigned inebriation. A group of bare-chested men, painted for the celebration, bounced in a traditional dance done with clubs.

And except for the clubs, not a weapon was in sight.

Khamisi adjusted the focus on his binoculars. He shifted

and lifted his field of view above the tall game fencing topped by barbed curls of concertina wire. He could make out movement in the jungle canopy beyond. Waalenberg forces had gathered along the elevated walkways, spying over the fence, guarding the borders.

"One minute," Paula intoned. She had a sniping rifle on a tripod under their tented tarp, hidden in the shade of a stinkwood tree. He was surprised to learn she had won gold medals in Olympic marksmanship.

Khamisi lowered his binoculars. The traditional Zulu attack strategy was termed "the Buffalo." The largest body, named the "chest," would lead a full frontal assault, while from either side, the "horns of the bull" would strike out at the flanks, cutting off any retreat, encircling the enemy. But Khamisi had made a slight modification, compensating for modern armaments. It was the reason he had scouted the grounds all night, planting his surprises.

"Ten seconds," Paula warned and began counting down quietly. She settled her cheek to the side of her rifle.

Khamisi lifted his transmitter, twisted the key, and held his thumb over the row of buttons.

"Zero," Paula finished.

Khamisi pressed the first button.

Beyond the fence, the charges he had planted throughout the night ignited in fiery detonations, shattering through the canopy, igniting sequentially for maximum chaos. Sections of flaming planks and branches sailed high while an entire forest of birds took wing in fright, an explosion of rainbow confetti.

Khamisi had planted C4 packets, supplied through British channels, at key junctures and supports for the elevated walkway. Explosions spread, encircling the mansion, crashing the canopy bridges, stripping the Waalenberg forces of the high ground, and inciting panic and confusion.

Ahead, Zulu warriors dropped blankets to reveal rifles or

knelt down and tugged free buried tarps that hid weapons caches, becoming the chest of the Buffalo. To either side, engines revved all around Khamisi as warriors mounted their vehicles, turning cycles and trucks into the horns of the bull.

"Now," Paula said.

Khamisi pressed the next buttons, one after the other.

The fence line for a full half mile exploded with a fiery twist of metal and barbed wire. Sections dropped flat to the ground, exposing the belly of the enemy.

Khamisi shed his tarp and stood. A motorcycle sped up from behind, kicking sand and dirt as it skidded to a stop next to him. Njongo waved him to mount. But Khamisi had one last duty. He lifted a siren horn over his head and squeezed the trigger. Its trumpet blast echoed across the homeland of the Zulus, sounding once again the charge of the Buffalo.

3:13 P.M.

The explosions echoed down from above, flickering lights across the Bell chamber. Everyone froze. Baldric stood with his grandson Isaak by the control board. Ischke guarded Gray from a step away, her pistol leveled at his chest. Eyes drifted toward the ceiling, questioning.

Not Gray's eyes.

His gaze remained focused on the power meter on the console. Its indicators slowly rose toward a full pulse. Deaf to Gray's pleading, Baldric had activated the Bell. A rising hum penetrated the lead cylinder encased around the device. On a video monitor, the outer shell of the Bell glowed a pale blue.

Once the power meter reached its peak, a pulse would

erupt and broadcast outward for five miles, killing Monk, Fiona, and Ryan wherever they hid. Only Gray was safe in the chamber, under the shield.

"Find out what's happening," Baldric finally ordered his grandson as the explosions died away.

Isaak was already reaching for the red phone.

The pistol blast startled all of them, coming on the heels of the muffled explosion, loud and intimate.

Gray spun around as blood splattered across the tiled floor.

Ischke's left shoulder bloomed crimson as she spun with the impact, shot from behind. Unfortunately, her pistol was clutched in her right hand. Knocked around, Ischke took aim at the shooter by the door.

Dr. Marcia Fairfield knelt in a shooter's stance, but with her right arm incapacitated, she had shot with her left, missing her kill shot.

Ischke was not so compromised. Even caught by surprise, her aim was rock solid.

Until Gray dove into her side.

Two pistols went off, deafening in the chamber—Ischke's and Marcia's.

Both missed their target.

Gray bear-hugged Ischke from behind, twisting her away from Marcia, but the woman was strong and fought like a wildcat. Gray managed to get his hand around Ischke's fist that held the gun.

Her brother ran toward them, a long German-steel dagger in his hand, held low.

Marcia fired from her stance, but she had no clean bead on Isaak either as Gray's and Ischke's tussling bodies blocked her shot.

Gray drove his chin into Ischke's bloody shoulder. Hard. She gasped, weakened slightly. Gray got her arm up and squeezed her fingers. Her pistol blasted. He felt the recoil in his own shoulder. But the shot was too low, striking the floor at Isaak's toes. Still, the ricochet grazed the man's calf, stumbling him a step.

Ischke, seeing her twin injured, savagely freed her arm and slammed her elbow into Gray's ribs. The air was knocked from him and pain danced across his eyes. Ischke broke free.

Beyond her, Isaak caught his footing, murder in his eyes, dagger glinting.

Gray did not wait. Lunging forward, he shoulder-checked Ischke from behind. The woman, still slightly off balance from breaking Gray's hold, flew forward into her brother.

Onto his dagger.

The serrated blade plunged into her chest.

A scream of surprise and pain burst from her lips. It echoed out of her brother. The pistol dropped from Ischke's fingers as she clutched her twin in disbelief.

Gray dove and caught her falling pistol before it struck the ground.

Skidding on his back, he aimed toward Isaak.

The man could have moved, should have moved, but he just held his sister in his arms, his face a mask of agony.

Gray fired from the side, a clean head shot, putting Isaak out of his misery.

The twins collapsed together to the floor, limbs entwined, blood pooling together.

Gray stood up.

Marcia ran into the room, pistol aimed toward Baldric. The old man stared at his dead grandchildren. But there was no grief in his eyes as he leaned on his cane, only a clinical detachment, dismayed by disappointing lab results.

The fight had taken less than a minute.

Gray saw the power meter for the Bell was in the red zone. He had maybe two minutes until the pulse. Gray placed the hot muzzle of the pistol against the old man's cheek. "Turn it off."

Baldric met his eyes. "No."

3:13 P.M.

As the explosions echoed away, the frozen tableau in the upper hallway of the Waalenberg mansion thawed. The hyena creatures had flattened to the floor as the booming erupted. A few had turned tail, but the remainder stayed near their trapped prey. All around, muscled bulks rose back to their feet.

"Don't fire!" Monk whispered urgently. "Everyone into that room!"

He waved toward a side door, where they could make a better stand, limit their exposure. Gunther hauled Anna. Mosi D'Gana stepped away from the beast he had impaled with a spear. He helped Major Brooks to his feet. Blood flowed thickly from a deep bite to the man's thigh.

Before they could move farther, a savage growl of warning arose from Monk's other flank.

His name was whispered. "Monk . . ."

Lisa crouched over Painter's limp form on the floor, near another doorway. A massive creature, the largest by far, rose behind the pair, sheltered in the door, shielded by Lisa and Painter.

It shouldered up, stance wide, guarding its prey. Its entire muzzle rippled back from razor teeth, growling, blood and saliva dripping. It eyes glinted crimson, warning them back.

Monk sensed if any of them raised even a weapon it would rip into the pair on the floor. He had to take the chance, but before he could move, a shout barked down the hall, full of command.

"Skuld! No!"

Monk turned.

Fiona stepped into view at the end of the hall. She stalked right past two of the creatures, ignoring them as they dropped, mewling, falling on their sides. A Taser crackled with blue sparks in one hand. She held another device in the other. The antenna pointed at the beast hovering over Lisa and Painter.

"Bad dog!" Fiona said.

To Monk's amazement, the creature backed off, growls fading, hackles lowering. As if under a spell, it lolled a bit in the doorway. Fire died in its eyes as it sank to the plank floors. A soft lowing moaned from it, half-ecstatic.

Fiona reached their side.

Monk stared up and down the hall. The other monsters fell under the same spell.

"Waalenbergs planted chips in the bastards," Fiona explained and hefted the device in her hand. "Had them wired for pain—and *pleasure*."

A contented mewl rose from the massive monster in the doorway.

Monk frowned at the transmitter. "How did you get—?"

Fiona stared up at him and waved the device for them to follow her.

"You stole it," Monk said.

She shrugged and headed down the hall. "Let's say I bumped into an old chum, and somehow it ended up in my pocket. She wasn't using it."

Ischke, Monk thought as he gathered the others to follow.

Monk helped Lisa with Painter. Gunther carried Anna under one arm. Mosi and Brooks leaned on each other. They made a sorry assault team.

But they now had backup.

Behind them, the pack trailed, a dozen strong, more joining, lured by the aura of pleasure emanating from the girl, their own little Pied Piper of monsters.

"I can't get rid of them," Fiona said, babbling a bit. Monk noted how her hands trembled. She was terrified.

"Once I found the right button," she said, "they followed me from their cages. I hid back in the room where Gray told me to wait . . . but they must have remained in the halls and rooms around here."

Great, Monk thought, and we run right smack into them, the perfect postcoital snack.

"Then I heard your yells, then the explosions, and—"

"Fine." Monk finally cut her off. "But what about Gray? Where is he?"

"He took the elevator downstairs. That was over an hour ago." She pointed ahead, where the corridor ended at a balcony overlooking a larger hall. "I'll show you."

She hurried. They stumbled along to keep up, checking periodically behind them to watch the pack. Fiona led them down a set of stairs to the main entry hall. Closed elevator doors were opposite the massive carved front doors of the mansion.

Major Brooks limped toward the electronic lock, flipping through a set of key cards. He swiped several before he found one that turned the red light to green. A trundle of motors sounded. The cage rose from somewhere below.

As they waited, the hyena pack slunk down the stairs, lounging, basking in the pleasurable glow from Fiona's device. A few padded the hall floor, including the one called Skuld.

No one spoke, eyeing the monsters.

Distantly, muffled by the door, screams and gunshots reached them. Khamisi was in the thick of his own war. How long would it take for him to get here?

As if reading Monk's mind, the double doors to the mansion slammed open. Distant gunfire shattered brightly, popping and blasting. Screams grew richer. Men poured in. Waalenberg forces in retreat. Among them, Monk spotted the black-suited figures of the elite, ice-blond siblings, a dozen strong, looking little fazed, as if they'd come in after a refreshing day on the tennis courts.

As war waged outside, the two forces eyed each other in the hall.

Not good.

Monk's team pressed back, pinned against the wall, outnumbered five to one.

3:15 P.M.

Gray stepped away from Baldric Waalenberg.

"Watch him," he ordered Marcia.

Gray slid to Isaak's former workstation, one eye on the Bell's power meter. He reached to a toggle he had seen Isaak flip before. It controlled the blast shield around the activated device.

"What're you doing?" Baldric asked, voice sharp with sudden concern.

So there was something that scared the old man worse than a bullet. Good to know. Gray snapped the toggle back. Motors rumbled underfoot and the shield began to lower. A sharp blue light pierced its top edge, blazing forth as the lead wall dropped from the roof.

"Don't! You'll kill us all!"

Gray faced the old man. "Then turn the goddamn thing *off*."

Baldric stared between the lowering shield and the console. "I can't turn it off, you *ezel*! The Bell is primed. It *must* discharge."

Gray shrugged. "Then we'll all watch it happen."

The ring of blue light thickened.

Baldric swore and turned to the console. "But I can erase the kill solution. Neutralize it. It won't harm your friends."

"Do it."

Baldric typed rapidly, his knobby fingers moving swiftly. "Just raise the shield!"

"After you're done." Gray watched over the old man's shoulder. He saw all their names appear on the screen along with an alphanumeric code marked GENETISCH PROFIEL. The man hit the delete key four times and the genetic profiles were erased.

"Done!" Baldric said, turning to Gray. "Close the blast shield!"

Gray reached to the toggle and switched it back with a *pop*.

A groan sounded underfoot—then something cracked with a ground-shuddering jolt. The lead shield froze in place, partly lowered.

Beyond the edge, a blue sun glowed in the heart of the blast chamber. The air rippled around the Bell as its outer shell spun in one direction and the inner in the other.

"Do something!" Baldric begged.

"The hydraulics are jammed," Gray mumbled.

Baldric backed away, eyes widening with every step. "You've doomed us all! Once fully powered, the Bell's raw and unshielded pulse will kill everyone within five miles . . . or worse."

Gray was afraid to ask what could be worse.

3:16 P.M.

Monk watched the rifles rise toward them.

Outnumbered.

The elevator cage hadn't reached this floor yet, and even if it had, it would take too long to get aboard and close the doors. There was no way to avoid a firefight.

Unless . . .

Monk leaned to Fiona. "How about a little pain . . ."

He nodded to where the hyenas had retreated to the stairs.

Fiona understood and shifted her finger on her device, switching from pleasure to pain. She pressed the button.

The effect was instantaneous. It was as if someone lit the hyenas' tails on fire. A mighty scream yowled from a score of throats. Creatures fell from balcony perches overhead, crashing to the floor. Others rolled down the stairs into the men. Claws and teeth lashed at anything that moved in a blind rage of fury. Men screamed. Rifles fired.

Behind Monk, the elevator doors finally chimed open.

Monk fell back, drawing Fiona with him, guiding Lisa and Painter.

Gunfire peppered at them, but most of the Waalenberg forces focused on the hyenas. Mosi and Brooks offered return fire as they retreated into the cage.

Still, it would be close. And what then? Alerted, the forces would simply chase after them.

Monk stabbed blindly at the subbasement buttons.

Time enough to worry about that later.

But one of their party was not one to procrastinate.

Gunther shoved Anna into Monk's arms. "Take her! I hold them off."

Anna reached for him as the doors closed. Gunther gently pushed her arm down and stepped back. He turned away, pistol in one fist, rifle in the other—but not before staring hard into Monk's eyes, sealing their silent pledge.

Protect Anna.

Then the doors closed.

3:16 P.M.

Khamisi raced through the jungle, hunched low over the motorcycle. Paula Kane rode behind him, rifle on her shoulder. Zulu warrior and British agent. Strange bedfellows. Some of the bloodiest history of the land had taken place during the Anglo-Zulu wars of the nineteenth century.

No longer.

Now they were a fine-tuned team.

"Left!" Paula yelled.

Khamisi twisted the wheel. Paula's rifle muzzle swung to his other side. She fired. A Waalenberg sentry fell back with a scream.

To either side, gunfire and explosions echoed throughout the jungle.

The estate's forces were in full rout.

Suddenly, with no warning, their cycle jetted out of the jungle and into a ten-acre manicured garden. Khamisi braked to a stop, skidding into cover under the branches of a willow.

The mansion filled the world ahead.

Khamisi lifted his binoculars from around his neck and searched the roofline. He spotted where the park helicopter had landed at the helipad. Movement drew his eye. He adjusted the binoculars, and a familiar shape focused into view. Tau. His Zulu friend stood at the roof's edge and studied the war below.

Then from the left, a shape entered the field of view, behind Tau, a pipe gripped above his head. Warden Gerald Kellogg.

"Don't move," Paula said behind Khamisi.

Her rifle's stock settled atop Khamisi's head as she aimed through her sniper's scope.

"I see him," she said.

Khamisi cringed but held still, staring through his binoculars.

Paula squeezed her trigger. The rifle blasted, ringing his ears.

Warden Kellogg's head snapped back. Tau almost fell off the roof in fright, but he dropped flat, unaware his life had just been saved.

Khamisi caught some of Tau's fear, a tremble of foreboding after the close call. How were the others doing in there?

3:17 P.M.

"You've doomed us!" Baldric repeated.

Gray refused to give up. "Can you slow the Bell from discharging? Buy me time to get below. To fix the shield."

The old man stared at the frozen blast shield, crowned by blue light. Fear reflected in his face. "There may be a way, but . . . but . . ."

"But what?"

"Someone has to go inside there." He pointed his trembling cane at the blast chamber and shook his head, plainly refusing to volunteer.

A voice called as the door pushed open. "I'll do it."

Gray and Marcia spun, lifting their pistols.

An amazing sight hobbled into the room. Monk came first, supporting the dark-haired woman who had just called to them. Most of the others were strangers. An older black man limped in with a clean-shaven youth in a military buzz cut. They were followed by Fiona and a tall athletic blond woman who looked like she had just run a marathon. The two supported an older man, limp, barely standing. Momentum seemed to be all that kept him on his feet. As soon as the women stopped, he sagged. His face, hanging down until now, raised, met Gray's gaze with familiar blue eyes.

"Gray . . . ," he mumbled numbly.

A shock of recognition passed through him. "Director Crowe?"

Gray hurried to his side.

"No time," the dark-haired woman warned, still supported by Monk. She looked little better than Painter. Her eyes studied the shield and Bell with a look of familiarity. "I'll need help getting inside the chamber. And he's coming with me."

She lifted a trembling arm at Baldric Waalenberg.

The old man moaned. "No . . ."

The woman glared. "We'll need two sets of hands on the polarity conduits. And you know the machine."

Monk motioned to the black man. "Mosi, help get Anna inside there. We'll need a ladder." He then faced Gray and clasped him in a brief handshake, leaning forward to touch shoulders in a more familial gesture.

"We don't have much time," Gray said in Monk's ear, surprised at how relieved he was at Monk's arrival. Renewed hope surged through him.

"Tell me about it." Monk unhooked a radio and passed it to Gray. "Get that contraption movin'. I'll get things going here."

Gray grabbed the radio and headed out. He had a thousand questions, but they would have to wait. He kept the radio channel open. He heard noises and voices, arguments and a few shouts. Footsteps followed him, running. He glanced back. It was Fiona.

"I'm coming with you!" she shouted and closed the distance by the time he reached the fire stairs.

He clambered down.

She lifted a transmitter with an extended antenna. "In case you run into any of those monsters."

"Just keep up," he said.

"Oh, shut up."

They ran the rest of the way, reaching the lower-level hallway and utility room.

Monk came on the radio. "Anna and the old bastard are inside the chamber. Course he's none too happy about it. A shame. And we were getting to be such good friends."

"Monk . . . ," Gray warned, focusing his man back on task.

"I'm going to pass the radio to Anna. She'll coordinate with you. Oh, by the way, you've got less than a minute. *Ciao.*"

Gray shook his head and yanked on the utility door.

Locked.

Fiona saw him tug on the door a second time and sighed. "No key?"

Gray frowned, pulled out his pistol from his waistband, and aimed at the lock. He fired. The blast echoed in the hall, leaving a smoking hole where the lock used to be. He shoved the door open.

Fiona followed. "I guess that works, too."

Ahead, he spotted the motor assembly and pistons for raising and lowering the blast shield.

A strange rhythmic static flowed over the radio, ebbing and flowing like waves on a beach. Gray realized it must be interference from the Bell. Monk must have passed Anna the radio.

Confirming this, he heard the woman's voice arguing through the static. It was a jumble of technical debate, an angry mix of German and Dutch. Gray tuned most of it out as he circled the motor assembly. Then the woman's voice spoke more clearly in English.

"Commander Pierce?"

He cleared his throat. "Go ahead."

Her voice rasped with exhaustion. "We have our fingers in the proverbial dike up here, but it won't hold."

"Hang tight."

Gray spotted the problem. A fuse smoked by one of the pistons. Using the edge of his shirt, he yanked it out. He turned to Fiona. "We need another one. Must be a spare around here somewhere."

"Hurry, Commander."

Static grew ominously louder, but not enough to cover Baldric's words, whispered to Anna urgently. ". . . join us. We could use another expert with the Bell."

Even frightened, Baldric was playing all the angles.

Gray listened more closely. Would she betray them? He motioned to Fiona. "Toss me that transmitter."

She underhanded it to him. He caught it and snapped off the metal antenna. He didn't have time to find a spare fuse. He would have to jump it. He jammed the antenna between the contacts and crossed to a control board with a massive manual wrench-lever. The operation was self-explanatory.

At the top was marked OP and below it ONDER'AAN.

Up and down.

Not exactly rocket science.

Gray spoke into the radio. "Anna. You and Baldric can get out of there."

"We can't, Commander. One of us has to keep their finger in the dike. If both of us let go, the Bell will blow instantly."

Gray closed his eyes. They dared not trust Baldric's co-operation.

Static had grown to a dull roar in his ear.

"You know what you must do, Commander."

He did.

He shoved the lever.

Distantly her last words reached him. "Tell my brother . . . I love him."

But as she lowered the radio, one final statement rasped out—whether to answer Baldric's offer, or to make a last declaration to the world, or simply to satisfy herself.

"I'm not a Nazi."

3:19 P.M.

Lisa knelt on the floor, cradling Painter. Then she felt the rumble of massive machinery below her knees. Ahead, the giant lead shield rose toward the ceiling, pinching off the blaze of blue light.

She rose half up. Anna was still in there. Even Monk took a step toward the closing blast shield.

A terrified scream erupted from inside.

It was the old man. Lisa spotted his fingers scrabbling above the edge, frantic, trying to catch a grip. Too late. It rose above his reach and smoothly clamped into the ceiling's O-ring.

His screams could still be heard, muffled, frantic.

Then Lisa felt it. In the gut. A *whomp* of power. It had no description. A quake that rattled without movement. Then nothing. Complete silence, the world holding its breath.

Painter moaned, as if the effect were painful for him.

His head lay in her lap. She examined him. His eyes had rolled back in his head. His breathing grated with fluid. She shook him gently. No response. Semicomatose. They were losing him.

"Monk . . . !"

"Hurry, Gray!" Monk called into the radio.

Gray pounded back up the steps, followed by Fiona. Below, he had delayed only long enough to find a replacement fuse and repair the shield. He didn't understand all that Monk had relayed, but he filled in the blanks with what he knew. Painter had some form of radiation poisoning, and the Bell held the only cure.

As he neared the fifth-floor landing, he heard a heavy booted tread stumbling down toward them. Gray pulled out his pistol. Now what?

A massive figure, heavy-browed and pale white, appeared above, half falling down the stairs toward him. His shirt was soaked in blood. A ragged scrape raked the side of his face from crown to throat. He held a broken wrist to his belly.

Gray raised his weapon.

Fiona pushed past him. "No. He's with us." And in a lower voice to Gray, she added with a nod, "Anna's brother."

The giant stumbled to them, recognizing Fiona, too. Eyes narrowed at Gray with tired suspicion. But he waved his rifle back up the stairs. *"Blockiert,"* he grunted.

Blockaded.

So the giant bought them time with his own blood.

They hurried down the hall toward the Bell chamber. But Gray knew he had to prepare Gunther. After Anna's sacrifice, he owed her brother at least that. He touched the man's elbow.

"About Anna . . . ," he began.

Gunther turned to him, tensing, eyes going pained, as if he expected the worst.

Gray faced that fear and explained in terse words, sparing nothing, ending with the final truth. "Her efforts saved everyone else."

The large man's feet had slowed with the telling. What his wounds couldn't bring low, grief finally did. He slumped slowly to his knees in the hall.

Gray paused. "Her last words . . . were for you, passing her love."

The man covered his face and curled to the floor.

"I'm sorry . . . ," Gray offered.

Monk appeared in the doorway. "Gray, what the hell are you—?" Then he spotted Gunther in a posture of pure grief. His voice died.

Gray strode toward Monk.

It was not over for any of them.

3:22 P.M.

"Lower the shield!"

Lisa glanced to see Commander Pierce stride into the chamber with Monk, both leaning their heads together. She stood over the Bell's control suite. She had spent the past few minutes familiarizing herself with the device. On the trek here, Anna had gone over in detail how the Bell functioned. The woman had feared she might be too debilitated to oversee its use. Another had needed to know. That onus fell upon Lisa.

"The shield!" Gray called to her again from Monk's side.

She nodded dully and flipped the toggle.

Motors clattered below. She turned to watch the blast shield drop. With the Bell quiescent, light no longer blazed out from inside. A step away, Painter lay on a tarp on the floor, attended for the moment by Dr. Fairfield. To the right, Mosi and Brooks dragged another tarp over the bodies of the twins.

What about the pair's grandfather?

The blast shield continued to lower, waist-high now. The Bell sat quietly in the center, waiting to be activated again. Lisa remembered Anna's description of the bell-shaped device. The ultimate quantum-measuring tool. It scared the hell out of her.

To the left, yelling a bit to be heard over the motor, Monk related the radioed message from Khamisi. The Zulu forces had secured the estate, driving any surviving Waalenberg forces into the mansion, where a siege was under way. A continuing firefight ensued above.

"Gunther blocked the fire stairs," Gray said. "And the elevator doors are jammed open. It should buy us some time." He waved to Brooks and Mosi. "Keep a watch on the outer hall!"

They lifted their weapons and headed out.

As they left, Gunther stumbled inside. From the expression on his face, Lisa knew he had been told about Anna. He had shed all his weapons. Each step was leaden as he headed toward the lowering shield. He had to witness the end. A final absolution for all the blood on his hands.

The shield settled to a stop. The motors went silent.

Lisa feared viewing the damage herself, but she had a duty here.

She crossed toward the Bell.

Anna lay on her side in the shadow of the device, curled like a baby. Her skin was ash white, her dark hair turned snowy, as if she had become a marble statue. Gunther stepped over the lip of the shield and knelt beside his sister. Without a word, expressionless, he bent and scooped her in his arms. She lolled limply in death, her head coming to rest on her brother's shoulder.

Gunther stood, turned his back on the Bell, and headed away.

No one tried to stop him.

He vanished out the door.

Lisa's gaze fell upon the other figure still sprawled atop the blast chamber's lead floor. Baldric Waalenberg. Like Anna, his skin had gone an unnatural white, almost translucent. But the radiation had burned away all his hair, too, leaving him bald, not even eyebrows or lashes. His flesh had also collapsed to his bones, giving him a mummified appearance. And something about his underlying osseous structure was . . . was wrong.

Lisa froze, horrified to step any closer.

With the hair gone, flesh sunken, the skull was plainly misshapen, as if partially melted, then hardened again. His hands were twisted, fingers oddly elongated, apelike. The word *devolution* filled her head.

"Get him out of there," Gray said with disgust, then faced Lisa. "I'll help you get Painter inside."

Lisa slowly shook her head, stepping back. "We can't . . ." She could not take her eyes off the twisted horror that was the former Waalenberg patriarch. She couldn't let that happen to Painter.

Gray came up to her. "What do you mean?"

She swallowed, still staring as Monk grabbed the monstrosity by the sleeve of his shirt, plainly afraid to touch his flesh. "Painter is too far gone. The Bell only held the hope of staving off or slowing the debilitation, not reversing it. Do you want to suspend your director in his current state?"

"If there's life, there's hope."

His words were spoken softly, gently. They almost succeeded in drawing her attention away as Monk hauled the old man's devolved form out of the device, bumping over the lip.

Lisa opened her mouth to argue against false hope.

Then Baldric Waalenberg's eyes snapped wide, milky and blind, looking more like stone than flesh. His mouth stretched in a silent and prolonged scream. His vocal chords were gone. He had no tongue. Nothing was inside him but horror and pain.

Lisa gave voice to the man, crying out, backing away until she bumped into the console. Monk recognized the true horror here, too. He lunged away, dropping Baldric on the tiles outside the blast chamber.

The mutated form collapsed. The limbs remained toneless, muscleless. But the mouth opened and closed, a fish out of water. Eyes stared blindly.

Then Gray stepped between Lisa and the horror. He gripped her shoulders. "Dr. Cummings." Her gaze, fluttering in panic, settled to his. "Director Crowe needs you."

"There . . . there's nothing I can do."

"Yes, there is. We can use the Bell."

"I can't do that to Painter." Her voice rose in pitch. "Not *that*!"

"It won't happen. Monk told me how Anna instructed you. You know how to set the Bell for a minimum output, for a palliative radiation. What just happened here is different. Baldric had amped the Bell up to a maximum setting, one set to kill. And ultimately . . . ultimately you reap what you sow."

Lisa covered her face with her hands, trying to block everything out. "But what are we trying to reap?" she moaned. "Painter is at death's door. Why make him suffer any longer?"

Gray pulled her hands down. He leaned to catch her gaze with his own. "I know Director Crowe. And I think you do, too. He would fight until the end."

As a medical doctor, she had heard such arguments before, but she was also a realist. When there was no hope, all a caregiver could provide was a measure of peace and dignity.

"If there was a chance to cure," she said with a shake of her head, her voice steadying, "even a small one, I'd take it.

If we knew what Hugo Hirszfeld had been trying to communicate to his daughter. His perfected code." She shook her head again.

Gray caught her chin in his fingers. She tried to break free, flaring with irritation. But his grip was sure and hard on her.

"I know what Hugo hid in those books," he said.

She frowned at him, but she read the truth in his eyes.

"I have the answer," he said.

16
RIDDLE OF THE RUNES

3:25 P.M.
SOUTH AFRICA

"It's not a code," Gray said. "It was *never* a code."

He knelt on the floor, a marker in hand. He circled the set of runes he had drawn for Baldric Waalenberg.

ᛚᛁᚷᛉᛗᛦᛏ

The others had gathered around him, but he kept his attention fixed on Lisa Cummings. The answer Gray had discerned made no sense, but he sensed it was the *lock,* and this woman, who knew more about the device than anyone else in the room, might hold the *key.* They would have to work together.

"Runes again," Lisa said.

Gray frowned at her for an explanation.

She nodded to the floor. "I saw another set of runes, a different set, drawn in blood. They spelled out *Schwarze Sonne.*"

"Black Sun," Gray translated.

"It was the name for Anna's project in Nepal."

Gray pondered the significance. He pictured the Black Sun symbol on the workstation below. Himmler's original cabal must have been split after the war. Anna's group to the north. Baldric's to the south. Once separated, the two groups diverged further and further apart until allies became adversaries.

Lisa tapped the runes on the floor, drawing back his focus. "The runes I decoded were a simple transposition of letters for symbols. Is this the same?"

Gray shook his head. "Baldric made the same assumption. It was why he was having so much trouble deciphering the runes. But Hugo would not bury his secret so shallowly."

"If it's not a code," Monk asked, "then what is it?"

"It's a jigsaw puzzle," Gray said.

"What?"

"Remember back when we talked to Ryan's father?"

Monk nodded.

Gray pictured that meeting with Johann Hirszfeld, the man crippled with emphysema, lost in the past, the family estate forever shadowed by Wewelsburg Castle and the family's dirty little Nazi secret.

"He described how inquisitive his grandfather Hugo had been. Always searching up strange things, investigating historical mysteries."

"It's what drew him to the Nazis," Fiona said.

"And in his spare time, Hugo was all about sharpening his mind."

Johann's words echoed through Gray: *Memorization tricks, jigsaw puzzles. Always with the jigsaw puzzles.*

Gray tapped the set of runes. "This was just one more mental brainteaser. But not a code . . . a jigsaw. The runes were shapes to be manipulated, rearranged, returning order out of chaos."

Gray had worked the puzzle out in his head over the past

day, letting the runes twist and turn in his mind's eye until
one shape formed. He knew it was the answer. Especially
knowing the angst at the end of Hugo's life, his expressed
regret for his collaboration with the Nazis. But what did it
mean? His eyes fell upon Lisa.

He redrew the six runes on the floor, one after the other,
reassembling them in their proper sequence. He completed
the jigsaw on the floor, inscribing the last rune and complet-
ing the spell.

Order out of chaos.

Absolution out of collaboration.

Holy out of unholy.

From the pagan runes, Hugo showed his true heritage.

"It's a star," Monk said.

Lisa lifted her eyes. "Not any star . . . it's the Star of
David."

Gray nodded.

Fiona asked the most important question. "But what does
it mean?"

Gray sighed. "I don't know. I have no idea what it has to
do with the Bell, with perfecting the device. Maybe it was
merely a final declaration of who he was, a secret message
to his family."

Gray recalled Anna's last words.

I am not a Nazi.

Was Hugo's runic code just another way to say the
same?

"No," Lisa said sharply, her certainty resounding across the room. "If we're going to solve this, we must act as if this is the answer."

Gray saw something fill her eyes, something missing a moment ago.

Hope.

"According to Anna," she continued, "Hugo went into the Bell chamber alone with a baby. Without any special tools. It was just him and the boy. And once the experiment was over, tests showed that he had succeeded, produced the first true and pure Knight of the Sun."

"What did he do in there?" Fiona asked.

Lisa tapped the Star of David. "This is somehow tied to it. But I don't know the significance of the symbol."

Gray did. He had studied multiple religions and fields of spiritual study during his youth and while polishing his Sigma training. "The star's meaning is diverse. It's a symbol of prayer and faith. And maybe more. Note how the six-pointed star also is really two triangles—one atop the other. One pointing down, one up. In Jewish Kabbalah, the two triangles are the equivalent of yin and yang, the light and the dark, the body and the soul. One triangle represents matter and the body. The other our soul, our spiritual being, our conscious mind."

"And joined together, they're *both*," Lisa said. "Not just a particle or a wave—but *both*."

Gray saw some edge of understanding, enlightenment. "What?"

Lisa stared toward the blast chamber. "Anna said the Bell was basically a quantum-measuring device that manipulated evolution. *Quantum* evolution. It's all about quantum mechanics. That's got to be the key."

Gray frowned. "What do you mean?"

Lisa explained what Anna had taught her. Gray, having

studied biology and physics in depth for Sigma, needed little elaboration.

Closing his eyes, he sat back, trying to find a balance between the Star of David and quantum mechanics. Was there an answer between them?

"You said Hugo went into the chamber with just the baby?" Gray asked.

"Yes," Lisa said softly, as if sensing she needed to let him run with his thoughts.

Gray concentrated. Hugo had given him the *lock*. Lisa had given him the *key*. Now it was up to him. Letting go of time's pressure, he allowed his mind to twist and turn the clues and pieces, testing, rejecting.

Like another of Hugo's jigsaw puzzles.

As with the Star of David, the right combination finally formed in his head. So clean, so perfect. He should have thought of it sooner.

Gray opened his eyes.

Lisa must have noted something in his face. "What?"

Gray stood. "Get the Bell powering up," he said, crossing to the console. "Now!"

Lisa followed him and began running through the procedure. "It will take four minutes to reach a palliative pulse." She glanced to Gray as she worked, eyes inquisitive. "What are we doing?"

Gray turned toward the Bell. "Hugo didn't go into the chamber without any tools."

"But that's what Anna—"

"No." Gray cut Lisa off. "He went in with the Star of David. He went in with prayer and faith. But mostly he went in with his own quantum computer."

"What?"

Gray spoke rapidly, knowing he was right. "Consciousness has baffled scientists for centuries . . . going all the way back to Darwin. What is consciousness? Is it just our brain? Is it just nerves firing? Where is the line between brain and mind? Between matter and spirit? Between body and soul?"

He pointed to the symbol.

"Current research says its there. We are both. We are wave *and* particle. Body *and* soul. Life itself is a quantum phenomenon."

"Okay, now you're babbling," Monk said, joining him, drawing Fiona.

Gray took a deep breath, excited. "Modern scientists reject spirituality, defining the brain only as a complex computer. Consciousness arises merely as the by-product of the firing of a complex interconnectivity of neurons, basically a neural-net computer, operating at the quantum level."

"A quantum computer," Lisa said. "You mentioned that already. But what the hell is it?"

"You've seen computer code broken down to its most basic level. Pages of zeroes and ones. That is how the modern computer thinks. Turning a switch on or off. The zero or the one. The theoretical quantum computer, if it could be built, offers a third choice. The old *zero* or *one*—but also a third choice. Zero *and* one."

Lisa squinted. "Like electrons in the quantum world. They can be waves or particles or both at the same time."

"A third choice," Gray said with a nod. "It doesn't sound like much, but by adding this possibility into a computer's arsenal, it allows such a device to perform multiple algorithmic tasks simultaneously."

"Walk and chew gum," Monk mumbled.

"Tasks that would take modern computers years to perform could be done in fractions of a second."

"And our brains do this?" Lisa said. "Act like quantum computers."

"That is the newest consensus. Our brain propagates a measurable electromagnetic field, generated by our complex interconnectivity of neurons. Some scientists conjecture that it is this field where consciousness resides, bridging the matter of the brain with the quantum world."

"And the Bell is hypersensitive to quantum phenomena," Lisa said. "So by Hugo joining the baby inside the Bell chamber, he influenced the result."

"What is observed is changed by the act of observing. But I think it was *more* than that." Gray nodded to the Star of David. "Why this? A symbol of prayer?"

Lisa shook her head.

"What is prayer but a focus of the mind, a focus of consciousness . . . and if consciousness is a quantum phenomenon, then *prayer* is a quantum phenomenon."

Lisa understood. "And like all quantum phenomena, it will and must measure and influence the result."

"In other words . . ." Gray waited.

Lisa stood. "Prayer works."

"That's what Hugo discovered, that's what he hid in his books. Something frighteningly disturbing but too beautiful to let die."

Monk leaned on the console next to Lisa. "Are you saying he willed that baby to be perfect?"

Gray nodded. "When Hugo entered the chamber with the baby, he prayed for perfection, a concentrated and focused thought, selfless and pure. Human consciousness, in the form of prayer, acts as a perfect quantum-measuring tool. Under the Bell, the pure quantum *potential* in the boy was measured, swayed by Hugo's focus and will, and as a result, all the variables settled into perfect place. A perfect roll of the genetic dice."

Lisa turned. "Then perhaps we can do the same to reverse the quantum damage in Painter. To save him before it's too late."

A new voice intruded, coming from Marcia, who still nursed Painter on the floor. "You'd better hurry."

3:32 P.M.

Monk and Gray rushed Painter into the blast chamber, slung in a tarp.

"Put him close to the Bell," Lisa directed.

As they obeyed, she called out final instructions to the others. The Bell was already spinning, its two shells revolving in opposite directions. She remembered Gunther's description of it. *A Mixmaster*. That pretty much described it. A soft glow also shone from its outer ceramic shell.

She sank to her knees next to Painter, checking vitals, the few that remained.

"I can stay with you," Gray said at her shoulder.

"No. I think more than one quantum computer might interfere with the results."

"Too many cooks in the kitchen," Monk agreed.

"Then let me stay," Gray said.

Lisa shook her head. "We'll only get one shot at this. If it takes focus and will to heal Painter, it might be best if the mind directing that focus was a medical doctor."

Gray sighed, little convinced.

"You did your job, Gray. Gave us an answer. Gave us hope." She stared up at him. "Let me do mine."

He nodded and stepped away.

Monk leaned down to her. "Just be careful what you wish for," he said, his words fraught with levels of meaning. He was not so much the dumb oaf he pretended. He pecked her on the cheek.

The pair left.

Marcia called from the console. "Pulse in one minute."

She twisted around. "Raise the blast shield."

As the gears ground below her, Lisa leaned over Painter. His skin had a bluish hue—then again maybe it was just the Bell's glow. Either way, he was moments from expiration. His lips were cracked, his breathing much too shallow, his heartbeat sounded more murmur than beat. Even his hair. The roots had gone snow-white. He was failing at an exponential rate.

The blast shield rose around her, closing them off from the rest of the group. Voices beyond, hushed already, grew muffled then ended as the shield locked into the roof.

Alone, with no one looking, Lisa leaned over Painter, resting her forehead against his chest. She didn't need to focus her will in some meditative verve. It was said there were no atheists in a foxhole. It was certainly the case here. But she didn't know what God to ask for succor at this moment.

Lisa remembered Anna's discussion of evolution and intelligent design. The woman had insisted it was quantum measurements that ultimately collapsed potential into reality. Amino acids formed the first replicating protein because life was the better quantum-measuring device. And if you extrapolated that further, *consciousness*, which was an even greater quantum-measuring device than life alone, evolved for the same reason. One more link in the evolutionary chain. She pictured it.

AMINO ACIDS »»» FIRST PROTEIN »»» FIRST LIFE »»» CONSCIOUSNESS

But what lay beyond consciousness? If the future dictated the past through quantum measurements, what desired consciousness to form? What better quantum-measuring tool lay further in the future, dictating the present? How far into the future did this chain go? And what lay at its end?

AMINO ACIDS »»» FIRST PROTEIN »»» FIRST LIFE »»»
CONSCIOUSNESS»»»???

Lisa remembered one other cryptic statement from Anna,
when Lisa had confronted her about God's role in all this.
While quantum evolution seemed to remove the hand of God
from sudden beneficial mutations, Anna's last words on the
matter had been *you're looking at it the wrong way, in the
wrong direction*. Lisa had attributed the cryptic statement to
the woman's exhaustion. But maybe Anna had pondered the
same question. What did lie at the end of evolution? Was it
merely some perfect and incorruptible quantum-measuring
device?

And if so, was that God?

She had no answer as she leaned over Painter. All she
knew was that she wanted him to live. She might hide from
the others exactly how deeply she felt for him—maybe even
from herself—but she could hide it no longer.

She opened her heart, allowed her vulnerability to shine.

As the Bell hummed and its glow swelled, she let go.

Maybe that's what had been missing in her life all along,
why men seemed to fade from her, why she ran. So no one
would see what could be harmed so easily. She hid her vulnerability behind an armor of professionalism and casual
dalliance. She hid her heart. No wonder she was alone on a
mountaintop when Painter stumbled into her life.

No longer.

She lifted her head, shifted over, and kissed Painter softly
on his lips, putting into action what she had sought to hide.

She closed her eyes as the last seconds counted down.
She opened her heart, willing the man a future, wishing him
to be healthy, hale, and whole, and mostly praying for more
time with him.

Was that the ultimate function of the Bell? To open a

quantum conduit to that great quantum-measuring tool that lay at the end of evolution, a personal connection to that final designer.

Lisa knew what she had to do. She let go of the scientist inside, let go of her own self. Her goal was beyond consciousness, beyond prayer.

It was simply *belief*.

In the purity of that moment, the Bell burst with a blinding light, joining them together, turning reality into pure potential.

3:36 P.M.

Gray flipped the toggle, and the shield began to lower. They all held their breath. What would they find? The motors grumbled. Everyone gathered around the shield wall.

Monk glanced to him, his eyes worried.

In the silence, a small chime sounded, coming from the left.

The blast chamber slowly cleared into view. The Bell, quiet and dark, rested inertly in the center—then Lisa appeared, crouched over Painter, her back to them.

No one spoke.

Lisa slowly turned, rising. Tears, held suspended by lashes, poured down her cheeks. She clutched Painter under her arm as she stood. He looked no better. Pale, weak, debilitated. But he lifted his head on his own and spotted Gray.

His eyes shone sharp and focused.

Relief spread through Gray.

Then the small chime sounded again.

Painter's eyes flicked in its direction—then back to Gray. Painter's lips moved. No words came out. Gray stepped closer to hear.

Painter's eyes narrowed hard on him. He tried again. The word was faint and made no sense. Gray worried about the man's mental status.

"Bomb . . . ," Painter repeated hoarsely.

Lisa heard him, too. She glanced in the same direction as Painter. To the body of Baldric Waalenberg. She then shoved Painter toward Monk.

"Take him."

She headed to the man's twisted form. At some point, unseen, unmourned, Baldric had finally expired.

Gray joined her.

Lisa knelt down and shoved up the man's sleeve. He wore a large wristwatch. She turned it over. A second hand swept over a digital readout.

"We've seen this before," Lisa said. "A heartbeat monitor tied to a micro-transmitter. After his heart stopped, it began a countdown."

Lisa twisted the man's arm so Gray could read the number.

02:01

As he watched, the second hand swept over the number twice more. It sounded the familiar chime as it dropped below **02:00**.

"We have less than two minutes to get the hell out of here," Lisa said.

Gray took her at her word and straightened. "Everybody out! Monk, radio Khamisi! Tell him to clear all his men as far away from the mansion as possible."

His partner obeyed.

"We have a helicopter on the roof," Lisa said.

In seconds, they were all running. Gray took Painter from Monk. Mosi helped Brooks. Lisa, Fiona, and Marcia followed.

"Where's Gunther?" Fiona asked.

Brooks answered. "He left with his sister. He didn't want anyone to follow him."

There was no time to search for him. Gray pointed to the elevator. Monk's group had jammed the doors open with a hall chair, to keep anyone from using it to come after them. Mosi yanked it out one-handed and threw it down the hall.

They piled inside.

Lisa hit the top button. Sixth floor. The elevator slowly began to rise.

Monk spoke. "I radioed our man up top. He doesn't fly, but he knows how to turn a key. He'll get the engines warmed up."

"The bomb," Gray said, turning to Lisa. "What do we have to expect?"

"If it's the same as back in the Himalayas, it'll be big. They've developed some quantum bomb using that Xerum 525 material."

Gray pictured the tanks stored at the deepest level.

Crap . . .

The elevator continued to climb, passing the main floor, which was deathly silent. And upward they went.

Painter stirred, still unable to hold his own weight. But he caught Gray's eyes. "Next time . . . ," he whispered hoarsely ". . . you go to Nepal on your own."

Gray smiled. Oh yeah, Painter was back.

But for how long?

The elevator reached the sixth level and opened.

"One minute," Marcia said. She had had the presence of mind to note and monitor the time.

They raced up the roof stairs and found the helicopter waiting, blades spinning. They ran for it, supporting one another. Once under the rotors, Gray passed Painter to Monk.

"Get everybody aboard."

Gray ran to the other side and climbed into the pilot's seat.

"Fifteen seconds!" Marcia called.

Gray cranked the engine speed. Blades screamed. He

yanked on the collective, and the bird lifted its skids off the roof. Gray was never so happy to leave a place. The helicopter took to air, rotoring up. How much clearance would they need?

He adjusted his blade pitch and fed more power.

As they swept upward, he yawed the bird a bit. He searched the grounds around the estate. He saw Jeeps and motorcycles racing in all directions away from the mansion.

Marcia started a countdown. "Five, four—"

Her precision was slightly off.

A blinding light suddenly blazed beneath them, as if they were lifting off the sun. But the most disturbing effect was the total and absolute silence. Unable to see, Gray fought to hold the bird in the air. But it was as if the air had vanished beneath him. He sensed the helicopter plunging earthward.

Then the light fell away around them with a loud clap, shedding like a wash of water.

The rotors suddenly found air again, bobbling in the sky for a long moment.

Gray stabilized the craft and banked away, frightened to his core. He stared back to where the mansion used to be. A massive, smooth-walled crater lay below, cut cleanly through rock and soil. It was as if some mighty Titan had taken a giant ice-cream scoop to the mansion along with most of the surrounding gardens.

Everything was gone. No debris. Just emptiness.

Pools and creeks, cut in half, poured over the lip in trickling waterfalls.

Farther from the edge, Gray spotted vehicles stopping and people glancing back, some walking closer to check. Khamisi's army. Safe. The Zulu people gathered along the borders, claiming back what they had lost so long ago.

Gray flew the chopper over them, banking to circle the

crater. He remembered the missing drum of Xerum 525, the one marked for the United States. He toggled the radio and began passing a long chain of security codes to reach Sigma Command.

He was surprised to hear someone other than Logan pick up the line. It was Sean McKnight, the former director of Sigma. Fear iced through Gray. What was he doing there? Something was wrong. McKnight quickly briefed him on what had happened. The last came as a blow to the gut.

He finally signed off, numb and shocked.

Monk had leaned forward, noting his growing consternation.

"What's wrong?" he asked.

He turned. He had to face his partner when he said it.

"Monk . . . it's about Kat."

5:47 P.M. EST
WASHINGTON, D.C.

Three days had passed. Three *long* days settling matters in South Africa.

Finally, their plane had landed at Dulles International after a direct flight from Johannesburg. Monk had ditched Gray and the others at the terminal. He had hailed a taxicab and taken off. Then the taxi hit congestion near the park. Monk had to force himself not to yank open the door and run on foot, but eventually the bottleneck broke up, and they were moving again.

Monk leaned forward. "Fifty bucks if you get me there in under five minutes."

Acceleration threw Monk back into the seat. That was more like it.

In two minutes, the jumble of brown brick buildings

appeared. They flashed past a sign that read GEORGETOWN UNIVERSITY HOSPITAL. Tires squealed into the visitors' parking lot, almost sideswiping an ambulance.

Monk threw a fistful of bills at the driver and leaped out.

He squeezed sideways through the automatic door, impatient when it opened too slowly. He ran headlong down the hall, dodging patients and orderlies. He knew which room in ICU.

He ran past a nursing station, ignoring a yell to slow down.

Not today, honey.

Monk winged around the corner and spotted the bed. He ran, fell to his knees in the last steps, and slid in his sweatpants up to the side of the bed. He hit the lowered side rail rather hard.

Kat stared at him, a spoonful of jiggling lime green Jell-O halfway to her mouth. "Monk . . . ?"

"I came here as soon as I could," he said, panting, winded.

"But I just talked to you ninety minutes ago on the satellite phone."

"That's just talking."

He shoved up, leaned over the bed, and kissed her square on the mouth. The bandages were wrapped around her left shoulder and upper torso, half hidden by a blue hospital gown. Three gunshots, two units of blood lost, collapsed lung, shattered collarbone, and lacerated spleen.

But she was alive.

And damn lucky.

Logan Gregory's funeral was set for three days from now.

Still, the pair had saved Washington from a terrorist attack, gunning down the Waalenberg assassin and stopping the plot before it could come to fruition. The ceremonial gold Bell was now buried deep in Sigma's research labs. The shipment of Xerum 525 intended for the Bell had been found at a shipping yard in New Jersey. But by the time the U.S. intelligence agencies had tracked the shipment—encumbered by the vast web of Waalenberg-owned corporations, shells, and subsidiaries—the one last sample of Xerum was found degraded, left too long out in the sun, gone inert due to improper refrigeration. And without the fuel source, the Bells, even those recovered from other embassies, would never ring again.

Good riddance.

Monk preferred evolution the old-fashioned way.

His hand drifted to her belly. He was afraid to ask.

He didn't have to. Kat's hand covered his. "The baby's fine. Doctors say there should be no complications."

Monk sagged again to his knees, resting the side of his head on her stomach, relieved. He closed his eyes. He snaked an arm around her waist, gently, careful of her injuries, and pulled tight to her.

"Thank God."

Kat touched his cheek.

Still on his knees, Monk reached to his pocket and lifted out the black ring box. He held it out, eyes still closed, a prayer on his lips.

"Marry me."

"Okay."

Monk opened his eyes, staring up into the face of the woman he loved. "What?"

"I said okay."

Monk lifted his head. "Are you sure?"

"Are you trying to talk me out of it?"

"Well, you are on drugs. Maybe I'd better ask you—"

"Just give me the ring." She took the box and opened it. She stared silently for a moment. "It's empty."

Monk took the box and stared inside. The ring was gone. He shook his head.

"What happened?" Kat asked.

Monk growled. "Fiona."

10:32 A.M.

The next morning, Painter lay on his back in another wing of Georgetown University Hospital. The table retracted from the doughnut-shaped CT machine. The scan had taken over an hour. He had almost fallen asleep, having rested very little over the past few days. Anxiety plagued his nights.

A nurse opened the door.

Lisa followed her inside.

Painter sat up. It was chilly in the room. Then again, he was wearing nothing but a threadbare hospital gown. He sought some manner of dignity, tucking and snugging, but finally conceded defeat.

Lisa sat down next to him. She nodded back to the monitoring room. A clutch of researchers from Johns Hopkins and Sigma had their heads bent together, the focus of their attention on Painter's health.

"Looks good," Lisa said. "All signs of internal calcification are receding. Your lab values are all returning to normal. You may retain some minor residual scarring to your aortic valve, but possibly not even that. The rate of recovery is remarkable . . . dare I say, miraculous."

"You may," Painter said. "But what about this?"

He ran his fingers through the white streak of hair over one ear.

She reached up and followed his fingers with her own. "I like it. And you're going to be fine."

He believed her. For the first time, deep down, he knew he would be okay. A shuddering sigh flowed from him. He would live. There was still a life ahead of him.

Painter caught Lisa's hand, kissed her palm, then lowered it.

She blushed, glanced to the monitoring window—but she didn't pull her hand from his as she discussed some technical matter with the nurse.

Painter studied her. He had gone to Nepal both to investigate the illnesses reported by Ang Gelu and as a personal odyssey, a time for private reflection. He had expected incense, meditation, chants, and prayers, but instead it had turned into a hellish and brutal journey around half the globe. Still, in the end, maybe the result was the same.

His fingers tightened on her hand.

He had found her.

And though they had been through so much together in these past days, they still barely knew each other. Who was she really? What was her favorite food, what made her let out a belly laugh, what would it be like to dance with her, what would she whisper when she said good night?

Painter knew only one thing for certain as he sat in his gown, all but naked next to her, exposed down to the level of his DNA.

He wanted to know everything.

2:22 P.M.

Two days later, rifles fired their last shot into the blue sky, cracking brilliantly across the green slopes of Arlington National Cemetery. The day was too bright for a funeral, a glorious day.

Gray stood off to the side as the funeral ended. In the distance, overlooking the clutch of black-suited mourners, rose the Tomb of the Unknowns, eighty tons of Yule marble quarried from Colorado. It represented loss without a name, a life laid down in service to the country.

Logan Gregory was now one of them. Another unknown. Few would know of his heroism, the blood shed to protect all of us.

But some did.

Gray watched the vice president pass a folded flag to

Logan's mother, draped in black, supported by his father. Logan had no wife, no kids. Sigma had been his life . . . and his death.

Slowly, after some milling, amid condolences and goodbyes, the service broke up. Everyone wandered toward black limousines and Town Cars.

Gray nodded to Painter. He limped with a cane, recovering from his debilitation, stronger every day. At his side, Dr. Lisa Cummings had an arm hooked around his elbow, not supporting him, just being near him.

Monk trailed as they headed together toward the waiting line of cars.

Kat was still in the hospital. The funeral would have been too much for her anyway. Too soon.

Upon reaching the parked cars, Gray stepped up to Painter. They had some matters to settle.

Lisa kissed the director on the cheek. "I'll see you there." She stepped back with Monk. They would be taking another vehicle to the Gregorys' home, where a small gathering would take place.

Gray had been surprised to learn that Logan's parents lived only blocks from his own parents in Takoma Park. It just showed how little he really knew about the man.

Painter crossed to a Lincoln Town Car and opened the door. They climbed into the backseat. The driver lifted the privacy screen as he pulled from the curb.

"Gray, I read your report," Painter finally said. "It's an interesting angle. Go ahead and follow up on it. But it would mean another trip to Europe."

"I've some personal matters to settle there anyway. It's what I came to discuss, to ask for a few extra days."

Painter lifted one eyebrow in tired levity. "I don't know if the world is ready for another one of your working vacations."

Gray had to concede that might be true.

Painter shifted, plainly still suffering some aches. "And what about the report from Dr. Marcia Fairfield? Do you think . . . believe that the Waalenberg lineage . . . ?" Painter shook his head.

Gray had read the report, too. He remembered when he and the British doctor had been skulking about the embryonic lab at the deepest levels of the subbasement. Dr. Fairfield had once claimed that the greater the treasure, the deeper it was buried. The same could be said for secrets, especially those kept by the Waalenbergs. Like their experiments with chimera, mixing human and animal stem cells in the brain.

But even that was not the worst.

"We checked the corporate medical records from the early 1950s," Gray said. "It's been confirmed. Baldric Waalenberg was sterile."

Painter shook his head. "No wonder the bastard had been so obsessed with breeding and genetics, continually battling to bend nature to his will. He was the last of the Waalenbergs. But his new children . . . the ones he used in the experiments? Is it true?"

Gray shrugged. "Baldric was involved intimately with the Nazi *Lebensborn* program. Their Aryan breeding program. Along with other eugenics projects and early attempts to store eggs and sperm. At the war's end, it seems the Xerum 525 program was not the only secret project that ended up in Baldric's lap. One other did. One frozen inside glass straws. And once thawed, Baldric used the samples to inseminate his young wife."

"And you're sure of this?"

Gray nodded. Down in the subterranean lab, Dr. Fairfield had viewed the real family tree of the new-and-improved Waalenberg clan. She saw the name typed next to Baldric's wife. Heinrich Himmler, the head of the Black Order. The Nazi bastard might have killed himself after the war, but he had a plan to live on, to birth the new Aryan supermen, a new line of German kings, out of his own corrupted seed.

"And with the Waalenberg clan eradicated," Gray said, "that monster is finally laid to rest, too."

"At least we hope so."

Gray nodded. "I'm in contact with Khamisi. He's keeping us informed on the cleanup at the estate. So far they've rounded up several of the guards. He fears some of the estate's menagerie may have escaped into the deeper forest, but most were likely destroyed during the blast. But the search continues."

Khamisi had been named interim head warden for the Hluhluwe-Umfolozi reserve. He had also been given emergency policing authority by the South African government, helping coordinate local tribal support with Chief Mosi D'Gana. Drs. Paula Kane and Marcia Fairfield were providing him with technical support in handling the international intelligence communities' response to the attack on the mansion and bombing.

The two women had settled back into their home on the reserve, happy to discover each other alive and well, but they had also opened their house to Fiona. The two spies had even helped Fiona get into an early-acceptance program at Oxford.

Gray stared out at the flashing scenery. He hoped Oxford had everything nailed down very securely. He suspected the petty crime rate around the university was about to have a sudden and significant uptick.

Thinking about Fiona, Gray was reminded that he needed to check on Ryan. With the murder of Ryan's father, the young man had put his family estate on the auction block, determined at long last to escape the shadow of Wewelsburg.

Just as well.

"And what about Monk and Kat?" Painter asked, drawing

back his attention. His voice was brighter, shedding some of the sorrow over the loss of his friend, or at least setting it aside. "I heard they got engaged yesterday."

Gray found himself smiling for the first time today. "They did."

"Heaven help us."

Again Gray had to agree with the man. They shared this small bit of happiness. Life rolled on. They went over a handful of other details, and eventually the driver wound their Town Car through the tree-lined streets of Takoma Park, settling to a stop before a small green-shingled Victorian.

Painter climbed out.

Lisa was already there.

"Are we done here?" Painter asked Gray.

"Yes, sir."

"Let me know what you find in Europe. And take those extra days."

"Thank you, sir."

Painter held out an arm. Lisa slipped into it. The pair headed toward the house together.

As Gray climbed out, Monk joined him and nodded to the woman and the director. "Any bets?"

Gray watched them climb the porch stairs. The two had been almost inseparable since leaving the Waalenberg estate. With Anna dead and Gunther vanished, Lisa was now the only living source for information on the Bell's operation. She had been spending many hours at Sigma, being questioned. Yet Gray suspected the debriefings were also an excuse for Painter and Lisa to spend more time together.

It seemed the Bell had done more than just heal the flesh.

Gray stared a moment at their joined hands as they reached the porch. He pondered Monk's question. *Any bets?* At this point, maybe it was too early to tell. If life and consciousness were a quantum phenomenon, then maybe love was, too.

To love or not to love.

The wave or the particle.

Maybe for Painter and Lisa, it was still *both,* a suspended potential that only time would settle.

"I don't know," Gray mumbled, answering Monk's inquiry.

He headed toward the house, thinking about his own future.

Like everyone else, he had his own reality to measure.

EPILOGUE

He was late.

As the sun sank toward the horizon, Gray marched across the green cast-iron bridge. The baroque span forded the River Oder, a flat green expanse polished to a mirror's sheen by the setting sun.

Gray checked his watch. Rachel should be landing right about now. They were set to meet at the coffeehouse across the street from their hotel in the old historic district. But first he had one last thread to tie up, one last interview.

Gray continued across the pedestrian bridge. Below, a pair of black swans sliced across the waters. A few gulls swept across the sky, reflected in the river. The air smelled of the sea and the lilacs growing along the edges of the waterway. He had started this journey at a bridge in Copenhagen, and now it ended at another.

He lifted his gaze to the ancient city of black spires, copper-roofed turrets, and renaissance clock towers. The city of Wroclaw was once named Breslau, a fortified township on the border between Germany and Poland. Large sections of the city had been flattened during World

War II as the German Wehrmacht fought the Russian Red Army.

The aftermath of that attack had also drawn Gray here . . . some sixty years later.

Ahead rose Cathedral Island. The twin gothic towers of the island's namesake, the Cathedral of John the Baptist, glowed fiery as the day ended. But the cathedral was not Gray's destination. There were scores of other smaller churches huddled on the island. Gray's goal lay only steps from the bridge.

His boots crossed from iron grate to stone street.

The Church of Saints Peter and Paul squatted humbly to the left, easy to miss, merging its rear facade with the brick river wall. Gray spotted a small coal door that led from the waterway's rocky bank to the back of the church rectory.

Had a certain child once played along there?

A perfect child.

Gray knew from recently unsealed Russian records that the motherless boy had been raised at the orphanage once run by the Church of Saints Peter and Paul. There were many such abandoned children after the war, but Gray had narrowed the possibilities by age, sex, and hair color.

The last of these parameters was most certainly *white-blond.*

Gray also found records of the Russian Red Army's search of the city, of their scouring of the mountains for the Nazis' subterranean weapons labs, of their discovery at Wenceslas Mine. They had come close to capturing SS-*Obergruppenführer* Jakob Sporrenberg, Anna and Gunther's grandfather, as he evacuated the Bell. Lisa had learned from Anna that it was in this city, in this river, that Tola, Hugo's daughter, had drowned the baby.

But had she?

It was this one possibility that had Gray and a handful of Sigma research experts delving into old records, following a trail long gone cold, pieced from bits and shreds. Then the discovery . . . a priest's diary, the one who ran the orphanage here, telling of a baby boy, cold and alone, found with his dead mother. She was buried in a cemetery near here, nameless until now.

But the boy had lived, grown up here, entering the seminary under the tutelage of the same priest who rescued him, gaining the name Father Piotr.

Gray crossed to the rectory door. He had called in advance to interview the sixty-year-old priest, posing as a reporter researching wartime orphans for a book. Gray lifted and tapped the iron knocker on the nondescript plank door.

He could hear singing rising from the church itself, a service under way.

After a few moments, the door opened.

Gray knew instantly who greeted him, recognizing from old photos the lineless old face and bushy white hair parted down the middle. Father Piotr was casually dressed in jeans, black shirt, white Roman collar of his profession, and a light, buttoned sweater.

He spoke English with a thick Polish accent.

"You must be Nathan Sawyer."

Gray wasn't—but he nodded, suddenly uncomfortable lying to a priest. But such subterfuge was necessary, as much for the old priest's sake as his own.

He cleared his throat. "Thank you for granting me this interview."

"Certainly. Please come in. Be welcome."

Father Piotr led Gray through the rectory hall to a small room with a warm coal stove in the corner. He had a pot of tea brewing atop it. Gray was motioned to a chair. Once seated, Gray took out a pad containing a handful of questions.

Piotr poured two cups and settled to a worn wingback, the cushions long contoured to the man's body. A Bible rested on a table beside a glass-shaded lamp, along with a few tattered mystery novels.

"You've come to inquire about Father Varick," the man asked with a soft and genuine smile. "A great man."

Gray nodded. "And about your life here at the orphanage."

Piotr sipped his tea and waved fingers at Gray to continue.

The questions were not that important, mostly filling in blanks. Gray already knew almost everything about the man's life. Rachel's uncle Vigor, as head of the Vatican's intelligence branch, had supplied Sigma with a complete and detailed dossier on the Catholic father.

Including medical records.

Father Piotr had lived an unassuming life within the church. There was nothing especially noteworthy about his accomplishments beyond steadfast devotion to his flock. His health, though, remained exceptionally good. Little to no medical history. A broken bone when he was a teenager, falling off a rock. But other than that, routine physicals showed a perfectly fit individual. He wasn't massive like Gunther or wickedly agile like the Waalenbergs. Just stolidly healthy.

The interview turned up nothing new.

Gray eventually closed his notebook and thanked the father for his time. Just to be thorough, he would obtain blood and DNA samples when the priest went for his next physical, again coordinated through Rachel's uncle. But Gray didn't expect anything much to come of it.

Hugo's perfected child turned out to be simply a decent and thoughtful man with resoundingly good health. Maybe that was perfection enough.

As Gray was leaving, he spotted an unfinished jigsaw puzzle spread on a table in the room's corner. He nodded to it. "So you like puzzles?"

Father Piotr smiled guiltily, disarmingly. "Just a hobby. Keeps the mind sharp."

Gray nodded and headed out. He thought of Hugo Hirszfeld's interest in the same. Had some insubstantial essence of the Jewish researcher been passed to the boy, imparted through the Bell? As Gray left the church and headed back over the river, he pondered such connections. Fathers and sons. Was it just genetics? Or was there something more? Something at the quantum level?

The question was not a new one for Gray. He and his father had never had a good relationship; only lately had bridges started to build. And then there were other issues, worrisome concerns. Like Piotr's jigsaw puzzle, what had Gray inherited from his father? He certainly could not deny his fear of Alzheimer's, a real genetic possibility, but it went deeper than that, back to their hardscrabble relationship.

What type of father would he be?

Despite being late, the question stopped Gray cold on the iron bridge.

In that one question, reality shifted for him. He remembered Monk challenging him on the plane ride to Germany, about Rachel, about their relationship. His words returned to Gray on the bridge.

I mention Kat's pregnant and you should've seen your face. Scared the crap out of you. And it's my kid.

Here was the root of his panic.

What type of father would he be?

Would he be his father all over again?

Gray found his answer in the most unlikely place. A girl strode past him on the bridge, tucked into a hooded sweater against the river's breeze. He flashed upon Fiona. He remembered the days of terror, her hand gripping his, needing him, but forever fighting him. He recalled how that felt.

He gripped the rails of the bridge, hard.

It had felt wonderful.

And he wanted more.

A short laugh escaped him at the realization, just a madman on a bridge. He didn't have to be his father. While the potential was there to follow in his father's footsteps, he also had free will, a consciousness that could collapse potential in either direction.

Freed at last, he headed again across the bridge, slowly allowing this one reality to collapse other potentials, falling like a chain of dominoes, one after the other, leading to one last teetering unresolved potential.

Rachel.

He stepped off the bridge and headed toward their rendezvous.

When he reached the coffeehouse, she was already waiting on the patio. She must have just arrived herself. She had not spotted him. He paused, shocked at how beautiful she was. It hit him anew every time. Tall, long-limbed, an inviting curve of hip, bosom, and neck. She turned, finding him staring. A smile bloomed. Her eyes, caramel colored, glimmered warmly. She combed a hand through her ebony hair, almost shyly.

Who wouldn't want to spend the rest of their life with her?

He crossed, closing the gap, reaching a hand out for her fingers.

In that moment, Monk's challenge again returned to him. It seemed so long ago. A challenge about where Gray and Rachel were headed. A challenge raised on three fingers.

Wife, mortgage, kids.

In other words, *reality*.

A relationship couldn't be suspended forever as pure *potential*. Both loving *and* not loving. Evolution would not stand for it. Reality must eventually measure it.

And so it did now for Gray.

Wife, mortgage, kids.

Gray had his answer. He was ready for the challenge of all three. And with this realization, that last domino toppled inside his heart.

To love or not.

The wave or particle.

Gray took Rachel's fingers. He saw it with clarity, yet the result still surprised him. He pulled her toward the small table, noting that a plate of scones rested atop it, along with two dark steaming mugs of caffe latte, already waiting for them.

Rachel's usual thoughtfulness.

He drew her down to one seat. He took the other.

He stared into her eyes. He could not keep the sorrow and apology out of his voice, but he allowed his firm resolution to ring forth, too.

"Rachel, we need to talk."

Gray then saw it in her eyes, too. Reality. Two careers, two continents, two people with separate paths from here.

She squeezed his fingers. "I know."

Father Piotr had watched the young man cross the bridge. He stood at the open coal door that led back into the rectory's wine cellar. He had waited for his recent visitor to vanish down the far street, then sighed.

A nice young man, but shadows cloaked him.

Poor boy had much grief ahead of him.

But such is life's journey.

A soft mewling drew his attention back down. A scrawny tabby brushed against his ankles, tail high, eyes looking up at him expectant. One of Father Varick's strays. Now his charges. Piotr knelt down and balanced a tiny plate of scraps on a rock. The river cat gave him one last rub, then minced at the food.

Father Piotr crouched and stared out at the river, ablaze with the last rays of the sun. He noted a bit of feathered fluff near his heel. A brown sparrow, its neck broken. One of the many gifts his orphans left on his doorstep.

He shook his head, collected the limp bird between his palms, and raised it to his lips. He blew upon its feathers, dancing them up, raising a wing, which caught air with a surprised flutter. From his palm, the sparrow took flight, darting and dancing back up into the sky.

Piotr watched it for a breath, trying to read something in the winged path scribed through the air. Then he brushed his hands and stood with a stretch.

Life forever remained a wondrous mystery.

Even for him.

AUTHOR'S NOTE:
TRUTH OR FICTION

Thanks for accompanying me on this latest journey. As usual, I thought I'd take this last moment of your time to *deconstruct* the novel, to reveal where research ended and imagination continued.

First on the minor side:

DARPA has indeed developed prosthetic limbs using revolutionary technology (though I don't think they have incorporated flash charges into their plastic composites).

Similar to the book's *ukufa,* Stanford University has actually produced a chimeric strain of mice whose brains contain human neural cells. Scientists are now contemplating trying to produce mice whose brains are one hundred percent human neural cells.

A German boy was born in 2004 with a mutation in the gene for myostatin, which resulted in a condition called double-muscling, resulting in increased strength and muscular tone. Is this the first natural-born *Sonnekönig*?

Shangri-La was discovered deep in the Himalayas in 1998, a lost oasis of free-flowing water and lush vegetation in the middle of the frozen peaks. What else might be hidden up there?

Moving on to the larger concepts:

As mentioned at the beginning of the book, the Bell itself is indeed real, proving truth is often stranger than fiction. The Nazis had constructed a strange device, fueled by an unknown compound named Xerum 525. Little is known about its true functioning, only that when it was powered up, a strange illness afflicted the scientists involved, reaching as far as neighboring villages. At the end of the war, the Bell vanished, the scientists involved were executed, and to this day, what became of the device remains a mystery. If you'd like to learn more about this strange bit of history, about the postwar race among Allied forces for Nazi technology, and about the Germans' fascination with quantum research, I refer you to one of the research bibles for this novel: *The Hunt for Zero Point* by Nick Cook.

In this novel, I also spent considerable time describing Heinrich Himmler's fascination with runes, the occult, and his search for the Aryan birthplace in the Himalayas. All of it is based on fact, including the set piece of Himmler's Black Camelot of Wewelsburg. For more information on these topics, I suggest Christopher Hale's *Himmler's Crusade* and Peter Levenda's *Unholy Alliance*.

Lastly, one book was instrumental in stimulating the core of this novel: *Quantum Evolution* by Johnjoe McFadden. This book offers a fascinating treatise on quantum mechanics and its possible role in mutations and evolution. It also delves into the evolution of consciousness, which is touched upon at the end of the novel. For a more comprehensive analysis on these topics, I highly recommend you pick up a copy.

Which brings up the final tenet of the book: the question of intelligent design versus evolution. I hope this novel raises as many questions as it provides answers. But ultimately, I firmly believe much of the current debate is misguided. Rather than focusing so intently on where we have come from, a larger question deserves even more fervent attention: *Where are we headed?*

To answer that, to follow that path, is mystery and adventure enough for anybody.

An ancient angelic script.
Holds the secret to patterns in our DNA?
A great explorer in the jungles of Southeast Asia.
Discovered a fate so horrifying he never spoke of it.
An intrinsic basis for evil.
Buried in our own genetic code,
can mankind survive . . .

THE JUDAS STRAIN
Available Now
Wherever Books Are Sold

Nothing stays buried forever—and it will be up to Sigma Force to face what will be unearthed: a plague beyond any cure, a scourge that turns all of Nature against mankind.

From the high seas of the Indian Ocean to the dark jungles of Southeast Asia, from the canals of Venice to the crypts of ancient kings, Sigma Force must piece together a mystery that, unless solved, will end all life on our planet. But even this challenge may prove too large for Sigma Force alone. With a worldwide pandemic growing, Director Painter Crowe and Commander Gray Pierce turn to their deadliest adversaries for help, teaming up with a diabolical foe who thwarted them in the past.

But can the enemy be trusted even now? Or will they prove to be another Judas?

James Rollins—for the thrill of it!

"I have not told half of what I saw."
—the last words of Marco Polo,
spoken upon his deathbed
when asked to recant his stories of the Far East

May 12, 1293
Island of Sumatra
Southeast Asia

The screams had finally ceased.

Twelve bonfires blazed out in the midnight harbor.

"Il dio, li perdona . . ." his father whispered at his side, but Marco knew the Lord would not forgive them this sin.

A handful of men waited beside the two beached long-boats, the only witnesses to the funeral pyres out upon the midnight lagoon. As the moon had risen, all twelve ships, mighty wooden galleys, had been set to torch with all hands still aboard, both the dead and those cursed few who still lived. Flakes of ash rained down upon the beach and those few who bore witness. The night reeked of burned flesh.

"Twelve ships," his uncle Masseo mumbled, clutching the

silver crucifix in one fist. "The same number as the Lord's Apostles."

At least the screams of the tortured had ended. Only the crackle and low roar of the flames reached the sandy shore now. Marco wanted to turn from the sight. Others were not as stout of heart, kneeling on the sand, backs to the water, faces as pale as bone.

All were stripped naked. Each had searched his neighbor for any sign of the mark. Even the great Khan's princess, who stood behind a screen of sailcloth for modesty. Her maids, naked themselves, had searched their mistress, a maiden of seventeen. The Polos had been assigned by the Great Khan to safely deliver her to her betrothed, the Khan of Persia, the grandson of Kublai Khan's brother.

That had been in another lifetime.

Had it been only four months since the first of the galley crew had become sick, showing welts on groin and beneath the arm? The illness had spread like burning oil, unmanning the galleys of able men and stranding them here on this island.

With the cruel fire, the disease was at last vanquished, leaving only this small handful of survivors.

Seven nights ago, the remaining sick had been taken in chains to the moored boats, left with water and food. The others remained on shore, wary of any sign among them of fresh affliction. All the while, those banished to the ships called out across the waters, pleading, crying, praying, cursing, and screaming. But the worst was the occasional laughter, bright with madness.

Better to have slit their throats with a kind and swift blade, but all feared touching the blood of the sick. So they had been sent to the boats, imprisoned with the dead already there.

Then as the sun sank this night, a strange glow appeared

in the water, pooled around the keels of two of the boats, spreading like spilled milk upon the still black waters. They had seen the glow before, in the canals beneath the stone towers of the cursed city.

The disease sought to escape its wooden prison.

It had left them no choice.

The boats—all the boats, except one—had been torched.

Marco's uncle, Masseo, moved among the remaining men. He waved for them to again cloak their nakedness, but simple cloth and woven wool could not mask their deeper shame.

"What we did . . ." Marco said.

"We must not speak of it," his father said and held forth a robe toward Marco. "Breathe a word of contagion and all lands will shun us. But now we've burned away the last of the pestilence with a cleansing fire. We have only to return home."

As Marco slipped the robe over his head, his father noted what the son had drawn earlier in the sand with a stick. With a tightening of his lips, his father quickly ground it away under a heel and stared up at his son. "None must ever know what we found . . . it is cursed."

Marco nodded and did not comment on what he had drawn. He only whispered, *Città dei Morti.*

His father's countenance, already pale, blanched further. But Marco knew it wasn't just plague that frightened his father.

A hand gripped his shoulder, squeezing to the bone. "Swear to me, my son. For your own sake."

He recognized the terror reflected in his fire-lit eyes . . . and the pleading. Marco could not refuse.

"I will keep silent," he finally promised. "To my deathbed and beyond. I so swear, Father."

Marco's uncle finally joined them, overhearing the younger man's oath. "We should never have trespassed there, Niccolò," he scolded his brother, but his accusing words were intended for Marco.

Silence settled between the three, heavy with shared secrets.

His uncle was right.

Marco pictured the river delta from four months back. The black stream had emptied into the sea, fringed by heavy leaf and vine. They had only sought to renew their stores of fresh water. They should never have ventured farther, but Marco had spotted a stone tower deep within the forest, thrusting high, brilliant in the dawn's light. It drew him like a beacon, ever curious, brave with two score of the Khan's men from the galleys.

Still, the silence as they rowed toward the tower should have warned him. No bird calls, no scream of monkeys. The city of the dead had simply waited for them.

It was a dreadful mistake to trespass.

And it cost them in more than blood.

The three stared out as the galleys smoldered down to the waterlines.

"The sun will rise soon," his father said. "Let us be gone. It is time we went home."

"And if we reach those blessed shores, what do we tell Tedaldo?" Masseo asked, using the original name of the man, once a friend and advocate of the Polo family, now styled as Pope Gregory X.

"We don't know he still lives," his father answered. "We've been gone so long."

"But if he does, Niccolò?" his uncle pressed.

"We will tell him all we know about the Mongols and their customs and their strengths. As we were directed under his edict so long ago. But of the plague here . . . there remains nothing to speak of. It is over."

Masseo sighed, but there was little relief in his exhalation.

Plague had not claimed all of them.

His father repeated more firmly, as if saying would make it so, "It is over."

Marco glanced up at the two older men, his father and his uncle, framed in fiery ash and smoke against the night sky. It would never be over, not as long as they remembered.

Marco glanced to his toes. Though the mark was scuffed off the sand, it burned brightly still behind his eyes. He had stolen a map painted on beaten bark. Painted in blood. Temples and spires spread in the jungle.

All empty.

Except for the dead.

The ground had been littered with birds, fallen to the stone plazas as if struck out of the skies in flight. Nothing was spared. Men and women and children. Oxen and beasts of the field. Even great snakes had hung limp from tree limbs.

The only living inhabitants were the ants.

Teeming across stones and bodies, slowly picking apart the dead.

Upon discovering what Marco had stolen from one of the temples, his father had burned the map and spread the ashes into the sea. He did this even before the first man aboard their own ships had become sick.

"Let it be forgotten," his father had warned then.

Marco would honor his word, his oath. This was one tale he would never speak. Still, he touched one of the marks in the sand. He who had chronicled so much . . . was it right to vanquish such knowledge?

If there was another way to preserve it . . .

As if reading Marco's thoughts, his uncle Masseo spoke aloud all their fears. "And if the horror should rise again, Niccolò, should someday reach our shores?"

"Then it will mean the end of man's tyranny of this world," his father answered bitterly. He tapped the crucifix resting on Masseo's bare chest. "The friar knew better than all. His sacrifice . . ."

The cross had once belonged to Friar Agreer. Back in the cursed city, the Dominican had given his life to save theirs. A dark pact had been struck. They had left him there, abandoned him, at his own bidding.

The nephew of Pope Gregory X.

Marco whispered as the last of the flames died into the dark waters. "What God will save us next time?"

"Who wants another bottle of Foster's while I'm down here?" Gregg Tunis called from belowdecks.

Dr. Susan Tunis smiled at her husband's voice as she pushed off the dive ladder and onto the open stern deck. She skinned out of her BC vest and hauled the scuba gear to the rack behind the research yacht's pilot house. Her tanks clanked as she racked them alongside the others.

Her husband climbed up with three perspiring bottles of lager, pinching them all between the fingers of one hand. He grinned broadly upon seeing her. "Thought I heard you bumping about up here."

He climbed topside, stretching his tall frame. Employed as a boat mechanic in Darwin Harbor, he and Susan had met during one of the dry-dock repairs on another of the University of Sydney's boats. That had been eight years ago. Just three days ago they had celebrated their fifth anniversary aboard the yacht, moored a hundred nautical miles off Kirimiti Atoll, better known as Christmas Island.

He passed her a bottle. "Any luck with the soundings?"

She took a long pull on the beer. "Not so far. Still can't find a source for the beachings."

Ten days ago, eighty dolphins, *Tursiops aduncus*, an Indian Ocean species, had beached themselves along the coast of Java. Her research study centered on the long-term effects of sonar interference on Cetacean species, the source of many suicidal beachings in the past. She usually had a team of research assistants with her, a mix of postgrads and undergrads, but the trip up here had been for a vacation with her old mentor. It was pure happenstance that such a massive beaching occurred in the region—hence the protracted stay here.

"Could it be something other than manmade sonar?" Professor Applegate pondered, drawing sigils with his fingertip in the condensation on his beer bottle. "Micro-quakes are constantly rattling the region. Perhaps a deep-sea subduction quake struck the right tonal note to drive them into a suicidal panic."

"There was that bonzer quake a few months back," her husband said. He settled into a lounge beside the professor and patted the seat for her to sit with him. "Maybe some aftershocks?"

Susan couldn't argue against their assessments. Between the series of deadly quakes over the past two years and the major tsunami in the area, the seabed was greatly disturbed. It was enough to spook anyone. But she wasn't convinced. Something else was happening. The reef below was oddly deserted. What little life was down there seemed to have retreated into rocky niches, shells, and sandy holes. It was almost as if the sea life here was holding its breath.

She frowned and joined her husband.

A sharp bark startled her, causing her to jump. She had not known she was that tense. Apparently the strange, wary behavior of the reef life below had infected her.

"Oy! Oscar!" the professor called.

Only now did Susan notice the lack of their fourth crewmate on the yacht. The dog barked again. The pudgy Queensland Heeler belonged to the professor.

"I'll see to him," Applegate said. "Leave you two love-birds all cozied up. Besides, I could use a trip to the head before I find my bed."

The professor gained his feet with a groan and headed toward the bow, intending to circle to the far side—but he stopped, staring off toward the east, away from where the sun had just set.

Oscar barked again.

Applegate did not scold him this time. Instead, he called over to Susan and Gregg, his voice low and serious. "You both should come see this."

Susan scooted up and onto her feet. Gregg followed. They joined the professor.

"Bloody hell . . ." her husband mumbled.

"I think you may be looking at what drove those dolphins out of the seas," Applegate said.

To the east, a wide swath of the ocean glowed with a ghostly luminescence, rising and falling with the waves. The silvery sheen rolled and eddied. The old dog stood at the starboard rail and barked, trailing into a low growl at the sight.

"What the hell is that?" Gregg asked.

Susan answered as she crossed closer. "I've heard of such manifestations. They're called *milky seas*. Ships have reported glows like this in the Indian Ocean, going all the way back to Jules Verne. In 1995, a satellite even picked up one of the blooms, covering hundreds of square miles. This is a small one."

"Small, my ass," Gregg grunted. "But what exactly is it? Some type of red tide?"

She shook her head. "Not exactly. Red tides are algal blooms. These glows are caused by bioluminescent bacteria, probably feeding off algae or some other substrate. There's no danger. But I'd like to—"

A sudden knock sounded beneath the boat. Oscar's barking became more heated. The dog danced back and forth along the rails, trying to poke his head through the posts.

All three of them joined the dog and looked below.

The glowing edge of the milky sea lapped at the yacht's keel. From the depths below, a large shape rolled into view, belly up, but still squirming, teeth gnashing. It was a giant tiger shark, female, over six meters. The glowing waters frothed over its form, bubbling and turning the milky water into red wine.

Susan realized it wasn't *water* that was bubbling over the shark's belly, but its own *flesh*, boiling off in wide patches. The horrible sight sank away. But across the milky seas, other shapes rolled to the surface, thrashing or already dead: porpoises, sea turtles, fish by the hundreds.

Applegate took a step away from the rail. "It seems *these* bacteria have found more than just algae to feed on."

Gregg turned to stare at her. "Susan . . ."

She could not look away from the deadly vista. Despite the horror, she could not deny a twinge of scientific curiosity.

"Susan . . ."

She finally turned to him, slightly irritated.

"You were diving," he explained. "All day."

"So? We were all in the water at least some time. Even Oscar."

Her husband would not meet her gaze. He remained

focused on where she was scratching her forearm. The worry in his tight face drew her attention to her arm. Her skin was pebbled in a severe rash, made worse by her scratching.

As she stared, bruising red welts bloomed on her skin.

She gaped in disbelief. "Dear God . . ."

But she also knew the horrible truth.

"It's . . . it's *in* me."